DISTANT STATIONS

by Jonathan Schwartz

DISTANT STATIONS
ALMOST HOME

DISTANT STATIONS
Jonathan Schwartz

DOUBLEDAY & COMPANY, INC., GARDEN CITY, NEW YORK, 1979

Library of Congress Cataloging in Publication Data
Schwartz, Jonathan, 1938–
   Distant stations.
   I. Title.
PZ4.S3995Di   [PS3569.C566]   813'.5'4
ISBN: 0-385-02431-2
Library of Congress Catalog Card Number 77–25607

Grateful acknowledgment is made for permission to use lyrics and poetry from the following copyright material:
"Street Fighting Man" by Mick Jagger and Keith Richard. Copyright © 1968 ABKCO Music, Inc. All Rights Reserved. International Copyright

for
Jane Mankiewicz
David Feinberg
Merry Aronson

"Every life is, more or less, a ruin among whose debris we have to discover what the person ought to have been."

José Ortega y Gasset

PART ONE

CHAPTER ONE

The President flew west that morning. Paul Kramer reported the trip on the seven o'clock news. Reading from the New York *Times* that was spread before him on a card table, Paul, twelve years old, began: "President Eisenhower and several of his top aides will leave Washington this morning for a five-day stay in the resort community of Palm Springs, California. The President plans to return to the White House early next week."

Paul skipped to local news, reporting with a concerned tone that Mayor Wagner had the flu. The baseball scores were delivered with attention to detail: ". . . And in the junior circuit, the Philadelphia A's vanquished the New York Yankees six to one as Bobby Shantz gained his fifth victory of the year against only one setback. In the only other game scheduled, the Cleveland

Indians, behind Mike Garcia's neat four-hitter, knocked off the Detroit Tigers three to two before a large throng at Briggs Stadium."

Paul ended with the weather: "Today, Friday, fair and mild. The high today in the low seventies, the high tomorrow near seventy. We can expect some clouds with the possibility of a shower or two tomorrow.

"And that's it. The seven o'clock report; a morning feature presentation of WPKF. This is Paul Kramer. Have a good day."

Paul, dressed in pajamas, closed the New York *Times.* He had spoken for ten minutes, almost to the second. He believed that a sense of timing was essential to a newscaster. He believed that the WPKF audience respected attention to detail. Each morning Paul's alarm rang at six forty-five. Usually he was awake a minute or so before. He would leap up, wash his face, and brush his teeth with Calox tooth powder (his mother had often told him that "powder gets the job done a thousand times the better"). With a bathrobe over his pajamas he would leave his room, scurry down the hall, unlock the front door, pick up the *Times,* and return to his room. He would scan the front page, pinning down the national and local news. International news was filled with unpronounceable names of diplomats and countries ("Ambassador Garzinhastitouf said today . . ." "Ethiopia suffers famine"), and so Paul rejected international news completely. At precisely seven o'clock, according to the Westclox by the bed, Paul would begin: "Good morning. On WPKF this is Paul Kramer with the news."

The station had been on the air of his imagination for over two years. Its call letters had been fashioned from his initials and his father's first initial, F, for Franklin. It was, after all, Franklin's copy of the *Times* that Paul used as a wire service; and it was Franklin's copy of the *Times* that now, as every morning, must be folded carefully back to its virgin state and returned to the entrance hall.

The WPKF broadcast schedule was a flexible one. With the exception of the morning news, rigidly begun at exactly seven, other programs would air at Paul's discretion. Music would air when Paul played the phonograph: "Hi there, Paul Kramer here with music for *you* on a cloudy Tuesday evening. To kick off the proceedings, here's Joni James." Classical music programs were conducted with more formality: "Good afternoon, this is Paul Kramer. We hear now a performance of Mozart's Symphony Number Twenty-nine in A major. The NBC Symphony Orchestra is under the direction of Arturo Toscanini."

And sports, especially baseball, played an important role in the WPKF program schedule. Paul would listen to Mel Allen broadcast a Yankee game, or Red Barber with the Dodgers, or Russ Hodges with the Giants. He would keep a record, pitch by pitch, so that his score card, at the end of the game, was unimaginably detailed. He would then, on another day, rebroadcast the game on WPKF, always beginning: "How ya doin', baseball fans. It's a perfect day for baseball, and this is Paul Kramer inviting you to pull up a chair, bring out a Ballantine, and enjoy all the action that I'll be bringing your way." After identifying the teams and reading through the starting lineups, Paul would announce with considerable authority: "The broadcast you are about to hear is intended only for the private use of our listening audience. Any rebroadcast, or any other use of this play-by-play description, without the express consent of Paul Kramer or his father, Franklin Kramer, is prohibited."

At the beginning Franklin was disturbed by WPKF.

"He's in there talking to himself," he said to Paul's mother.

"There's nothing wrong with *that*," Carol said. "I mean, I can't see that it does any harm. He's alone a lot, you know."

"How true." Franklin's compassion showed. This child of his was burdened with solitude. His mother had been ill since his birth, and had drifted in and out of the Rockefeller Institute for experimental medication. On several occasions she had submitted herself for months to a hospital in Durham, North Carolina, where she lived on a diet of rice. At home, surrounded by capsules and pills, she remained in bed with *Gourmet* magazine that was filled with photographs of glorious meals forbidden to her. She read of her illness in medical journals, searching for clues, weepy and determined, her medication altering her moods: euphoric highs, and embittered lows charged with accusation and despair. Fatigue surrounded her, accompanying her sedentary life like a heartache. She would slip into sleep, and awaken at desperate hours in the night. Overwhelmed by hunger, she would choke on cold rice in a dark kitchen. On the way to her room she would open Paul's door and stand by his bed in the studio of WPKF. Her stranger of a child, restricted in his home, his energy suppressed by his mother's fragile presence—"Don't slam the door, you'll wake your mother"; "Keep your voice down, your mother isn't feeling well." She sat by his bed and whispered, "I love you, Paul."

Franklin had watched his son shield himself whenever he could from the confusing world outside his bedroom. His behavior at school was troubling and inflammatory. His homework was often sacrificed to WPKF.

"Why the letters WPKF?" his father had asked on one of the many walks the two of them took after dinner. "I understand the WPK, but what's the F?"

"It's for Franklin. I wanted you to be a part of the management of the station."

"I'm delighted. I accept the job." Franklin understood that what his son was asking for with the F was his father's authorization for the whole project, a kind of parental FCC. Wishing to know if Paul understood this, Franklin asked: "How much of a part do I play? I'm only one of four letters."

Paul thought for a moment. "A big part, but not a decision-making part. I got two letters, and the fourth is neutral." He said this very warmly. In his tone was the suggestion that this flagrant construction of his mind—this WPKF, New York—was grasped by its conceiver as the temporary necessity it was.

That morning, Paul's mother was awake early. The family sat at the breakfast table.

"We have an English test today," Paul said.

"Vocabulary, or what?" Carol asked.

"*David Copperfield.* I'm way ahead, so it's okay."

"Will it be an essay or facts?" Franklin inquired. English was Paul's only strength. The road to college would be rocky.

"Don't know. I like essays. Everything else at school is facts. Facts, facts." Paul laughed. "I got a lot of facts, but I don't *know* anything. You know?"

"But you need facts, don't you?" Carol asked. She had a cup of black coffee in front of her.

"Two X equals four, X equals two. How important is that for a radio announcer to know?"

"It might turn out that you won't become a radio announcer," Franklin suggested.

"Oh no?" Paul said dryly. Then, with a glance at his mother, he used a pet phrase of hers. "We shall see what we shall see," Paul told his father.

It was loving mimicry, and Carol was comfortable with it, even flattered. Any parroting of her by her son made her feel noticed. She needed to know that Paul was conscious of her, not simply of her darkened bedroom, her silk nightgown, her steaming rice. He could get away with almost anything by nodding hello.

In a while, Paul left for school: a crosstown bus, a subway ride to Van Cortlandt Park, and a climb up the hill to chapel. "Faith of our Fathers, Holy Faith/We will be true to Thee till death. Amen." Paul imagined the assembly in song: "Ask the man for Ballantine. What kind? *Ballantine.* Amen."

Franklin sat with his wife in her bedroom. He had long ago moved into the study at the other end of the apartment. Carol's restless nights had regularly awakened him. She had insisted that he sleep away from her so that he might have peaceful rest. And she had lovingly and frankly insisted upon a sexual life for Franklin in whatever corners of the city would reward him. Her own appetites, voracious at the start of their marriage, had been diminished and finally extinguished by sickness. She inflicted marital abstention on her greatest and closest friend and was staggered constantly by an overriding guilt. She was possessed by her own futility. "See other women," she told Franklin. "This is no life. Please. This is no life."

Franklin said no.

Franklin Kramer was a playwright and an actor who frequently traveled on the road with second companies. He was a thin, dark-complexioned man who moved with grace and dignity. Through a long and somewhat unnoteworthy career on the stage, he was often cast as a lawyer or a doctor or a distinguished scholar. He seemed to have compassion for his fellow actors and their multiplicity of characters. One felt that there was no rage in Franklin Kramer. Even in the most histrionic appearance, Franklin suggested with a lift of his head or a hand gesture that there was humaneness in this theater, on this stage. Villainy was softened by the wisdom Franklin Kramer projected. Maybe he was in touch with God. Though he was an agnostic Jew, a spiritual ambiance surrounded his performances. He commanded a paternal respect, and the younger women on his stages were beguiled. For years a moral and faithful husband, he took his first adulterous pleasure with a sad-faced girl named Wendy, his daughter in a play about infidelity. They merged in the Bradford Hotel in Boston. Afterward, Wendy held him and whispered, "My bunny."

Franklin Kramer, the playwright, concerned himself with frivolous ideas about entangled men and women. The people in his pages played Parchesi, and giggled, and smoked cigarettes. Mirth. That was the word. Mirthful and urbane, Franklin's couples posed slyly and toyed with tapioca sex. They were charmingly devious, with names like Robin and Wilfred. Two of Franklin's plays, written in the same year, drew praise and audiences. Franklin appeared in one, as the gentle neighbor of the entangled protagonists, and played it on the road, and later in revival to a less enthusiastic response. His two plays enabled him to save money, although these savings were constantly depleted by Carol's medical bills. But their lives were perpetuated through the years in theaters around the country, and Franklin Kramer lived on his modest royalties and acting jobs.

"It's such a lovely spring morning," Carol said. She was sitting in bed wearing a blue bathrobe over her nightgown. She had washed her face and freed her hair from the bun that had contained it through the night. It was light brown and fell to her shoulders. Franklin saw that his wife had applied lipstick. Her face was oval, her eyes hazel and filled with life; their messages of expectation and defiance had been successfully transmitted to her son's. Paul's eyes were darker, more intense. They suggested the secrets of another language, perhaps a foreign language of which his mother spoke only a few confusing words. Secrets of the heart—lightning flashes of desire. Franklin Kramer caught glimpses of these secrets. His son's eyes put him in touch with the woman he married: with the streak of the wild; impulsive trips to the moon. A feminine, open woman, unprofessionally naive, vulnerable, stung by gestures, imagined implications, and the shine of deceitful smiles. But she moved ahead anyway, skipped across minefields, trusted the outcome. She was spectacularly affirmative, Franklin Kramer's find, a bit of the Scottish, a bit of the Irish, and much of Protestant America. He had deflowered Carol in Glen Ridge, New Jersey, in the bedroom in which she'd grown up. The only child of two schoolteachers had permitted an actor fifteen years older to come to her home with chrysanthemums only three quarters of an hour after her parents had left for Vermont on a hot July afternoon. She had given him wine, and embraced him, and led him by the hand to her room, where the power in the air changed hands. Franklin Kramer, without restraint, became the third teacher of the house.

"I was thinking of doing a little shopping today," Carol said. "I feel okay. I feel up to it."

"Would you like to eat at Longchamps tonight? You could have liver," Franklin suggested.

Once a week Carol was allowed specialties: liver, skinless chicken, a baked potato.

"Maybe I'll let Emma off and make something for you and Paul. How about lamb?"

Emma, the black cook, was a sullen, whining woman who slept in a small room by the kitchen. Carol and Franklin had talked of replacing her; the negative bite of her ignorance was seeping into the apartment and infecting them all with sour lethargy.

"Why don't we order a leg of lamb and then wait and see how you feel?" Franklin said.

Carol nodded. She smiled at her husband and took his hand. "How's it coming in the study?" she asked.

"Slowly," Franklin told her. He was writing a play, his first in years. "Sometimes I feel like Michael Arlen," he had laughed on more than one occasion. "A passé dandy, a one-shot playwright. It seems I'm stenciling the same pages over and over."

"If a play of yours opened, do you think Paul would read the review on his radio station?" Carol asked.

"Possibly," Franklin replied, "but I have a feeling his station will be off the air by the time I get something on the boards."

He stood.

"Nine-thirty," he pointed out. "I've got some calls."

"My dear Franklin," Carol said softly.

Franklin, at the door, embraced his wife with his eyes. They touched each other often this way. He held her gently from afar.

Robert Garment fancied himself a connoisseur of good food and good wine. On that mild spring morning in his history class, he sat back, feet on his desk, and told his students of culinary adventures that he had quite personally vividly experienced in the country of France—in the city of Paris and in the town of Menton and in the village of Beaulieu. His reveries had sprung from a lecture on the France of the thirties, "The France before the Germans," he had declared, with a disdainful gushing out of the word "Germans." Garment despised the Teutonic mentality. "They rise up every twenty-five years like a black cloud," he was apt to say. That he himself loathed the Jews who dominated the student body was only a part of his hypocrisy. His style was military; he marched the aisles of his class as he lectured pedantically to the sixteen young men alphabetically distributed in the room. He pulled or twisted the ear of a distracted student. "Attention!" he commanded. He would receive wrong answers with a contemptuous grin.

"Your ignorance is matched only by your acne," he said to Richard Tornitzer, whose acne was unmatchable. It was a favorite construction of Garment's. "Your stupidity is matched only by your obesity." It was true that Billy Steinberg was round. "Your shallowness is matched only by your deformity." No argument there. Richard Aaron, in the first row where the A's were grouped, had been born without three fingers on his left hand.

Garment was tall and balding. His two eyes led separate lives, one drifting far to the left, the other focusing on Larry Zimmerman to the right. Paul had concluded that Garment was double-jointed in the eyes, that he was capable, somehow, of unusual feats and possessed great physical power. He was a well-built man, with hairy arms and wrists. The overall impression was one of devastating strength. After a Garment ear-twist the pain would linger for several days. Paul thought: just think what would happen if an arm or leg got the same treatment!

But for now, Garment was in a mellow mood. The names of wine and cheese fell from his lips in a soft and musical stream. The lightness of the sound permeated the room and set Paul to dreaming. Perhaps a sports round-up show on Sunday mornings. He could use "Stars and Stripes Forever" as a theme. All the Saturday action could be described in detail. It could be a program without a time limit; if it worked out that fifteen minutes covered it all, then fine, fifteen minutes it was. If a half hour was needed (standings included), then a half hour was just perfect.

Garment was driving through the French countryside. He was stopping at an inn. The local wine was *superb*. "We had never tasted anything like it," Garment was saying. "You will learn someday what wine is all about, and then, and only then, will your lives begin."

Paul wondered with whom Garment, a bachelor, had traveled. Perhaps a friend in France. At twelve, Paul did not consider the question of gender. As an adolescent, he would have guessed the truth. For now, he felt that maybe Garment had vacationed with his father. Garment's mother wouldn't have had the strength or the energy to accompany them on such a lengthy excursion.

The classroom overlooked the athletic field. The freshmen were out in maroon shorts, romping without direction at the start of their hour. Two years ahead of Paul, they appeared worldly and imposing, their games orchestrated by conspiracy. Paul would have been annihilated in their company. There was a bright sun and a clear blue sky. A whistle blew. From the habit of a winter playroom, the boys, who were scattered across the field, fell languidly into line.

The barren winter playroom, moist and drafty, its frightening acoustics exaggerating sound, was structured for dodge ball —fifteen to a side, volleyballs or soccer balls hurled like bullets. If an opponent caught the ball and held it, the boy who had thrown it was disqualified. If a dashing soldier, racing in terror across his territory, was nicked or caught squarely, he was out. Hovering in a corner, overlooked until the end, Paul became the target of Thomas Lawler. Slam! The ball whipped by Paul's nose, crashing into the cement wall a few feet behind his trembling body. The echoes of the playroom magnified the slam and frightened Paul like a backfire. Slam! Lawler bearing down on his target. Paul Kramer; short brown hair, short legs, swift, dodging, with his mother's round face, the secrets gone from his eyes, the son of an actor, the announcer of news, the reconstructor of professional games. He was wearing maroon shorts. He was shirtless because his team was shirtless.

It was Lawler and Paul, the last two soldiers on the field. Lawler's ball slammed against Paul's wall with such force that it bounded back to Lawler, standing at the chalk line in the middle of the playroom. It was all Lawler, huge and red-haired, a freshman. Slam! And back to Lawler. Paul was racing crazily. "Get him!" Tornitzer yelled to Lawler. Tornitzer had been on Paul's side. "Get him!" Paul, out of breath, stood motionless in the corner. From the line, Lawler considered him. The playroom fell silent. Lawler evaluated the target. The target, he understood, would stay still. The target had no breath and no will. The target was a coward. Lawler, in maroon shorts and a tee shirt, brought back his arm. The bullet flew. Paul was caught on the side of the face. He buried himself in the corner, determined not to cry. "Lawler's the king!" shouted Andy Baker. Paul could hear the rain on the window. He had never in his life exchanged a word with Lawler. Lawler did not know his first name. In the corner, covering the side of his face with his hand, he spoke softly to himself: "My name is Paul Kramer. Hi, there, my name is Paul Kramer."

Calisthenics on the field, the lines of boys bending and turning. Mr. Bentini, in charge of the activity, performed the exercises with his charges. He was a grossly muscular man with a low opinion of troublemakers. "Kramer, where are your sneakers?" Paul was wearing street shoes in the gym. "I guess they just snuck away," Paul replied. "You're a low-life, kid. Get out of my gym," Bentini hissed. The low-life shuffled out, his leather heels clicking noisily on the sleek gymnasium floor.

Paul watched the calisthenics end and the group disperse. Quickly, Bentini organized two softball games back to back, one at the far end of the field, one directly in Paul's line of vision. Paul tuned in to Garment for a moment. The wine was still flowing, it was easy to hear. Garment now had himself addressing a group of wine lovers at the Commodore Hotel, miles and miles from the France before the Germans.

Paul observed that the softball games drifted into one another. The outfielders in both contests seemed to be gathered together, grazing in a neutral pasture. Now and then a ball would be struck that would find its way through the defense and roll elusively from its own designated area into the territory of the other game. A fielder would chase it down, rushing recklessly into the teeth of the action, through the infield, and just to the right of the pitcher's mound, where he would pounce on it. It occurred to Paul in history class that perhaps the games could be combined in a complex series of arrangements whereby certain fielders in one game were permitted to participate in the other; certain ground balls could be retrieved and acted upon by a congress of performers so that the four teams would accumulate in a way that Paul would work out, one final total of scoring, subdivided by a judge or referee, such as Bentini, according to specific skills that he alone defined and acknowledged. A fascinating concept.

"Mr. Kramer, the answer isn't out the window."

Garment charged into Paul's scheme.

"Pardon, sir?" Paul said, awakening to the confrontation.

"I said, and I won't say it again, that the answer isn't out the window." Garment's feet remained on the desk. His tone, to Paul's surprise, lacked its usual cruelty. It sounded almost conversational.

"Oh, but it *is*," Paul replied earnestly. "Really it is. The answer *is* out the window, you know?" Paul spoke seriously, and for the very first time to Garment, with a slight degree of passion.

Garment took his feet off the desk and leaned forward in his chair. For a moment he stared at Paul. Then he asked, "Would you care to explain yourself, Mr. Kramer?"

Paul, exhilarated, said: "I just think that—I just think that sometimes there are no facts that can give you an answer, you know? What I mean is, I like to try and figure out a different kind of answer."

The class giggled.

"You mean an answer of your own invention?"

"Yes, that's it. I don't mean right or wrong, the answer, that is. I mean just that it's something I feel good about, or I think about seriously, without a book or a test, or, you know, an answer." Paul spoke quietly.

"When did the Japanese bomb Pearl Harbor?" Garment wanted to know.

"December seventh, nineteen forty-one," Paul replied quickly.

"Now, that's a fact, isn't it?" Garment asked, with more severity than before.

"Uh-huh," Paul said, sensing his case was lost.

"That answer *isn't* out the window, Mr. Kramer. It's not

anything you *feel*. It's right there in the books, it's right there on the tests, tests that you have had extreme difficulty passing. Isn't that right, Mr. Kramer?"

"I guess," Paul said, despondent.

"My advice to you, Mr. Kramer, is to pay attention to what goes on in the classroom and cease your indolence. Do you understand me?" Garment, avoiding the overkill, spoke these last words to Paul with a paternal flavor, even with a suggestion of affection in his slight smile.

He turned away from Paul and, leaving the Commodore Hotel behind, returned at last to the France before the Germans.

With despondency came fear. Paul felt tears somewhere. He riveted his eyes on Garment. He didn't hear a word. He imagined his mother swimming in the green ocean. She waved at him from far away. He was standing at the water's edge. His mother swam through the waves and came to him on the shore. She held him.

Franklin Kramer made dinner. He had given Emma the day off and had cautioned his wife about fatigue; she had visited the shops in the afternoon and had returned with a light feeling in her body. She always described it as "a floating sensation; as if I'm walking in the air by the ceiling, and rising higher, like a helium balloon."

"I want total rest for you," Franklin had told her.

Broiled chicken, and rice to accompany Carol's, and sliced tomatoes, and Schrafft's chocolate ice cream. Carol sat with them for a while, then went back to bed. Franklin could get a good meal on the table, and Paul could broil meat, defrost frozen stringbeans, bake a potato, tear a head of lettuce into small pieces in a glass salad bowl and pour bottled dressing, usually in excess, onto the lettuce. They both enjoyed preparing food. It was partly due to Carol's passion. She was an instinctive and brilliant cook, and though she could eat nothing that she made, she would read recipes aloud from *Gourmet* magazine; before entering the kitchen she would write them out in longhand, adding a little, subtracting a little. Casseroles were her favorites: moussaka, beef bourguignon, sweetbreads chausseur, and a bouillabaisse. She permitted herself not even one taste along the way. "I'm like a blind man playing the piano," she said.

"Would you like to know my favorite things to eat in the world?" Carol asked her family as they sat around her bed after dinner. "Make a list," Paul suggested.

On a yellow legal pad, and with a ballpoint pen, Carol wrote:

> artichoke
> Camembert
> draft beer
> lobster
> corn on the cob
> fresh clams
> asparagus
> avocado
> caviar (tied with artichoke)

"That's it," Carol said with pleasure. Paul took it from her and looked it over with his father.

"Asparagus shouldn't be on there. It's too stringy," Paul declared firmly.

"I bet you change your mind on that," Carol told him.

"Never," Paul said.

"You shouldn't be so positive about things," his mother advised. "Leave room for change."

"Not on asparagus."

"We shall see what we shall see."

"Four of your favorite things are really one big dinner," Franklin observed. "Lobster, corn on the cob, clams, and beer."

"I guess that would be my favorite combination." Carol

remembered such a meal with Franklin in the first year of their marriage. In Truro, early in a sultry August. They had rented a house and hired a cook. The fog rolled over the Cape at five. They lay together in a bedroom above the sea, resting gin and tonics on their naked bellies. Later, at twilight, at a wooden table in a garden, they were served with care by their silent chef from Bangor, Maine. Mozart chamber music from an old Capehart by a window helped them along. The night turned clear and deep and glittered with stars, and lit their garden with the last full moon before the harvest. A breeze played with the candlelight. Dahlias and cosmos daisies surrounded their table.

"How about a walk and a Good Humor?" Paul asked his father. It was their custom after dinner, at least twice a week, to go out for a stroll, a neighborhood stroll, with the prize a Popsicle.

"I'm going to nap a little," Carol told them.

"You need anything?" Franklin asked his wife. "Magazines? Books? The *World-Telegram?*"

"Maybe *Vogue,* if the new one's out."

Franklin leaned down to kiss Carol. "Truro?" he whispered.

"Truro," she said softly.

Franklin and Paul walked over to Fifth Avenue and took the park side down through the Eighties. The night was warm and clear and sleepy with spring humidity. Paul, in khakis and cordovans and a Dodgers cap, felt at ease in the company of the tall man striding beside him. They had walked together often, occasionally at war: more respect for your mother. More sensitivity to her illness. More attention to schoolwork. Less emphasis on WPKF. There are other people in the world besides Paul Kramer, you know, and you've got to start to deal with them

rather than draw away or cause enough trouble for them to want
to draw away from you.

And Franklin bought presents for Paul: chocolate cake
from Hamburger Heaven; an electric hockey game; a miniature
pool table; a stop watch; dice; dark glasses; a carton of Double
Bubble gum; books: *The Brown Bomber; The Babe; The Jackie
Robinson Story*; and records: "I'm My Own Grandpa"; "My
Heart Cries for You"; "The Tennessee Waltz." These presents,
carrying Carol's weight, infected Paul with continual expectation. "Will you get me some comics?" "Will you get me an
official National League baseball?" "Will you get me some records?" "Could I have some records?" Hi, there. Paul Kramer
here. "Somewhere there's music, how faint the tune/Some-
where there's Heaven, how high the moon."

Silence worked well for them. They could walk together,
pick things up in midstream, navigate gracefully. Their shorthand had honed their intimacy.

"Indolence," said Paul. They were passing the museum.

"Indolence," Franklin repeated, declaratively.

"Indolence, indolence," Paul said, picking up his father's
scheme.

"Indolence," Franklin repeated. He could wait.

"I would like to know," Paul said finally, "if indolence is
bad."

"You would like to know what indolence *means*. Am I correct in assuming you would like to know what indolence
means?" Franklin dug up some stage resonance for the occasion.

Paul was on the ball: "You are correct in assuming that I
am assuming that you know what indolence means."

"Indolence means lazy; sluffing off on the job. Primarily it
means laziness, or not inclined to work at the task. Who called
you indolent?"

"What do you mean? I don't know what you're talking
about." Paul spread his arms, his palms up.

"Who called you indolent?" Franklin persisted.

It was clear to Paul that his incredulity was doomed. "Garment," he said.

"In what context?" Franklin wanted to know. "Did he simply say 'Good morning, indolent Paul'?"

"I was lookin' out the window." Paul dropped his g's in a crisis. Cuteness couldn't hurt when his back was to the wall.

"I see," Paul's father said. And after a pause: "Do you think you're indolent?"

"I think sometimes. But it's not laziness, you know?"

"Just indolence. A good old case of indolence."

"My mind wanders away sometimes," Paul said with a smile.

"Where does it go?" Franklin asked.

"I don't know. Places."

"What places?"

"Baseball. My programs. Stuff like that."

"Your mind has a mind of its own," Franklin said. "Like mirrors in a barber shop. Have you noticed that when you're at Michael's getting a haircut you can see dozens and dozens of reflections of yourself?"

"It's weird," Paul replied. "I try to count them sometimes."

"Well, that's what your mind is like. A mind within a mind within a mind."

"Everything's scrambled sometimes. And fuzzy. Like steam gets on all the mirrors."

Franklin thought this a splendid analogy for a twelve-year-old. "Yes. That's a nice way of describing it."

Franklin stopped walking for a moment. They were standing at the corner of Fifth Avenue and Seventy-ninth Street, about to cross the street and head to Madison, where a Good Humor truck lingered in the evenings.

"You know something," Franklin said, catching Paul's eyes, "the thing to do is to not let the room steam up so that the mirrors get steamy and fuzzy. Do you understand what I'm trying to say? If you can keep things in a certain order, not necessarily any rigid order, but just a certain kind of clearness that's never totally wiped away by daydreaming, or looking out the window as Mr. Garment caught you doing, then you can, in effect, keep the heat down in your mind. There will be less fog in the room. What do you think?" Franklin was curious about just how much of this was working.

Paul stood at the corner without speaking.

"What do you think?" his father repeated.

"I think it's hard to do," he said. "For me it's hard. Do you think I'm a screwball?" Paul asked this with a large grin. Franklin knew that the packaging of his son's questions was important.

"I think you're not a screwball at all," Franklin told Paul seriously. "I think you are thoughtful. I think you are strong and creative. I think you can see into every mirror in Michael's, and then some. What makes you think you're a screwball?"

"I think about it sometimes, that's all," Paul replied. "I mean, it's just a dream, is all it is."

They both had orange Popsicles which shed their sherbet cocoons, revealing vanilla ice cream.

They could see the blinking images of a televised ball game through the window of a bar. They stood for a while, finishing their Good Humors and looking into the dark saloon.

"That's Hank Bauer batting," Paul pointed out. "I hate Hank Bauer."

"Why?" Franklin asked idly.

"Ever see his face? You'd hate that face."

Bauer singled.

"Let's go," Paul said. "Bauer's always getting on."

In a while, Paul asked his father: "Who's your favorite player?"

"I'd have to think," Franklin answered. His relationship with baseball was remote, and almost entirely manufactured for his son. Paul, in his Dodgers cap, put Franklin in mind of Carl Furillo; somewhere along the line Franklin, if only subliminally, had made the connection. Furillo's name was the name he chose.

"Do you think the Dodgers will win all the marbles?" Paul asked.

"Yes," Franklin said. "Certainly."

"Do you think they'll ever win the World Series?"

"Isn't the World Series all the marbles?"

"To me that's just the pennant."

"I think they'll win the World Series."

"When?"

"This year."

"Why?"

"Why do I think that? I just do."

"You wouldn't make a very good interview guest," Paul said.

"Why not?" asked his father.

"Your answers are too short. You gotta really talk if you're going to be a guest."

"Do you ever do any interviews on your station?"

"Sometimes in 'Sports Extra' after a game I'll interview one of the players."

Paul and Franklin continued on without talking. They were only a few blocks from home.

"Do you know what I'd like?" said Paul, at last. "I'd like to interview you. Just for practice."

"I'd be delighted," Franklin replied.

"When we get home let's just practice, okay?"

"Tonight?" Franklin had looked forward to reading in his study.

"Not for long. Okay?"

"If it's not for long."

"I've never interviewed anyone, you know, real."

Franklin wondered how deeply his son had hidden the consideration of fantasy. At what point would the dam spring a leak and pour through Paul, flooding the transmitter of WPKF, condemning it forever to silence?

They sat opposite each other at the card table in Paul's room.

"All right, are you ready?" Paul asked. "This is just practice."

"I'm ready," Franklin said.

"Good evening," Paul began. "This is WPKF, and I'm Paul Kramer. Tonight our guest is Franklin Kramer, the actor and play writer. How are you tonight, Mr. Kramer?"

"I'm fine, thank you," Franklin replied. He was amused to find himself slightly nervous.

"I'd like to ask you, first of all, are you planning to write a new play?"

"As a matter of fact, I'm working on one now, my first in a long while. It's called *The Shade of the Apple Tree.* Is that a long enough answer?" Franklin was aware that he might disrupt the interview by speaking out of the character of a guest.

Paul ignored his father's aside. "When will it be produced?" he asked, his voice assuming a persuasive radio flow.

"I hope sometime next season. Perhaps a year from now." Franklin was relieved that Paul had let it pass.

"Well, now, tell me," Paul continued, "What are your upcoming plans?"

"You mean professionally? I plan to continue work on *The Shade of the Apple Tree,* and to look after my family, my son Paul, and my wife Carol, which is all, of course, on the personal side. There's a possibility of a tour in a play called *The Man Who Came to Dinner* for sometime this summer."

"I see," Paul said. "And your family? What are their summer plans?"

"My wife Carol will remain in New York. If I should do the play in July and August she'd have a part-time nurse to make sure that things were in order around the apartment. My son Paul will be returning to Camp Robinson Crusoe for his second summer. Last summer was somewhat difficult for him, but I think that now that he's a bit older, he'll enjoy camp life more."

"I don't think so," Paul said seriously.

"Why not?" Franklin asked the interviewer.

"Because everything is so competitive at that camp. And there's a schedule for every hour. And I hate the kids."

"Maybe there'll be some new kids this year."

"There's never any new kids."

"You were a new kid."

"I was the only one. Maybe there was about three."

"But you won't be new any more."

"There's something about being new. Once you're new, you're always new."

Silence. Franklin thought he would let Paul struggle with the issue on his own.

Then, from the hallway outside Paul's closed door, there came an unusual sound. Both Paul and Franklin picked it up at once, but at first neither could make any sense of it. Paul had the eerie feeling that a large dog had stationed itself in the hallway and was wagging its tail against the wall.

They sat motionless for half a minute. Then in a quiet voice, with an almost electronic texture, Franklin said to his son: "Your mother's dying."

Paul read his father's lips, but the sound failed to reach his ears. Paul heard nothing but the thumping of the dog's tail in the hallway. He was unaware of his father's jolting departure from the room. It struck Paul that a game had been interrupted by a roll call; that certain players were absent and their names were being repeated on the radio. He listened for the names.

On the floor, in the hallway, a few feet from Paul's door, Carol, on her knees, struggled to stand. Franklin surrounded her with his arms. She was vomiting blood in a steady stream. Her mouth was filled with white foam. She was choking on her excretion. Her silk nightgown was soaked with blood. Her arms and ankles and feet were painted a black-red. Her hair was tangled over her face and covered with blood. Now she struggled to stay on her knees. Franklin, with his mouth to her ear, repeated over and over: "Carol easy love easy love Carol love love." Bloody foam splattered on him and clung to his face. Carol's knees gave way and she slipped to her side. Her nostrils spewed blood. She attempted to speak but gagged on a gush of foam. "Carol easy easy love Carol easy easy." Franklin kept speaking into her ear over and over. He held her tightly to him. He was bathed in her blood.

Paul came to the door. He stood on the threshold of his room. Was someone calling his name? Was he wanted on the phone? Was he missing a program? Oh no. Oh no. Oh no.

"Paul, get Morris up here. Get Morris up here, and after that I want you to go in your room and close the door and stay there until I come in. Get Morris now." Everything that Franklin had said had been spoken quietly, as if someone were asleep nearby. Paul went down the hall right away. He rang the elevator bell. A short man came up. He faced Paul. Paul said: "Come."

Morris ran down the hall.

"Get Dr. Spiro and an ambulance," Franklin told him.

Morris said: "Jesus."

Morris used the phone by Carol's bed.

"I want you to go to your room and stay there until I come

in," Franklin told his son again. Paul did as his father asked. He shut the door to his room and lay down on his bed.

Morris ran through the hall to the elevator. Franklin lay next to Carol on the floor, his chest pressed to her back. Her head rested on his arm. Franklin repeated over and over and over: "Easy love easy love Carol love." He whispered to her, his mouth pressed directly to her ear. And then softly, and clearly, and with her eyes closed, so that she appeared to be speaking from within sleep, Carol said to her husband: "Thank God for you both."

"Easy easy love," Franklin said to her.

Paul lay on his bed in his clothes, his face buried in the pillow. He was nowhere near tears, although he tried to induce them. Then sleep surrounded him and disengaged him from his mother and father. He slept dreamlessly with the lights on.

He was awakened in the middle of the night by a knock at his door. He swung quickly into consciousness. He checked the clock. It was four-thirty. He wondered why his mother was knocking, why she didn't simply come in, just open the door and walk in. Paul thought that she needed a glass of water, that the faucet in her sink had run dry, and that he would be able to help her.

The door opened slowly. Paul faced his father. Franklin's face was white and his eyes were black. Paul assumed that he was wearing make-up, that he had just come off the stage, that he had flown in from another city to be with his family on a special occasion.

"Your mother died at midnight," Franklin said from the doorway. "She had a stroke and she died. She's gone." At first he spoke softly, his eyes focused on Paul. But then, with a bit more strength in his voice, he continued. "She was the bravest woman I've ever known. The bravest human being. The most courageous." Franklin's eyes filled with tears. "She had a will to live that I've never seen the likes of. She was determined to go on with her life."

Paul had never seen his father cry. Now he watched, amazed, as tears streaked his father's face. Why was his father crying? This gentle and composed man standing in the doorway, why was he crying so late at night with the lights on?

"Why are you crying?" Paul asked.

"I'm lost," Franklin answered.

They faced each other in silence, Franklin remaining at the door.

"Carol is gone," Franklin said, finally, more to himself than to his son.

"Is she dead?" Paul asked. He was sitting on the bed, his legs dangling over the side.

"She's gone, Paul. She loved you. You don't know how much she loved you." Franklin moved into the room. He sat down at the card table, his arms at his sides. His gray cashmere sweater and blue slacks were caked with blood.

"We're alone," Paul said. He hadn't formed the words in his mind, or thought them out. They just came from him.

"That's right," Franklin said. "That's true."

Again there was silence, a silence so heavy that Franklin's tears, at first quiet and even peaceful, now flowed steadily, and became sobs. Franklin closed his eyes and cried. Paul, on the bed, extended his right arm, his fingers reaching for his father. Franklin covered his face with his hands.

The alarm rang at six forty-five. Paul got up and put a bathrobe on over his clothes. The lights were off, his father gone. A dim early-morning sunshine filtered through the blinds. Paul went to the bathroom. He washed his hands and brushed his teeth (powder gets the job done a thousand times the better).

He went down the hall in something of a hurry, for it was almost seven. Paul saw that the door to his father's study was closed.

"Good morning. On WPKF this is Paul Kramer with the news."

He was right on time.

"President and Mrs. Eisenhower arrived in the desert resort community of Palm Springs, California, this afternoon for a weekend of rest and golf. They will remain until midweek and plan to return to Washington by Thursday morning.

"In other news, Mayor Robert F. Wagner is reported improved today after a severe case of the flu. The Mayor has been confined to bed since Tuesday.

"In Major League baseball, in local activity, the Yankees beat the A's nine to five, the Dodgers overcame the Phillies four to two, and the Giants lost to the Braves eight to one."

It was here that Paul stopped for a moment to fold the paper together, and close it, and lay it gently on the floor. Then, resting his arms on the card table, he looked straight ahead of him for half a minute before beginning again.

"I have an announcement to make," he said. "There is a news story that is not in print this morning that must be reported by WPKF. My mother, Carol Kramer, died last night. She had a stroke and she died. She died at midnight. She was forty-one."

Again, silence. And then, at last:

"I wish you a good day. The sun has risen. This has been the seven o'clock news. Tune in tomorrow morning at seven o'clock for more news from the studios of WPKF in New York. This is Paul Kramer speaking."

PART TWO

CHAPTER TWO

Paul was dreaming. He was singing at the Acropolis to a large international audience standing in front of him in formal attire. He was accompanied by a symphony orchestra scattered in the ruins behind him; they were sitting on stone stools with sheet music in their laps. Paul, in a tuxedo and a Dodgers hat, was singing childhood lyrics to "Smoke Gets in Your Eyes":

> They asked me if I knew
> Raccoon shit was blue;
> I turned to them and said
> Bullshit you've been fed
> Raccoon shit is red.

There was enthusiastic applause from the audience. Paul picked out familiar faces and waved and doffed his hat. Charles

Aznavour was there, and Jennifer Rosen from Brandeis, and Jeb Magruder, and Preacher Roe.

Jennifer Rosen and Paul were off to Mykonos in a helicopter. A severe wind buffeted the aircraft. Jennifer Rosen was nude from the waist up, her large breasts bouncing wildly. "I'm ready just in case," she said. Paul caressed the nearest breast, the right breast, and aroused the nipple with his thumb. The helicopter was having a difficult time with the wind, and Jennifer was thrown against him. She held him tightly.

Paul was awakened by the shuffling of playing cards.

"Interested in gin rummy?" The passenger seated next to Paul, a chunky pink-faced man in a jacket and tie, had observed that Paul's eyes had opened.

"Are you up for defeat?" Paul asked.

"I'm a shrewd player," the man replied, continuing to shuffle on his tray.

"I've never lost a game of gin rummy in a moving vehicle of any kind. My game suffers in parlors and studies." Paul dug his watch out of the pocket of the seat before him. "We have an hour before Los Angeles. Can you be shrewd for an entire hour?"

"Would you care to lay a wager?"

"How's ten dollars to the winner? We'll play to a hundred."

"If you wish." The pink-faced man was already dealing.

"You didn't cut," Paul pointed out. "Doesn't matter, go ahead and deal."

"My name's Billings," declared the dealer.

"Paul Kramer, nice to know ya."

Paul drifted back to Jennifer Rosen over the Aegean Sea. He could feel her pendulous breasts in his hands, and was distracted by the heat of the memory.

"Down with four," Billings announced a short while later. "Spades," he added, displaying his hand with pride.

"I'll be back in a minute," Paul told him.

"I told you I was shrewd," said Billings with a championship smile. "Take your time. You'll need it."

In the lavatory Paul stared at himself in the mirror. He addressed his reflection: "Should I jerk off?"

He mulled this over for a while. Then he turned from the mirror and, with difficulty in the tiny cubicle, undressed completely, hanging his pullover sport shirt, blue jeans, and underpants on the door handle. Dressed only in moccasins he stood before the mirror once more, his head swimming with Jennifer Rosen by a pool in Beverly, Massachusetts. He and Jennifer Rosen were entangled in the grass. Fixed on this image and staring into his own eyes, Paul Kramer achieved orgasm onto the floor and into the sink of the lavatory. Occupied. Occupado. There was no Kleenex. There were no paper towels. Fuck American Airlines. Dear American Airlines: After jerking off in one of your filthy lavatories, I discovered that there were no paper towels, no Kleenex, no washclothes, no clean-up pads of any kind, only your cheap, sleazy wax toilet paper, which does not absorb sperm off the hand or the cock. It only spreads it like paint and makes a fucking mess. From now on, TWA gets my call.

Billings was dealing as Paul returned. "Thirty-three zip," Billings said.

It was Paul's hand all the way; an easy forty-one points.

"I'll go down with three," Paul told Billings the third time around.

"You got me," admitted Billings. He had a whole pack of Trident spearmint gum in his mouth, but his jaw hardly moved at all. Occasionally it stopped altogether as he considered his cards. When he spoke, it was without any suggestion that his mouth was full of gum. Paul wondered: Where is he hiding it? Perhaps it was stored away in his considerable jowls, or under his tongue, or perhaps Trident had special properties that encouraged easy storage in the hollows of the mouth, the gum itself thinning out into nothingness, only to regain its bulk at the discretion of the chewer.

Billings rallied. A flurry of winning hands: six, thirteen, twenty-one points. Paul saw that the man was sweating.

"You're closing in, Billings," he said, somewhat concerned.

The seat belt sign was on. After two discards Paul knew he had Billings pinned. Billings, with his Trident, studied his cards. He shuffled them around. He was taking his time. They were on top of Los Angeles. Franklin Kramer passed through Paul's mind: something Paul had said had made his father laugh. They were out-of-doors.

Paul to Billings a minute later: "What's the name of the game?"

"What?"

"What's the name of the game we're playing?"

"Gin."

"*You* said it, *I* didn't." Paul displayed his clinching hand. Billings studied it, searching for errors or tricks.

"I offer you my congratulations," he said wearily. From an inside pocket Billings produced a fistful of crumpled bills, and handed two fives to Paul.

"You play an interesting game," Paul said, understanding that he was angry with this perspiring, overweight opponent, this flaccid loser. Why angry? Paul had no idea. He extended friendship with a handshake. "You're a tough player, Mr. Billings. I hope we meet again."

The two of them stood in the aisle together, waiting for the ramp.

"Here on business?" Paul asked idly.

"My brother passed on yesterday. He lives here."

Paul was tempted to correct the "lives," but instead said: "I'm sorry to hear that."

"And you?" Billings inquired, with airplane-aisle politeness.

Paul thought of lying, but the truth popped out: "I'm visiting my dad. He lives here and he's retired."

"I see," Billings said.

Paul thought: and that is that.

Billings was met by three elderly women who embraced him solemnly, one by one. Paul watched them walk slowly down the stairs, clustered together, consumed by the gravity of the day.

On the lengthy moving ramp to the street a man in a ten-gallon hat rested a noisy radio on the railing. Paul was in earshot. "Billy Graham, in a telephone interview with an Associated Press reporter yesterday, said that we should pray for the Judiciary Committee and for the President. Dr. Graham said that the language in the transcripts is, quote, 'not the language I've ever heard him use,' and then he said, 'The Lord is listening all the time. The Lord has got his tape recorder going from the time you're born until you die.' "

In the bus to Budget Rent-A-Car Paul thought of Jennifer Rosen at Logan Airport years earlier. When she had lost him during a severe Boston winter she had cried: "I am permanently grieved."

"Permanently grieved," Paul said in the back of the empty bus, gazing out at the hazy afternoon.

Paul drove aimlessly in a Dodge Dart. At the Farmer's Market he wandered up the aisles of avocados and tomatoes and settled on a tostada from a Mexican stand. Feeling restless and blue, he was putting off seeing his father. Ducking out of the May heat, Paul adjusted himself to the darkness of a porno house on Pico and stared distractedly at three men and two women furiously at work. The tension in the auditorium was disturbed by the laughter of an aging gentleman in the last row. The laughter was shrill and persistent; it grated on the other patrons. "Shut up, motherfucker!" someone yelled from near the front. The laughter subsided for a moment, then continued as before. Paul detected a defiant increase in its volume, confirming that the deranged old fart in the back had his angry wits about him.

Paul slipped away and back into the Dodge Dart. The laughter stayed with him, infecting the car like stagnant air. Rock and roll radio loud, May, Los Angeles, California:

> Everybody, have you heard
> He's gonna buy me a mockingbird;
> And if that mockingbird don't sing
> He's gonna buy me a diamond ring.

The string of a Tampax had been clearly visible on the screen, dangling from the vagina of a young blond girl in the Pico porno house. Could that have amused the motherfucker?

> I might rise above,
> I might go below;
> Ride with the tide
> And go with the flow.

Crescent, Maple, Rexford, Elm, Roxbury. Paul, driving through Beverly Hills, fastened on fantasy: the Paul Kramer estate. Avocado trees, string quartets, the privilege of considering the possibilities.

There was money here in this languid territory. Abundant white homes, manicured lawns, Japanese gardeners crouched near sprinklers. The rows of the rich, from Sunset to Santa Monica, roped off from the rest of time, men and women traveling in season, invading these immaculate castles. The sleepy perfection of excess.

"Senator, where do you project yourself three years from now?"

"Do you mean in the Pennsylvania Avenue sense of the word?"

"Which word?"

Paul and the Senator together on New York television. Paul was known for his irreverence. His programs on radio and on television were removed from the air, and returned, and discontinued. Ebb and flow, Paul had observed.

Gathering fifteen thousand dollars from the ebb and flow, Paul was thinking of wandering. "I'm going to go out and see my dad. Then maybe San Francisco. Then, who knows? I'm thirty-two, and there's only me to worry about. I've got a little savings. I want to drift. What do you think?"

The question was asked of Michael Holland, a friend from Brandeis, a doctor. In the last year he had become Paul's doctor.

"Mr. Kramer, here are your facts: Height: six feet. Weight: 180. Blood pressure: 130 over 90. Cholesterol: 310, too high. No eggs, less beef, no shellfish, but all the fish you want."

They were having lunch at King of the Sea. Holland was a thin, youthful man with a sparkling, compassionate smile. Often, Paul thought of him playing tennis at Brandeis in a red bathing suit: Holland, racing to his right for a surprising return, had stretched himself to his very limits, comically determined, pursuing the unreachable with tenacity. Holland hung in, but not—or so it seemed to Paul—on behalf of victory; rather, in deference to the afternoon and to the severely competitive spirit of Sharon Childs, and with affection for the art of structured combat: I will play against you in this game. I will attempt, by ability and cunning, to strike the ball with my racket and place it on your side of the court with speed and accuracy, so that you, try as you might, will be unable to return my placement and unable to match my expertise and strength. I will accumulate more points than you, and arrive at the concluding sixth game an obvious but gracious winner. This victory, however, will not preclude our mutual nudity within the hour. I will nail you on the bed, licking your sweaty armpits, subduing your thrashing legs, entering your unwilling body, encouraging you to sit upon me. Direct our show, Sharon Childs. You move with the music of Mantovani. Your eyes are shut. Sweaty Sharon Childs, writing with tennis defeat. Wipe it out as you move. Sharon Childs. Sharon love. Six love.

Michael Holland was leaning forward in his chair at King of the Sea. "I can't argue with a drifter. He's gone before your case is made. And I have no argument anyway. It's time for you to drift a little."

"I think so," Paul responded. "Time to get my shit together. We got it made, baby, we Eisenhower children got *choices*. We're a select group. We're to be envied. We can remain uncommitted in Hyannis Port until the convention actually gets on the blower and calls us, *implores* us. For the good of the party."

"Los Angeles?"

"Los Angeles."

"How's your father?"

"He's okay. He's fine. He's thinking about writing his memoirs."

"Does he live alone?"

"Yes, but he has friends out there. Thirties Broadway people, New Deal people. Screenwriters, a couple of actors from the Walter Slezak mold. I get the feeling that he's got a good life."

Franklin Kramer in Paul's mind: filled with champagne, he was in a tux, he had a cane, he had a piano and a piano player, he had an audience—his son and his wife. "I can't give you anything but love, baby/That's the only thing I've plenty of, baby."

"Shrimp defeats the purpose of the fish," observed Holland.

"This is a celebration, Holland," Paul replied. "American Airlines a week from Tuesday, no movie."

"How long will you stay in L.A.?"

"Whatever feels good," Paul said. And after a pause: "What a difference between you and me. Your life decisions are made. Wife and children, and a doctor's office with a Plaza exchange. I'm still looking over the possibilities."

"You know, Paul," Michael Holland said seriously, "you travel your own road. It's all a matter of need."

Paul took a room at the Château Marmont and fell asleep in the late afternoon. He was awakened by a woman's shrill voice in the hall: "Listen, you sonofabitch, don't Dory Previn me!" The remark went uncontested.

It was eight-thirty. Paul lay on his back, fighting depression. He considered calling his father: Dad I'm here how are ya that's good I'm at the Château Marmont and I'm depressed and I'll be right over.

Eight-thirty. It had always been a threatening time for Paul. Slipping into darkness and solitude in the unfamiliar shadows of this hotel room, Paul wondered why. Hi, there. Paul Kramer here, and to kick off the proceedings tonight, here's Peggy Lee.

> Lover, when I'm near you
> And I hear you speak my name,
> Softly in my ear
> You breathe a flame.

Paul ordered a bottle of Scotch and some ice. He went through his bags, searching for a book that had floated into his mind. He had two suitcases, containing six tee shirts, three pairs of dungarees, sneakers, black shoes, ten pairs of underpants, many black socks, a small radio, two white shirts, a blue suit, two dark ties, tennis whites, a blue terry-cloth bathrobe, two bathing suits, a jockstrap, a medicine case stuffed with Ultra Brite toothpaste, Valium, nail clippers, an electric razor, fifteen joints in a plastic soap dish, a small bottle of Scope, and three toothbrushes. And books.

Paul was after a favorite paragraph of his from *Slouching Towards Bethlehem*. He stood naked in the middle of the room and read it out loud. An old friend, that book.

After a second drink Paul sat on the side of the bed by the phone. He believed that his passage from day through dusk and into night was made treacherous by the deprivation of alternatives. Imprisoned by the dark, he was robbed of peripheral vision, cunning, defense, and the clarity of hope. Night had one dimension: survival. The manners that Paul assumed at night were designed to carry him through intact. He observed: there is very little truth around here after the sun done gone down.

"Hi Sandi with an 'i.' "

"Hey!"

"Can I come over and play?"

"You in L.A.? Where are you?"

"Beverly Hills Hotel."

"How ya been?"

"Under control."

"I'm menstruating?"

"Think of it. In spite of that, I'd like to see you."

"Gee, okay."

"If a pretty girl is a week, you is a decade."

"What?"

"C. P. Snow."

"What?"

"See ya later."

"If a pretty girl is *what?*"

Sandi Cummings. Fashion coordinator. Alexander's in New York, now Robinson's in Los Angeles. She had gathered up thirty-seven pairs of shoes, clothing that filled a vast walk-in closet, three large Del Monte boxes of cosmetics, *This Is My Beloved* by Walter Benton, seven thousand three hundred dollars' worth of jewelry, and traveled West on her own, unencumbered by substantial thought, or severe heartache, or complex human arrangement. That she was annoyed at her dismissal from Alexander's there was no doubt. Surely she had been opportunistic, and occasionally devious, at war through smiles with her sly and sleek superior. It was known throughout the store: Sandi had drive; the heir apparent in her department, a fashion dynamo, and an absolute *love*. Her friend Bob, in the shoe department, a bald homosexual with a penchant for bow ties and checked shirts, had said of Sandi: "The sweetness of the earth is contained in her heart. If I were a girl I'd go for her."

Sandi was a perfect and vapid beauty. Her light-brown hair was cropped short. She was rouged and lipsticked and earringed. She smiled easily and laughed warmly. Her face, noncommittally structured, gave away no ethnic information, no town or state, no contempt or passion. Her eyes were hazel and small; she would enlarge them cosmetically in the early-morning hours before Alexander's. She arose at six and began work almost at once. Occasionally Paul would watch the process from semisleep. Sandi naked: she was thirty-three years old. Her breasts were ample, her limbs were thin, her belly bulged ever so slightly. "I'm only seven pounds over my modeling days," she had told Paul with childish and delightful pride. Her pubic hair, trimmed and triangled, was a shade darker than her hair.

Sandi would stand before the mirror and stare severely at her reflection. In her apartment the implements were numerous. In his apartment she had stocked only the essentials. At both homes, in the nude, she smoked Kools, and ashes would fall to her feet.

"Let's see ya burn your box," Paul said.

"What an awful thing to say," Sandi responded. It was a pet phrase. She trotted it out in lieu of anger or real gut irritation. She would accompany it occasionally with a small and somewhat tentative smile. She seemed to be asking: "That's not true, is it? I mean, I'm really nice, no?"

"Your silliness is overwhelming." Paul glared at her in mock rage.

"What an awful thing to say."

"No one needs a thousand pairs of shoes."

"What an awful thing to say."

"I hate nail polish on toenails."

"What an *awful* thing to say."

"Putting nail polish on toenails is like putting adhesive tape over your ears or eyes."

"I don't understand—what?"

And now, in May, Paul sought her out again. She had appeared on his television program with others in her field. He had taken her to dinner that evening. Later, sleepy with wine, they had fornicated on full stomachs and had fallen immediately asleep. It was only the next morning in sunlight (no one had pulled the blinds) that the extent of their hunger for each other had become apparent. They went after each other voraciously, seeking out orifices, sucking and playing, coming in easy silence.

"I'm into hitting," Sandi had confided, as they lay exhausted in beams of sunlight.

So, as it turned out, was Paul. Kneeling before her, her legs in the air, installing himself in her body, and retreating, and slashing in again, Paul had smacked her smartly across the cheek, arousing them both. "Oh, baby," he had said. I'm not angry. Hit her. Hit her good. Slam her.

"You bullshitter," Sandi had hissed.

Now *that* made him mad.

He slapped her with more strength. Her cheeks were aflame. She froze in orgasm. He came in tears.

"And a guy named Donald gave me a lovely bracelet. Look."

Sandi was speaking. They were sitting in a small, carpeted living room on Doheny Drive with the heat on.

"Why is the heat on?" Paul asked.

"*Is* the heat on?" Sandi bounded up. "Off it goes," she said, cheerfully. She was wearing a green silk bathrobe. Her toenails were pink, her hair longer than Paul remembered. She was smoking a Kool. A backgammon set was open on the card table. With the sound off, the "Tuesday Night Movie" blinked at them from a large color set. Sandi stared at it from the couch.

"Are you happy out here?"

"Oh, yes. The store respects me, with New York and all."

"Is it the same job exactly?"

"Uh-huh. I'm presenting part of the fall line to the branches a week from Thursday."

The "Tuesday Night Movie" lost out to Robinson's. Sandi had some sketches of the fall line, and would Paul like to see them?

"Yes."

Sandi had a slick little speech:

"There is a conscious, avant garde fashion change for fall of this year. The feeling is loose, big and easy. Styles are romantic and fun. Fabrics and colors are rich. Easy designs are beautifully balanced and proportioned, with an aura of exquisite quality about them. Even casual and camp are chic, neat, and tidy. A new-found conscious desire seems to have emerged, especially on the part of the young, toward a whole new, well-balanced, groomed approach to dressing. We're entering a new fashion era, with totally new shapes and silhouettes moving to the fore. The skinny, body-binding shapes are loosening up and moving away from the body. Hemlines are dropping, and the Big Pants scene is losing the race to the Big Skirt.

"The dress is making a strong comeback, softer, more romantic than in past years. The most important word describing the fall fashion scene is Big. But it is with a sense of softness and width—effortlessness and ease of movement. Shapes are easy and looser, with lengths going from just below the knee to ankle length. Boots are the perfect complement to all these lengths with a high-heeled shoe, without platform, worn with sheer, color-matched toes. Accessories play a big part in the total scene. Scarves are riding high on almost everything. If it's not a scarf tied above the neck, it's multiple beads or delicate flowers. It's a totally coordinated picture, with handbag and shoe colors matching again. Colors remain in the neutral category—strong on beiges, browns, rusts—with olive and burgundy, or aubergine, following close behind. And the cape is coming strong, with fur trim, super-wide shapes; hooded, peasant styling. Fabrics run the gamut from fake fur to strong tweed and lodens. Ombré-textured plaids are standouts with Cacharel and Sonja Rykiel."

Paul hung in there for the first couple of seconds as Sandi turned the pages of sketches. Rat-a-tat-tat, Sandi had got it down pat. Paul sipped his Scotch and water. Sandi was drinking too. Paul imagined that they would screw, and later eat Monterey Jack in the kitchenette. Paul slipped his hand under Sandi's silk robe. She didn't miss a beat of her speech.

"Whaddaya think?" Sandi asked, finishing up her routine.

"Do you stand up while saying all that?" Paul knew that a question or two would show his interest. He could move gracefully through her answers and steer the ship to bed. He removed his hand. This gesture, he thought, strengthened his credibility.

"I'll be showing slides. I'll probably be sitting down." Sandi was thoughtful, considering whether she'd be sitting or standing.

"Do you have anything to eat?" Paul asked.

For the most part, non sequiturs slipped by Sandi: look over here, Sandi, doyouhaveanythingtoeat? and that's where Sandi would go, except perhaps if she was angry she'd hang petulantly around the previous ground, slow to get her coat on and her shit together to move over to doyouhaveanythingtoeat? But Paul knew her anger: little driplets of whining and a God damn it and a what an awful thing to say. Paul cajoled and comforted, and occasionally apologized before he felt it was safe to move on.

"I got salami?"

Sandi often tacked a question mark onto her replies.

"It's eight-thirty?" "It's made of leather?" "Scrambled eggs?"

Paul was touched by this. Sandi was afraid of him, and of everyone. Her question mark protected her from catastrophe. Suppose eight-thirty was too late or too early. That leather was loathsome. That scrambled eggs were not acceptable.

Her question-marked salami moved Paul to surround her with his arms and kiss her cheek with tenderness. "I love salami," he whispered to her.

In bed, naked, they embraced each other.

"I'm menstruating?"

Replying with his hand, Paul positioned Sandi on her back. He caressed her breasts and her belly, letting his palm brush over her loins. Her cunt was dry. His fingers probed and established an entrance. He found the string and carefully tugged the Tampax away. "All gone," he told her, giggling, suggesting muffins and childhood and Cream of Wheat. He played with her. She moistened slowly.

"Wait," she said. She was up, and in the bathroom. Paul took a glimpse at Johnny Carson, silenced like the "Tuesday Night Movie."

Sandi was back with Lubriderm. "Here," she said. Crouched beside him, she was generous with Lubriderm. "Okay?" she wanted to know.

"Okay," he told her. He slid inside her.

Sandi had things to say: "I miss you. You fuck good. Sometimes I love you. Slower—ah, there. Don't wait for me, I can't come."

This time, with Scotch and salami and the oppressive heat in the tiny room, Paul accepted this. "For me this time," he whispered. He was telling her that in the morning he would make amends.

"For you for you, I love it," Sandi said.

Paul took it for his own, the right speed at the right time. Shut up, motherfucker! Paul heard it again. He was taking this one. It was his.

Ride with the tide and go.

CHAPTER THREE

It was noon and cloudy. Sandi, at seven in the morning in her new world, had sat naked before the mirror performing her familiar ritual. Paul had been able to catch a piece of his own supine figure in the glass. It had occurred to him that it would not be at all unpleasant if Sandi's western mirror could, with some juggling of its properties, discard the tiny bedroom in which she sat, considering her countenance, and replace it with his own appealing quarters in New York, leaving the nude star at center stage, mind you, simply reflecting her as the chief attraction in another theater. There they would be: himself in his own reassuring bed, having moments before completed slow and successful cunnilingus. His books and records, a framed photograph of him with Jackie Robinson, gold curtains from Bloomingdale's, a bulletin board displaying cartoons, snapshots of a girl named Leslie, a Los Angeles Dodgers schedule, typed questions for Jason Robards, a large black-and-white photograph of Franklin Kramer in his California garden: Franklin was standing by a tree in a long-sleeved sport shirt and light slacks. It looked as if he was smiling, but Paul couldn't tell for sure. It might have been that that was Franklin's idea of how a seventy-six-year-old retired playwright/actor should appear in a black-and-white photograph to be sent to his son: reflective, subdued, distinguished, at ease. At ease. If not now, when?

Franklin lived on the ground floor of a two-family house on Highpoint. Paul had helped him find it four years ago, and had returned three times in ten months to smooth his father's transition. The people above, an elderly couple named Meyer, with a number of cats on the loose, were the landlords. They stayed up there, reclusive and silent, their cats drifting through Franklin's garden, and up Franklin's tree, and every now and then into Franklin's very digs. The cats were haughty company for him. He had taken to leaving bowls of milk in the garden.

Paul was waiting, sitting in his Dodge Dart across the street. Maybe his father would emerge for a stroll in the gray early afternoon. It was possible that Franklin was out for lunch. Paul guessed the Brown Derby. Franklin Kramer: twenty years a widower, a trim man full of cautious pep, with a keen and inquiring mind. In his uncrowded days he contemplated his memoirs and tended to his garden and talked with his friends on the telephone. They were others like him, single men with theater in their past. They knew George Abbott and Billy Rose, and had stories to tell. Malice had evaporated with the years. They were cheerful ghosts, attached to each other by Roosevelt and Churchill, and the theaters of the east: the Music Box, the Colonial, the Wilbur, the Booth. Their sons and daughters battled with their own adolescent children in New York and Chicago and Washington and Seattle, keeping an eye on the gentlemen in the west. In some cases there were still scores to be settled, accusations to be made, peace to be established. Franklin and Paul, only briefly at war, and long ago, shared a tacit understanding that their weapons were dismantled and their explosives defused. Grievances were stored in the attic with cobwebs and dust—they had no bearing on today. Franklin's and Paul's unwritten treaty spelled it out: the attic was off limits, the ladder was rickety, the door jammed, the light chain broken.

Paul lurked in his rented car, flicking the radio from station to station. He lingered: "Among the many statements issued last week was one from Senator Byrd that said: 'If the President were to resign due to such pressures as are now engulfing the country, and by doing so terminate the impeachment inquiry now under way in the House, a significant portion of our citizens would feel that the President had been driven from office by his political enemies. The question of guilt or innocence would never be fully resolved.'"

How many times had Paul laid in wait, huddled in automobiles, the ignition off for fear of attracting attention? He had remained shivering on King Street in New York through a January morning and afternoon, anticipating the emergence or return of a girl named Judith. At dusk she had come out with a tall blond man who wore earmuffs and no overcoat. They had walked up Seventh Avenue to Sheridan Square and the subway. Paul had followed on foot, sneaking along the avenue forty yards behind them. Judith had curled her arm around the blond man. Later, in the car, Paul had wept. Only a month before, he had observed Judith's defecation, as she had sat blatantly naked on his toilet. What did this blond warm-eared asshole know of such intimate things.

One September Sunday afternoon, Paul, in a black Volkswagen, had waited out Robert Kennedy. Paul had parked at Seventy-sixth Street and had listened idly to a Yankee doubleheader while consuming a mammoth Mr. Goodbar. Around five, Kennedy, alone, had popped out of the Carlyle Hotel and had started north on Madison. Paul, crawling along in the VW, had felt that the Senator, in a black pinstripe suit, would be easy prey for a determined lunatic. Hello! waved passers-by.

Hello! waved Robert Kennedy. Paul had trembled with admiration. At Eighty-fifth RFK turned west. At Fifth Paul had left him. It was clear that the apartment of the former First Lady was the Senator's destination.

For whom does a lurker lurk? Paul asked himself this on Highpoint. Considering Judith and Kennedy, Paul observed that he now awaited another, more formidable hero. Fresca bottles and pinstripe suits paled by comparison. And yet the chances of Franklin Kramer actually appearing—one, two, three, just like that—accommodating his one child in a rented car, were, if one were to peek at the chances, almost nonexistent. Paul thought: I will not sit here a minute longer. Why am I here? I am obviously afraid of that man in that building, or I would have barged in right off the plane.

Paul found an answer. He was drifting now. His father would see through it, condemn his wandering, and show dismay. Franklin's lucid logic would anger Paul Kramer. "Return to your job. Fortify your credentials." Paul, knowing that to this minute here on Highpoint he had not thoroughly explored his departure, or examined his motives and the possibilities of return, felt vulnerable to an avalanche of perception from the Golden West. His homework was incomplete. His room was in disorder. He was late for chapel. "And in baseball, the Brooklyn Dodgers, behind Don Newcombe, nipped the Pittsburgh Pirates three to two last night before twenty-four thousand fans at Ebbets Field. Roy Campanella slammed his thirteenth homer of the year to lead the Dodgers' eight-hit attack."

Paul on television: What music do you listen to in your own home?

Pop Singer: I like all kinds of music.

Paul: But what do you especially like and choose to listen to in your own home?

Pop Singer: I'm partial to serious music. When I'm alone I like something more weighty.

Paul: Like what?

Pop Singer: I favor Percy Faith.

There was Franklin Kramer! What were the odds against this? Paul's father, across the street, was walking toward his car, a beige Maverick. He looked to be dressed in the same clothes he wore in the photograph. He was walking slowly, taking in the afternoon. Was this his first time out-of-doors today?

Paul found himself near tears. There, a few feet from him, was Franklin Kramer, well into his eighth decade, making his way across a rented lawn in the state of California on a cloudy Wednesday in the month of May. His hair was gray, almost white. He appeared less imposing than Paul had imagined him, less broad of shoulder, slightly frail. But not sickly by any means. Paul had last seen him at Christmas. Franklin had come east for the holidays and had taken a room at the Biltmore, though Paul had urged him to stay in his apartment. "It will be more comfortable for both of us," Franklin had explained.

Paul thought that maybe his father would be disappointed. Possibly he was housing a mistress. Quickly now or he'd be gone.

Paul got out of his car and slammed the door forcefully, hoping to draw his father's attention across the street. Franklin looked up. His son, in dungarees, a cotton sport shirt, and moccasins, stood seventy-five feet away. Franklin was stunned.

"Paul?" he finally shouted out, questioning what looked to be the astonishing truth.

"Hi!" Paul, with a big smile, walked quickly to his father. It crossed his mind to run, but he held back.

"Well, my God!" Franklin was positively mystified, and extraordinarily pleased. The two men held each other.

"Dad," Paul said into Franklin's shoulder. "I thought it would be fun to just show up."

"Is everything okay?"

"Of course. Just fine."

They broke their embrace at a mutually acceptable moment so that neither had to endure the other's concluding hug.

"Where are you off to?" Paul asked.

"I was just going over to get the mail."

"Where?"

"Post office. On Robertson. Come on with me."

In Franklin's car they were delighted with each other.

"Try to hold the speed down," Paul kidded his father, who was very much of a right-lane turtle.

"Never an accident, never a ticket. And I'm all in one piece." Franklin patted his son's knee.

"You look fine. You look well," Paul said.

"Well I *am* fine! Absolutely. Tell me. What and how and when? What a surprise! Are you sure everything's okay?" It might have occurred to Franklin that Paul's east was aflame.

"I got in an hour ago and I'm perfectly wonderful. Honestly, Dad, things couldn't be better. I was doing a television show. You saw it at Christmas, right? I was doing that show, and I picked up gossip in the hall that they weren't happy with it, and I beat them to the punch. You understand? It was the best thing for me in the world."

"Why weren't they happy with it?"

Paul moved cautiously: "I don't think the ratings were all that special. But there were some good things on the show."

"You resigned?"

"I told them I wanted to take a leave of absence."

"Did you specify any time period?"

Franklin wanted it all out in the car.

"They just said fine, we'll talk when you get back. And that's it." Declarative sentences. Facts. Nothing but the facts.

"Wait." Franklin had pulled to the side, and he was out and into the post office.

Paul, alone for a moment, considered a lie: they said that when I return they'll expand the show and introduce some new elements, possibly some sort of news reporting.

Back in the car, Franklin, with the *Wall Street Journal* and two circulars, was quick to pick up the flow. "Do you have any plans?" He was conversational. He could have asked: "Did you enjoy *The Music Man?*"

"Nothing that's all that definable. I just want out of New York for a while. I don't want to work. Let's face it, Dad, I want to drift."

There it was, right out on the old table in a beige Maverick. I WANT TO DRIFT. The truth.

Franklin was thoughtful at the wheel. Paul felt it could go either way: fortify your credentials, or drift with my blessings. Paul had imagined conducting this conversation over Polynesian food.

"Will you stay out here for a while?" asked Franklin. "Just exactly what are your travel plans?"

The verdict wasn't in yet.

"I don't know. I think I'll stay here. Somewhere in California. Big Sur. The desert. Somewhere. I don't know." Paul understood that with vagueness he was encouraging the avenue of credential fortification, so that if he won in the end, he would win big.

"Golly, I envy you," Franklin said without expression.

"Why?" Paul asked.

"Because you're a young man with adventure still to discover. I never thought you would starve. Will you stay with me for a bit?" Franklin glanced at his son.

Well, now. A big and moving win. We find the defendant not guilty of reckless and self-destructive behavior. In short, we find him sane.

Paul touched his father's arm. With a certain kind of smile he was able to tell his father that he was grateful, and that his roots would find their soil in time, and that he loved the driver of this particular automobile above all other human beings. And that he would stay with him for a bit.

Paul awakened at five in the morning on a Castro in his father's den. The room was small and lined with books. Its one large window overlooked the garden and faced east, so that in the morning it was filled with sunlight. Now, before dawn, Paul lay with his eyes open in the dark. His father's bedroom across the hall was silent, the door ajar. There was only a sliding partition for the den, and Paul felt observed and threatened by the lack of enclosure. It had been this same uneasiness that had invariably awakened him in the den on other visits to Los Angeles. He had watched the garden introduce the dawn, awaiting his father's awakening. "You up?" he had asked from behind his partition. "Good morning," Franklin had replied. "Coffee?"

This morning Paul slipped quietly down the hall and into the kitchen. He took a Coors from the refrigerator and returned to the den. Sitting at the desk, he switched on the light and listened for movement from his father's bedroom. There was none. The house was quiet. Paul, usually a nude sleeper, was wearing underpants, a trace of modesty around his father.

The beer was not cold enough for Paul. Franklin disliked severe refrigeration, a preference that Paul equated with his father's cautious driving.

Paul recalled their evening talk. They had eaten dinner at Chasen's and had touched on the past.

"Do you remember coming with me to visit your mother in North Carolina?" Franklin had asked.

Paul did. A midnight train, the taste of cherries, and

Charlie (Choo Choo) Justice. His mother had appeared well, even vibrant, which was puzzling to her son. Paul had imagined the entire American Southland as an enormous outdoor hospital, with Negroes in the fields gathering rice for the white patients from the north. He remembered wondering, If his mother was as healthy as she appeared, why was she incarcerated so far from home and for so long? He had told all of this to his father at Chasen's, who had smiled before replying. When, at last, he had responded to Paul's memories, he had uttered only one word: "Yes."

Paul was thinking about this at the desk. He examined his father's "yes": a reasonable notion for a child of ten, was what Franklin acknowledged: Negroes, out-of-doors, good health. It was understandable that, removed from the gloom of her bedroom, his mother in a foreign land would appear to her son abundantly well, her infirmities locked in her New York apartment. She was in the south on a vacation from those infirmities. They did not make the trip with her.

Also, Franklin's "yes" said that he himself might have shared, so many years ago, bits and pieces of Paul's puzzlement, and that now, hearing of it in Chasen's, it was ringing true. Franklin had longed to release his wife from sickness. With Carol in Durham, hiding out in a college town, could her illness possibly follow her south to discover her in seclusion and infect her again, so many miles from home?

They had talked, as well, of taking a trip together.

"I haven't been to London since 1949," Franklin had said. He had gone, at that time, to participate in a production of a play of his. The British had loved it. There was a formality about Franklin's writing: characters *addressed* each other. They mused together. Their indiscretions were harmless, packaged as they were in language of civility. Their passions were fully clothed. Offstage sexuality, spoken of affectionately, as one would recall a good meal, was conducted under parasols, genitalia joining gently in the pleasant breezes of late afternoons.

"Maybe we'll go to London together," Paul had said. He had envisioned such a trip as a burden; his responsibility for the tricky navigation of a seventy-six-year-old man through a one-thousand-nine-hundred-year-old city would accompany him like a clinging child. Paul had been guilt-stricken by this realization. He had attempted to conceal it from his father by bubbling enthusiastically: "We'd have a *marvelous* time together."

Franklin had given no sign that he had grasped his son's duplicity. He'd had three Bourbons, and drifted lovingly to Paris.

"Your mother and I stayed at a charming little place on rue Vaneau, as I recall. It was the spring of 1946. What a time that was! Glorious Paris just after the war. We turned a corner one afternoon, and there was Notre Dame. We hadn't known how close we were!"

"Where was I?" Paul had wanted to know.

"We had a woman named Doris looking after you in New York, as I recall. That was the last trip your mother and I ever made together."

There had been sadness in Franklin's voice, and longing. Your mother is dying. Paul could hear the words from the studios of WPKF.

In the early morning the desk light made a mirror of the window. Paul, in Franklin's swivel chair a few feet away, turned to examine his reflection. He imagined that Michael Holland would see, quivering in the window 180 pounds and a cholesterol of 310. Franklin would recognize his son—clearly, unmistakably, that's my son. That's Paul, grownup now. He came through high school and he came through college, and not without trouble, let me tell you. You understand his mother's illness had a lot to do with the trouble. But he has been a radio and television journalist. He has never married. But he will. I'm not rushing him. He's a good-looking young man with intense eyes. He's a good listener, like his mother was. He makes fun, but not malicious fun. I think he's a gentle lad.

Paul, facing the window, observed that he was a man. He was always surprised by subway mirrors and city windows to discover himself as an adult. His hair was dark brown with a little gray here and there. His body was firm and large. His presence was that of an athletic male with considerable strength. His eyes were young. They were interesting eyes, participating defensively. They governed a fleshy, oval face constructed for laughter. Everything swung up: the corners of the mouth, the nostrils, and certain private pockets of the eyes themselves. There was a great potential for noise.

Paul imagined himself as an adolescent; the sixteen-year-old Paul Kramer reflected back into the den. This awkward fellow recalled by Paul was physically determined but lacking sexual access. He was feverishly masturbatory. He was insolent and self-absorbed. He was academically troubled and at odds with acceptable procedure. He lived with his father on Central Park West in an apartment with a small terrace above the park. On more than one occasion, at night, he had climbed over the railing on the nineteenth floor and hung from the metal bars over the side of the building, like a man forced from his home by fire and taking refuge in the one last possibility. Open my hands. Let my fingers loose one at a time. When I count three: one . . . two . . . *now!* The hands will not open tonight. The fingers are locked in place. The moon is high and full. And that's the news, Paul Kramer reporting.

Paul hated Franklin. They cohabitated in volcanic silence. They prepared their own meals and ate behind closed doors in separate rooms. Franklin's friends were appalled by Paul. They urged boarding school and psychiatry for the vicious kid down the hall. "Listen, you cocksucker, you ruined my mother's life and you're ruining mine!" That's what Paul Kramer believed. "You're a fucking cocksucker!" This, a present for a sixty-year-old man from his sixteen-year-old son.

Paul got up and went back to the kitchen for another beer. He considered drinking it in bed, but returned instead to the desk. The sun was beginning to rise, and traces of the garden were beginning to show, replacing the mirror with a window.

What was in Franklin's top desk drawer?

Canceled checks, pencils and erasers, obituaries: Agnes Moorehead, Dorothy Fields, Katharine Cornell.

There were loose sticks of Doublemint gum, pennies and dimes, a number of rubber bands, an unmailed letter from Franklin to the Chemical Bank, Branch 116, in New York concerning the disposition of a checking account, and a Xerox of a letter to a woman named Lillian. It was typed, double-spaced, and immaculate. Paul thought that his father must have worked it over and over, starting from the beginning at any sign of a typo. The letter, copied on plain white paper, had not been dated:

Dear Lillian,

I haven't heard from you since that extravagant outpouring of words in early April, and I miss hearing from you. I had, and in fact *have*, come to count on your correspondence as comforting punctuation in my days. You have explained that you are a spasmodic letter writer; that some kind of seizure must overcome you to propel you to your writing "tablet," a word I very much admire in your hands, as I appreciate its lack of affectation and the very lovely parody you were letting me in on, somewhat like explaining a sweet practical joke about to be played on a third and significantly appealing party. I throw myself at your feet, no groveling around down there, but down there nonetheless, to encourage you and your tablet to reconcile. There is a somewhat flustered elderly gentleman who would read and reread what you had to say from New York. Even from the depths of catatonia, where I doubt you've been in a number of years, your message would be lovingly received.

As for me, I am here. I am social, but I know my potential for reclusivity. I have cronies—how's *that* for a giveaway word from a geriatric? Cronies. That means games of chance played on a table by groups of people numbering five or six on a regular and in fact regulated schedule, surrounded by merriment based on reminiscences and accompanied by somewhat alcoholic beverages such as beer or Weibel rosé.

I enjoy seeing women, exceptional women, and talking with them, and occasionally I'm invited to homes where such women congregate. I met Lillian Hellman the other night—of course I thought of you through the "Lillian," and I imagine that I'm writing to you two or three weeks sooner than I had planned because of it, counting as I was on the natural flow of our correspondence to provide for me a note from you before I plunged in again (as you can see, I'm throwing pride to the wind). She's very talkative and beautiful and I found her without guile. I am ashamed to report that although I am older than Lillian Hellman I am still active in guile, the only difference being, I suppose, that after all of these years I can watch it happening, stepping aside, as it were, offstage and down into the auditorium to witness, as part of the audience, the conception of trickiness and falseness. Deceit is too strong a word. I am not deceitful. I am cunning and Charming (my capital C nods knowingly to your "tablet") and not entirely truthful. Sitting there in the audience watching all this, I am battle-weary on behalf of the trickster on the stage. I have access to his motives. I have empathy with his needs, I want to reach out to him, put my arm around him, and take him over to the side of the stage to whisper last-minute instructions. And last-minute they would surely be, and futile I suppose, coming so late in the third act.

You are in my mind much of the time. When I dream, and can recall the dreams, I find that I have mixed you up, in my Waring mixer of a brain, with Carol. You have taken on each other's identities in my dead of night in a not altogether unpleasant way. Even the funereal dreams that usually begin with my own violent demise, tend to straighten out in loving and lovely reverie. That is, I am remembering Carol, or you, in subdued blues and reds, after silent processions to graves, to burials, to my own aloneness. I seldom awake in despair. The dominating mood of the dream or dreams is the blue-red love for both of you. I have given thought to this phenomenon and have come to believe that I am preparing for my own passing. It's not that I feel it's imminent. It's just that my fears of it are gone, whereas, say, ten years ago (and I remember talking to you about it once) I was hypochondriacally involved with my own minor maladies. I now consider the number of days I have muddled through in perfect health—without even head-aches or indigestion, and observe the mere handful of 24-hour cycles when I have been indisposed and generally out of it, either in some kind of pain or discomfort. Why, the ratio is staggering! My preparation for death, therefore, is a private acknowledgment that as illness is some kind of companion of health, so is death an extension of life. I'm not talking here, as I'm sure you understand, about "Life After Death"; rather, about death after life. How presumptuous of me to meddle with the process by stirring up my own stupid agitation and the agitation of my more vulnerable cronies who huddle in fearful groups with their eyes on the clock. I do not inflict them with any Pollyanna nonsense. I don't feel Pollyannish. Let me tell you what I feel: quiet. I feel quiet. Also, lonely. I think of my son, whom I adore, with concern for his unpredictability. I miss speaking with him on a regular basis. I am lonely for the opportunity to make progress with him. The opportunity takes on a personality of its own. The opportunity lives in New York and rings me up now and again. The opportunity and I talk for ten or fifteen minutes every two weeks or so. I would like to write the opportunity a letter. I would like to start the ball rolling, to begin to dig into the center of that remarkable lad. Do you ever watch his program? I understand he handles himself quite well. From the couple of shows I saw last Christmas he looked to have much power, much presence. He's rather feisty, and it works to his advantage sometimes. Perhaps you'll give me a report in a letter one day.

And I am lonely for you. Our impossible situation causes me grief. I often imagine you making your way to Doctors Hospital to face your speechless and helpless husband. My heart goes out to you, and to William in his awful chair. You are a great lady and I love you. I saw you in the eyes and in the magnificent face of Lillian Hellman (she was eating lima beans). I dream of eating summer squash with you, and other thrilling vegetables, like broccoli and asparagus and artichokes and beets. Please write to me.

With love,
Franklin

Paul read through the letter twice before returning it to the drawer. Then, switching off the desk light, he swiveled again to face the garden, bathed now in sunrise. Two cats were on the prowl, circling the fruitless persimmon tree near the window. Their bowl from Franklin was empty. Pulling on jeans, Paul returned to the kitchen for a carton of milk. Quietly, so as not to awaken his father, he opened the screen door and slipped into the garden. As the cats watched from a distance he filled the bowl.

Back in bed, Paul closed his eyes. The room was alive with morning light. He could feel tears on the way. He allowed them to fall in silence. He pulled the covers over his head.

Paul on radio: I carry around in my mind little things I've read, and I'll use certain phrases or combinations of words as my own and hope nobody remembers the source. Have you had this experience with your writing?

Writer: I wouldn't admit to any actual plagiarism. (Smiling) Certainly there are shadings that, from respect for an author, or poet, have become subliminally a part of how I attempt to express myself.

Paul: How about construction?

Writer: Do you mean the actual architecture of a book?

Paul: Yes. And I'm talking about decisions like flashbacks or the dilemma of tense. Things like that.

Writer: If I decide, for example, to use the present tense I'll look up authors who have gotten away with it in the past. Updike's two *Rabbit* books are good examples of present-tense writing. Using the present tense is very restricting and difficult and often results in a certain kind of flow in language, or lack of flow, that is difficult to overcome. The thing about it is that if halfway through you discover that it's too cumbersome, you can always go back and change it.

Paul: Wouldn't that necessitate a considerable rewrite? I mean, after all the "ises" and the "hases" have been transformed into "wases" and "hads," don't you then, to follow through on what you said for a moment, have new breathing room, and an opportunity for different and possibly more eloquent language?

Writer: That's a good point. I would have to say that, to an extent, the answer is yes, although I assume an author would like to preserve the spareness that the present tense almost invariably is responsible for, so that elaborate adjectival rewriting wouldn't become desirable.

Paul: Of all American fiction, which book or books would you like to have written yourself?

Writer: You mean the books I admire most?

Paul: Not only admire, but books with which you are empathic.

Writer (pausing): I would have to say *Herzog* and *Gatsby*. And *The Web and the Rock*. There are many others, but I'd have to give them some more thought.

Paul: Those are good choices. Moses Herzog's letters overwhelmed me. And in the context of Herzog's tragedy they were poignant and grotesque, and brilliant.

Writer (smiling): You took the words right out of my mouth.

Paul: Am I too talky?

Writer (laughing): Not in the least.

Sandi and Paul were picnicking in Griffith Park on a sunny Monday afternoon. Into two large canvas bags Sandi had piled Camembert and cold roast beef and red and white wines and imported caviar and black bread and three Mars bars.

Sandi knew all about picnics. Sandi knew all about bargains. Sandi knew a little about music. Sandi knew a lot about movies. Sandi knew something about sports. Sandi knew all about drinking, and smoking grass and hash. Sandi knew about sexual intercourse with men. Sandi knew about hygiene. Sandi knew about perfume. Sandi knew about Bonniers, top to bottom. Sandi knew about Commack, Long Island. Sandi knew about El Morocco. Sandi knew a good deal about survival.

"The thing about you, baby," Paul was saying in Griffith Park, "is that you know how to, and where to, but not why to."

"What an awful thing to say. I don't understand?"

"Do you mean you don't understand what I said? Or do you mean that you think what I'm saying is that you don't understand?"

"Nothing." Sandi was pouting. She had gotten together a beautiful feast, and she was wearing green velvet slacks and a lovely sleeveless silk blouse, and this guy over here, this Paul, was telling her something she didn't like. She didn't quite know what it was, but she didn't like the sound of it, that's for sure.

"Come on, sweetheart," Paul was saying. "I was just kidding."

"No, you weren't."

"Sure I was. Can't you tell a joke?" Paul leaned over and caressed her arm.

"Sometimes your jokes aren't funny, you know?" Sandi was looking him straight in the eye.

"The answer is for me to make fewer of them, and to wait for the best ones."

"I even remembered a corkscrew," Sandi said with a smile. Zip. She was happy.

"You are remarkable," Paul told her.

"See?" said Sandi, finding the corkscrew and holding it up.

Later, Sandi sat beneath a tree with Paul stretched out in the grass, his head in her lap. His eyes closed as she stroked his hair. They were quiet for a while.

"This is nice," Sandi said, finally.

Paul was thinking the same thing. He was unthreatened by this appealing fashion coordinator. She had fed him in the leaves, and would, in her sublet at sunset, place a breast to his mouth. A silent Walter Cronkite would complete the *ménage à trois*.

Sandi and Paul would break bread together again this evening. Paul considered this phrase: "break bread." They would consume foodstuffs together. They would share nourishment at the same time. The bread would be broken, a loaf of French bread, hard to break. At angry meals everywhere, the bread was broken like bottles in a Western saloon: the combatants, with the jagged nerves of bread held before them, circled each other at their tables, their rage nourished by absolute loathing. Paul felt that many dinner tables were covered with blood each night in the week.

"How many nights a week do you eat alone?" Paul asked.

"I'd say two or three." Sandi was thoughtful.

"What do you eat? Do you cook large meals for yourself?"

"Sometimes a TV dinner, if I'm tired at all. Sometimes, you know, chops or a steak. I'll never make anything fancy just for myself."

"What do you do during those dinners?"

"Watch TV?"

"Do you ever eat dinner by yourself without the TV on?"

What answer should she give? Paul was up to no good. Was it better *not* to watch TV during dinner, or was it better to *watch* TV during dinner? What would get her past this point intact? She decided to tell the truth: "I usually watch TV."

"On those nights when you're home alone, do you have many drinks?"

Sandi was surprised to have slipped by on the TV question so easily.

"A few. Scotch." She laughed. "What is this, an interview? 'The Paul Kramer Show'?"

"I'm just curious." Which was fairly accurate. Paul was idly gathering pieces of Sandi together.

"How about you?"

"How about me what?"

"Do you watch TV during dinner?" Sandi was turning it around. A dose of his own medicine.

"Sometimes," Paul replied. He had no intention of spilling any beans on this tranquil afternoon. Through their spasmodic affair in New York he had dribbled only fragments of truth and had cloaked them in language that was difficult for Sandi to grasp. He would hide from her now, his head in her lap.

"Do you drink every night?" she asked.

"Sometimes."

"Come on."

"That's the truth. Next question."

"What do you think of me?"

This surprised Paul. He had thought that booze and the tube was as deep as she'd go.

"What do I think of you?" Paul bought time.

"Uh-huh."

"Who wants to know?"

" 'The Sandi Cummings Show' wants to know."

"Well, I'll answer." Paul looked up in her eyes. It was clear that she was waiting expectantly for his reply. "What do I think of you? I think you are beautiful. I think you are very honest. I think you're a terrific lover. I think—"

"What makes me a terrific lover?"

"Well, for one thing, tenderness. And you're naturally sexy. You enjoy a man's body. You're into strange good things."

"Like what?"

"Like slapping around. Like buggering."

"Uh-huh."

"And that's what I think of you."

"Anything else?"

"I like being with you." There was much truth there.

Sandi was smiling. She was pleased.

No more questions. The air was filled with answers. They fell into a long silence. Paul drifted to sleep. He was awakened —how much later?—by a kiss. He found that the two of them were alone, their small corner of the park deserted.

"How long will you stay out here?" Sandi asked.

"What time is it?" Paul asked.

"Late."

"How long did I sleep?"

"An hour?"

"It must be six."

"How long will you stay in California?"

Paul perceived that during his nap Sandi had experienced romantic reverie. "I'm not sure," he told her. "I'm just kind of hanging out right now."

After a pause: "What will you do?"

"Do? You mean every day? Every moment?"

"I suppose," Sandi replied softly. Was he irritated?

"Maybe I'll get a job. I don't know."

"On TV?"

"Sandi, love, I'm as free as can be. I have options. Do you

understand? I've been working since I was twenty-two. I want some time alone."

"Uh-huh. Well, yes. I mean, yes." Sandi was trying to tell him that she agreed with that plan; that, heaven knows, she found nothing wrong with it.

Paul smiled at her, and reached up and ran his fingertips lightly over her cheek. "Whaddaya say, baby, let's go home and get in bed together."

"I've got to shower?"

"Together we'll shower?"

"Paul?"

He waited.

"Do you see any other girls?"

"No."

"Are you going to see any other girls here?"

"No."

Sandi lowered her head. Another kiss for a sleepy Paul.

CHAPTER FOUR

Paul spent time rummaging through his feelings. The euphoric highs and bottomless lows that had been so dominant throughout his life had been replaced, he felt, by neutrality, his passions and ambitions subdued, his course of action unclear. He defined himself as a witness, at least for the moment, with a somewhat deeper understanding of the unpredictable fires of the extremes that had burned through most of his life. Had he, in an unrealized accident, extinguished them, leaving him to wander through the unfamiliar ruins of a more inhabitable territory? But if they were ruins, why did he imagine they were desirable? Wasn't he deceiving himself by wishing away his highs and lows?

Priorities. He would scribble lists in the margins of magazines: a fuller receptivity to change; an attempt at an increase in candor; a diminution of rage; a more thorough gathering of personal facts.

"What was so galling to me?"

Paul and Franklin were in the den after dinner, each with a brandy. Paul knew that he had misplaced information concerning chunks of his life; his adolescence was something of a blur. He was asking his father about anger.

"Do you mean, What was so galling about *me?*" asked Franklin.

"Why was I so removed from you, and furious? There we were living together, just the two of us. This was from when to when? How old was I?"

"Your last three years in high school." Franklin, in his swivel chair, crossed his legs. He added with a smile: "Those were not easy years."

"I don't remember moving to Central Park West. I have no idea how we got there."

"I wanted to keep us in the old place so that you wouldn't be disrupted twofold; that is, your mother's death, and then having to move immediately. As it turned out, we stayed on a few years. I do know that I was ambivalent myself about leaving. I didn't want to cut away from the place. On the other hand, it was important that we did."

"Did the trouble start there?" Paul wanted to know.

"It was born in the period following your mother's death, but it flowered, shall we say, later on." Franklin let out a little laugh.

"What was at its roots?" Paul, on the couch with his legs crossed Indian-style, was facing his father.

"Ah," said Franklin, considering. "A myriad of things. A resentment of me. I think also a guilt you might have had about you keeping me in the old place. In other words, that I did it for you. Which was to a large extent true."

"Did you ever tell me that specifically during the years we stayed there?"

"I don't recall."

"It's possible?"

"I would think."

Both of them knew that there were no charges against anyone in the small book-lined room looking out on a garden many years after the fact.

"I can't remember," Paul told his father. "I just remember being angry."

"You know," Franklin replied, "I think another upsetting factor was that I was away and working. That left you with a maid, or occasionally with a surrogate father, like a college kid or someone like that. I hired them to entertain you on weekends, to supply some kind of masculine figure for you."

"I remember."

And then, after a pause, Franklin said: "I didn't know what in the world to do."

What in the world to do. Didn't know what in the world to do. An only child hissing at his father: "cocksucker!" Franklin was caught up in that ancient sadness. Paul saw it at once. "And here we are," he said emphatically, "in your beautiful apartment, and with a *garden,* for Christ's sake. And we are *survivors,* you know?" He smiled broadly, easing his father forward.

"I do like this place." Franklin extended his arm to take in the den and the hallway and the bedroom and all of his home and most of his cronies and his good health and his sufficient funds and his son across the room.

Paul agreed with him, nodding, regarding the actual living quarters: all white, with Degas lithographs in a blue-carpeted living room, a cozy kitchenette larger than Sandi's—it was a dining room too, with a small white table against the wall, and zinnias in a green vase in the middle. Franklin's bedroom had red throw rugs on a gleaming wooden floor. An original Grandma

Moses hung over the bed; Paul knew the painting from the apartments of his childhood. There were familiar little things everywhere: a glass coffee table in the vestibule; a framed photograph of his mother in a brown dress—she was standing on a New York street corner in a bonnet, looking quite young and pleased. There were plates and silverware from many years ago, and two Steuben deer heads on lamp tables, all from Central Park West. There was a small gold clock in the bedroom that Paul remembered at his mother's side, and a glass bowl in the kitchen that a long time ago had been filled with peaches. Ornaments of the past surrounded Franklin. They were filled with light. Franklin's home was airy and open. Paul imagined that his father would live forever.

Paul went into the kitchen to pour them both another brandy. He felt they were making contact. In the first days after Paul's arrival they had dealt primarily with the mechanics of their life together in Franklin's household. They had established understandings: dinnertime, the locking of doors at night, the general keeping up of order. Paul had been displayed to his father's cronies, and Sandi had been exhibited over drinks—Franklin had been permitted only a fleeting glimpse of her. "She's *charming*," he had told his son. "He's distinguished-looking," Sandi had told Paul. "Isn't he," Paul had replied.

"What do you feel about marijuana?" Paul was back in the den with their drinks, and had resumed his position on the couch.

"I don't really think about it," Franklin replied. "Why do you ask?"

"It occurred to me that we've never talked about it. I don't know what your feelings are about it."

"To be perfectly frank, I don't know much about it. I've read articles, I've *heard* about it. It seems to me that it would lead to harder stuff, no? That's been my feeling, anyway." Franklin sipped his brandy.

"Why do you think that?"

"Wouldn't that be the natural course of events?"

"Why aren't there millions and millions of junkies? I mean, if marijuana led naturally to heroin, think of the number of people who'd be into heroin." A non-negotiable point, Paul thought.

"Are you interested in getting me to try some?" Franklin had a smile on his face.

Paul was surprised. "How do you know I know anything about it?" He laughed.

"I don't." It's as simple as that. So there.

"Would you be interested at all? In just a little?"

"You mean *now*?" Franklin asked.

This was always a tricky one. You mean *now* you wanna ball? Right here at Lexington and Sixty-third? You mean *now* you wanna go swimming? Right this *minute*? Paul understood that there was a built-in "no" in "You mean *now*?" and had invariably shot back a "No, silly, not *now*, sometime in the *future*." Paul had always meant *now*.

"I don't mean *now*. I mean sometime," is how he replied to his father's question.

"How about right now?" Franklin was serious. Paul was incredulous.

"Are you sure? I mean, I didn't mean *now*."

"Are there any side effects?" Franklin wanted to know.

"Not a thing. And you probably won't feel it. It never seems to work until the acceptance level is high. It's safe, there are no side effects, it's completely harmless."

"I can't see that it would do any damage." Franklin appeared to be set on it. So quickly had he approved the idea that Paul held up a bit.

"Why don't we finish our drinks first, and then we'll see?"

"I'll bet you never thought I'd be open to such a thing," Franklin said. "How about the mixture with brandy?"

"Not to worry," Paul assured him. "The truth is, I never really thought about you and grass together, probably because it was such a farfetched notion." And that was the truth, to be sure.

"You simply smoke it like a cigarette?"

"You hold it in your lungs as long as you can." Paul got his plastic soap dish from the medicine cabinet in the bathroom. "Watch," he told his father.

Franklin observed the demonstration, and, receiving the joint from Paul, imitated his son's inhalation.

"Hold it in there," Paul urged. "Hold hold. Now let it out." He was standing by his father. Franklin coughed. "That's okay," Paul said. Franklin tried again. "You sure are determined," Paul laughed, accepting the joint back.

Franklin let the smoke out. "It hasn't hit yet."

"You know what to do? Shake your head back and forth as if you were saying no. This is Tai stuff. Heavy stuff."

Franklin shook his head back and forth. "Maybe I'm too old. Possibly men of my age are immune to certain potions. Isn't that a marvelous word, 'potions'? It's a Halloween word, 'potions.' A witches' brew. Served in a ladle." Now, that was a word that made Franklin laugh. "Ladle," he repeated. "A potion in a ladle. My my."

"Your your?"

"Yes. My my." Now Franklin was laughing somewhat more noisily.

"Are you immune?" Paul asked.

"To what?"

"To the potion."

"The potion in the ladle? I don't see why not."

"You want some more grass?"

"I'm fine."

"Here. One more." Paul returned the joint to his father.

"I can see now," observed Franklin, a moment or so later.

"What can you see?" Paul, as witness and participant, felt lovingly directorial.

"I can see, I can see what all the fuss is about." Franklin swiveled to face his desk.

"You mean the potion?"

"It's a, well, you know."

Paul didn't say anything. He let his father come around. In a while, Franklin had an observation or two: "You can hear very well."

"*I* can?"

"One can."

"One? You mean a general word for just a person."

"Myself. One. Myself. Very clear."

"Yes."

"Is it wrong to have had brandy?"

"You mean morally?"

"What is 'morally'? I mean, well, what is moral?" Franklin swiveled back to his son.

"Spiritual ethics."

Franklin thought about this. "That *sounds* nice," he said, "but will it play?"

"Spiritual ethics?"

"Is it actually accurate? Spiritual ethics. Does that mean anything? Isn't it really just a high-falutin' redundancy?"

Paul shifted slightly to the defense. "It moved morality up a notch. Not to any religiosity, but just to the plateau of the spirit." He felt he was covering his tracks.

"But that just complicates the redundancy." Franklin hung right in there.

"Morality goes far deeper than good or bad. The very essence of its definition is of the spirit."

"The essence of its definition." Franklin pondered this. Then he said: "Essence of Definition, I'd like you to meet Spiritual Ethics."

Paul was comfortable with this gentle onslaught. "You're watching me like a hawk."

"I have my ways and means."

"Committee," Paul added.

"What?"

"Committee," Paul repeated.

"Oh, yes, yes. Gotcha." Franklin nodded with a smile.

In a while Franklin said: "My mouth seems dry."

"It is," Paul responded. "It gets that way."

"Would you say I'm up-to-date?"

"You mean smoking grass?"

"Up-to-date. Up to the moment. The way things are done these days. You know?"

"You're a man of the seventies," Paul told his father.

"That's very flattering. I'm really a man of the thirties in disguise."

"But you're not *stuck* in the thirties." Paul put the roach in the soap box. "How do you feel? Physically."

"What's the difference between marijuana and LSD?" Franklin wanted to know.

"I've never had LSD. The only thing I've ever had, other than grass, was something called MDA. You just get all mellowed out. It's a very positive trip. Friendly. Acid is the king."

Paul went into the kitchen and snooped around. He returned with chocolate-covered graham crackers and a quart of milk.

"I feel fine," Franklin told his son. "It's interesting that when you focus on an idea how three-dimensional the idea becomes. It's all I can do to keep my attention on all that's happening."

"I understand. You want some crackers and milk?" Paul offered the carton of milk to his father.

"I think not."

"Try some. Really. It'll taste really good."

"I'll pass."

"Okay."

In a short time Paul had a question: "Do you feel totally good about this?" The idea had been growing in his head that Franklin might just simply up and die, that the introduction of a foreign substance might overcome him and make Paul a villain with a smoking gun in a soap box.

"It's very strange. It's a very nice feeling. It seems that sweet things come into my mind."

"Food?"

"No, not that. Memories. Events. I, uh, you know?" Franklin smiled at Paul.

"Tell me," Paul said.

Franklin put his feet up on the desk. "For some reason I've been thinking of Milton Cross. I'm sure it was he. This happened many years ago. Your mother and I were listening to a radio broadcast of symphonic works. It was Mozart's Fortieth. And Milton Cross was the announcer. And in a very pompous way he introduced the symphony." Franklin dropped his feet to the floor and leaned forward to quote Milton Cross: " 'We hear next, a performance of Mozart's Symphony Number Forty in G minor, Köchel listing five hundred and fifty. The Philadelphia Orchestra is under the direction of Eugene Ormandy.' Now, *that's* when he should have stopped. Right there. But he was apparently so consumed with his own resonance and with the regality of the occasion that he couldn't help but continue, even though there was nowhere else to go, nothing else to say. But Milton Cross said, and this is an *exact* quote from at least thirty years ago: 'Mr. Ormandy will conduct the Philadelphia Orchestra,' and he stopped there realizing he was just repeating himself and he was frantically looking for some way out, and so he finished the sentence by saying that Mr. Ormandy would conduct the Philadelphia Orchestra 'with his baton.' "

Franklin and Paul roared. Their laughter subsided only to

start up again. They gave in to it, allowing it its own course until, winded, they finished up.

"Well now, tell me, are you all right?" Paul asked a little later.

"I'm having a hard time keeping things in order," his father replied. "I can't stay with anything."

"That's okay."

"What would happen if I lay down?"

"Are you sleepy?"

"I don't know."

"Why don't you lie down. I'll come next to you." Paul stood, and walked with his father to the bedroom.

Franklin placed himself carefully on the bed, propped up a pillow and cautiously rested his head down.

"You okay?" Paul asked, concerned.

"Fine. My thoughts are in a whirl. It was a good idea. I like it. I like the disunity."

Paul sat by his father on the bed.

"I hear music," said Franklin.

"Mighty fine music?"

"The singing of a sparrow in the sky."

"The perking of the coffee right near by."

"Sure that's music."

"Mighty fine music."

Franklin asked: "When the people at My-T-Fine go out and rent a car, do they put My-T-Fine Incorporated on the form?"

"Franklin, you're stoned," said his son.

Franklin, who had closed his eyes, opened them. "I have a lot of questions," he told Paul.

"What are they?" Paul asked.

"Oh, they're not for you. They're not for any particular human being."

"Who are they for?"

"For me, I suppose."

"Like?"

"I can't say."

"Can't or won't?"

"A little of both. I'm beginning to feel cheated."

Paul was surprised by this. "Of what?" he asked.

"I don't know. I don't know. I, uh, I haven't accumulated a great deal of wisdom. It's too late."

"I think you—"

"This isn't anything for you to respond to. It's just, it's just some thinking. Fear in aloneness. There's aloneness but there's no *completeness*. It seems that the natural order of things have been speeded up. I've arrived *physically* at the solitude, but I'm still thinking about long ago. Do you know what I mean? The natural order of things."

Paul understood his father. He could find no adequate response.

"I'm sleeping," Franklin said. "Did I say that or think that?"

"A little of both," Paul replied. "Would you like some iced tea?"

"I think I'll have iced tea for lunch tomorrow. I'll look forward to it."

Franklin's eyes were closed. Paul, still sitting by his father, allowed himself to realize that the natural order of things was out of the question.

CHAPTER FIVE

Paul had secrets. Covert rooms and hallways. He sought them out, discovered them. In childhood, a hidden staircase behind a boiler room within a dormitory; an attic in Roslyn, Long Island; a moist and sandy basement by the ocean. They were used for weeping, for covering one's face with one's hands, for rocking, cheeks pressed to knees, shivering, crying. They were used for becoming invisible, for moaning, for not knowing, not understanding, for whispering "why," and "why why," for sleeping, for waking, for trembling with fear. Mortuaries hidden in cobwebs and dust behind dripping pipes and wooden beams, steamy with heat, damp with rain, they were Paul's secrets.

There were others. Conference rooms in the Manhattan Hotel, with spinets that Paul could play in the dark, a drifter off the streets: the elevator to the mezzanine and it was just a mat-

ter of an unlocked door. A piano in the corner was all Paul
wanted. Sixteen years old in a Dodgers windbreaker, he would
sit at the conference table making no sound at all, waiting in the
dark. Maybe an hour would pass. One o'clock in the morning.
The spinet was out of tune when Paul began to play. Strange
and haunting melodies in minor keys improvised in the corner
became familiar when he sang.

> This will be my shining hour,
> Calm and happy and bright,
> In my dreams your face will flower
> Through the darkness of the night.

Later, in a winter daybreak, Paul would slip away. He
knew where the pianos were: the empty ballroom of the Pierre,
the windows in its men's room overlooking the zoo, and a Bald-
win in tune on a slightly elevated stage. His voice rang out in
the generous acoustics:

> If I loved you
> Time and again I would try to say
> All I'd want you to know;
> If I loved you
> Words wouldn't come in an easy way,
> Round in circles I'd go.

The Waldorf had a piano and a celesta in a private dining
room on the third floor. Paul found a half bottle of wine on a
service table near gold curtains. In these secret rooms he learned
about drinking. Haig in a wired bottle—just a little in an empty
coffee cup. Warm Miller High Life from the can, Gilbey's gin
from frosted glass with leftover Schweppes, Bourbon diluted
with the cool water from the bottom of ice buckets on the floor.

> How sweet you are,
> How sweet you are,
> How dear your tenderly smiling face;
> Through days all bitter and gray and grim,
> Through nights when even the stars are dim.

"What are you doin' in here?"

An infrequent security guard in the doorway, the shocking light of the hall scorching Paul's privacy from above the shoulders of authority.

"Nothin'."

"Smart ass."

"Yup."

"You're gonna get out of here."

"Nope."

"I'll drag your ass outahere."

"You and what army?"

"You fuckin' wise cocksucker."

"Get the police."

"You bet your fuckin' ass."

The light vanished as the door closed. Paul had orchestrated the exchange on the piano. A light-spirited G major chord after his "nothin'." "The Caissons Go Rollin' Along" in C after "You and what army?"

Paul would wait it out, testing, gambling, as he had hung from the terrace above Central Park West. He would scoot away and vanish at the last instant, down the stairs, onto the street, exhilarated and furious, with tears in his eyes, Haig in a wired bottle an ally well before his seventeenth birthday.

Midnight. There was news on the radio from behind the paper-thin wall separating rooms Forty-three and Forty-four: "Senator Ervin continued, 'There are two ways to indicate a horse. One is to draw a picture that is a great likeness. And the other is to draw a picture that is a great likeness and write under it *This is a horse*. We just drew the picture.'"

From beyond his window: "You may be good for me, but I'm not good for you."

"Because you're sinister."

Paul thought that "sinister" was quite a word, that it really did the job. He was lying on a bed in a motel room on Hillhurst.

He had gravitated to a secret place and had waited for someone to use the pool outside his window. A man and woman of middle age obliged him. The sinister man, Paul observed from behind closed curtains, was wearing a yarmulke. The woman was in a one-piece light-colored bathing suit and had pulled a bathing cap tightly over her hair. Paul was reminded of his mother in the ocean.

"I don't care what they think, you know," said the man. "They can convict me if they want, it makes no difference to me."

"It may make no difference to you, but it makes a difference to Sheila." The woman was doing the side stroke the length of the pool. It was a very small pool with a pink child's slide at one end. There was no really deep area, and it was possible to stand anywhere in the water.

If this sinister man was convicted, Sheila would care. Where was Sheila now? Praying, maybe, to a God of Severity, a God of Frugality, a God who had the goods on Sheila. Why were these people in a tiny swimming pool at midnight in a cheap motel in East Los Angeles? Their exchange suggested bitterness, but their tone was conversational, even pleasant. The woman swam, the man stood, not caring if he was convicted, oblivious of Sheila, rather comfortable on a hot and humid night. How heinous was his crime? Could it have been tax fraud? Paul had declared every penny, having read that George S. Kaufman had been permanently hounded after a one-hundred-dollar oversight. Surely the man in the yarmulke had committed no sexual indiscretion; there was something in his flaccid cheeks that ruled it out. A petty thief? Paul had stolen from others: dollar bills from Franklin's pockets, but not for years; books from Brentano's under the New York *Times*; bottles of liquor from parties, in winter overcoats. How much more guilty than he was the man in the yarmulke?

Paul returned to the bed and lay in the dark with his eyes

open. Franklin believed he was in La Jolla with Sandi Cummings. Sandi Cummings believed he was in San Francisco with Dr. Michael Holland. Michael Holland in New York believed he was somewhere in Los Angeles, and Holland was therefore in touch with the truth. Paul mulled over the possibility of calling Holland. Three in the morning in New York. On what pretense could Paul awaken his industrious physician? Chest pains? Spitting blood? Pressure on the spine?

Jennifer Rosen. Boston, Massachusetts. Married to a psychiatrist, Dr. Lawrence Tellman. Paul imagined the two of them asleep in a queen-size bed, dressed in pajamas in the frigid winds of 15,000 BTUs on Pinckney Street. Settled. Serene. Sublime. What were Tellman's thoughts just prior to orgasm? I'm coming. I love my wife. Is Lou Boudreau still alive? Jennifer's breasts. Jennifer. Jenny, Jen, I'm comin', I love. Christ, that was a bitch of a come. Honey, Sweetheart. Jenny. Wife. Lou Boudreau *is* alive. Does color for the Cubs. Or the White Sox. Midwest somewhere. The *Tigers*.

Tellman was paid fifty dollars an hour to think about Lou Boudreau.

Paul sat on the side of the bed. He picked up the phone. "Information, on Pinckney Street the number for Dr. Lawrence Tellman. Residence. Thank you." "Operator, station to station, calling Area Code 617, 523-4802."

"This is Dr. Tellman."

Right out of a deep sleep: This is Dr. Tellman.

"Tellman?"

"To whom am I speaking?"

"Lou Boudreau works for the Tigers, and besides that I think you're a shady practitioner."

"Who's this?"

"You're a *schmuck,* Tellman." Paul hung up. He was concerned that because his conversation was so brief the motel would come on the line before Tellman hung up. Mr. Paul

Kramer, is your call finished? the operator would ask. Jennifer, it's that guy Paul Kramer. Paul, this is Jennifer, what do you want? It's three o'clock in the *morning*, I mean *Christ*, what can we *do* for you?

We.

My dearest Sandi,

This is not the easiest of letters to write, and I want you to understand the amount of thought that I've given to it and the reasons for it.

I've got to be on my own at this time in my life. I can't become as dependent on you as I'd like, dependent on your constant presence, your reliability. It's my own dependence on myself that's got to be cultivated, and this is a job I can only accomplish alone. I realize I have been taking up your time, monopolizing your days, demanding things, acting on whim, being punky about obligation and not concerned with your feelings. I know you are filled with feelings, not only for me but for all the things you do, all the people you encounter. You are very vulnerable to the vulnerable parts of other people. They in turn find a sympathetic shoulder and a wonderful spirit in whom to confide and on whom to rely. I've seen it not only with me but with friends of yours both here and in New York. You are a major source for other people's light. It should be in the playbill: LIGHTING BY SANDI CUMMINGS. You are extremely generous with your lighting, more generous than most people and more trusting despite difficult encounters. You do not give up. You are a fighter. And it is precisely this strength, *your* strength, that I must try to live without.

I don't know what my plans are. I'm getting to feel a little restless. My father and I get along fine. It's wonderful to have so peaceful a relationship and one so devoid of hidden angers. I'm beginning to find living with him somewhat confining and a little bit claustrophobic. It's *his* place, it has *his* things, and even though we're solid together, I feel a parental atmosphere in the house that I'm sure he's not even aware of. On the top of my list of things to do is to find some place of my own. So you see, Sandi, it's not just you that I am attempting to remove myself from, it's the dependence on other people for my needs—for companionship, for things sexual (and God knows you and I have got it fine on that score—all your tenderness is reflected in the way you make love). I want to decide what career I want. I've thought of doing some writing at some point in the future. Or do you think I'd be any kind of actor at all? Or maybe my television show again someday, if they'll have me. I don't know. But whatever. I don't want to hold you down or hold you back. You are a beautiful and sensitive girl and much more settled than I am and deserving of something more lasting than what I have to offer right now.

Please forgive me the suddenness of this letter, as I realize I've given you no hint about my thoughts and should, under the best of circumstances be confronting you face to face with all this.

I wish you great joy and great success at work. Robinson's is lucky to have you, to have your kind of original thinking in the building, and your grace, and your loveliness.

All my love,
Paul

Paul,

You hurt me badly. Can't I see you and talk? I can't write stuff down. You really are a shit. I mean, you come out here and you get things all started again and then you pull out. It's like coitus interruptus. I'll never trust you again because you've made me hard-boiled, and mighty glad to be on *my* own. So there. *Buster*. Can I call you and talk to you, just to say goodbye?

Sandi

Paul liked bars. He liked smooth wood and Spanish nuts and the gradual procedure of intoxication. He liked to contemplate the jukebox, losing quarters to rock and roll. He was anonymous in a Los Angeles saloon, his television face unknown. He programed for himself, repeating what he wanted to hear over and over again until an objection was raised: "Hey, *Jesus*, enough with that thing!"

> I might rise above, I might go below,
> Ride with the tide and go with the flow.

Bars were for dreaming, for focusing on possibilities. Bars were for watching what other people drank, and where they placed their hands, what their eyes contained. Bars were for measuring oneself against another and finding oneself generally the better off. Bars were for organizing ideas into frivolous order, for dreaming of women, for composing dialogue that would remain unspoken, for remembering a red skirt or a white arm or the welcome disorder of intimacy.

Paul found the Dorado in Venice near the ocean. A clean little room with a red-tiled floor, the Dorado offered chili, which Paul often ordered late in the evening. The jukebox did not overwhelm, the beer mugs were kept in a freezer, and men and women were sandaled, and mostly young, though there was a lack of merriment in the place, a lack of cheery energy so frequently associated with youthful drinking. In groups, in the booths, there was quiet talking, no bursts of sound, no great gales of community laughter. At the bar there was solitude. Paul saw the place in slow motion. People drifted by carefully, wearing sombreros and bonnets, and glided with deliberation *through* each other. Paul felt they brought no issues, harbored no anger, hid no weapons. They slid through the arrangement of California, touching shoulders, sipping skin like liquid, bobbing aimlessly on a mellow sea. What they said had mainly to do with an absent third or fourth party. There was sexual babble but no sensuality. There was gossip without a wink or a sneer; there was only inference. Paul imagined that there was no sexual progress, only a maze within a circle. Sombreros and bonnets would fall away and the graceful bodies, nude but for cordless earphones, would merge in familiarity. Sheets would remain pressed throughout all events. Paul had always searched for strands of duplicity on morning pillows, knowing little of unwrinkled bedding.

On a Monday evening around ten, Paul regarded a slim girl in white slacks and a long-sleeved orange pullover who had come into the Dorado with an unusual intensity. She stood at the bar waiting for assistance, and it was clear that she was impatient. She was holding coins—probably quarters—that she shook in her right hand like dice. She remained at the far end of the bar close to the entrance, so that by swiveling to his right he could look directly at her from about thirty feet. Her face was lovely in its urgency. High cheekbones and a prominent chin. Dark, deep-set eyes and a hollowing of the cheeks suggested difficult times, or hard work, or general debilitation. Her hair was curly and short and light; Paul couldn't be sure of the shade. Her hands were small with long fingers that Paul believed were nail-bitten. It was possible she was chewing gum, as there was a barely perceptible movement of the lips; he imagined she was toying with a canker sore.

"Somebody needs service at the far end," volunteered a man on a stool a few feet from Paul. The bartender, in a blue tank top, turned his head.

But the man on the stool had, all the while, been facing the jukebox in the back of the room. Paul realized that he himself had been conscious of this and had invented a reflection of the girl above the jukebox to accommodate both the volunteer and his own perception. There was no mirror, there was no reflection above the jukebox, or anywhere at all in the back of the Dorado, only a solid wall of brick. Paul saw that the volunteer, the man on the stool, the only other customer at the bar, was unaware of the girl with the coins.

"What did you say?" Paul asked him.

"What?"

"Did you say something? Did you say anything?"

"No, man, howya doin'?"

Paul knew him to be a surfer, a solitary guy, a regular at the Dorado. "Can you tell me who's at the bar by the door?"

The surfer turned to look. "Don't know her. Thin, yeah?"

"I never saw her myself," Paul related.

"They come in here and, like, they're gone. It's like that a lot."

"What's she doing?" Paul wanted the surfer interested in this. "What do you think?"

"She wants an egg, I think. Yup, ya see?"

An egg for coins, an abbreviated smile, and a tidy departure, clean and soundless.

"I thought you told Willie she was there," Paul said. "Didn't he tell you she was there?" Paul was standing, addressing the bartender.

"Dunno. She was down by the end's all I know."

"Know her?"

"Don't know her." Willie was shaking his head.

Paul realized that there wasn't a great deal of interest he could legitimately generate without appearing lascivious and clumsy. He issued a nasal laugh designed to say "sexy broad, right, man, you wanna drink." He wished no role in any matter at the Dorado. He wished to distribute no opinions, convey no responses, share no ideas. This awkward outburst was irritating to him, and mortifying.

At home in Franklin's den Paul came to believe that the two men at the Dorado hadn't found the girl a sexy broad, right, man, you wanna drink, and that his nasal laugh might very well have been taken as unpleasant bravado, sexual applause for the infirm. It wasn't so much the girl's thinness that might have spoken of infirmity. It was the coins in her hand, the dark and insistent eyes, the bustling purchase of a single egg, the immediate, immaculate withdrawal.

"Somebody needs service at the far end." He was sure he had heard it spoken. Seemingly he had created it out of the blue, so necessary was it for him to italicize her appearance. She was powerful, the twitchy little thing, darting in and out of the Dorado. Had she come by car? Had there been, all the while, a chosen thug waiting at the wheel?

Paul fell slowly asleep with unanswered questions. He felt helpless. He whispered the word to himself. He wished he could sleep forever.

Ball Player: On that occasion I think I had things going for me stuffwise. He hit a good pitch. A slider low. You got to keep the ball low to him. He hit a good pitch. Said so himself. He just made contact and that was the ball game.

Paul: Do you remember any special thoughts when the winning run scored?

Ball Player: I just sort of felt empty in my stomach. It's a kind of thing you can't describe. Sometimes you feel very lonely on the field. It doesn't have to be a crisis kind of situation like that one was. You know, now, I'm a pitcher, but I think this is what we all feel now and then. You look around, you see the fans, you see the players in the dugout, you see your defense behind you, you can pick out certain faces in the stands, kids eatin', guys watchin' you, you see a girl or something in the aisle, there's movement, you know? And you feel, like, this incredible loneliness, you out there, you know, alone. Like your life has come down to that, just standing out there in a uniform, and you make your living out there with the lights on and everything, and sometimes it's drizzling and you feel like it's just a big joke, that whoever thought it up was makin' up a joke. It's crazy, if you look at it closely. All those faces thinkin' their thoughts and nobody knows anybody else's thoughts. It's all so alone. And you're the loneliest one because everybody can see you, but nobody can see you at all. Am I makin' myself clear at all?

Paul took his father shopping. In the aisles of the supermarket he observed Franklin from distances. He would separate himself from Franklin, drifting to the soft drinks forty feet away so that he might witness his father's activities in private. An old man. Paul had never felt it so keenly. The hurried tempo of the market whirled around Franklin's tiny island of contemplation; a melon, a tomato were gathered up, considered, and returned to the stand. The steps were slow to the onions and potatoes. It wasn't a shuffle. It was, Paul felt, cautiousness, defensive shopping by a man aware of his own fragility. Paul had always counted on his father's strength. Paul always believed that this constant man could swoop into the midst of chaos and settle things. In no way massive, just ordinarily constructed, a trim six-footer, Franklin possessed the suggestion of power. Don't tangle with FK is what Paul knew to be fair warning.

No longer. Was there a slight stoop? Maybe ever so slight. In other markets, in other rooms, in restaurants and theaters, on the frantic streets of New York, Paul would receive his father's arrival: an entrance with a subtle flourish. Heads would turn. Franklin's back was straight. His right hand was slipped into his pants pocket. His hair was black, his suit was gray, his tie was maroon, the handkerchief in his jacket was navy blue. He was smiling. Paul would stand, an instinctive gesture, as for an anthem. On a corner they would embrace. Paul would fly to him. This man of strength, his arms wide to engulf his son, would reassure Paul in a darkened bedroom. If Paul would only tell him the troubling facts of the day, Franklin could move them around, place them in an alleviating order. Paul could grasp the order. Yes, I see. I understand. Will I be all right? Is everything going to be okay? I'm getting sleepy. I love you too, Daddy. I love you, Daddy.

And other thrilling vegetables. Paul recalled it from his father's letter to Lillian. He had never told Franklin that he had read, that he knew, that he had rifled a desk and had wandered around in his father's secrets. He wouldn't be condemned. However, there would be, Paul imagined, a very slight alteration of their business together, the intrusion of doubt.

Paul joined his father at the thrilling vegetables.

"You can't get really good bean sprouts in New York," Paul said. "They're bitter and brown. These are marvelous."

"And these are probably the last of the artichokes for the summer," said Franklin, lifting one from its row. "Did you ever see them grow? They sit on top of their plants close to the ground, like hats. Thousands of them. Thousands of little green hats. They're glorious. *And do you know what?* They're a meal in themselves."

Paul remembered: *And do you know what?* His father would grab his attention anywhere along the line. *And do you know what?* Inserted into an algebra lesson, into a discussion of law and order, into Milton himself. *And do you know what?* It was riveting. Franklin would use it at crucial moments. He accompanied it with wide eyes, his mouth open slightly, anticipating, relishing his seduction. Paul Kramer was hooked by such a device. There was, he knew, always the possibility, however remote, that the *and do you know what?* would turn out to shoot miles away from the action, into a playground down the street, or, as in *and do you know what? We're going to get some chocolate ice cream!* Even now, standing beside his father, who held an artichoke to his heart, Paul felt the energy of surprise. He imagined that down the next aisle, around the corner amidst cans of Rosarita refried beans and bottled mushrooms from Taiwan, they would come upon Paul's desk from twenty years ago, right in the middle of the aisle, with shoppers making their way

around it, and there would be Paul and Franklin sitting side by
side with pencils and erasers and notebooks of equations. *"And
do you know what?"* Franklin would be saying, "X equals
twenty-four!"

In the checkout line Paul's Master Charge card was refused
under a sign that encouraged its use.

"On what grounds?" Paul wanted to know. He was dealing
with a squat, middle-aged woman whose pace never faltered.
Paul had observed her on other occasions working steadily
within concentration, never pausing or turning away or glancing
up to face the faces of her line. Paul, on other lines, was able to
watch her automation, her wretched industry, her icy visage.

"Over fifty dollars," she announced. "You have liquor."

"That's a lot of crap," Paul told her, anger welling up. "You
just don't want to take the time because you got to call the office
for anything over fifty dollars and they take a while to answer."
He leaned forward, placing his face inches from the woman's.

"Are you being snotty with me?" She was slowing up just a
piece.

"No, ma'am. I'm just telling you what the truth is. Master
Charge is accepted here and that's the way I'm gonna pay." Paul
moved back from her and rested his hands on the counter.
Franklin, at his side, stayed quiet.

"Not allowed," the woman said, grinding to a surprising
halt. Paul saw that she was trembling. In moments like these
signs of weakness would ignite him. He would attack in vitriolic
whisper. "You pathetic old woman, you tragic little person," he
would be likely to spew with an enormous smile, a wicked challenge to weak sisters. Conscious of his father, Paul held back.
"Get the manager," he snapped.

"No, sir," was the reply.

"Dad, would you find the manager. I'll keep things cool
here."

"I have the cash," Franklin said.

"Now, listen to me," Paul said. "Find the manager and we'll clear this up. Okay?"

"But I have the cash," Franklin persisted.

"Dad"—and now Paul faced his father—"find the manager for me, would you?"

"Where might I find him?"

"Go to the inquiries desk. It's in the center aisle. See it?"

"You'll have to get out of line, sir," Paul was ordered by the woman.

"Now, I want you to understand something," he replied quietly. "I'm not moving. I'm not going anywhere. We'll get the manager's verdict on this, then I'll move along. That's the way it's going to be." He spoke precisely and slowly. He leaned forward to examine her name tag. "That's the way it's going to be, Martha Gordon."

"God damn it," piped an old guy who was next in line, holding two enormous packages of Bell's potato chips in his arms.

"Why don't you go through right here in front of me?" Paul suggested magnanimously.

"No one's going through until you move," said Martha Gordon, her trembling increasing.

"Then no one's going through," Paul told her.

There was a rumble of discontent on the line. Paul imagined Franklin drifting cautiously through the store in search of a stranger. How many other fatherly excursions had he ventured into on his son's behalf?

Martha Gordon stood perfectly still, her arms at her sides.

Franklin returned with a tall black man with a severe countenance. Paul became conscious of his own hair, which had grown fairly long in California. He felt it could be a deciding factor. Severe black men were not likely to take a shine to long hair and tee shirts. Paul knew, too, that there was about himself an air of defiance, the unattractive presence of condescension easily detected by the frequent Martha Gordons and authoritative blacks with whom Paul had exchanged differences through the years.

"Martha won't take Master Charge because our groceries are over fifty dollars," Paul told the manager. "I've been coming here for a while and that's never been a problem. What's the story?"

The black man, Daniel P. Lang by tag, turned to Martha Gordon. "This gentleman's got a Master Charge card?"

"I never saw it," Martha Gordon said, her eyes cast down.

"See it?" Paul said, displaying it widely. "Your ship is sinking, sweetie." A present for Martha.

"You can take over fifty dollars in this line," Daniel P. Lang told Martha Gordon.

"Mr. Sepulveda instructed me not to take anything over fifty dollars."

"I'll talk to Mr. Sepulveda," Daniel P. Lang said.

Paul had it won. He would ease up on Martha. Franklin stood out of the line in the front of the store, framed by bags of charcoal.

"I didn't mean to cause you any trouble, Martha," Paul told her with a nice smile. "Thank you, Daniel," he continued, gracious, beneficent.

Martha filled two large bags in silence. Daniel stayed for a moment, overseeing, and walked away purposefully in response to a page.

Through the turnstile. Bags in hand. Father waiting. Suddenly Martha Gordon was beside him, away from her post, her eyes calm, her lips in a slight smile. She had something to say to Paul, and she said it in a whisper that rivaled his own: "You come through my line again and I'll cut your fucking balls off." And she was gone, back behind her counter, toting up the Bell's potato chips.

Franklin hadn't heard what Martha had had to say. "Well,

now," he observed, with false cheeriness as they walked to the car. "Well, now," he repeated. "We survived. I'm still intact. I'll go on with my life. Well, now."

Paul could feel his father's relief. "I'm sorry," he found himself saying.

At night at the Dorado Paul thought about his sorrow. He was sorry. I'm sorry. Sorry. I apologize. Will you forgive me? I'm *most* sorry. He heard himself through the years: phone calls asking forgiveness, abject sorrow in bedrooms and kitchens and in airports and on beaches. Letters of apology, special delivery, typewritten documents of self-disdain. Paul Kramer making his sorrow known, setting things straight, Paul Kramer 'fessing up, Paul Kramer assuaging, Paul Kramer admitting, Paul Kramer working at emerging from trouble with things in order. Paul felt there was too much at stake with every human entanglement, too many wounds to inflict and endure, too many evasive eyes, too many truths unspoken, too many jagged edges perceived, too many plans altered, too many emotions brutalized. Brief volleys of language could result in annihilation of the heart. The shift of a hand, the turn of a head were as devastating as war. And war itself infected the soul with grief and fatigue. How many chunks of his own spirit had been blown away on the front lines?

"How much remorse do you feel?"

Paul was talking to his father in the kitchenette. They sat together with drinks late on a Sunday night in July.

"I'm not sure I know what you mean," Franklin replied.

"As you go about your business on an average day—an average day I'm talking about—what do you feel about decisions you've made, the way you've handled people, what you've said to them, and so on."

"I've made mistakes," Franklin said.

"I'm not talking about mistakes. Not mistakes. It's something more intangible, like inflicting hurt, like expressing anger on inappropriate occasions. I mean, your treatment of people."

"I see. Well. I see. There have been many times, yes. I've acted irrationally."

Paul saw that his father was uncomfortable with this. "Irrational is too strong. I mean, *irrational* is so funny, it's so dopey, if you know what I mean, that it often doesn't count." Paul chuckled.

"I've made some wrong decisions," Franklin confessed. "I've been responsible for a number of difficult episodes that involved other people. I could have been easier, made things easier, I suppose."

"Why didn't you?"

"Because I was weak." Franklin looked away from Paul, fixing his gaze on a bottle of Lemon Joy.

"I've always felt there was so much I didn't know about you," Paul said. He spoke softly and with tenderness so that Franklin wouldn't mistake his words for ridicule.

"Well, you know," Franklin replied, after a moment, "I'm a very private man." This was difficult for Franklin. Paul sat back in his chair and took a sip of his drink.

"I haven't really had many close friends," Franklin went on, his eyes still averted.

"Why do you suppose that is?" Paul asked.

"It's just that I'm very private."

"Who's your closest friend out there in the world?"

Franklin answered at once, returning his eyes to Paul. "Your mother," he said.

"I always felt that the two of you had an understanding."

"We're good friends. I feel we're still good friends."

"I know," Paul replied.

"I've envied you sometimes," Franklin continued. "You've always had a really outstanding group of friends. You never inherited my private character."

Paul didn't say anything. How could he begin to tell his father of boiler rooms and midnight pianos? There was little he wished Franklin to know. What Franklin accepted was a public man with a thousand questions, a man of candor and intelligence, a man of dialogue and energy with an impressive group to receive his private stock. It was too late now to let Franklin Kramer in on abuse, immobility, and deceit. It was out of the question that Franklin be told of rifled desks, motel rooms, sexual gluttony, and everlasting evasiveness. Most of all, most significantly, Franklin must never discover that Paul's privacy was valued more intensely than his own, and that his youthful son's secrets were locked away for all time.

"You know, I had a dream the other night," Franklin said, getting up from the table and going to the refrigerator for an ice cube. "It was one of those very clear dreams that impresses itself on the following day. In the dream your mother and I were planning a trip to the West Coast to visit *me. Here.* In this house. We were talking about *me* as if I were a third person, just a man to be visited who happened to live on the West Coast. We were packing our things and we were in a very happy state of mind. We were very enthusiastic about the trip." Franklin returned to the table and plopped the ice into his drink.

"We flew out," he continued, "on a 747, and I was showing your mother its features because she had never seen or been on a 747."

"Never heard of?" Paul asked.

"It was more that she had never been on one, *in* one. She was acquainted with the 747. There was a bed for her on the plane, but she told the stewardess that she didn't want the bed. She said she had no use for it and that there was no reason for her to lie down.

"We got to Los Angeles, and you and that girl you used to go with, Jennifer Rosen . . . ?"

"Jennifer Rosen."

"You and Jennifer Rosen met us at the plane and told us that Franklin would be very happy to see us. I was thinking that it was really funny and that we were all involved in a practical joke, but no one was admitting it.

"And so then you drove us to an apartment like this one in somewhat the same kind of neighborhood as this, and I told your mother to wait in the car and that I would go in first, by myself. Which I did."

"What happened?" Paul asked, softly.

"I came into the house, which turned out to be the house I grew up in. You know how dreams are. And I shouted 'Franklin, Franklin,' going along with the joke even though I was by myself. I went upstairs to my room because I knew the house and I knew where the room was, and I assumed that that's where I would find Franklin.

"I opened the door and it was my room all right, with all my childhood stuff scattered about. And of course, you know dreams. There was Franklin, *me,* on the bed, asleep. But it was quite evident almost immediately to me, it was quite clear that I had died. I was an old man.

"I stood in the doorway for a little while and then I went downstairs and out to the car and I told your mother that Franklin was on vacation and that he'd be back in a couple of weeks, and that we should go back to New York. Your girlfriend asked how I knew when Franklin would return. I replied that he had told me so. Instead of you driving us back to the airport, I drove. Just your mother in the car, and me. We didn't say a word the whole time."

"Dreams," Paul said, dropping his eyes.

"And so," Franklin added, musing.

"There's too much riding on everything," Paul observed, almost to himself.

If Franklin missed it, it didn't show.

CHAPTER SIX

Robinson's in search of Sandi. Paul, responding to her letter, had decided on neutral ground; no kitchens or hallways or showers or bedrooms. A business dissolution, an understanding.

Sandi had an office. She shared a secretary, to whom Paul gave his name. Expressionless, Sandi appeared from behind swinging doors.

"Can we talk?" Paul asked.

"Why have you come here?" she asked, coldly.

"Can we talk?" Paul repeated.

"About what?" Sandi wore a beige suit. She had cut her hair.

"Come on."

"Did you get my letter?"

"Of course I got your letter." Paul was standing a few feet from her.

"Well, then."

"Well, *what* then?"

"The letter speaks for itself." Indignant.

"The letter says we can talk."

"It says more than that." Sandi was maintaining her ground.

"Do you want to talk about it right here, in front of these nice people?" Paul swept his arm back to encompass two women on a couch and the young secretary directly behind him.

"You've caught me on a busy day."

Paul wasn't sure if she was holding or relenting.

"I've only got a few minutes?" she told him.

Her office was a cubicle, lavished with photos and drawings of women's clothing. A haughty model wearing only panties attracted Paul's eye.

"That's Clarissa. She wouldn't like *you*, buster." Sandi sat behind her desk, all business.

"I'm sure you're probably right," Paul said.

"Well, what is it?"

"I came to apologize for the way I treated you."

"Too late."

"For sending you a letter instead of coming directly to talk to you."

Silence.

"My letter was honest and it expressed my feelings. I regret having written it. My life is muddled."

"It sure is."

"Come off it, kid. You know what I'm talking about."

"It's too late now."

"It may be too late for you, but it's not too late for me." Paul took another glance at Clarissa.

"You mean you're asking my forgiveness?" Sandi sat back in her chair.

"I'm asking you to understand where I'm at. I consider this conversation an expansion of my letter."

"Oh, you do, do you?" Sandi nodded sarcastically.

"That's *right*." Paul was toughening up.

"Well, I don't know about it."

"What don't you know about?"

"It."

"What?"

"The whole thing. First you write me a letter and you pull away from me, just like that. Why did you even *call* me in California?"

"I wanted to see you."

"You wanted to see *someone*, not me?"

"You. Someone, yes. *You.*"

"Then you show up here at my place of business. I mean, I don't know what to say about that. It's rude."

Were there tears?

"Why rude?" Paul asked.

"Because it's so out of place. Here in the office, and all. I can't make sense of anything."

"Did you read my letter carefully?" Paul asked, softly.

"Did I read your letter carefully?"

"Did you read my letter carefully?"

"I read it a hundred times. I *care* for you."

There were tears.

"And *I* care for you."

Nobody said anything.

"You're just a bum." Sandi spoke with a touch of a smile, her eyes reddening.

"I know it. I am a bum." Paul felt no emotion. You come through my line again and I'll cut your fucking balls off. What was Martha's last name?

"I think I was in love with you." Sandi lowered her eyes.

"Sweetheart, it's my fault." Paul got up and went to her. He leaned down and took her face in his hands.

"I'm getting old?" Her eyes lifted involuntarily to meet his own.

"Bullshit you're getting old." Paul kissed her cheek. Paul kissed her mouth.

"I miss you," Sandi whispered.

The phone.

"I'll call them back," Sandi told the secretary. "I'll call later."

Paul knelt in front of her chair. She took his head and drew it to her lap. "You're a little boy. You're wandering around. You're a big shot little boy wandering around. What am I going to do with you. I don't know what." She caressed his hair.

"You're warm," Paul said, from her lap.

"I've been promoted," she exclaimed, suddenly, brightly.

Paul felt the familiar shot of depression at her inevitable inattention. It was all he could do to force a "Terrific" from the folds of her skirt.

"I'm one of the two assistants to Helen. She's the overall boss, you know? So now I'm like right behind. Isn't that super?"

It was super, yes it was super. Paul couldn't keep his head in her lap. He rose and went back to his chair. Super super, he assured her.

"I'm getting up in the world?" Gone were the tears. Only red eyes remained, bathing in smiles.

"You're going to do very well here," Paul said. He felt trapped in her cubicle.

"I'm glad I'm in the west. They don't have people like me around. People with drive." Sandi was nodding, agreeing with what she was saying.

"Sandi, do you understand at all where I'm at?" Paul

thought to get her back to business so a comfortable resolution could be found.

"I understand. I mean, I read your letter." Serious eyes once more.

"You know that I don't mean you any harm?" Paul sat forward in his chair.

"Could we see each other? Every now and then?" Sandi asked him shyly, preparing for the worst.

"Sure. Sure we can. I didn't mean that we shouldn't be in touch. We're too close not to be in touch." Paul gave her a tender look.

"Well, you mean, Don't call us we'll call you?"

"I mean, whatever *feels* right we'll do. Whatever we're comfortable with. There are a lot of ways of dealing with things. There are a lot of ways of treating each other. There are a lot of ways to have a good time."

"A good time?"

"What I'm trying to say is, that there are many kinds of relationships. It doesn't mean that a change in our relationship means automatically that we're out of touch. It just means a different space for us, a different approach. Do you understand what I'm trying to say?" Paul sat back and waited for her reply.

At last: "I guess, as you said, this is just an extension— what did you say?—an expansion of your letter." Sandi's eyes fell again.

"An expansion, I suppose. An extension with some new ideas," Paul replied.

"I get you," she told him, without a smile of any kind.

Paul drove slowly through Beverly Hills. Clarissa lingered in his thoughts, lurking above Sandi Cummings on the cork of her cubicle. At first, Paul imagined her a participant in theater, a pouty and aloof character drawn by the playwright photographer. Paul could enter the auditorium and observe her from a distance, as Marjorie, or Barbara perhaps, a concoction for the stage, emitting language, posing as directed to convey the essence of a fictional creature.

And yet. Clarissa the model would herself be undraped upon the stage. The fragile notion of fiction would surely disintegrate in the erotic flames of reality. It would be *Clarissa's* body revealed in nudity, *Clarissa's* belly fondled by masculine fingers. Paul concluded that no theatrical pretense could obscure the arousing truth. He understood that public nudity in the name of art exposed only the poser. It was entirely from within clothing that an actor could credibly work, a dependable messenger employed by the author to seek out the audience and share with them the secrets of the evening.

Paul was on his way to Sunset for records and cassettes. Rodeo Drive had at one time been divided by a bridle path; Paul remembered the horses from a childhood trip with his father. He had watched them gallop under the overhanging trees. They came up from Santa Monica, their riders cut from fine leather with their crops at the ready, their riding hats concealing their eyes. They were formal and perfect. They glided north across Carmelita and Elevado, slowing at Lomitas, disappearing finally into Sunset Boulevard. Paul imagined a massive dismounting at Tower Records. In a while, they would return to the saddles with cassettes of the Doobie Brothers and Jimi Hendrix. Pieces of time, shuffled, would swirl around the legs of the horses. Hiroshima and Normandy, Seoul and Saigon, the Doobie Brothers in leather pockets on a sultry afternoon in July. Already the bridle path is gone. Clip-clop through Beverly Hills. Clip-clop through Estes Kefauver and Frankie Laine, clip-clop through Seymour and Zooey and Frank Robinson, and Donald Segretti in Marina del Rey.

At the intersection of Beverly, Cañon and Lomitas, Paul spotted a flash of orange in a yellow Volkswagen. The girl from the Dorado crept cautiously out of Lomitas, across Beverly and Cañon, moving west. Ungoverned by stoplights, she was unsure of herself in the tangle of roadways.

The same orange pullover. Unmistakably it was she, picking her way through Beverly Hills. Paul took off after her. South on Camden. West on Elevado. He hung fifty feet behind, exhilarated, and without any rational motive. The girl with two quarters anxious for one egg on a summer evening. Likely as not she had driven this same Volkswagen to the Dorado, alone with her impatience. She had a long and graceful neck. Her two hands were placed high on the wheel. She drove with more than average speed and with an authority that showed she knew the way. She could drive it in her sleep. Zip zip. A native. Never heard of Paul. "The Paul Kramer Show." His credentials would be empty blather up against this orange pullover.

East on Santa Monica. Well, then, why west on Elevado? And now a stoplight at Crescent. He was directly behind her. She lit a cigarette. A quick left on Crescent without a signal, and a second or two before the green light. He had to wait for the cars going west on Santa Monica.

Paul speeded up on Crescent, spotting her two blocks up. She wasn't stopping at intersections, only slowing for a quick check. The girl had picked him up, maybe from the start, and was winding craftily through Beverly Hills in an effort to lose him, lose him cold.

In Riverdale, in the Bronx, Paul had learned his tricky business. Twenty years old, in the company of WQXR, Paul would select a victim. Nighttime. His lights bore down on Buicks. Mahler, Gustav; Schumann, Robert; Shostakovich, Dimitri. Loud, like the Stones, before the Stones. Grosvenor, down the hill to Fieldston, over the bridge across the Henry Hudson Parkway and all the way to Mosholu Avenue. The Buicks parked in panic. Paul passed with his lights off. "It's eleven o'clock. Every hour on the hour the New York *Times* brings you the latest news bulletins."

The orange pullover in the yellow flash jammed into Sunset traffic. Paul followed automatically. A right on Alpine without breaking speed. Paul was with her. If she didn't know before, she knew now. She was picking up real velocity. A right on Lomitas. A left into an alley: back yards, avocado trees. She jostled a garbage can; the top leaped up and fell in front of Paul's wheels, crashing like a pair of cymbals. Paul was laughing. The pursuee was taking a look at him through her rearview mirror. She was out of the alley at Carmelita. She made a shocking left and a daredevil U-turn as Paul emerged from the alley, narrowly missing Paul's rear fender. All the way over to Rodeo. She was bound by Santa Monica and Sunset, avoiding traffic lights, whipping through the undisciplined roadways of Beverly Hills. Another alley—watch out for the kid! A garbage can overturned. Paul kept it in front of him like a soccer ball. Grapefruit peel on the windshield. The orange pullover was really flying. Paul fooled with his radio: "Mr. Sandman." "No." "Mr. Railsback." "Aye." "Mr. Wiggins." "No." "Mr. Hogan." "Aye."

Back where they came from: Beverly, Cañon, and Lomitas. The orange pullover didn't stop, didn't slow down, no checking right or left, a roll of the dice, a roll of the quarters. She was across safely, but just barely. Paul, with more caution, lost her to a right on Rexford but found her at Carmelita on a long shot. She was off again, determined. Paul was with her. Christ, somebody's gonna get killed. What the fuck is this? Pull out of it you cunt, you motherfucker!

But no. Bedford, Roxbury, Linden, up to Sunset for a right, fuck the light, past the Will Rogers Memorial Park and all the way to Hillcrest and south on Hillcrest, that rearview-mirror look at her eyes, she's making a U-turn on a guy's lawn and he's out there giving her the finger, and she's moving north again on Hillcrest and she's through Elevado again and Lomitas again and she's gonna *zip* across Sunset and she's gonna get killed, *we're across!* We're making sharp turns and *moving west,* into the hills and west, we're well above the Beverly Hills Hotel, "Article One is adopted and will be reported to the House," we're climbing, we're climbing. Orange pullover makes a left. This is it. Dead end. She smashes through a fence and stops.

Paul was twenty feet behind her. They were beyond the houses and alleys. Off with her ignition. Off with his ignition. They sat in their cars, garbage on windows and doors. Radio off. Silence. Late afternoon. Rearview-mirror eyes and the haze of the hills.

Two or three minutes. Paul ran possible dialogue through his head: "I thought you were somebody else, I'm really sorry." "I just wanted to tell you that your passenger door was open." Orange pullover: "It's closed, you shit heel!" Paul: "It looked open to me. I'm sorry. I'm really sorry. No harm done."

No harm done? Paint scraped, fenders bruised, avocado skins clinging to windshield wipers, orange seeds stuck to hoods, grapefruit, *God* knows, everywhere.

The orange pullover got out. The Dorado girl, absolutely. Jeans this time. A no-nonsense kid heading his way.

Paul got out. The girl stopped ten feet in front of him. "Now, there's *gotta* be an explanation, right?" Her hands were on her hips. She didn't appear angry, or in any way frightened. She simply wanted to hear what Paul had to say before deciding on a penalty. Her glove compartment was filled with penalties. Paul had the feeling that she traveled with penalties and doled them out as she saw fit. Notarized penalties just waiting for him on a dead-end street above Beverly Hills.

"Don't you think that fifty cents is too much for one egg?" Paul asked her most seriously, as if they were confronting each other in an official place of business. It was, after all, his only point of reference.

"Fifty cents yes, thirty cents no."

"Do you know what I'm referring to?" Paul was immediately sorry about "referring." "Do you know what I'm talking about?" he asked her.

"I know who you are," the girl replied, without the slightest warmth.

"You're a better man than me," said Paul, bemused.

They were standing on a small plateau overlooking the town, framed by the broken gray fence and the edge of a modest cliff at the front wheels of the yellow Volkswagen. It was late in the day. The sun was beginning to set, lighting their stage with pale white and splashes of soft purple.

"Why all this?" the girl asked, a little less severely than she'd spoken before.

"You know who I am?" Paul asked in return.

"Forty-four West Eighty-eighth Street."

"You mean you're from New York. That's your address." Now Paul had something to work with.

"I saw you in that place," the girl told him.

"The Dorado?"

"I don't know. Just that place."

"I didn't think you were aware of anything. You were in one mess of a hurry." Paul edited: let me tell you, lady.

"There were two of you at the bar. The other guy was blond. The bartender had a blue shirt on. He had a turquoise ring on each pinky. "Paperback Writer" was the music. There were four people in one of the three booths. There was a very pretty blond girl in a bathing suit."

"Smart kid." Paul was pressing for an advantage.

"What are you chasing me around town for?" No smile, but not unpleasant.

"What are you running for?"

"A guy puts a tail on you, you move."

"You said you knew me."

"Still. You move."

"I was having fun," Paul told her. Risky business.

"I could have been dead ten times."

"That's life. That's what all the people say."

"Did you have your fun?" Sarcastic.

"Did you have *your* fun?"

No answer. They stayed ten feet away from each other. Paul leaned an elbow on the top of his car. The girl remained with her hands on her hips, relaxing her posture just a little.

She was a beauty. There was some red in her short light-brown hair. She was pale, naturally and smoothly pale. Her large dark eyes were filled with possibilities. They were wonderfully dishonest eyes, conniving and secretive, unmalicious, mirthful, richly wicked, and profoundly accessible. She wore no make-up. Her lips appeared to be dry, somewhat crusty. Her nose might very well have been broken along the way; there was a slight imperfection at the bridge, an indentation, in fact a tiny scar. Paul resisted an impulse to examine the scar, to touch it, to kiss it.

The girl wore no jewelry except for gold hoop earrings. Her neck went on forever and disappeared enticingly into the orange pullover, too warm a garment for a summer afternoon. Her fingers were slender, her nails manicured. Her feet were bare within sneakers. She was shorter than Paul had imagined from the Dorado. "Diminutive" was the word that came to his mind. She was small-boned, delicately crafted. And the eyes. Too easy to decode. Paul had a line on her. This time around, her penalties would remain in her car. Paul felt bulletproof.

"Well?" she said at last, still standing there facing him.

"Why didn't you put a stop to this before it really got off the ground?" Paul asked.

"I didn't think you'd persist."

"If this were a court of law, you'd be up to your ass in it too."

"Bullshit."

Ah, bullshit. They were flowing together on their little plateau. Bullshit, with an emphasis on the *bull*, a slight jab of the
head toward him, a quick visual punctuation mark.

"You are an accomplice," Paul told her, letting her have a
piece of a smile, telling her he'd go any way she wanted on this.

"You're either remarkably stupid or just plain irrelevant,"
she said, glaring at him with empty menace.

"What's the next step? Do we exchange licenses?" Paul
wanted to know.

"We could just clear right out of here. Right directly out."
The girl took a step backward.

"Do you have any opinion of my television persona, Miss
Forty-four West Eighty-eighth Street?"

"None whatsoever."

"Do you know Adrian Manilow?"

"No."

"She lives at Forty-six West Eighty-eighth Street."

No response.

"Here are the facts, as I see them," Paul said to her. "We
are here on this mountain. It's a fact that I followed you up
here. It's the first time that anything like this ever occurred to
me, and I followed through on it and I don't regret it in the
least, seeing as though we're both in one piece, no cuts or bruises
even. Now, that's a real piece of luck, considering our circuitous
trip. It's also a piece of luck that the fuzz ain't up here with us,
don't you agree? So. This afternoon I bought a bottle of Scotch
and it's on the back seat, somewhere back there. Would you like
to have a drink with me? Or do you want to call it a day?" Paul
just stood there, waiting for her reply. It came in a few seconds
and missed a crucial beat.

"Well."

"Well, what?"

"I'll have a sip of your Scotch whiskey." The girl moved
back to the yellow Volkswagen to check it out. She wiped some

debris off a side window with the cuff of her pullover. She was busy. A lot of things to do up here on this little clearing. That's what she was telling Paul: go get the booze. If you must you must. I'm doing research on Dr. William Moskeroski, I'm translating *Heart of Darkness* into Swedish, the two men with whom I live, the two *studs,* are expecting me home in ten minutes' time. But if you insist on taking a swig I'll have a quick sip and be on my way, thank you very much.

When Paul approached her with a bottle of Black and White and two plastic cups from his own glove compartment, she settled down a bit. She held her cup, he poured. They found a rock with a view and sat down, a foot or so apart.

"I've got to tell the truth," Paul said, looking over the town below. "I've thought about you occasionally since that night at the Dorado."

"I was in there for ten seconds."

"Why were you in such a hurry?"

"I was working." The girl took a good-sized swallow of her Scotch.

"What were you working on at ten o'clock at night?"

"I'm a writer." The girl addressed the side of his face.

"What do you write?"

"I write articles and children's books." She was really quieted down now.

"Of the *Stuart Little* genre?" Paul turned to her.

"No. No, it's more, let me put it this way: I don't deal with rodents or other animals."

"I understand." Paul looked at her seriously. She doled out her very first smile. "What have you published?"

"As I say, articles on a number of subjects, and I'm working on this book for children I mentioned."

"Do you have a title?"

"*The Equator of This Day.*" She averted her eyes.

Paul thought about that. "Good," he told her. "I think it's a wonderful title."

"Thank you," she said quietly.

"What function of the equator are you most concerned with?"

"Mental equators. Do you know what I mean? I mean, in all of us there's that point in the cycle, the daily cycle, though I'm referring metaphorically to the process of life, that is *safe* ground, a point equidistant from the war-torn poles. A raft protected from emotions that get out of hand." She spoke earnestly, and in a soft voice.

"More a witness than a player?"

"More a witness than a player with a blindfold on running wildly. You know?"

"Equidistant," Paul remarked, after a pause. "There's always been something scary about that word to me. Division, distance, space, time. Thousands of miles, thousands of miles. I suppose for some people, 'equidistant' would conjure up security. For me it's forbidding stuff." Paul sought out her eyes. She granted him, although without a sparkle, the first imperfect signal of trust.

"There *is* something awesome about equidistant," the girl agreed. "Planetary escapades, arithmetic precision, a complete divestiture of guesswork. Isn't it funny about words? Equidistant. Now, that's a good example. I mean, just *this* kind of exploration is possible with a word like that. You can sink into it and move around in it, or *on* it, as if it were a geographical location. You say it's a scary place, and I know what you mean. But you ask someone else about it and they bring out a slide rule and light up a Marlboro."

"Yes, sir," Paul said, nodding. "But the word 'faith' might make them uneasy."

They stared into their plastic cups for a while.

"Are you doing any work out here?" the girl asked Paul.

"No." He shook his head.

"What state is your career in?"

"Dormancy, temporarily. I'm moving around a little this summer. I'm visiting my father, who lives here. I'm hanging out. I'm going to do a little traveling, but I don't know where I'm going to do it. I'm conveniently fixed here without any real responsibility." Paul thought to slip his television program in, to coax some praise out of her, but did not.

"You're loony," she said. "That was a loony chase we put on down there."

"Yup." Paul gave a laugh. "I'll say." And then, after a moment had passed: *"The Equator of This Day."* He was thinking it over. The girl understood that he was not being seductive.

"It's a little hazy today, isn't it," she said.

"Whose fence is it, do you think?" Paul asked.

From their rock they took a look at the damage. "The township?" Paul suggested.

"Do you think we should leave our names on it and say we'll pay, and everything?"

"I have a pen," Paul told her, rising.

"I have a crayon," she replied, getting to her feet more slowly than he.

"What are you doing with a crayon?"

"I baby-sit and I wound up with a crayon in my bag."

She dug the crayon out of the car and together they walked over to the fence, a fence splintered badly and broken almost directly in the middle.

"The equator of this day," Paul pointed out, glancing at the fence. "We've been sitting on our raft."

TOWNSHIP, she printed, in large blue letters, WE ARE RESPONSIBLE FOR THIS DAMAGE. WE ARE . . . She handed the crayon to Paul, who printed his name and his father's phone number.

Then, under his own, and in slightly smaller letters than before, the girl set down, quite neatly, and most deliberately, her name. Paul leaned over to look closely. He said her name out loud. "Emily Keller," he said. "Emily Keller," he repeated.

CHAPTER SEVEN

Paul: Where does an idea for a novel start? For you, I mean. Is it something that's been in an amoebic state for years and gradually weaves a more complex system? Or do you seek out an idea as one would, let's say, seek out a running mate, interviewing scores of prospective ideas before making your decision?

Writer: The three books I've written began in the same way. They began with a mental picture of something, much like a photograph, and they grew out of that photograph.

Paul: Is the original photograph always contained in the book intact?

Writer: No. For example, my first book revealed itself to me when I was driving in the South of France. I was with my wife, and we passed a lovely château that had extraordinary coloring about it, a kind of light silver. We stopped because it was so compelling. Very powerful.

There was a grand balcony above a terrace, and it seemed as if at any minute some sort of drama would be played out for our benefit. The château was set not far off the road or obscured by trees or barriers, so that we had an excellent view of the place.

As we sat in the car—I had turned off the ignition to hear the sounds of the countryside—a young boy, maybe fifteen, but certainly no older, appeared on the balcony. He looked frail and was dressed in a silk robe that had very much the coloring of the château itself. He looked to be an extension of the place, but without its physical grandeur. I remember thinking that he might have just gotten out of bed, even though it was late afternoon.

From the balcony he gazed about, at the garden below and up at a somewhat cloudy sky. He didn't see us, as I had parked in the corner of the driveway's entrance and was therefore not in his exact line of vision, though I suppose that, had he studied the situation, he would have seen the hood of the Peugeot.

Then, suddenly, he turned his back to the garden to face someone standing in the doorway of the balcony, someone who was out of our view. They held a conversation we couldn't really hear, except for wonderful little splashes of Italian. It is this memory, that fraction of a moment in the French countryside, that suggested my first book, though the moment itself was never fictionally drawn.

Paul: One can feel its implication in the book, though.

Writer: Oh yes.

Paul: The second?

Writer: Again, a feeling, a scene, something rapid and, in this particular case, unsettling. My sister getting on a bus in Yarmouth, Massachusetts, on a wintry morning. She reached up to place her coat on the overhead rack, which I noticed her do from the street. She remained standing even as the bus pulled away and disappeared from my sight. At that exact instant it began to snow.

The third photograph, and the one that led to my current novel, was very comical to me. I was at the Provincetown Airport seeing a friend off. We were in that small waiting room they have, and we were standing by a window looking out at the field and at the small plane that would fly my friend to Boston.

From around the corner of the building we were in came a chunky mail truck, one of those square, determined vehicles without regular doors. In big bold letters on the side were the words AIR MAIL. I got it into my head that ever so slowly the mail truck would pick up speed, gradually, gradually gathering velocity until it would rise, somewhat unsteadily at first, and then ascend over the bay on its airmail way to Boston. The whole feeling of that notion runs wild in this new book of mine.

Paul (laughing): Absolutely. It's quite clear to me. That's a terrific little event. I know that airport. I chartered a plane there once from a drunken pilot because the Provincetown Airlines was booked up months in advance—it was August. We had a harrowing trip into that tiny airport tucked away by LaGuardia—what's it called, Butler? I think so. Fifty dollars to fly fifty feet above Long Island Sound late on a Sunday afternoon with thunderstorms on the brink of exploding in our faces. I've always wondered if the pilot got back to the Cape safely.

Writer: Didn't you know the airline would be booked solid?

Paul: Yes, but I had to leave suddenly. I just had to get out of there fast.

Writer: Why?

Paul (laughing): I was escaping. A bunch of sheets tied together, over the wall, back to New York.

Writer: Were you a prisoner?
Paul: Without any doubt.

Same birthdays. Same date, same year. July 1, 1942. In New York. Different hospitals. But there it was. The date they shared. They couldn't believe it. Who was older? Emily, by maybe ten hours. They were asking each other for facts in an Italian restaurant that very night. When were you? How were you? Why did you?

Paul got his praise. Emily felt he was easily the brightest guy in the media. So there it was. But he had to work for it. How many times have you seen my show? Did you see the one with? (she hadn't seen the one with). Did I appear well researched most of the time? And then her matter-of-fact compliment—strictly speaking, a professional evaluation with nothing romantic in the air. The brightest guy in the media. Paul didn't want romance attached to it; he just wanted the facts: and in other news, Emily Keller of Venice, California, informed TV personality Paul Kramer that he was easily the brightest guy in the media. Ms. Keller told Kramer of her feelings at Liverri's Italian restaurant in Westwood. The two diners, who had met earlier in the day after an extended automobile chase through Beverly Hills, exchanged ideas at the popular eatery after returning to their homes from the hills and driving later in the evening, in separate cars, to the appointed rendezvous.

No orange pullover. Instead, a simple short-sleeved white blouse, a gold necklace—a wisp of a thing, light-blue slacks, the hoop earrings.

"I fell asleep when I got home," she told him.

"Are you very social in your waking hours?"

"You mean, am I involved with a man?"

"Allow a fellow some caution."

"Not involved."

And here, sitting right in front of her was the brightest guy in the media, sitting right in front of this uninvolved authoress, sitting right in front of her and he was sipping Coors rather than whiskey, wishing to remain sexually alert.

"Why do you live in Venice?" Paul asked. He didn't wish to convey incredulity or disdain, but felt that something in her reply was defensive.

She said: "It's funky. It's dirty. It's got a gentle charge. It's near the beach. I live on a canal."

Little spurts of information. Declarative sentences. Paul thought to mimic it, but knew it would be counterproductive.

"You live on a canal?" Very sweet he was. Canal? Really? A charming canal? Tell me more.

"The ducks can drive you crazy sometimes. Quack, quack, in the dead of night." Emily smiled. She hadn't issued a real quack, only the spoken word. Quack. No throaty qu-u-a-ack with a slight visual aid around the lips. Paul felt it took a certain kind of derring-do to go the distance with quack in a sedate restaurant on a first date. Maybe while sitting on the john a year from now: qu-u-a-ack. Emily Keller naked, not worried about the visual aid around the lips. She would even do a gorilla with her arms and hands, a gorilla grunt. But for now, just quack.

" 'Chicks and ducks and geese better scurry.' " He spoke the words without expression.

" 'When you take me home in your surrey.' " Emily was right with him, deadpan.

"I've always been amazed by accumulated stuff," Paul said. "Somewhere in the air you picked up that lyric. It's a piece of luggage, along with square roots and who Roy Cohn is, and the difference in taste between canned and fresh asparagus. And area codes, and Rutherford B. Hayes, and the name of Sylvia Plath's husband. And where was I all this time? You know? Basically speaking, except for absolutely personal experience, it's the same luggage out there."

Emily listened intently. Then, from a shoulder bag on the floor by her chair, she plucked out a pack of Camels and lit a cigarette with a small gold lighter. "How many songs from *Oklahoma!* can you name?" she asked.

Paul ran down the list. "I have lots of this kind of luggage," he said, concluding.

"Is that the whole score?" Emily asked him, seriously.

"Yup." Confidence.

"How about 'Many a New Day'?"

"I see. Loaded dice."

"Luggage," said Emily, with a slight smile.

"There's another thing," Paul told her. "The difference between luggage for men and luggage for women has got to be taken into account. Stuff that has to do with virility, and menstruation. Don't you agree?"

Emily agreed. "I've thought about this accumulated luggage that you talk about, especially in romantic dramas, my *own* romantic dramas. With whom did *he* see *Through a Glass Darkly?* What does blue look like to *him?*"

Paul noticed the plural in the company of the first acknowledgment that either of them had ever experienced sexual pleasure. She was telling him about dramas, this thirty-two-year-old woman. Affairs, bodies entangled, genitals explored, semen visible. She was telling him she knew about semen, while he had skipped harmlessly by with Rutherford B. Hayes. Romantic dramas. No marriages sitting invisibly at the table looking over their shoulders; that had been established way back, fifteen, twenty minutes ago: "Have you ever been married?" "No. Have *you* ever been married?" "No." They were left with romantic dramas. Lovemaking. Fucking.

Emily continued: "I don't invest that kind of daydreaming in relationships that are emotionally irrelevant, or relationships that are *parentally* oriented. I'm not talking about fatherly lovers, to whom I have ridiculously gravitated on occasion. What I mean by 'parentally' is, I guess, passionless teaching, Mr. Fix-its or pedantic Joycian experts. For me, *luggage* thinking is most always *romantic* thinking. I see that waiter over there, not for a minute do I wonder what he feels about James Ageé, or if he's ever tasted endive. In order to wonder at all, you've got to wonder *intimately*."

Paul was touched. He said so. He had tender feelings, which he withheld. Lust was reshaping itself as desire. Things were out of his hands.

He ordered another beer, and a martini for Emily, and thought for a moment of Jennifer Rosen. What was she up to in these waning days of July? Dr. and Mrs. Lawrence Tellman. Martha's Vineyard? Somewhere along the Cape?

Emily Keller bore a resemblance to Jennifer: pale skin, smooth skin, and the heart of any matter flagrantly in the eyes. But for Mrs. Lawrence Tellman there was the problem of conveying what she wished with clarity. There were false starts and jumbles of words, mangled from the beginning into jagged clumps. Everything ran together without any revealing punctuation. Emily Keller was a smoothy—a good, clear, metaphorical thinker with unusual lucidity and the spice of toughness. One couldn't slip things by her. Deceits packaged in smiles or ambiguity would be subjected to a devastating apparatus that would strip away the ribbons and bows. Emily was on the lookout for devious declarations and weapons that could sabotage an evening. Aha! She would exclaim, arrest this man! Paul saw the truth and prepared himself for her regal scrutiny. You live by a canal? How sweet, tell me more. He had known then. Her eyes said bullshit! and set him to wondering if all was lost right there at the start over olives and celery.

But here they were with cups of coffee and pecan pie and a brandy for Paul. He had discovered that Emily blushed. How strange a contradiction. "You have extraordinary eyes," Paul told her. "You have a very warm laugh," Paul told her. The truth, yes, emerging from desire, that reprehensible appetite. Paul Kramer bulldozing his way through the women of the land. Here, in the company of Emily Keller, he felt that his constant motive was repulsive. And yet, there was a blush and another, from his lofty companion, reaching out to tell him that what he wanted he would have, reciprocally, no less, an undeserved bonanza for one so sly. If she had all the facts, would the blushes speak as formidably?

"The impression I get is that you've chosen a kind of isolated life," Paul said. They sat at a centrally placed table. They were the only ones left in the restaurant. They lowered their voices as Italian chatter drifted out from the kitchen.

"What's your proof?" Emily asked.

"It's not a matter of proof. I mean, the word 'conclusive' never entered my mind. Why did you leave New York? Not that that's a criterion. It's just that you don't seem plugged in to the electric circuit. You're running on private batteries."

"That's nice," Emily said, smiling.

"Heavy duties," he added, hastening to tell her that he wasn't implying that the power was weakening.

"I was in love with a man who lived in California, and I came to live with him." She stopped. Paul gave her a second or two to get it rolling again.

Emily lit a cigarette and rested her elbows on the table. She presented him with an easy smile, informationless. Just: well, now.

"Where's the man who lived in California?" Paul asked.

"In California," she replied, in something close to a whisper.

"No ducks for him these days?"

"None."

"Does he come to call now and again?"

"None."

"Of your own doing?"

"Collaborative."

"Where do you stand? Heart a-broken? Relieved?"

"No feeling. Solitary."

"Solitary tells the world the heart's a-broken."

"It used to, when *we* were growing up. These days it could tell the world a thousand different things. And don't forget something else." Emily paused for a moment to capture the missing corners of his eyes. "Don't forget something else," she repeated. "I don't have diplomatic relations with the world. And I don't advertise."

"Are you at war?" Paul asked her.

"Of course not. That would mean obligations. Phone calls, negotiations, maneuvers."

"But not at peace. No diplomatic relations, remember?"

"*Now* you got it," Emily said, with surprising passion.

"I got it," Paul replied. "The equator of this day."

"Ah." Emily sat back and folded her hands in her lap. Her eyes dropped away from his, down to the tablecloth. Down.

"Let's go somewhere and take off our clothes."

Nothing from Emily. Hands in lap.

"Is that all right with you, Emily Keller?"

Up came her eyes, slowly, tentatively to his own. She said: "Come to my house tomorrow night when it's dark."

"What's the code word?" Paul laughed to let her know that he meant no harm. To his surprise, she had a code word handy:

"Possibly."

"I can live with that," he said.

Then, pulling her bag to her lap, and with a slight but thoughtful nod, she said to him: "We're out of here."

"I'm out of here," Paul said to Franklin in the afternoon. Franklin had been kept in the dark. As far as Franklin knew, Sandi was on the scene and his son was in San Diego or Malibu.

Paul was at the Pussycat Theater in Santa Monica watching a film called *Teenager*. Roberta and Jerry left no sexual stone unturned in a bedroom with a bookcase visible in the top left-hand corner of the screen. A handful of books, upright. As Roberta's belly button received Jerry's ejaculation, Paul's head tilted so that his ear touched his shoulder and he could make out the titles: *The Young Lions* (hard cover); something about backgammon; *The Pete Rose Story*—close-up of sperm on belly, books off camera. Long shot of Roberta and Jerry embracing, books back for just a second with their titles out of focus. Medium shot of ringing phone on bed table, books visible, titles in focus: *The Young Lions* (paperback); *Tip on a Dead Jockey*. A tribute to Irwin Shaw. Dear Mr. Shaw, yesterday at the Pussycat Theater in Santa Monica, during a rather well-made pornographic film called *Teenager*, I noticed three books of yours on a shelf in Roberta's bedroom, Roberta being the heroine, a nice-looking and very young girl with a tendency to lick her lips while being spoken to. There was both a paperback and hard cover of *The Young Lions* and a hard cover of *Tip on a Dead Jockey*. I found this remarkable in view of Roberta's very young age and certain personal habits of hers that would ordinarily preclude a literary interest. I myself treasure my first edition of your excellent collection *Mixed Company*, which I stole from Bennett Cerf's office when I interviewed him there many years ago. That fine man had stepped out of the room for a moment and I slipped *Mixed Company* into my briefcase. The office was in the Villard Houses. He had a beautiful corner office that overlooked Madison and Fifty-first, an office I am sure you've been in many times because of your long association with Random House. In fact, I also removed a Cheever book on that regrettable day. I am, yours sincerely, Paul Knight.

At the conclusion of *Teenager*, the lights came up and Hawaiian music began. To Paul's right, four seats away, two men embraced. The Los Angeles *Examiner* lay across the lap of an old man in an aisle seat in the row in front of Paul. A Longine's clock with a wide white face told the time: five-thirty. Killing time on a Sunday at the Pussycat. Come to my house when it's dark. Paul was under orders. He saw himself as subservient, creeping into Venice at sunset to seek out a born boat-rocker.

The boat-rocker lived near a car wash. Paul pulled in and watched his leased Dodge Dart slide slowly through the soapy water. He held an open can of Bubble Up, which he did not drink. He considered calling his father. What for? How are ya, Dad, I'm in a car wash, are you goin' out for dinner? For din-din, doo-doo, boo-boo, Boo Boo Tannenbaum. Daddy, I got to make a doo-doo. Mommy, I got to make a doo-doo. Mommy, can you hear me, Tommy, can you hear me, Mommy, can you hear me. Mommy, can you *hear* me?

Disconnected. That was the word. Paul felt tied to nothing. He had, or so it seemed to him on Pacific Avenue in Venice, California, broken friendship, withheld truths from a loving father, sexually bamboozled a fervent fashionist, excused himself from professional obligation, mistrusted tailors and tellers and all other members of his peripheral populace, and, furthermore, had installed himself in motels and other public houses of regret to spy on the bewildered and accumulate shabby bits and pieces of their despair. A concocter of dreams and savage pleasures, he felt he was a transient invalid. He had informed Michael Holland that he would drift—he had cleaned up his intentions that afternoon at King of the Sea for the bright-eyed measurer of cholesterol. "I'm on the run," would have been more like it. And hey, Dr. Holland, what about the fatty tissues of the soul? What's my reading, pal? And mental triglycerides? What thoughts do I cut down on? What ideas should occur to me no more than twice a week?

A lurker in a parked car fiddling with the radio. He would, in an hour, cross a canal, trudge across a decaying bridge, and find his way along the embankment to the proper address and into the home of a woman he knew little about to look around and encourage a consummation of a confusing and tenuous alliance.

"As the press secretary put it: 'The President remains confident that the full House will recognize that there simply is not the evidence to support this or any other article of impeachment and will not vote to impeach. He is confident because he knows he has committed no impeachable offense.'"

An attractive dark-haired woman wearing an Oakland Raiders tee shirt and cut-off jeans emerged from a grocery store across the street. She carried a large paper bag in one arm and a baby in the other. It had become too dark for details, but Paul was sure that the woman was crying. He thought about following her slowly, but did not. He sat with the murmur of the radio and watched the woman disappear.

> Sing, sing a song,
> Make it simple to last your whole life long;
> Don't worry that it's not good enough
> for anyone else to hear,
> Just sing, sing a song.

Nighttime. Paul walked by the canal searching for Emily's building. There were the ducks. No noise out of them. They sat huddled at the water's edge, crouched in the mud.

The sounds of Venice in the evening. Music dominated— country rock, a less than urgent tempo falling from upstairs windows. A moment of laughter from behind a picket fence. "Bonnie baby" shouted from an alley. "Bonnie baby, Bonnie baby!" No crisis, of that Paul was sure. Just Sunday-night pleasures, and bobbing and weaving under the trees.

"Hi," Emily Keller said, dressed in a light-brown sleeveless leotard and dungarees.

"Hello Emily, is it dark enough?"

"It's light enough," she said with a smile.

Emily lived in the downstairs apartment of a two-family

dwelling. There were candles in a small living room, a fluffy white rug, and a mahogany coffee table sleekly reflecting the candlelight. And paintings; it was too dark to get a close look. Ferns hanging low from the ceiling brushed Paul's temples like leafy cobwebs.

And there was Emily Keller. From orange pullover to white blouse to the soft nudity of a skin-colored leotard. An ample bosom and thin arms, a back held straight and a glorious long neck. No jewelry.

She was in the kitchen and back again with beer.

Two small couches of light orange were separated by the coffee table. Emily and Paul faced each other, pressed into soft cushions. The painting above Emily was of a couple dancing in the rain. It appeared they were in a field.

"I've thought about you," Paul said.

"That's nice to know," Emily said.

"Do you work every day?"

"It's off again, on again."

"Did you work today?"

"Not really."

"The night I first saw you you'd been working."

"When I work it's late, usually."

"As I told you yesterday, you were in a piss of a hurry."

"I get tangled up in tension."

"Does your book have a plot? I mean a real plot you could tell me?" Paul sat forward.

"It's about my father."

"How old will your readers be?"

"Early teens."

"*The Equator of This Day.*"

"It's about my father and his safety. Equidistant."

"You told me last night that your father is dead. What was his safety?"

"He found a way to express himself without commitment. He created a Ziegler. An inanimate object, a witless surrogate."

"How? What do you mean?"

"What do you think?" Emily smiled.

"Was your father an entertainer?"

"Yes."

"Was your father a ventriloquist?"

"Yes."

"Jesus," Paul whispered. He was chilled by this news.

"So," Emily said. "It's about the safety of not having to do much of anything under your own name."

"What was *its* name?"

"The dummy? Ah, my childhood sweetheart. Temmy."

"Timmy?"

"Temmy."

"Androgynous."

"You said it."

"Were you and Temmy good friends?"

"Our feelings for each other were mixed." Emily dropped her eyes to her lap.

Paul decided to pursue this no further. Although he had been with her for only a handful of hours, on the hilltop and at dinner and now these few moments here, he understood that her eyes to her lap was a signal of retreat, a modest and feminine announcement that her intentions were to slide back from him.

"Do you have any music we could hear?" he asked, quietly.

No answer, but she rose and left the room and disappeared down a hallway. Alone, Paul sat in silence. Aha, a quack from the canal. One little quack, an almost plaintive quack from beyond the candles that now, with the night full, were the only source of light. Five heavy candles with wooden bases, Bleecker Street stuff so far from their roots.

There were speakers that he hadn't noticed, under the Boston ferns and wrapped in Indian tapestry. Just audibly, music crept into the room, chamber music, one of the Beethoven quartets. When Emily returned he took a guess:

"The Tenth?" he asked.

"That's impressive," she replied with a nod.

"I have a lot of that kind of luggage."

"Still, to pin it down."

"I think the quartets are the greatest body of work in all of music. Most everything else grovels in the dirt by comparison."

"Not so fast. Mozart's *Concerto for Flute and Harp?* Bach's *Double Violin Concerto?* She stood in front of him with her hands on her hips in much the same way she had stood in the hills.

"I said *most* of everything else. Are we *really* musicologists?"

"No," Emily answered. "I fell into attitudinizing a lot."

Paul was pleased with her candor. "Sit down, for God's sake, and drink 'em up."

"You want some grass?"

"That would be fine."

Emily removed a small turquoise pipe and accoutrements from a silver box on the coffee table. Forming a working diamond between crotch and heels by folding her legs on the couch, she set herself to the preparation.

"Do you want to talk any more about your father?" Paul asked, watching her get things together.

"Not particularly."

"Do you know what I'd like to know?" Paul said, with enough earnestness to force her eyes up. "I'd like to know about the man who lives in California."

Eyes back down to the pipe, but she was willing. "He's a man of exceptional qualities. He is very spiritual, and people are likely to follow him around. There's incredible energy there. He is personally captivating. One feels—at least *I* felt—that he

knew exactly why *I* was on this planet, but that he had decided
to let *me* do the discovering on my own."

"You speak of him with reverence. You're dealing with om-
niscience."

"It sounds that way, doesn't it."

"Spiritual?"

"Yes. Powerful." Emily looked up. "I'm not equating the
two. I'm just reading the list."

Paul didn't say anything.

"Here." Emily leaned forward to hand him the pipe. He
met her across the coffee table as she held a match above the
bowl.

"How long did you live with him?" Paul asked after a
while.

"Half a year."

"And?"

"I lost my voice." Emily pulled her feet beneath her.

"Where was this?"

"In Oxnard, by the ocean. And do you know something? I
literally *lost* my own voice. It was like the ultimate case of laryn-
gitis. I could hardly make a sound." She smiled. "It's all part of
the process, right?" The smile broadened.

"And do *you* know something, Emily—he sounds to me
like a closet midget. Less to him than meets the eye, for whatever reason."

"Ah," Emily said. And after a pause, "His secret was the
enormity of his contempt. You're right. The hypocrisy made the
midget."

"But isn't there any room in the spiritual for contempt?"

"The thing is, Paul, and it was the *essence* of his secret,
there was no room for the legitimately spiritual in the truly contemptuous." Emily got up to turn the volume up. When she
came back they gave in to the music. Their eyes would meet and
drift apart. Paul stifled a fleeting notion to tell her that he loved
her. Which wasn't true at all, he reasoned. He was desirous of

her. He wanted to touch her. He felt the need to overpower her, to wrestle her down, to pin her, to exact from her a whisper of devotion.

What were her plans? Was there steamed broccoli to face? And curry and grapes and more facts on the table, neatly pushed together like a pile of crumbs?

"Are you hungry?" he asked.

"I eat late. Is that all right?"

"That's fine. This is good strong grass. And so far I'm not hungry."

"Let's be naked." Emily was sitting with her back straight and her legs crossed on the couch. She held her glass of beer in her right hand. She looked directly at him with serious eyes. Let's discuss Peter Rodino for one hour and nine minutes. Let's play chess. Let's dance. The boss with the straight back was in charge, amidst the candles and the music, on her own turf, defining the evening. He would do as she told him.

"What?" Paul said.

"You heard what I said. Don't fuck around with me."

"Calm your ass, kid. You've got to allow me my rhythm, however false it rings. I'm not fucking around with you."

They stared at each other. They stayed with it, and soon they scented the air and cleared the room of foul play. Beethoven became Joni Mitchell who merged with the Stones. They were on the floor, on the fluffy white rug, clothes under the coffee table and on the couches. Emily Keller, totally naked, lay flat on top of him, kissing him, holding his head in her hands, squirming on his body, trapping his cock between her thighs, rolling onto her back and pulling him with her. He held her arms above her head, imprisoning both wrists in his left hand. Her breasts flattened, her belly fell in, tight and thin, emphasizing her ribs. Paul felt her liver as he massaged her deeply. He wanted her organs in his hands. He put four fingers in her cunt, massaging and fishing, finding the string of an IUD, pressing the walls of her vagina. He removed his fingers from her body and rested on his side. He kissed her lips and masturbated her, still holding her wrists with his left hand. Her eyes were closed. He kissed them. They were shut tight. She wasn't ready to see. Her eyelids were the only clothes she wore.

When he released her wrists her arms remained above her head. He spread her legs with his hands on her inner thighs. He wanted to study the map of her cunt, but the light was dim and deprived him. He licked and sucked and held her breasts and squeezed her nipples.

In a while her body tensed. The veins in her neck and arms swelled and pushed at skin. Paul watched her orgasm closely: eyes tightly shut, but everything else available. As she came he pushed his middle finger into her ass. She made no sound. Her torso rose from the floor. Her arms extended themselves even further over her head. She pulled her knees up, allowing him more access. Her mouth opened, but she said nothing. Her ribs stuck out from her body—washboards on either side of her chest. "You're naked," he whispered, "and I'm watching." She was tight as a drum, frozen, almost all of her off the floor. Paul said, "Emily." That brought forth an utterance: "Ahhh." He stuck with her clitoris and pushed his finger deeper into her ass.

Slowly her muscles began to relax and her back descended. On his knees between her legs he removed his hand from her genitals and ass and slipped his cock into her cunt. He lay on top of her. Her arms circled him. He moved slowly. He thought it was possible that he would cry. He put his right arm under her head. He kissed her with tenderness—her lips, her closed eyes, her forehead, her ears. The floor prevented elaborate movements of intercourse. His knees rubbed against the rug. He moved circularly inside her. He did not announce his orgasm. He came, without the tears he had expected, holding her face to his, pressing his cheek to hers. Her arms were around his back.

Bellies together, they rested. He withdrew his arm and set

her head gently on the floor. They found each other's mouths and kissed without fire. They pecked at each other and squashed each other's lips, and finally they lay quietly as he deflated. He moved his lower body occasionally to prolong his erection and maintain his time inside her.

In time, he rolled from her.

They lay on their backs for a while, their sides touching. He rested his hand on her pubic hair and toyed with it idly. His mind filled with eyes and flashes of events from the past. His mouth was dry from the grass. He was attempting to reconstruct a certain Brooklyn Dodgers team: Hodges, Robinson, Reese, Cox. Furillo, Snider, Pafko. Pafko? Where was Andy Pafko at this *exact* minute? Chicago, maybe. Wasn't Pafko *from* Chicago? Did Pafko remember a catch he made against the Braves at Ebbets Field? With his back to the plate? Joe Adcock hit the ball. Adcock. Add cock. Add cock to Emily Keller.

"Did you ever hear of Joe Adcock?" Paul asked softly.

A reflective pause. "I don't think so," Emily said. "Why?"

"I was just wondering. He came into my mind."

"Who is he?"

"An athlete."

That was enough. Emily stretched, rising a little. Her lubricated cunt received Paul's affectionate finger. He withdrew it when she settled down.

"Emily?" It was a statement, with a Sandi Cummings question mark pinned to its tail.

"Uh-huh?" Emily picked up the question mark.

"You're a sexy girl."

No response.

"You're erotic."

"When we were together, I knew where you were going all the way through," she said. "It felt good."

"No surprises?"

"Plenty. But very comfortable. I *belonged* with you, you know?"

"The music's over. You had it all cleverly programed, you turkey. You been here before?"

"No."

"You mean you've never been up here before? Oh, these weekends are fun. Grossinger's goes all out."

"I wish the pool was heated."

"Yeah, I know. Isn't it a drag?"

"But I liked *Singin' in the Rain* last night."

"You'd never seen it?"

"No."

"I was there. Where were you sitting?"

"In the middle."

"Who were you with?"

"My friend Maggie."

"Debbie Reynolds. I hear she's, well, you know."

"I heard that, too. But I don't believe it."

"Why don't you believe it?"

"Just because."

"So you were at the movies."

"Who were *you* with?"

"My buddy Richie."

"Is he a short guy with blond hair?"

"Yeah."

"I met him at the Secret Love dinner."

"*You* were the girl who sang at the table?"

"Uh-huh."

"He *told* me about you. He said you had big mamms and that you just sang out, right at the table."

"You wanna hear me sing?"

"You mean right here? In the snowmobile?"

"Uh-huh."

"Okay."

"No. I can only sing on the floor."

"Then let's go back to the floor."

"We're out of here."

"You programed the music cunningly. You been here before?"

"No."

"The plants are hung really low in here."

"I like them at eye level so you don't see the pots."

"My knees are red from rubbing against the rug."

"Was it worth your while?"

"Decidely."

Paul leaned over her face and kissed her lips. "Sing," he whispered into her ear.

"We're back."

"Sing."

Emily hesitated for a moment, and began. She sang in a quavering voice, but held onto the melody all the way through, gathering confidence with her eyes closed. She was musical, tentative, and charming. The sound that she made, soft and sad, filled the room with peace. She sang slowly, and with her hands clasped together on her bosom. Paul, resting on an elbow, watched from above her.

> I know that each of us is all alone in the end,
> But the trip still seems less dangerous if
> You've got a friend.
> If through all the madness
> We can stick together
> We're safe and sound;
> The world's just inside out and upside down.

Paul kissed her. Then he sat beside her and held her hands. Emily finally opened her eyes. "These weekends usually don't turn out so well. I guess we just got lucky," he said.

Oh the banners! The streamers! What a glorious day, an autumn day, with the microphones of WPKF along the way, eager reporters waiting for Paul. No, he had no statement at this time, not on such a day as this, not on a celebratory afternoon in Central Park. He strolled through the banners and waved and smiled. There was Dickie Tornitzer behind a WPKF microphone beckoning to him. Just a few words, Paul? No, Tornitzer, no words for you with your PKF microphone shoved in my face. You were a schmuck then, you're a schmuck now. Hello, back there in the crowd! What a splendid day! So this is what it's like: *honored by your fellow citizens.* "He married the girl with the strawberry curl/and the band played on." Try it as a torch song, Frank. It's the saddest song ever written. It's perfect for you. Take the waltz out of it, Frankie, and you got yourself the blues. And here now, ladies and gentlemen, is the girl with the strawberry curl. Ladies and gentlemen, *Emily Keller!* Emily on a slab of ice, naked. Dead. Having ceased to live, her head shaved except for the strawberry curl, all of it a surprise to Paul. His mother, taking him by the wrist, pulling him around, *snapping* him around: *"You have ruined this day."* No, Mommy, please, Mommy, it's not *true.*

Emily, asleep beside him, stirred as he left the bed. He stood by the door until she settled down.

In the tiny bathroom across from Emily's bedroom Paul, in the dark, aimed his urine at the side of the bowl to prevent the noise of splashing. For a second he pissed on his foot before finding the toilet again. Women could never piss on their feet, he thought.

Paul wiped his foot with a towel and closed the toilet without flushing. He made his way down the hall to the living room and sank into one of the couches. What was it, four or five in the morning? Why was he cursed with dawns in unfamiliar rooms, his head whirling with sad waltzes and accusing eyes.

A beer. Yes, a beer. Careful not to wake Emily with the refrigerator door. Careful not to offend, careful not to wound, careful careful through all the days and nights of his life, through morning Coors and phone calls to his father and whispers to lovers on living-room floors.

Emily Keller on the living-room floor, and later in her own bed, refused him her eyes as they made love to each other; they were shut tight, though she performed miraculously, coaxing him to come in her mouth, permitting another come in her ass, kissing his lips, receiving him on her back, a blind girl, confortably navigating the streets of him. Falling asleep she had murmured, "Now there's got to be an explanation for this," and had slipped her arms around his neck. He had laid her on her back in her pajamas with her arms at her sides, and she had slept.

And yet what care had he taken with Sandi Cummings? Hadn't Jennifer Rosen told him, with snowflakes on her face, that she was permanently grieved? There they were, two of the women parading before him for whom he had taken little care, throwing cherry bombs through their windows, shoving firecrackers up their asses, maiming. Meaningfully maiming. Here he was in his thirty-third year, indecisive and cautious, wandering through the home of a vivid girl with an absolutely *gorgeous* mind. The information that Emily had on hand—literary theories, political savvy, the innate good sense to get things rolling with a Beethoven quartet—had stampeded his genitals, arousing him. Would he keep the firecrackers away from her ass and leave the cherry bombs at home? Would he *care* about this woman? Would he, arriving at her door through the decade of the sixties, all hollered out and bruised up, drifting across an undetermined land with a blank map in his pocket, declare this woman through Customs? Yes, gentlemen, I take responsibility for this package. I *declare* this woman.

Emily worked in a small room with a desk and typewriter at the far end of the apartment. One Boston fern hung low from a corner of the ceiling, and two unframed lithographs in gray and black were pinned to the wall. Paul found his way into this room. He closed the door quietly and lit a candle on a bookshelf next to the desk. He took the candle to the desk and sat down.

Another desk to leaf through, only this time he was interested in a black school notebook on top of the desk by the typewriter. Emily's rich longhand suggested his mother's, flowing and graceful on lined paper. There were just a few entries, and Paul looked them over:

> With the death of the father the voice of Terrence is muted. I must attempt to make that voice ring, toll, as a matter of fact, long after the book is finished and closed. It is the voice within me, ever alive, ever tolling, the child born to the father and daughter, a fearsome essence. I must try to transmit the horror.

> If God were a ventriloquist it is possible that his act would be evangelical and that there would be no exchange between his little partner Invisibility, and Him. Invisibility would speak as a monologist, occasionally glancing over at God for confirmation. The visible aspect of the act would be only the slow and persistent dripping of human blood.

> We, as mortals, are constantly testifying against one another in God's presence. The testimony is funneled through sophisticated channels and reestablished as fresh testimony even before the original accusation has been completed. God uses this recycling as a toy, knowing well that we are all turncoats.

"Turncoats." The word excited Paul. Clearly he understood that he was falling in love with the woman who had selected it, who had placed it carefully, in ink, in a child's notebook.

In drawers Paul found pornography, a stack of ten-dollar books, published by Classic, displaying attractive, embroiled men and women. They occupied him for a long time, until he became aware of the beginning of dawn and a slight and subtle change in the room, a breeze. An open door.

Emily was in the doorway in her pajamas, hands on hips, serious eyes. The candle flickered.

"Come to bed," she said.

"Do you disapprove of me?" he asked.

"No. Naturally not. Do you disapprove of me?"

"Naturally not. I'm all horny with these books."

"Let's fuck."

On their knees, on the bed, they faced each other. Paul unbuttoned her pajama top. She stood, bouncing a little on the mattress, to remove her pants. She sat on him, inserting him with her hand. She rose and fell, her eyes open and with him. He reached for her breasts, but she brushed his hands away. Paul imagined himself within her brain, establishing language and recalling fleeting pictures of other men beneath her. I'll wait for him to come and then I'll come. I'm full of him. Did he read my notes? Is he frightened of me? I want to make him come now. I don't want him to touch me. My breasts want his hands but I won't do it, just me on top of him fucking him. He's a soft comer. I've got him. Come on baby, come to me, come to me, sweetie, come to me my love, juicy lovely coming in me, in me is all I want, sweetie . . . Paul lost her. He was hooked on the books in her drawer. He was back, involved in his own presence and Sandi Cummings douching and back to Emily, oh shit of course! the girl is a ventriloquist! Holy Jesus shit, *she can do it!*

"What's the matter?" Emily felt his deflation.

"Do it," he said.

"What do you want me to do?" she asked, baffled.

"I want you to talk like Temmy."

"So." They remained motionless, still connected.

"Come on."

"I did it in the bar."

"You can actually throw your voice."

"Actually. Not very well, but actually."

"Do it."

"I just can't, just *do it*."

"Talk like Temmy. Let me hear what he sounded like."

"Paul . . ."

"Come on."

Her lips moved just a little and there came forth a hoarse whisper, clearly enunciated, low of pitch, the voice of an adolescent. "We had a lovely box of toys. Mother asked me to get them from the top of the wardrobe. On the way downstairs I dropped the box and all the toys fell out." And in her own voice: "What happened then?" Emily didn't miss a beat: "I put the toys back in, but I dropped the box again. They call me a dirty old man." "Why?" "Because I like boxes."

"I don't believe it." Paul pulled out of her and rolled onto his stomach.

"Now the distant voice is like people shouting from a long way off. It's real hard and it can't take close scrutiny."

"At the Dorado."

"I can only do it for a second. I can make it seem as if somebody a little distance away from me has spoken. They taught me."

"*They?*"

"My father and Temmy. You got it?" The room, filling with light, let Paul see her smile.

"It's just, you know, amazing. Fucking amazing."

"Why?" She put a hand on his shoulder.

"I've always been afraid of ventriloquism. I've never thought it was amusing."

"Neither have I."

Not a word was spoken for a minute or two.

"I'm sorry about the sex," Paul said.

"There's more, my love. We have more, you know?" She ran her hand down his back.

"How well I know."

"I can smell booze on you."

"Beer."

"What woke you?"

"It's not unusual. I'm up a lot."

She rested beside him on her elbow.

"We're going to a party, do you know that?" Emily said, with a touch of excitement.

"When are we going to a party?"

"Tonight."

"What party?"

"*A* party."

"We're going to have dates together."

"I haven't had a date in a long time," she told him.

"What's playing at the Trans-Lux Eighty-fifth Street?"

"*Love Is a Many Splendored Thing.*"

"Seen it."

"See it again?"

"Okay."

"You want a Mounds bar?"

"Bonbons."

"How much money ya got on ya?"

"Fifty dollars."

"Betcha ya don't."

"Betcha I do."

"Put your money where your mouth is."

"Come on and kiss me, you turkey."

And Emily did. He rolled over and she lay on top of him.

"How much do you weigh?" Paul asked.

"A hundred and fifteen." Emily kissed his chest.

"How tall are you?"

"Five foot five or six." Emily surrounded his cock with her lips.

"I thought you were much shorter. What's your cholesterol?"

No answer. She was engrossed.

"What's your cholesterol?" he repeated.

Emily raised her head. "Shut the fuck up," she said.

"Okay. It's *your* house."

And in her house, on the sheets of her own bed, through a dawn of considerable clarity, she drew a hard-on out of him and reinstalled his cock in her body, rising and falling, leaning forward to allow him full access to her breasts. He came quickly, clutching her breasts, overwhelmed by Emily Keller. Straddling him, she masturbated, staring him straight in the eyes. Her hand froze on her cunt, her shoulders caved in, her mouth opened fully, completely. She crumpled to his body and surrounded his head with her arms.

An hour later, with the ducks announcing the morning, they drank coffee in the living room, naked on the orange couches.

"Do you want to live with me?" Emily asked him, casually.

"Absolutely," he replied. No doubt at all.

"Fair enough."

"You've done this before? On two days' notice?"

"Once."

"And?"

"Disaster."

"And?"

"And so. Do you want to live with me?"

"Absolutely."

"Well."

They held each other's eyes.

"What's the plan?" he asked, after a moment.

"Get crackin'. Get yourself together."

"And tonight?"

"Celebration. Let's cook up something deadly tonight. Let's surprise ourselves."

"Risky stuff."

"You got it."

"You're an *eevil* motherfucker."

"I ain't hidin' it from you, baby." Emily laughed, a nice warm laugh.

"I'd like you to meet my father along the way."

"But of course. Let's face it, sweetheart, we got *plans.*"

"Do you know what I'm thinking of? *The Equator of This Day.* I read some of your notes." Paul took a final sip of coffee.

"I figured you did."

"So here we are." Paul stood up and went to Emily and leaned down and kissed her. "We're on the high seas," he whispered into her ear.

"And the raft is ashore. *Think* of it!" she said.

PART THREE

CHAPTER EIGHT

"This is Robert Miller of the Los Angeles *Times*," Paul said. "I'm calling because we're doing a story on salt, diuretics, and related material, and we would like to know precisely how much salt is added to an eighteen-ounce can of your product, Sacramento tomato juice."

"How much salt contained therein?" replied Norma Sullivan, a Borden's nutritionist.

"Therein," Paul said.

"I would have to inquire from our office in San Francisco."

"Where are you located?"

"Columbus, Ohio."

"Why?"

"Why?"

"Why?"

"Because the Borden's headquarters is located here."

"And what of the headquarters in San Francisco?"

"What is your name again, sir?"

"Robert Miller of the Los Angeles *Times*. That is my full name."

"And you're doing a story on salt?"

"Correct."

"Fine. Well, I'm going to have to get back to you."

"I'll be here for two hours. We're running the piece tomorrow, and would appreciate any help you might be able to give."

A call to New York and a tie line to Columbus, Ohio; a network of Borden executives strung around the country. San Francisco consulted because of a persistent fraud, alone in his father's house in Los Angeles, acting out. "You don't have to *act out* all the time," Jennifer Rosen had told him on more than one occasion. "I mean, my *God*, you *want* what you *want* when you *want* it."

True, Paul thought, gathering some of his things together. Salt, retaining water in the body, bloats. Tomato juice, though lower in calories than orange juice, could, because of the salt, be more of a villain to the weight-conscious than orange juice. This was what was on Paul's mind. He reasoned that he had followed through, not acted out. "Not *acted out*, Jennifer," he said aloud.

His books would stay, and a change of clothes. He would tell Franklin that he'd be staying with Emily off and on. Off and on. Nothing elaborate, no strings, just off and on. A new friend in Venice, surely a charmer. She would charm Franklin Kramer.

"There are four grams of salt in an eighteen ounce can," Norma Sullivan reported back, early in the afternoon. And could the Borden people be sent a copy of the article? Oh, yes, Paul assured her, unless the piece was killed. And what is your address, Norma Sullivan? One-eighty East Broad Street, Columbus, Ohio. And the zip, please. Paul was thorough. Four three two one five. Thank you, Norma, and once again, thanks for your help.

"Hey," he said.

"Hey," Emily said. "When are you coming?"

"Around six."

"What have you been doing today?"

"Details."

"Have you told your father?"

"I haven't seen him. But I will later." The sound of Emily's voice unsettled him. What was the color of her eyes? The length of her hair? For a second, he lost her entirely.

"Paul," she said, softly.

The sound of his own name brought her back. "Anything is possible," he said, reassuring himself.

Paul drove to the Farmer's Market for a late lunch. He would bring Emily vegetables and fruit—avocados and grapes and artichokes out of season—and tomatoes, and cheese; Camembert and Brie. And pumpkin pie, a bottle of Scotch, three pounds of walnuts, a large jar of red caviar, a warm loaf of pumpernickel bread. And at the Market a tostada for himself at a table in the sun.

Paul called Michael Holland from a phone booth in the parking lot.

"Are you with a patient?" he asked.

"It's all right," Holland replied. "How are you?"

"I've met a girl," Paul said.

"Exhibition game?"

"No. League game. Four-game series. Pierce against Ford in the Friday-night game."

"I *see*," Holland said.

"Is everything okay with you?" Paul asked. He could hear himself reaching for Holland. Help me, Michael, is what remained unspoken.

"It's been a nightmare-hot summer, and you haven't missed a thing," Holland said.

"What does the New York press say about you-know-who?"

"That he's a cocksucker."

Would Holland have used that word in the presence of a patient? Was he by himself but not anxious to talk? Did he give a shit?

"What's her name?" Holland asked.

"Emily."

"Are you okay?"

Holland was picking up something.

"I'm okay."

"Are you sure a whole four-game series?"

"Pretty sure."

"Careful. You know?"

"I miss you, Michael."

"Same thing here."

Paul left the Freeway to drift through Westwood. He parked, and got out to wander around UCLA. Summer classes and summer dresses. Flashes of notebooks and sex. A joint passed around a circle and a radio hanging from a low branch of a tree: "Just what is abusive conduct? I suggest that it is an empty phrase, having meaning only in terms of what we pour into it. It must reflect our subjective views of impropriety, as distinguished from the objective views enunciated by society in its laws."

Paul bought an orange Popsicle and sat in the sun on a vast stretch of lawn. Was he, he wondered, recognizable as an elder statesman languishing by choice among the laughing and unformed faces of this summer campus? He was harmless enough in his jeans and white tennis shirt, and he looked young. Could his power be felt? He felt powerful, detached from regulation, and wise to the ways of the world. No longer a schoolboy, in charge now of his own schedule, governed only by his private morality. Were these children with naked thighs and teasing smiles aspiring to his spot on the map? Maybe not. Maybe his spot, fed by tributaries of indecency and aimlessness, was not nirvana after all. Was he, Paul Kramer, comfortable on this swaying sea? How dare he assume an omniscient pose when he recognized the shifty bungler in charge of his own reckless performance.

Paul could feel the orange flavor pushing him back, in the heat of the afternoon, to his father. The Franklin Kramer of long ago, the Fifth Avenue companion after dinner, strolling with an orange popsicle, his mother drowsy at home, and Franklin asking about indolence and solitude and WPKF, the two of them returning in overcoats to the darkened hallways of the infirmary. "We're home, darling," Franklin would say from the bedroom door. "How you doing?"

How you doing? Carol Kramer, how you doing? Wiggens, stop for a moment, please, with your subjective views of impropriety. I'd like you to meet Carol and Franklin Kramer, my parents. Wiggens, these are good people. They're not in your constituency, but they hold opinions about abusive conduct. Can you see them, Wiggens, my mother propped up in bed reading *Gourmet* magazine, my father in the doorway asking, "How you doing?"? I'm in my room, if you want to know, but I hold no opinions about abusive conduct. I'm indolent, prone to exaggeration and fantasy, and I revere Carl Furillo. But take a look at the other two, just for a moment, Wiggens, though I know you have a national forum waiting for you. What you are saying to that national forum is not acceptable to those two people, Carol and Franklin Kramer. They know of pumpkins and typewriters and pinkies and Commies. The man, my father, has read transcripts and heard testimony, and he, *they*, as a matter of fact, are not prepared to accept your position on this matter. You would have to visit their *lives* to understand. You'd have to sneak into their history and watch them from a corner of the room. Hear what they have to say, see their devotion to each other, watch my mother in the kitchen and observe my father with his son. Do you see the kindness? That's your opposition, Wiggens. Talk about impropriety and society and laws till the cows come home. You are missing the point.

From a phone booth in Westwood Village, Paul called Franklin.

"I'd like to meet the girl," Franklin said, after Paul's careful announcement.

"But of course," said Paul.

"And you say she lives in Venice?"

"On one of the canals."

"And you say she's a writer?"

"She writes for children."

"Will I ever get to see you?"

"I'm not going anywhere drastically or permanently," Paul said. "It's something I think I believe in."

"I see."

And then from Paul: "How you doing?"

"I'm a little tired this afternoon. Sometimes heat debilitates the middle-aged."

"Ah," Paul said. "One of these days I'm going to become older than you."

"I'd like to meet the girl," Franklin said.

"But of course," Paul replied. "You got yourself a deal."

They listened to the vote of Article Two in Paul's car.

"Twenty-eight to ten," mused Emily.

"Sandman doesn't really count," Paul said.

At a party on Doheny Drive in a large apartment painted entirely black, there was an open house. Emily had filled him in: chili and grass and coke and rock. The hostess was Mona Nine, a dealer, a small long-haired girl about twenty-five, who lurked in the far ends of her black corridors in constant negotiation. Two blond women in white saris hovered around a bowl of guacamole, while three shirtless young men sipped beer from cans in silence. In a black den lit only by candles, a group of children sat on a shag rug staring at a soundless color television set.

Paul could find only one book in the apartment: *Better Backgammon*, and that in a closet with eight-track tapes, hundreds of eight-track tapes.

"Hiya," he said to Mona Nine, as he passed her in a corridor. And, surprising himself, he encircled Mona's waist with one arm and kissed her with passion. "See ya," he said, when they disconnected. "Right," Mona Nine said.

"You know, that's all right," Emily said. She had watched Paul and Mona from a sitting position on the floor of the living room, flooded in eight-track Rolling Stones.

"I wouldn't call it the world's most important romance," Paul said, surprised but not uncomfortable with the knowledge that Emily had seen them.

"It's all right," Emily said. "I like to watch things like that." She put her hand on his arm.

"Have you ever watched the whole orchestra and not just two soloists?"

"I have, but I prefer only the string section. Otherwise it gets too cluttered and loses its appeal." She fluttered her eyelids and presented a poker face.

"You are *some* turkey." He took her chin in his hand and gently shook her head.

"Do you know what's best?" she asked him. "When you've got something riding on it. When you have feelings about one of the soloists."

"You mean, when one of the soloists has read your private notes and pissed in your pot."

"Even more." Another touch of his arm.

"Anything riding on it for you tonight?" he asked, trying to ease this one through with a nice big smile.

"Oh, yes," she answered seriously. "Somewhere between the piss in the pot and the even more." She lowered her eyes with what Paul felt to be careful design.

"So. Your buddy, Mona Nine. What's her real name?"

"Sugarman, and she's not my buddy. She's an acquaintance from Oxnard."

"Was it possible that your man from California might have been here tonight?"

"The night is young."

"Do you want to see him?"

"No."

"What's his name?"

"Joshua."

"Then why come?"

"I like cheap risks."

Paul took her head in his hands and kissed her. They stayed at it in their rock-and-roll room. "You're too smart by a half," he told her in a while.

"Jesus, don't I know it. Do you want to see something?"

Emily stood up and took Paul down one of Mona's black corridors to a small room next to the kitchen, a room that Paul had missed when he had explored the apartment.

The door, closed but unlocked, swung open on dozens of medium-sized transparent garbage bags stuffed with marijuana. The one piece of furniture in the room, a plain wooden desk of no particular character, was crammed with small Handi-bags of grass that were sealed with rubber bands. A glass vase adorned the desk. Perhaps a foot high, it was filled to within an inch of the top with pure white coke, and capped with aluminum foil.

"That's ten thousand dollars right there," Emily said, gesturing at the vase.

"And the fuckin' door is *open*," Paul said, incredulously.

"And the fuckin' door is open. That's Mona."

"Mona fuckin' Sugarman. Where's she from?"

"Yonkers."

"What's Oxnard?"

"Oxnard's above Malibu, above Trancas. I told you once."

"I wanna take."

"Take. Quick and careful take." She shooed him on with her hand.

One Handi-bag in a back pocket of his jeans.

"A token take," he said, concerned with passers-by in the hall; Emily had left the door ajar.

"More," she urged.

"No. That's it, baby." He backed toward the door.

"Chicken shit," said someone behind him.

Paul whirled around. There was no one there, and no one in the hall. He went to Emily and stood in front of her. Suddenly, and without any warning from his eyes, he slapped her hard on the right cheek. She held her ground. She stared at him without expression.

"Never do that again," he told her, holding her eyes with his. "You got that?"

There was a smile somewhere on Emily's face. Just a wee bit of a thing within the corners of her mouth. "I don't promise nothin'," she said. She held out her hand to him. He took it.

"You'll kill us all," he said.

They stayed at the party for an hour or so, cuddled in a corner under the Rolling Stones.

"Emily, my dear," Mona Nine said, joining them for a moment.

"Are you hanging in there?" Emily asked, shouting above the music.

"Did you know that Artie's dead?" Mona asked, without any special emotion.

"I heard," Emily replied, in much the same tone.

"Have you seen Joshua recently?" Paul asked Mona.

"I think he's in New York," Mona said.

"I don't know," Emily said.

"I crashed last week," Mona said.

"Where, at the beach?" Emily asked.

"Santa Barbara," Mona said.

"Why is this place black?" Paul asked Mona.

"I like it," Mona said.

"You got any Linda Ronstadt?" Paul asked Mona.

"I didn't . . ." Mona said.

"We're going to split soon," Emily said to Mona.

"That's cool," Mona said.

"So you're okay?" Emily said to Mona.

"Dynamite," said Mona. "See you guys."

Their hostess drifted away. Emily and Paul remained in their corner for a while. They shared a joint and ate some cheese. They slipped their arms around each other's waist. Paul closed his eyes. He imagined himself in a heavy rain, walking across a field. In no hurry.

"I've never known how to do it. I always use one of those machines, those little rollers." Paul watched Emily prepare a joint, distributing Mona's grass carefully, evenly, rolling, and then moisturizing with her mouth.

"A perfect tough little joint," Paul said, respectfully.

"It's easy. I love to do it. I could do it for hours."

They were sitting at her small kitchen table. It was midnight.

"Stolen goods," Emily said, lighting up.

"Have you ever taken anything out of there before?" Paul asked.

"Yes," she replied, after a deep inhalation.

"And it's never missed?"

"You saw the setup. You can take a handful of M&M's from a bushel, who's to know?"

"But the handfuls mount up."

"We're talking peanuts, pal." And here now the peanuts passed from her hand to his.

Paul was fascinated with Emily's use of the word "pal." The word had never carried any dangerous freight; it was, Paul felt, more blustery than belligerent, more charming hotshot than tough guy. Okay, pal. He had said it himself now and again. It contained a "see ya," and a "I've got your lovely little number." Pal. From a woman with delicate hands rolling joints on a midnight kitchen table, it was sweetly contradictory and casually sexual.

"Mona Sugarman Nine," Paul said. He was comfortably high. "Answer questions."

"Well, first of all, it's a pleasure to be on your show," Emily said, leaning forward with her elbows on the table.

"Why Nine?"

"Her lucky number."

"Has she ever been busted?"

"No."

"How come?"

"Let me put it this way: you can park your car by the out-of-town newsstand in Times Square, see a movie, have a bite, and you can come back to your car and it's still there, and with no ticket, even."

"What?" Paul said.

"Nobody looks for the obvious under their own noses. They're too busy shining flashlights into corners." Emily put the joint out in an ashtray.

"But ten thousand dollars worth of coke!"

"It is exactly where it belongs. Under their noses."

"Sugarman. Yonkers."

"And she has a six-year-old kid named Sky at a house in

Malibu. Never married. A classic little Jewish girl from New York who parks in Times Square. That's the whole story. Got it?" Emily leaned back with a smile.

"She's rich?" Paul said.

"She has a good deal of money. Believe it."

"How do *you* know?"

"Don't we have to take a commercial break?"

"Come on, turkey. How do you know?" Paul leaned toward Emily.

"I've checked it out."

"Another case of M&M's?"

"Mr. Kramer. I see your time is up. It was a pleasure to have—"

"How much? How many times?"

"I am not a crook. It would be wrong."

"Twenty-eight to ten and twenty-seven to eleven is where that'll get you."

"Once, and nothing big. Peanuts."

"I'm interested in the ethics."

"How do *you* stand on the ethics?" Emily asked this very quietly.

Paul took his time with it. At last he said: "You and I are not strangers."

"What does that mean?"

"It means what you think it means."

"I think it means that you know all about Times Square parking."

"That's what it means, sweetie."

"Then you've been on top of this thing from the beginning," Emily said. She appeared to be somewhat surprised to find that the tricky brand of power she'd been flashing had been quite gracefully sabotaged. "Do you do devil's advocate work for a living?"

"Come on now," Paul said. "I didn't want you to see my cards until I was sure I had a partner and not a priestess."

"You aren't dealing here with a woman of the cloth." Emily meant business.

"While we're talking," Paul said, pushing his chair back and resting his feet on the corner of the tabletop.

"While we're talking," Emily repeated.

"It's interesting to me the *kind* of talk we have. The quality of the talk. Do you know what I mean?"

"Define."

"We seem to bring out in each other a very lucid cynicism. I like it. I'm attracted to it. I like the dialogue. I'm not often compelled in this direction on a continuous basis."

"We have an understanding." Emily said, with a smile.

"Yes, we do," Paul replied. "I'm just kind of speaking as a witness now. I mean, you charge me up, and I'm watching."

Paul understood that what he was withholding could plunge them, so early in the game, into a cautious waltz, their swords held in their gowns and cummerbunds. Emily, we are glib and we are smart. We are facile and speedy because we dance and whirl with our hearts filled with the fears of children in the night. We are terrified of each other, and if we were to acknowledge it, we would become prisoners of that admission. Our weapons would be at the ready as we paraded in costumes, and we would grow to despise each other while the evening was still young.

These thoughts stayed with Paul as they joined in Emily's bed. He spent a long time in her body, kissing her shoulders and lips. He moved quickly, then remained still. He caressed her hair. He started up again, ignited by the movement of her hips. He opened her closed eyes with his fingers, and she kept them open, for the room was dark and there was no danger of a confrontation. See, Paul, my eyes are open, she could very well have been saying. I'm giving in to you, don't you see? Ah, but Emily, it's pitch-black in here. Your gift is empty.

Why so doubtful and suspicious? The woman was in it with her eyes open and her body naked. Paul felt ashamed at his unrelenting condemnation. The crucial issues would be theirs to negotiate when the roadway across their land reached a measurable distance. For now, he reflected, with only a few feet covered, it was unreasonable to challenge open eyes. He, every bit as accomplished a thespian as Emily, had no right to call her on anything so soon.

"Are you okay?" she whispered, receiving from his body the perplexities of his mind.

Her sensitivity touched him and discouraged his rambling. He returned to her sexuality with an amorous heart. Yes, indeed, he loved the girl, oh, yes, indeed.

At his high school, there had been a white picket fence that had separated a playing field and a driveway. Paul had often leaped over it, comfortable with the grass that accepted his weight, and leery of the pebbles of the driveway when his derring-do originated from the field. It was this white picket fence that he found himself leaping over when, at long last, through the slowly tumbling thoughts, he came in Emily. This white picket fence, buried in the past, absent from any conscious consideration for seventeen years, placed itself directly behind his eyes and forced tears out of him. He slumped onto Emily and rested his head on her shoulder.

"Darling," she said, so softly. "Darling man."

But the tears were not for Emily, and he would never tell. Another secret locked away.

"I love you, Emily." How unforgivable of him to exploit her tenderness. Paul felt himself a coward, out of touch with any kind of truth.

"I'm on the way there, my darling," Emily told him, and stroked his hair.

Paul stifled his tears. It was the least he could do, having led her so far astray.

Guiltily he began to manipulate her clitoris. She lay on her back with her hands at her sides. He worked for her, imagining himself impaled on the white picket fence—a careless leap, his shoes slipping on the pebbles. Impaled, wearing Cordovan and corduroy. He worked hard for Emily Keller. He could feel it in her breathing. He slipped another "I love you" to her. It didn't carry its weight. Did she know of his shallow soul? He dipped a finger into her and drew his own sperm out to apply to her gently. Now that did it. Emily Keller, you motherfucker. Come to papa, come to papa do, my sweet embraceable you.

Paul lay beside her, their legs touching. Paul thought: I am forever covering my tracks.

Paul said to Emily: "I am invisible."

Was she asleep?

Emily Keller at work. A typist, and a smoker of Camel cigarettes. The afternoons and evenings were the best for her. She was able to sit for long hours. Occasionally she would fall asleep with her head on the desk. Frequently she would blow her nose. Often she would write in her notebook. But there she would sit, the light in the room changing with the passing of the day. She would not leave her chair except to go to the bathroom. She would not pace, or lie on her back on the floor.

Paul felt threatened by her discipline. He thought she wrote beautifully. He told her that as a daughter of a ventriloquist she had the good fortune of original material. He encouraged her and praised her and wandered through the city with the car radio on.

From a phone booth at La Brea and Pico he called Sandi, and hung up when a man's voice answered with a "Howdy." Sandi had found her howdy. It was an older man's howdy, unexpectant, perfectly and absolutely friendly, a sure-of-itself howdy, committed to Sandi Cummings, maybe revering her and all the hope in her eyes, revering her style, and her ability to deflect the worst news of the day, revering the generous sexual woman with a cubicle at Robinson's—by now, who knows? An office and a window and frequent conferences upon which much depended.

"I have come to the conclusion that the public interest is no longer served by repetition of my previously expressed belief that the President is not guilty of an impeachable offense. Therefore, as Vice President I will respectfully decline to discuss the matter further."

Paul, eating a taco in the car, turned the dial, leaving grease on the knob.

"Previously expressed belief . . . ," "respectfully decline to discuss . . . ," ". . . clusion that the public interest is no longer . . ."

> And if that better way ain't so
> I'll ride with the tide and go with the flow.

Paul pulled into a gas station to wash his hands. On the gray wall above a filthy sink was written in pencil: THE TRUTH IS LOUSY. An adult's longhand, the message slanted only slightly upward. No penis, no breast, no lewd invitation. Just: the truth is lousy. A traveler on his way through Los Angeles, a man in his mid-forties tasting matrimonial or vocational defeat, fleeing in a Hertz Camaro, trying to make some tangible sense of the mysteries in his cluttered drama. A quiet man, Paul imagined, not prone to verbosity, lashing out at a Shell station on Pico Boulevard. The truth is lousy. Maybe the full extent of his rage was yet to be felt. Maybe right now he was pulling off some freeway in his Camaro to write another denunciation over a similar sink under an Exxon sign. His temper inflamed by hours of solitary driving, he could unleash his vitriol to the fullest:

TRUTH IS FUCKING SHIT, he might scrawl, and become appeased.

In Franklin's garden at sunset, Paul and his father had drinks together. They sat facing each other in canvas chairs.

"What will I think of this girl?" Franklin wanted to know.

"I think you'll think she's smart. She might appear a little cold at first. She's certainly glib enough. I think you'll think that she's very appealing-looking. *I* think she's beautiful, but what do I know? You'll like her in stages, is what I think."

"Where does she come from? What's her . . . ?"

"Background." Paul filled it in for Franklin.

A parental word, "background." A nice word, Paul thought. What ground has Emily covered back there? What ground did her parents cover that laid the groundwork for her background? What religious beliefs does she hold, and on what grounds? Is she monetarily on safe ground? Was her education grounded before college? Back there. How far back there? Is she luminous, or unprepossessing, with a tendency to remain in the background? Paul understood that these were the things his father wanted to know. "Where does she come from?" Paul echoed, taking his time, caught in the background.

"Is she an eastern girl?" Franklin asked.

"She's from New York. She's a New Yorker every bit as much as we are," Paul said.

"And you say she writes?"

"She's working on a book about her father. Let me give you three guesses. Her father was: A) a lawyer, B) a professional magician, C) a ventriloquist. What do you think?"

"Well, obviously he wasn't a lawyer, or you wouldn't be giving me choices. Was he a magician? The other seems . . ."

"It's the other," Paul said.

"A ventriloquist," Franklin mused. "Extraordinary."

"Tom Keller by name, ventriloquist by game."

"Is he deceased?" asked Franklin.

"Both her parents are deceased," Paul said, stopping himself from saying "dead." Dead was too strong a word for Paul and Franklin to toss around. Franklin's "deceased" was a matter of style, and, Paul thought, the least odious choice.

"Was he a man of means?"

"He made a living," Paul said. "Emily has an inheritance. Sometimes she traveled with him in the summer, and occasionally was part of the act on stage. They'd both banter with the dummy. That's Temmy. In her book Temmy is Terrence. Emily can throw her voice. She's very skillful at it."

Franklin said nothing.

"Her mother died when she was a child," Paul continued. "And here's something for you: we have the same birthdays. I don't know whether that's ominous or sensational, but she was born on the first of July, nineteen forty-two. Now. Here are three things that Emily knows a lot about. She knows a lot about literature, and music, and she knows all there is to know about boarding schools. And she can throw her voice, which is, I will admit, eccentric. And she has a sense of the undercurrent. Do you know what I mean?"

Paul stopped there, and finished his drink. The sun was almost gone, and the light had become mellow and filled with color. Paul realized that he had not delivered so detailed a dossier to his father since Jennifer Rosen. Jennifer's dossier had been written in his child's hand. He had called Jennifer "neat," and possibly even "groovy." He had told his father that Jennifer Rosen was "profoundly sensitive." Profoundly sensitive and neat. Mrs. Lawrence Tellman was a groove. Now, twelve years later, Emily Keller had a "sense of the undercurrent," and was beautiful. And, Paul found himself adding, "She's not a usual woman, I'll tell you that." If Emily was a woman, as he, to his own surprise, described her, then he, the son of the man facing him in a canvas chair, was a man. No kid or boy. Man. Adult. At thirty-two, he still resisted the idea.

"It certainly sounds hopeful," Franklin said, rising to stroll around the garden.

"I don't have any grand designs," Paul said.

"What I'm saying is that she sounds like a splendid girl."

"Yes," Paul said. He stopped himself from describing Emily as mischievous.

More drinks. Scotch for them both. Paul went into the kitchen to make them. On the way back to the garden he slipped into the den for a quick look around. On a scrap of paper on the desk he noticed that his father had scribbled the word "Lillian" and written a phone number below it. He memorized it, imagining it as a third-quarter basketball score: 89–80. The Atwater exchange was easy enough.

In the garden, in the darkness of the early evening, they talked about old times. Durham, North Carolina, the Colonial Theater in Boston, an evening with Toscanini in a country house near a waterfall.

Lillian. Who was Lillian? Paul wouldn't ask his father. Paul imagined late-night phone calls and hushed voices, and fabricated excursions for Carol and Paul to believe in. And Paul, feisty in his father's eyes, sitting before the television camera. Before Lillian? Lillian, observing Franklin's only child, was the quiet recipient of Franklin's elegant love, the caretaker of letters from the west from a charming man in his seventies. Did Lillian have them all? Were they locked away, out of sight? The disclosures of Franklin Kramer. Paul himself would avert his eyes from the lot of them while surreptitiously peeking at what might be left unconcealed.

"Now, tell me the truth," Paul said. "Did you think I'd make it in the world? You know, all grown up and everything?"

"At times it wasn't the easiest thing to believe in. There was disorganization. You were helter-skelter, and that seemed to me the most difficult obstacle you'd have to face." Franklin finished his second drink.

"Do you look upon me as a success?" Paul asked.

"I do. Surely I do," his father said, unhesitatingly.

"What about now, here in California? Emily sits at her desk, hour after hour. She tells me that she's always been in sufficient control of her work. I'm just a gypsy."

"But you worked all those years."

"I was just asking again—I know I've asked before—I was just wondering how, I was wondering . . ." Paul trailed off. "You know," he continued a moment later, "Emily said something interesting the other day. She was talking about her father. She was telling me about him, and she said that his marriage had been a failure from the beginning because he had only been *umbilically* committed to his wife—those are Emily's words. And she said that his male offspring was nothing more than a theatrical extension of himself. He made his life's work out of displaying his store-bought son. Ventriloquists are vulnerable to pontifical psychological interference, and Emily knows it. Still, she always felt kind of secondary, something of a mistake."

"Tom Keller," Franklin said, attaching the name to the umbilically committed.

"Emily said that he spent most of his life on trains, or on long bus trips, with Temmy in a case, like an instrument. Which I guess is not a bad analogy."

"Did he have any other characters? Anyone besides Temmy?"

"He didn't. I asked her. And listen to this: Emily would overhear them."

"Do you mean—?"

"I mean that Keller would hold private meetings and conduct private arguments. *Arguments.* At night. Late. So you see? That's what we have here. A thirty-two-year-old woman who learned from her father that it was possible to deal with things out loud, *alone.* She says that when she was young she would hold conversations with herself, playing both parts. Both parts named Emily. The other night, in the middle of the night —and it might very well have been sleep-talking, I don't know —Emily said, and this is an exact quote: 'Why don't you organize the thing more efficiently.' And then she said: 'Because once organized, the chanciness would be removed.' I'm telling you, that's what she said."

Paul was aware that he had acknowledged a physical proximity that implied a sexual arrangement. It was not something he felt comfortable with around his father. He wanted a neutral packaging for his own carnal behavior; a tie and jacket and discretion; asexuality. Franklin's eyes were to be shielded from his son's lascivious scrambling.

"WPKF," Franklin said.

"I know," Paul said. "Emily's WPKF lacked only the transmitter and microphone I supplied for myself. If I'd met her twenty years ago, I could have shown her the way to do it."

"You could have done a show like Dorothy and Dick."

"And look what happened to *them*," Paul said.

"And look what happened to them," Franklin said.

The question of mortality was very much in the air. Paul was sorry he had plucked it from his father's harmless radio reference. It was, like sex, a tricky theme. Seventy-six-year-old fathers would live forever, and thirty-two-year old sons had intercourse only as a gesture of parody. These were the rules Paul had learned from his father's plays. Parasols and wine and flowing white skirts and crusty old gentlemen frozen in time. Urban octogenarians. Sex and death were imprisoned off stage, barred forever from Franklin's theater. With Franklin's back turned, however, Paul was on the sexual rampage, puzzled by the passage of time and the heartlessness of senility.

"Someday I'd like to interview you," Paul said. "I've mentioned it in the past, right? A private interview, on tape. Just about our facts. My mother, and your courtship. A chronology.

I'm very blurry on much of the . . . much of the movements. We were talking a few weeks ago about Central Park West, that general period. I'd like to have it all on tape."

"I feel a little strange about it," Franklin said.

"Why?"

"I don't know."

"The taping?"

"It's not that, I suppose."

"Strange?"

"I'm sure it would be all right," Franklin said. They were now sitting in the dark. Paul drew his chair a little closer to his father's.

"Tell me what you mean by 'strange.'"

Franklin didn't answer for a while, and Paul didn't rush him. When Franklin did speak, his tone was gentle and his voice soft. It was clear that what he had to say was difficult for him to convey. That he did so surprised Paul. "I would feel that after the tapes were made, and all of the chronology detailed, I would die. As a natural course of events."

Paul was moved, and told his father that he understood. "I would never press such a thing on you," he said. "It would just be an attempt on my part to, as Emily said, organize the thing more efficiently."

"A natural course of events," Franklin repeated in the same soft tone.

"*You* will outlast *me*, my good man," said Paul, half believing it.

"I'm getting feelings," Franklin replied.

"What feelings?"

"I'm not a young man."

"What has that got to do with anything?" Paul asked, thinking himself foolish and devious.

"Just feelings."

"I have those feelings about myself. Doesn't everybody?"

Franklin didn't answer.

"Things are just beginning," Paul continued.

"These days I'm inclined to think along the lines of things ending," Franklin said.

"Nonsense."

"Relationships. And will."

"I don't understand," Paul said.

"Well. In New York . . ."

"What in New York?"

"I shouldn't be so gloomy, should I?" Franklin gave a little laugh, self-mocking, but not through-and-through.

"I didn't know you were gloomy." Paul reached over and touched his father's knee.

"I'm not. Really, I'm not. Ends are beginnings and beginnings are ends, and all that."

"What in New York?"

"Nothing at all," Franklin replied, his voice louder than before. "It's just feelings."

Lillian. Atwater 9-8980. Was it possible she had been about to be revealed? Paul could feel her presence in the garden. A phone number scribbled, and the natural course of events, and ends are beginnings and beginnings are ends, and relationships and will. And *will*. Franklin's secret, unacknowledged for so long, would not be probed by Paul.

"I'm glad we're in the same town," Paul said, leaving his fingers on his father's knee without any pressure of the hand.

"Yes," said Franklin. "Oh yes."

CHAPTER NINE

Paul: What's your history? How did you become a general manager? Did you work in radio all your life?

General Manager: I came out of sales. I was with the company in Washington, and in Philly, and then eventually in the Big Apple.

Paul: What qualifies a salesman to become a general manager? It seems to me that most general managers have come from the sales end of the business. A general manager has got to know music, if it's a music station like yours. Do you have a music background?

General Manager: I would say a general manager has got to have precision. In dealing with people I—

Paul: What do you mean by precision?

General Manager: What do I mean by precision? Okay. I mean, you know, you've got to have a fiscal mind.

Paul: Do you have a music background?

General Manager: I enjoy music.

Paul: What kind of music?

General Manager: All kinds.

Paul: But do you have a *knowledge* of music? Any kind of background or training?

General Manager: You see now, here's where instinct, an instinct for people comes into it. I have a top-flight program director. He knows music, he knows policy. And he can handle the horses we've got on the station. He's a musicologist.

Paul: A musicologist?

General Manager: He's incredibly informed. He knows what's been popular over the last *thirty* years.

Paul: He sounds to me like a *hit*ocologist.

General Manager: Same thing. He's a top-flight guy. He'll make it work for you. He's got stability.

Paul: How long has he been with you?

General Manager: Four months. He's just really getting a feel—

Paul: Where was he before?

General Manager: I brought him in from Philly.

Paul: And before that, where was he?

General Manager: Cleveland.

Paul: Sounds to me like he's been around.

General Manager (with a chuckle):   Would you like his resumé?

Paul: What do you like most about radio?

General Manager: The possibilities.

Paul: What possibilities do you mean?

General Manager: When you sell time there are real possibilities. It's all tied in to the ARB ratings. Now, I don't personally believe in ratings, but they're here and you've got to live with them. The industry lives with them, so what can you do? You increase your rating-card structure when you have the numbers. The sales possibilities are enormous with a station that's maintained a low profile in a market, and then takes off. That's what I mean by precision.

Paul: I don't follow you.

General Manager: In the managerial end.

Paul: What kind of radio do you yourself care for?

General Manager: Radio that can be sold. And you've got to have professional horses in order to sell radio. The audience is cattle, and you've got to understand that.

Paul: You say your people on the air are horses and your audience are cattle. It sounds to me as if you're running some kind of ranch.

General Manager: I didn't know this was going to be an interrogation.

Paul: I'm just trying to get the feeling of a general manager.

General Manager: What I'm trying to say is, everything at a radio station is a team operation. Without good people at your critical posts, you're dead. You can't do it all yourself.

Paul: Why do radio people have the reputation of being somewhat shallow?

General Manager: I wasn't aware of that reputation at all. Some of the deepest people I know are radio people. Real intellectuals. I know you know what I'm talking about; you've worked in radio. There are real sensitive guys and gals in the industry.

Paul: Would you work in any market in the country that the company sent you to?

General Manager (with a chuckle): The company is only in six markets.

Paul: Would you enjoy living in certain cities more than in others?

General Manager: There's only one Big Apple. But there are other nice places. Philly's a nice town. Detroit is a good radio town.

Paul: What do you mean by "a good radio town"?

General Manager: Where there are sales opportunities. That's what I like. I like the challenge.

Paul: Is Top Forty radio more financially realistic than other formats?

General Manager: Depends on the market. Many of the kids these days are into FM. They outgrow the Top Forty stuff. You've got to analyze the market.

Paul: Is there any format you wouldn't work with?

General Manager: I like them all. It's the *challenge*.

Paul: Where is radio heading?

General Manager: It's got a big future. If you understand the meaning of radio, and you know your market, *then* you're in business.

Paul: What is the meaning of radio?

General Manager: You want it simply stated?

Paul: Sure.

General Manager: This is a country tied together by the wires of communication. Once you decide on your demographics, you shoot for that age group. And communicate with them. *Know* what you're selling them. And above all—and I don't mean to be sanctimonious—but above all, don't, I repeat, *don't* sell 'em a bill of goods. People are smart. They *know* when they're being communicated with and when they're not.

Paul: Do you believe in radio?

General Manager: That's what it's all about.

"We can be proud of it—five and a half years. No man or woman came into this administration and left it with more of this world's goods than when he came in. No man or no woman ever profited at the public expense or the public till. Mistakes, yes. But for personal gain, never. You did what you believed in. Sometimes right, sometimes wrong. And I only wish that I *were* a wealthy man—at the present time I have got to find a way to pay my taxes."

Emily and Paul lay in bed. Paul wore a Los Angeles Dodgers tee shirt. Emily was naked, smoking, balancing an ashtray on her belly. It was six in the morning, and a touch of summer light already pushed at the dark.

"I remember my old man," the wobbly black-and-white image flickering in cableless confusion said. "You know what he was? He was a streetcar motorman first, and then he was a farmer, and then he had a lemon ranch. It was the poorest lemon ranch in California, I can assure you. He sold it before they found oil on it."

And Franklin's ranch: had he sold before the oil? An actor in Chicago and in Baltimore—long-distance telephone calls; "It's me! It's your dad!" Much excitement. Philadelphia, Boston. Playwright discreeto. Modest funds, a generous heart. Could he have sought out the oil on his own land? "I Picked a Lemon in the Garden of Love." Carol Kramer, a shut-in. A lemon.

"My mother was a saint. And I think of her, two boys dying of tuberculosis, nursing four others in order that she could take care of my older brother for three years in Arizona, and seeing each of them die, and when they died, it was like one of her own. Yes, she will have no books written about her. But she was a saint."

A carpet to the helicopter. They were told it was red.

Air Force One.

Analysis.

It was light now. The set was off, the room was still. From a radio in a neighbor's bathroom:

> I deal in dreamers
> And telephone screamers

Lately I wonder what I do it for
If I had my way
I'd just walk out those doors
And wander
Down the Champs Élysées
Going café to cabaret
Thinking how I'll feel when I find
That very good friend of mine

Emily brought them coffee. Her nudity stirred Paul. This girl was allowing him to see her naked. Everything. But everything. This had always been an erotic consideration. She allowed him the information: her ass, her crotch, her nipples. Her spine. Spine. Ribs. A naked scurry to the kitchen. The nudity of her face.

"So," said Paul.

"Joni Mitchell," Emily said, on her knees on the bed, spine straight, drinking coffee.

"These little huts are sure jammed up against each other."

"It's like Provincetown a little. You get used to the noise."

"I imagined my own father up there on that podium," Paul said, inventing.

"Did you?"

"Not in defeat, really. I mean, not necessarily in defeat. Just seizing the chance for oratory."

"I'm afraid, reporter Kramer, that you have lost your abjectivity." And a smart-ass smile, too.

"You know something," Paul said, "sometimes you're no pun to be with."

"That's just stupid," Emily said, leaning back to put her coffee cup on the floor. Slim belly and breasts. Cunt exposed with an opening of the legs.

"That's enough shit," Paul said.

They wrestled. Emily was difficult to pin. Her arms: they fought and fought. No weak sister here.

"Let's do this outside by the canal," Emily whispered into his mouth.

"It's seven in the morning," Paul said. "You're on. By way of celebration."

They rolled in the mud near the canal, their feet in the water. Three ducks, alarmed by the disturbance, took to the shore for safety.

They scratched at each other. They rolled over and over in the mud. A couple on a balcony applauded. Paul crashed into Emily, on his knees, holding her legs high, pressing them back to her face. He observed the observers. He would fuck her on that podium, on that red carpet, in front of the asshole saint, in the helicopter itself. There was mud on his cock as he slammed into her. Were her eyes ever open! One duck made a tentative inquiry. Their feet were submerged in the putrid water. It was a gray and foggy morning; August in Venice, California. The couple on the balcony slipped their arms around each other's waist. "The war is over!" yelled the girl, a pretty blonde in her twenties. Emily muttered, "Just do it." She flung her arms above her head. Paul reached back for mud. He coated her chest with it, and her face. "I'm coming," she whispered. "Watch!" Paul shouted to the balcony. Emily's arms froze. Her back arched way off the embankment. "Cunt come," he said to Emily. Paul was angry. He accompanied her orgasm with it: "Cunt come!" Three black dogs, the mongrels of the canal, joined the spectators. More brazen than the ducks, they sniffed at the muddy bodies. Paul imagined the sight from the balcony. He was not at all embarrassed, and was furious with Emily for wiping away the rules and regulations. Oh, how he loved her! This muddy orgasmic motherfucker, coming in a canal at seven in the fucking morning. He was on the edge a minute or so after her back settled back. For a second he lost it to a Franklin thought: Franklin with his bowl of milk for the cat in the back-yard. "Chickenshit," Emily hissed at him, feeling his minor distraction. He thought to come on her face; after all, they had gone this far for the balcony. But his sperm visible, his own ejaculation so completely visible; no. In her. Quietly. Dignified. He closed his eyes. He said: "I love you," when he caught the handle of his orgasm. He considered: slut. Instead: "I love you." And then: "Emily."

Paul fell on top of her. He wiped away the mud from around her mouth, and kissed her.

Applause from balcony. Paul looked around. Only the ducks and dogs and the accepting audience above. No harm done. "Let's go in," he said. He pulled Emily to her feet.

Was this girl nuts?

"I think the world is crazy, if you wanna know, if you really wanna know."

"In what way?" Emily asked her friend, Maggie Furth.

"There's no real contact between humanoids. Humanoids don't look each other in the eye. They just pretend, which is the mark of craziness."

"We're looking each other in the eye."

"We're friends. You know what I mean. We know each other. Christina knows you. I know you."

"But once that wasn't true."

"Right." Maggie Furth nodded, agreeing. A beautiful twenty-six-year-old girl from Canada, an actress, a girl whom Joshua knew and Emily kept up with for access to Christina, Maggie's ten-year-old daughter. And also, Paul suspected, for word of Joshua the truly spiritual. This Emily denied.

"He never comes up. I never ask and she never volunteers. She's almost totally daffy, out of it, *way* out of it. I mean, off the wall. She lives in the middle of a jigsaw puzzle that's just been dumped onto the card table, and occasionally she picks up a piece and slides it into another and it fits, and that's a major victory that she thinks is knowledge, when all those other pieces

are still scattered on the table, and a couple on the floor, and
she's got two pieces together and that's *everything* for Maggie.
She has no idea what the finished product might even be; it
came in an unmarked box."

"What does Joshua the truly spiritual see in her?"

"Even the truly spiritual like to fuck."

So a trip to Trancas. An evening at Maggie Furth's, above
the sea, sunset and all. Christina, carrying a silver tray of Fritos
around the room, and a cheese dip that she had made herself—
"prepared" is how her mother described the process. And a joint
passed around, shared by Christina, declined by Walter Decker,
a bald, obese little man in an ill-fitting gray suit. He drummed
his fingers in the air as if he were playing a piano. Walter
Decker cast his eyes to the ceiling as his fingers drummed away.
He looked absurd in Maggie's living room: beige brick walls, a
floor of small, triangular terra-cotta tiles, a redwood ceiling, and
large glass sliding doors that looked out on the Pacific.

And Maggie Furth. On her own at fifteen, a Catholic from
Quebec, quite a beauty: white skin, dark hair, a voluptuous girl
in a blue turtleneck and dungarees. Barefoot, prominent cheekbones, not uninteresting eyes; God knows what she knew. Paul
recognized a touch of Sandi in Maggie's eyes; there was a piece
of that hope, and a dopey and poignant kind of trust that had
prevailed, Paul imagined, in the face of egregious manipulations
of this overtly available young lady. Quite clearly, Maggie Furth
was obliging and not despairing. If the world was crazy and
humanoids didn't meet each other's eyes, so be it, pass the salt.
The next humanoid down the road might meet the eyes and declare, for all the world to hear, that Maggie's two fitted pieces
were the stuff of scholarly humanoids. And besides: crazy like a
fox, that world, it knew a good thing when it saw it. Maggie
Furth had been invited to participate in one hundred and fifty-
six television episodes, seven motion pictures, and in two work-
shop productions at the Mark Taper. And: one innocuous nude

photograph. Sex Stars of the Seventies. Maggie Furth: "I live for my man. That is all I care about." The caption to the right of the Maggie Furth tit. Christina's father: the man with the Nikon, in Spain at that very minute tracking down Orson Welles. On not one of the six occasions of their lovemaking had Christina's father and Maggie Furth awakened in the same bed together. Maggie decided not to abort. "I cannot defy a life force," Paul had read somewhere years ago. And here he was eating chili rellenos personally made, prepared, by a sex star of the seventies who wished for eye contact between humanoids.

At dinner, Walter Decker spoke. He addressed the group as if he were describing a sporting event; drifting in and out of italics, he drummed his piano and jabbed at the air. "And *I'd* like to say that this is *simply* one of the finest of the *finest*. Let me tell you one thing, strictly *entre nous*. Margaret Furth, when it comes to food Mexican, you're well on your way to the *top* of the heap. You are cognizant of every little flavor, every, shall we say, *nuance*, and that makes for great cooking."

Paul saw that Decker was stuck in parody, parody grown so complex through the years that it had become all-encompassing. Somewhere along the way he had lost the thread of what he had started with, so successful must he have been with it at such an early age. Now, Decker, grown flaccid and bald, had allowed the parody to take over and render him ludicrous.

"I would like to suggest," Decker said, spreading both hands wide as if trying to reach octaves, "that we celebrate the occasion with a glass of this *excellent vino* supplied by Margaret and poured by Christina. A toast, then, to our lovely lady of the evening."

Paul was irritated by the "Margaret." It implied a certain kind of formal intimacy, a never-to-be-achieved knowledge of Maggie Furth except by this grotesque little man with flailing arms. It suggested that only *he* knew the secrets, and because Maggie raised no objection, it appeared there was an understanding between these two incongruous people, maybe even an unusual carnality inside a midnight language they had written together. Just the word "Margaret" out of Decker was enough to incite Paul's lust. He imagined himself taking an angry sexual stab at Maggie Furth while Decker watched helplessly, impaled on a toothpick.

After dinner they gathered in stuffed white chairs in a semicircle around the fireplace. Sports rolled out of Decker. He was delighted to find Paul knowledgeable. "You understand, don't you, that West or Baylor should have taken the last shot. *And*, my dear man, can you tell me *who* took the last shot?"

Paul, his answer ready, prolonged the moment. "We're talking here about nineteen sixty-two, right? The seventh game, right?"

"That is right, that is *correct*. On a gray day in Boston the two teams met to decide the championship of the nineteen sixty-one–sixty-two season. It had been a long, hard struggle for them both, and now it all came down to *one* shot, *one* last shot that, if made, would *win* the championship for the Los Angeles Lakers; if missed, would send the game into overtime before a screaming, partisan Boston crowd."

"Frank Selvy took the shot," Paul said.

"Frank Selvy did *indeed* take the shot! It bounced *high* off the rim as Bill Russell pulled down the rebound to create an overtime."

"You know your stuff, Decker," Paul said. "Mine was just a lucky guess."

"I don't believe so, my man. It was right on the money."

Decker was excited. He recalled the overtime, the fans streaming onto the court at the end of the game. "Another championship banner for the Hub!" he announced, and took a sip of wine.

"Have you ever been a broadcaster?" Emily asked. "You're quite good."

"No, I'm afraid I haven't. The microphone has eluded me, though, strictly *entre nous*, I've been told my talents are extraordinary in this field."

Decker, who had been sitting at the edge of his chair, slid back and sank—or so it appeared to Paul—more deeply than one would have thought possible. Paul imagined this little fellow sinking into the very bowels of the chair, slowly, slowly disappearing, talking away, announcing, the words "Roger Maris" the last anyone heard. The springs would surround him, consume him, and the chair from that night on would look to be ever-so-slightly more lumpy, more bulky, than its companions in the semicircle.

The facts came out as the evening progressed. *Why* Walter Decker, twenty minutes north of Malibu on a summer night in a thin-striped tie. *Why* Walter Decker, with his small dark eyes and his piano of the mind. A Maggie Furth Selection: come around, my sweet, and I will feed you food Mexican and you will meet my friend Emily Keller with her new lover, Paul Kramer, a New York hotshot, or so I'm told. The facts: Walter Decker the chocolate king: Whirls, Kingles, Honeydews, Cho-Chews. Rufus Decker, turning out those Cho-Chews and Whirls for Gatsby's America, for Herbert C. Hoover—remember the photo of Hoover with a Whirl bar in one hand and a cigar in the other? Rufus Decker on the stump—oh, how vicious he was. FDR: Filthy Democratic Rodent. The New Deal was "poisoning the bloodstream of this great country of ours!" Rufus Decker, the bearer of one offspring conceived two nights before an FDR plurality of three-and-a-half-million and born four hours after Hiroshima. Here now, twenty-nine years and twelve days after Major Thomas Ferebee snapped open the bomb-bay doors of the *Enola Gay* above Japan, sat the chocolate king himself, star-struck and energized, interested in producing "for the cinema," reading scripts, "conversing with directors" in his bungalow at the Beverly Hills Hotel, happy to be talking with Paul

Kramer—"Your questions on TV are *right* on the money."
Walter Decker was looking for "a vehicle" for Margaret Furth.
Approaching thirty, he wanted to, "shall we say, branch out."

"So you want to give producing a whirl?" Paul asked.

"You devil, you," Decker replied, with an awful wink, his
whole face crinkling up into it.

"Where are your headquarters right now?" Paul asked.

"I'm very cosmopolitan, don't you know," reponded Decker,
with a wave of his hand. "Basically speaking, New York is my
beat, though to tell you the truth I love the desert. I have a
house in Palm Springs. That's where I like to spend my time.
I've always believed that a bunt is *not*, I repeat, is *not* a first-class
hit. I admire the long ball, the Ballantine blast. I admire the
men and women who work in the industry *we* call the motion
picture industry. The other business, the family business, you understand, I have placed in the hands of gentlemen with great
fiscal mentalities and perspicacity. I can assure you that my father would be pleased. There's a difference, you know, between
Rufus Decker and Walter Decker."

A pause.

"And what is the difference?" Paul asked.

"Ah, my friends. So much, so much." A sip of wine.

Paul realized the fellow had been putting it away.

"Walter Decker is a generous individual. Rufus Decker
was, shall we say, more conservative." Decker sighed.

"I'll say," Maggie Furth laughed.

There it was again; a tie to Walter Decker. The poop on
Rufus was familiar stuff to her. I'll say. That meant hours of talk
in the midnight language. Clearly, Walter Decker was into these
coveted pants, a rankling fact for Paul Kramer.

Christina, stoned and red-eyed, spoke up: "There's blue in
the fire."

"You *must* visit me in Palm Springs," Decker continued.

"Have you ever been to the desert?" He leaned forward to ask this of Emily.

"I haven't," she replied, "and I'd like to come."

Very pleasant. Very conversational. Emily Keller, what's going on here? Paul felt himself out of place, an outsider, out of it. Was there a plot afoot?

"The desert is quite an extraordinary place, actually," Decker continued, finishing his glass of wine. "Now, as it happens, I enjoy the competitive game of tennis. The community of Palm Springs provides ample facilities for such an enthusiasm. And you have your people in the motion picture industry with whom to converse. And the nights are cool and the days are splendid. A paradise."

"Would you like some more wine?" Maggie asked.

"But of *course*, my dear," Decker answered. With an awkward flourish he was on his feet, glass in hand, moving to the dinner table. "I'll handle it, I'll handle it. An excellent vintage."

"You know," Decker continued, back in his chair, his glass filled, "there's a fine little restaurant up in the Malibu Hills. Margaret and I have dined up there several times, though the drive is treacherous and winding. The menu is limited to a very fine cut of steak served with a perfect baked potato. Or, if shellfish is your game, the other *entree* is a lovely bowl of steamed clams. Beer, wine, but of course. The establishment is called *El Besame Mucho*. It's got beautiful food. Wouldn't you say that was apt, Margaret?"

"I'd say so," Maggie agreed, seriously, and warmly, true to Decker's spirit, with no derisive hint in the eye, no impish aside for the crowd.

Paul caught Emily's eyes: they were pockets of neutrality, with no private message for Paul. Around the lips: was that the suggestion of a smirk? Paul thought: I'll take it.

"A vehicle for Maggie," Emily said, after a moment.

"Something that shows her extraordinary diversity, her

range," Decker said, a surprising softness in his voice. "I believe Margaret is capable of practically anything. As we know, she is outstandingly photogenic. Every time she goes to bat her reviews are favorable, encouraging, ecstatic. To be frank, *ecstatic*. I met Margaret at a very large party on Rexford Drive, and I knew right then what the future held for her."

"You must be an extremely wealthy man," Paul said, smiling broadly at Decker to disguise what he knew was an inappropriate response. It had been an angry response, a condemning one, and Paul was irritated to see that Decker had pulled him into it, one step at a time. If it wasn't for Paul's smile, suspect at best, he would be seen as the aggressor. To his dismay, Paul found that Christina was taking a good look at his eyes, a good and stoned ten-year-old look.

They all fell silent. Even Decker, deep in his chair, considered the fire and was quiet.

"Does anybody want to call their service?" Paul asked.

"You know something," Maggie Furth said, her hands behind her head, "it wouldn't matter if the future didn't exist. You know? I really don't feel it's all a big rainbow stretching out. It doesn't matter. Christina has seen the sea, and that's about as far as we ever get, really. Seeing the sea. You know what I mean? There's nothing we can *do* about it, except to marvel. It wouldn't be a disaster if there was, like, an announcement that this was it."

"That the ball game was over," Decker said.

"Yeah, you know? Nobody gets hurt or anything. It's just the way it is. Walter's vehicle is a very generous vehicle, whatever it is, or might be. But it won't make any *real* difference. There will still be nothing we can do about the sea, its bigness. Our hands are tied, and that's the truth." Maggie smiled.

"Walter is generously disposed toward you," Emily said.

Was Emily asking or musing? Paul imagined a furious physical attack on her, striking her repeatedly, drawing blood.

"Walter *gives*," Maggie Furth said, addressing Emily.

"But don't hand me *all* the credit," Decker interrupted. "I am, as Paul noted, a very affluent man. I like money. I'm enthusiastic about money. I'm embarrassed to tell you this—here, let me show you."

Decker pulled out his wallet. Leaning over, he placed on the floor, at the foot of his chair, ten one-thousand-dollar bills. "I'm embarrassed, really," he said. "Unlike Rufus Decker, I keep money around me, and I give money, I *contribute* money. And I am *not*, repeat, I am *not* taking credit for being a philanthropist. Mine is a very specialized form of giving. To tell you the truth, I'm embarrassed by my attitude in relationship to things financial. I'm reckless and thrifty at the same time. But unlike Rufus Decker, whose funds were *concealed*, I keep money around me. And I'm not trying to be a big shot. I hold the opinion that a big shot is a quiet shot. My funds reflect gracious living, but I am nobody's professional beneficiary. When I see a talent like Margaret Furth's, I want to, shall we say, surround it with the right vehicle."

The ten one-thousand-dollar bills went back into the wallet.

"In his way, Walter *is* a philanthrophist," Maggie Furth said respectfully.

"It's philanthro*pist*," Paul said.

"I know. I just didn't want to say 'pist,' " Maggie said brightly.

"I'm sure you'll succeed," Emily said to Decker.

"But it doesn't matter," Maggie Furth told them all. "What matters is the morning and the sea. How about staying over and making the drive back in the morning? Whaddya say, Emmy?"

"Paul, whaddya say?" said Emily.

"Does Maggie have the room?" Paul asked Emily.

"Margaret has the room," Decker said to Paul.

"Christina, do you think it's time for bed?" Maggie Furth asked her daughter.

"It's getting there," the child said. "Sleep-over guests are terrific."

Christina got up and went to the kitchen. She returned with a tray of bite-size Cho-Chews.

"You devil, you," Decker said, accepting a handful.

Maggie Furth lit a joint and set it traveling around the room.

"None for me," Decker said. "It makes me hungry."

"What a time in the history of things," Maggie said, wistfully. "The country, the sea, the leadership. Where are we heading, I'd like to know."

"You just wait," Decker said, peeling the wrapping from a Cho-Chew. "There's a fine man out here. Presidential material, in my humble opinion. And as Margaret pointed out, I am *not* an ungenerous man."

"Reagan," Emily said, declaratively.

"President Reagan," Decker said, holding his fist as an imaginary microphone, the announcer turning from the world of sports to things political. "A spokesman for President Reagan said today that—"

"No, no," Paul said, "you've got it all wrong. Jimmy Stewart for President, Ronald Reagan for best friend."

Decker replied with a mouthful of Cho-Chews. "We'll see, my good man," he said, accompanying himself on the piano. "We'll see who'll take the last shot."

CHRISTINA ANN FURTH. It was carefully printed in ink. It titled the watercolor on the top of the paper, middle of the page: a young girl on a stool, combing her hair in front of a mirror. She sat in a room with green walls and a red bed. A Raggedy Ann doll lay on the floor, its black dot eyes suggesting bewilderment, though not, Paul decided, irreversibly; the left eye, lower than the right, held visible mirth. Paul ran the tip of his index finger over the eye.

He had to take the painting off the wall and over to the window to examine the mirror's reflection. It was early in the morning and the light was dim. Maggie had framed it decently enough in a plain silver molding, though it was heavier than he had expected.

Opening the drawn curtains just a bit so as not to awaken Emily, Paul found that Christina had made it quite clear: there was no little girl in the reflection, only a fire, burning through barren winter trees. Paul could feel the orange blaze on his face, as if he were staring into a furnace. No leaves or limbs on those trees, but trees they were, and had been until this conflagration, while the young girl on the stool, running a comb through her hair, sat placidly in pajamas as the only witness.

Emily and Paul had stumbled, stoned, to bed, filled with Cho-Chews and Kingles. Maggie's pleasant little guest room, white and pink, was a doll's house above the sea: little wooden chairs, a small wooden desk, a light-blue throw rug on terra-cotta tiles.

It was six-thirty. Paul pulled on his pants and sat on one of the wooden chairs. He had left Christina's painting near the window. Taking another look at it from across the room, he got up and rehung it above the bed, above Emily. She slept on her stomach, her face turned away from him, a quilt pulled to her shoulders.

El Besame Mucho. Beautiful food.

Was Decker in the house? Emily and Paul had left Maggie, Christina, and Decker by the fire. Awake now, shirtless and barefoot in the early morning, Paul felt a transcending sorrow. Hurled into the midst of strangers, his mind jostled by Rufus Decker and Franklin Kramer and other voices, Paul whispered: "Thank God for you both."

"And in other news . . ." The thought of Decker's little

hand with nails untrimmed, squeezed into a fist of a microphone, moved Paul. Nearly thirty years old, Walter Decker saw
himself branching out, wandering around the country, looking
for the right vehicle.

Emily stirred, and mumbled something in her sleep. It
might have been the word "butter." We all miss each other by
miles, Paul thought. Franklin and Lillian, and Carol Kramer
and her son the announcer. And Jennifer and Lawrence Tellman. It was twenty to ten in the morning in Boston, Massachusetts. Were they sharing an English muffin? While he and
Emily had put away the Cho-Chews, were Dr. and Mrs.
Lawrence Tellman surrounding each other with their arms?
Had they held each other through a humid Boston night? Perhaps their 15,000 BTUs were in disrepair, and they were left
to face the face of August in pale nudity, clammy and cranky in
the heat.

The right vehicle.

In the living room Paul rummaged through Emily's bag on
the white ottoman where she had left it: spare Cho-Chews,
Camel cigarettes, a scrap of paper with a phone number scribbled in pencil, a small notebook and a ballpoint pen, a check-
book with a balance of two hundred and forty-seven dollars, a
large Kent hairbrush, seven keys on a gold chain, one bent super
Tampax, two New York subway tokens, a small black wallet
with sixty-three dollars and an American Express card, and a
poem, typed on a half sheet of rumpled onion-skin typing paper,
folded over and over and tucked between dollar bills. Paul read
it through a number of times:

> Time does not bring relief; you all have lied
> Who told me time would ease me of my pain!
> I miss him in the weeping of the rain;
> I want him at the shrinking of the tide;
> The old snows melt from every mountain-side,
> And last year's leaves are smoke in every lane;

But last year's bitter loving must remain
Heaped on my heart, and my old thoughts abide.
There are a hundred places where I fear
To go, so with his memory they brim.
And entering with relief some quiet place
Where never fell his foot or shone his face
I say, "There is no memory of him here!"
And so stand stricken, so remembering him.

Emily had penciled in an E. MILLAY at the bottom, barely now an E. Millay, caught in the folds of the paper that was ravaged by its seeker.

Back into the wallet it went, like Decker's thousand-dollar bills. And here: a photo Paul had never seen. Emily's father and Temmy, tuxedoed side by side, sitting behind a desk, Temmy in a highchair that gave no sense of infancy, rather of convenience. Nothing extraordinary about the two of them; Paul had run across their kind before. As Franklin Kramer had drifted collaboratively through the theaters of the land, so these two solitary companions had found their way to Buffalo, and beyond. Temmy, with a breaking adolescent voice, put up with Tom Keller, made do, affectionately. Paul, holding the photo in front of him, could hear Temmy. Emily had it down. It *had* to be perfect, must have been: nasal, occasionally dropping down with a punch line around the corner, squeaky and slightly petulant when Tom Keller held the upper hand: "It's time to go now, you haven't behaved." "I haven't behaved?" "Say goodbye to everybody, we're going home." "Do I have to?" "Yes, Temmy, you have to." Set and match to Keller, but not without a struggle. A pretty good struggle at that, from a guy in a highchair.

And what of Emily's notes? A new little book with a phone number or two, and one entry of interest:

They lived together testily but took delight in each other's successes (maybe lived together acrimoniously?). They relied on no one, only on their complicated companionship, their daily squabbles, their devotion. With the shades drawn and the afternoon stretching before them they would sit across from each other, perhaps at a table, and work on their dialogue. Terrence, out of his wooden costume, was just a shade shorter than Uncle Willie.

Paul went into the bedroom and peeked at Emily. She was still asleep, and in just the position he had left her, her face turned to the far wall, away from his search.

And so stand stricken, so remembering him.

Would he himself ever inflict her with such heartache? This girl with soft skin, shooing him forward, dragging him along with her: whaddaya say, chickenshit, are ya comin' or not. He was coming with her, all right. Where else was there? Paul imagined himself in the third person: think carefully, Paul Kramer. Paul Kramer in love. Always Paul Kramer felt sexual toward Emily Keller. But wait now: Paul Kramer was barely a month into her, without a proper fix on her, only scattered pieces, a half of an E, and a K left on the classroom blackboard from English at ten-thirty. Now, in Algebra at one-ten in the afternoon, equations were meticulously drawn and conclusions were methodically reached. How could such an old man make such tiny numbers with a piece of chalk? But traces of the E and K remained, shining dimly through the tiny numbers and methodical conclusions. Even a second erasure didn't do the job; the stem of the K held fast. Paul Kramer had the stem of the K pinned, and the E. He had the whole E in his pocket. Everything else was a gamble.

Maggie's door, around the corner and down the hall, was ajar. Two single beds with pure white blankets and candy-cane sheets, were placed at right angles. Decker lay on his belly in a Swiss rib sleeveless undershirt, his bald head joined to Maggie's ear and caressed by her flowing dark hair. The room, with the curtains open, was filled with morning light.

Decker's wallet. Paul could see its shape in Decker's gray

pants, which lay in a heap with his other clothing on the floor near the door.

These people were asleep. Serious business, this sleep, and they were at it. Absolute stillness.

Paul pushed at the door cautiously. It inched open soundlessly. Nerves of steel, nerves of steel. Nerves of steal. Paul imagined it all on a blackboard: "A tough alloy of iron with carbon." "To take another's property, especially dishonestly."

Not the slightest movement from Decker or Maggie. Paul felt sexual desire, crouched as he was, only a foot or two from Maggie's hair.

Decker's wallet slipped out easily. From a bulky accumulation of cash, Paul selected one one-thousand-dollar bill, two one-hundred-dollar bills, one ten-dollar bill.

He took a quick look through other compartments: a half-dozen credit cards, a stick of Wrigley's spearmint gum, two Trojans, for God's sake, a handful of business cards, Decker's and others. Paul took one of Decker's, returned the wallet to the gray pants, and with his four bills and one Walter Decker business card, he backed slowly out of the room. No more fooling with the door; he left it where it was. Trembling in the hall, he pushed what he had taken into one of the tight side pockets of his dungarees.

First of all, a beer from the kitchen.

Out on the terrace, facing the sea with a can of Coors, Paul felt elated and guiltless and inclined to wake Emily with the news.

Then he was torn with the tormenting need to return the money at once. Caught in the act, he would say: "I was *returning* it, don't you *see*? I just wanted to count, I wanted to, I, blah, blah, blah."

In the bathroom Paul masturbated. He stared into his eyes in the mirror above the sink. Maggie's hair surrounded his mind; an open purple robe is what came to him, though there had been no evidence of one. A shrug of the shoulders and Maggie was naked. She put her arms around him and pressed her breasts to his back.

What to do with the towel that he used to put things right, the one towel in the bathroom, filled now with semen? Crusty in the hamper, it would give him away. In a cabinet high in the kitchen there were gadgets and pans and rags. The towel could spend weeks up there buried in those rags, months maybe, and by then the villain would be anybody's guess, so transient the homes of the sex stars of the seventies.

Paul remembered Christina: "Sleep-over guests are terrific."

There had been a lake, and a raft anchored well out from shore. Paul, ten years old, had sat next to his mother in a rowboat. His father, conscious of his wife's fragility, had carefully negotiated their little rented vessel across the span of water that stretched to the raft's metal ladder. Unpenetrated by swimmers on the late-autumn afternoon, the lake lay absolutely still, except for the commotion, the plunge and draw, of Franklin's oars.

Paul, first out, had taken his mother's hand, helped her up the top step of the ladder and onto the raft. His father, tying the boat to the raft, had followed a moment later. They had lain together on their backs, Paul between his parents, listening to the crunch of the side of the boat against the side of the raft. The sun was warm. Could it have been November?

Paul, on Maggie Furth's terrace, could feel that raft, the comfort of its subtle sway. Guarded by the bodies of his mother and father, Paul had felt contentment. He had understood for the first time that he could isolate it, poke around in it, observe it as a spectator. It was then that he had hit upon the confounding sadness that this very understanding produced. He had closed his eyes to hold back tears, confused by the contradiction.

In a while, Christina joined Paul on the terrace. She squinted out at the ocean in pajamas and a maroon robe. Her eyes were filled with sleep.

"What time did you get to bed?" Paul asked, tossing his empty beer can over the railing and down the cliff.

"We were late. Mommy and me were stoned."

They both watched the beer can roll, finally coming to a halt in the weeds.

"You smoke a lot?"

"Mommy says it's up to me. You shouldn't throw things down there."

"I know. It's thoughtless, isn't it?" Paul edited out an apology.

"It's gonna be hot," Christina said, turning to face the house.

"I saw your painting," Paul said, trying to regain the footing he might have lost with the beer can.

Christina didn't say anything.

"I think it's fantastic," Paul told her.

"You do?" Christina asked, pleased.

"Here are the things I like about it. The reflection in the mirror. The fire and the trees. And I especially like the eyes of the doll."

"What about the girl?" Christina asked, her back to him.

"The girl is in everything in the painting, and *that's* what I like the most."

"I did it last year," Christina told him.

"What about the fire and the trees?"

"Spirits. They're the spirits."

"I see what you mean," Paul told her, addressing her back. She turned to him. "I see what you mean," he repeated to her eyes.

"You like it?" she asked.

"I told you. I think it's fantastic."

"It has a title, but I didn't put it on."

"What is it?"

"*Spirits.*"

"Why didn't you put it on?"

"It wouldn't have looked good."

"You put your name on, like where a title would be on a story."

"I'm sorry I did it," Christina said.

"Why?"

"Because it doesn't look good."

"You interested in a walk on the beach?" Paul glanced down at the ocean, wishing only Christina's reply, not her facial consideration that could, he knew, do a little damage.

"There are terrific shells," Christina replied, in a moment.

It was safe to take a look at her. "You want to get dressed?"

"I'm okay."

"It can be cold so early."

"You don't even have a shirt," she said.

"I'm getting one," Paul said.

"I'll meet you back here," Christina said.

"You're on."

"Sometimes you can find shells that are actually red inside," Christina told him.

They had climbed down a long flight of rickety wooden stairs. The ocean was calm, the beach deserted. Maggie's house looked unspectacular above them, gray and small.

"You don't have neighbors smack up against you," Paul said.

"You can play music loud," Christina told him.

"What music do you like?"

"Loggins and Messina," she replied without hesitating.

"Do you have any playmates?"

"You mean friends."

"I'm sorry. I was using a word from *my* childhood. I mean friends. Friends around here."

"Debbie Ross. You see *that* house? One, two, three, four from my house? She's up there."

"What do you think she's doing up there?"

"You mean right now?" Christina laughed. "I *know* what she's doing right now. She's eating grapes. She's always eating grapes."

"Seedless?" Paul asked.

"The yellows. She never stops. You can't have a conversation with her without her eating grapes. Throughout the conversation, from beginning to end. It's one grape after another. She stuffs 'em in. She eats about a thousand grapes a day. That's what she's doing now. Right up there. See? That house right there. Debbie Ross is eating grapes. She looks like a grape, sometimes. Round. I like her. She's never cried, and never vomited."

"She's never had the time between the grapes," Paul said.

"Maybe," Christina said with a smile. "Her dog runs around down here. Her father's a director. Steven Ross. Her mother's dead. Debbie likes Loggins and Messina, especially the *Sittin' In* album, and especially "Vahevala" on that album. I like the "Trilogy" on that album. It's more daring."

"Why 'daring'?"

"It's three songs together. It's long—eleven minutes and fifteen seconds. "Vahevala" is four minutes and forty-five seconds. I don't mean that just because the "Trilogy" is longer it's better. "Same Old Wine" is eight minutes and fifteen seconds and it's boring."

"You sure know your Loggins and Messina," Paul told her, impressed.

"I know a lot about rock." Christina picked up a shell and discarded it.

"Does the music bother your mother?" Paul asked.

"No. She likes it."

"How about Walter?"

"He's not around that much. And he's deaf. I don't mean deaf, really *deaf*. I mean—"

"He doesn't hear great."

"That's what I mean."

Their eyes met, and Paul was careful not to exploit it. It would have been too easy right then and there to sabotage Decker. To Christina, he was deaf. Paul didn't need anything more.

"So," he said, breaking a comfortable silence.

They were well down the beach. They had climbed over rocks and had eased their way around boulders. The bottoms of their jeans were wet and sandy. Christina held onto one white oval shell.

"You wanna see something?" Christina said. "Look."

She led Paul away from the beach and up a slight incline toward the highway. Quickly they came upon a winding little stream. There were sycamore trees on each side of the stream, and chaparral, and manzanita.

"It's sweet water all the way from the mountains," Christina told him. "This is like the little bottom of a canyon. The end of a canyon. It's dense in here, all the bushes and the trees."

"You come in here a lot?" Paul asked.

"Not too often. Every now and then. It's a surprise, isn't it? No one would ever imagine it being here, just like this."

Paul suggested they sit down for a while. They found two flat rocks that were hidden from the sun by the sycamores. "This is wonderful," Paul said. "You're right. It *is* a surprise."

"It's spirits," Christina said, quietly.

"What do you mean?"

"It's by itself. I don't mean it's a mystery spirit. I mean, because it *is* such a surprise, and peaceful, it has a spirit that's different. It's one of a kind. That's what I like. If you can just make something of your own spirit so that other people can learn from it, that's it. Do you know why Debbie Ross is a terrific friend? Because her spirit is just Debbie Ross. Maybe grapes are the only thing her spirit can eat, and that's why she eats them all the time." Christina pulled her knees to her chin. "I know you won't tell Mommy."

"One question," Paul said. "How do you know I won't tell Mommy?"

Christina answered at once. "You won't tell Mommy because you'll never know Mommy well enough to tell her."

Christina stood, rolled her pants up to her knees and waded in the stream. "Sometimes I can't believe it comes from the top of the mountains and under the highway and all the way down here. Did you know that they're actually the Santa Monica Mountains, but that everybody calls them the Malibu Hills?"

"So they're two things," Paul said. "As a matter of fact, they're three things. I've heard them called the hills behind Trancas."

"Uh-huh," said Christina. She leaned down and picked up a handful of pebbles from under the water.

"Like your painting is more than one thing," Paul continued. "It's the girl in the room and it's the reflection in the mirror. And it's the girl who's in both, who's in everything in the picture."

Christina didn't answer. Crouching in the stream, she let the pebbles fall, a couple at a time, into the water.

Paul examined her from his rock. Uncharted territory. Few had gone in there, exploring. Christina lived on her own reservation, fenced off from the town. She didn't resemble her mother. She offered no ethnic news. Her eyes were blue, her skin was as pale as her mother's, her hair was sandy and shoulder-length. She was thin, but not yet gawky, though gawky was in the cards. She was pretty in an uncommanding way. Her smile was pleasant and gratifying; one was pleased to receive it, as one might be pleased to receive an unexpected birthday present. And she was good company, comfortable company, keeping her distance while dropping hints. She had been left, Paul was sure, to her own devices, and had spent much of the time hammering the fence into the earth, declaring her land, dissuading explorers. Had the man with the Nikon ever tried?

On the beach, returning home, Christina said: "I liked coming down here with you."

"I did, too," Paul told her. And then, to divert them from embarrassment: "In the east the summer's almost over. Not here. Here, the real summer lies ahead."

"October's fabulous," Christina said.

With nothing specific in mind, Paul asked: "What do you think will happen?"

"You mean in general?"

"Exactly."

"Do you wanna know?" Christina, a little ahead of him on the sand, stopped, and turned to face him.

"Yes." Paul stopped.

"Not real happy," Christina said. "You wanna see something?" she asked immediately.

A headstand, her right pants leg still rolled to her knee, her left pants leg half-and-half. A long headstand.

"Terrific," Paul said.

Beyond Christina's acrobatics, down the beach toward home, high on the cliff at the top of the stairs, caught in the sun as if in a spotlight: Emily. Waving, waving. Good-morning waving, some nice excitement to it. And a wave back from Paul. Good morning, good morning, good morning, good morning. I love you, I love you, I love you, I love you.

Christina and Paul arrived at Maggie's terrace out of breath.

"A hundred and seventeen stairs," Christina announced.

"Sweetheart," Paul said, embracing Emily.

"Does she give good walk?" Emily asked, with a wonderful smile.

"Positively the best."

"What a beautiful morning," Emily said softly.

"Who *loves* you?" Paul whispered into Emily's ear.

"You."

"What do you think will happen?" Paul asked Emily, holding her. Christina had twirled into the house.

A kiss for Paul. An arm around his waist at the railing. A staring out at the ocean. And then, from Emily, quietly: "You don't need a weatherman to know which way the wind blows."

CHAPTER TEN

Not on the ride home. Not during lunch in a fish restaurant in Westwood, where Paul ordered lobster and champagne.

"A celebration," he told Emily.

"What are we celebrating?" she asked.

"You understand, don't you, that if I were at liberty to tell you, I would tell you."

"But you're not at liberty."

"I am not. But possibly I will be at some point. No fretting."

"Who's fretting?"

"Just no fretting."

"Do you want to know what Maggie told me about Joshua?"

"She told you *nothing*."

"Oh, but she did."

"What did she tell you."

"Do you *really* want to know?"

"I'm not trading you."

"You'll never know what Maggie told me about Joshua."

"I don't give a shit what Maggie told you about Joshua."

"Oh yes, you do."

"You're a loser, honey."

They wrestled amiably through the meal. Paul felt that they were at their best together with even something modest at stake; that maybe their tragedy might turn out to be the *need* for something at stake, something around the bend or under the table. It gave them the opportunity for parody, metaphor, playful deceit, challenge. Their jostling was their fuel. Paul thought it might do them in.

He had watched Maggie and Emily together, yapping away. A sex star of the seventies with billowing hair and startling breasts dissolved before Paul's very eyes, leaving only Emily's excited and extraordinary face, and the depth of her marvelous, wicked eyes. He revered her information, the sheer weight of it, the monstrous size of her reference library, the nimbleness of her movements within it: smack! to the right shelf and the right book and the line on the page that defined and supported her contention. Are there any other questions, schmucko, as the book refiled itself and the issue became intensely personal—how to recover, how to crawl across the rug to pick up the pieces of loss without looking undignified on your hands and knees, hearing your own righteous babble subside, aware that Emily's troops were gathered just down the hall in the event of any threat of battle. They were down the fucking hall on their fucking *horses* and she's just sitting there with a smile, smoking a cigarette. *Any* sex star would dissolve beside such a formidable citizen. Emily Keller the citizen. Could it be only cheap risks that so attracted Paul? The cheap risks of the truly miraculous? And Emily Keller was just that. Paul was elated. He leaned across the table and kissed her.

"Can you change a one-thousand-dollar bill?" Paul asked the waiter.

Customers in jeans and tee shirts with a one-thousand-dollar bill. Shady stuff at The Seafare Hut?

Paul could explain everything: "Strictly *entre nous*," he said. "Caesar's Palace is a gold mine."

"Do you have anything smaller at all?" asked the waiter, a pleasant young man, possibly at UCLA, postgraduate something. Nothing snide or unctuous; just a young man in the summer.

"Of course," Paul said. "I wanted to break it, if possible."

"I'll see what we can do," said the waiter.

"A lot of money," Emily said, when he left. On the conversational side, and, or so it seemed, without a thing to ask.

"I keep money around me. I *contribute* money," Paul said, without expression.

"Do you think it's reasonable to pay a sixty-seven-dollar check with a one-thousand-dollar bill?" Emily asked.

"I think you are missing the point," Paul said.

And then Emily smiled at him, a point-getting smile.

"Are you following me?" he asked.

"Now this is really something," she said. "One of the most interesting things about this is that you didn't tell me until now. We had coffee in Trancas, we had two little rendezvous on the terrace, we had an hour-long drive, a full meal, a *lobster* meal— no little hello-and-goodbye lunch—and you were able to wait around with news like this."

"Are you interested in the facts?" Paul asked.

"Please, my love. I can't think of anything more exciting. Now this is *really* something." Emily had a cigarette lit in no time.

Paul told her the facts.

"Jesus Christ," she said. "This is really something."

A thousand-dollar bill was too large for The Seafare Hut. Paul left a one-hundred-dollar bill on the table.

"First of all, there's no way in the world that that dismal little guy is going to miss that money," Emily told Paul, as he drove them home. "There isn't any process of organization in his mind. He has no way of knowing what he has and what he hasn't. It's just money. A lot of money. You didn't even make a dent in it. And the truth of the matter is, Maggie adores him. He's kind to her. He feeds her opportunism. And he's generous with his time, as far as Christina is concerned. He's not a dope, as you surely know. You know what he is? He's an exaggeration. He's an exaggerated fascist, he's an exaggerated piece of theater, he's an exaggerated physical Jew, he's an exaggerated lost cause. I'm not saying that he won't succeed. As a matter of fact, it's my guess that he'll pull something together; he'll grab a little piece of whatever it is he wants. He's playing to his father and those millions of Cho-Chews, even though the motherfucking father's a corpse. You see how Maggie fits in? A daughter-in-law that Rufus would truly admire. She's a beautiful child-woman, she's successful, and she loves his son. Rufus, baby, it's hard to believe, but it's true. Never mind that she's got a child, and particularly, never mind that she's not a Jew. She *is* a Jew. Walter can make of her what he wants. Whatever truth he wants to invent, then that's fact. People with a lot of money do that. They just make things up. Nobody's gonna tell on them. Rufus is a corpse, but Maggie is announced as a Jew. You see? Rufus *lives*. But you've got to remember something: basically, Walter Decker has never taken any notes, and he has no files, and he doesn't know where anything is."

"The other thing, Emily, is that I stole money. Walter Decker or no Walter Decker." Paul was serious.

"I know," she replied.

"Over a thousand dollars."

"I know."

"What now?"

"We spend it on grass and coke and acid. We simply *give* it to Mona. It's gone. It's grass. It's drugs. That's the end of it."

"Easy," he said, irritated.

"Do you want to buy a pulpit for me? Should I flog you in a house of God? Paul, you want to be admonished?" Emily touched his arm.

"Not by you," he said, sharply.

"I love you."

They were at a red light on Pacific Avenue. Emily kissed him.

"Well," he said. He found her duplicity confusing and moving. "We will have known each other a month," he said, softly. "I love you, too. Just plain old dumb luck, wouldn't you say?"

"Never done acid? Look at this. You see? It's little chopped-up pieces of mushroom. Organic, from Hawaii. It's not a hallucinogen."

Emily had the ingredients of a small pharmacy vial spread before them on a copy of *The Saturday Review*.

"What does it taste like?" Paul asked.

"Like mushroom. It's not gourmet stuff, I'll tell you that. I've done it, maybe five times, six times."

"Alone?"

"Twice alone."

"And who with? Joshua the truly spiritual seems like a safe bet."

"We'll do it together on a rainy day." Emily made a funnel of *The Saturday Review* and returned the chopped-up mushroom to the tube.

They had dropped in on Mona Nine on Doheny Drive. She had been dressed in bikini bottoms and had tied a scarf around her small breasts. She had shown no surprise at the appearance of a thousand-dollar bill. She was listening to Pink Floyd.

"Could you turn it *down?*" Paul had asked.

"Let's trip someday," Mona had said to Paul. "Em and you and me, 'cause it's a good combo and you won't be disappointed in my stuff and I can guarantee I can mellow you guys out, and no freak-out stuff or anything like that 'cause—"

"Would you turn the *music down* just a little more? Thank you."

"I got good shit for you, Em."

"Whatever you think—"

"I don't need all this bread. I mean, you—"

"It's symbolic bread. That's how Paul describes it."

"I never said 'symbolic.'"

"But you and I know, sweetie. We're not buying any Bibles, you notice?"

"It's an inaccurate analogy, the whole thing."

"No nitpicking."

"You guys got somethin' goin'?"

"Mona's speeding."

"Em knows me."

"It's so fucking dark in here."

"That's where Mona lives."

In the evening at the kitchen table, with Paul dressed and Emily in a terry-cloth robe after a shower, they shared a pint of beer.

"I once turned my father on," Paul told her. "I didn't think in a million years he'd ever try it."

"How was it?" Emily asked, with her elbows on the table and her chin in her hands.

"Wonderful. Very sad and very funny. He asked if there'd

be any side effects, and then we got into a language thing. He pinned me to the wall for the pompous ass I am. I got into something about verbal ethics, something like that. Wordy stuff. His attitude was to mimic me. I mean very quietly, very dignified. He's a very dignified man. You'll see that on Thursday night. And—I had forgotten about this; he said that he knew that he hadn't accumulated a great deal of wisdom. Those were his exact words. 'I haven't accumulated a great deal of wisdom.'"

"That's a very candid and dignified perception of your father's."

"Yes, it is, isn't it? But, you know something, he's a very playful man. And he's not a whiner. There's no self-pity. I can't remember anything remotely resembling a whine coming out of him. Anger, yes; whine, no." Paul finished off their can of beer. "I'm still a little high. I had two tokes, right? Mona didn't cheat us."

"What have you told your father about me?" Emily asked, up and at the refrigerator for another beer. She was barefooted and wet-haired. Paul could imagine no one as beautiful.

"I've told him you are one of the most beautiful women I've ever met. I've told him your family history. I've told him you're a writer, and that you're good, a good writer. I've told him that you're facile with language, and that you'd grow on him."

Emily returned to the table, nodding, considering what Paul had said.

"Here's the truth, as I see it," she announced. "I'm good-looking, I'm very sexy. One of the things that's sexy about me is that I somehow suggest intriguing possibilities."

"'Suggest' is the understatement of the year."

"I'm modestly good at what I do," Emily continued. "I've never tried to really make a living out of it because I've always had a little money. So, you see, the pressure isn't there. Though I do feel that when I'm working my habits are sound. I don't have any great professional ambitions, and I'm really incredibly unresolved about what course of action to take, on any front, really. And this has always been the case, very likely because of my transient childhood. Just wandering from here to there.

"Also, there's no question about something. And that is, that I don't feel absolutely mentally in place. I'm not totally the director of my play." Emily paused for a moment, and dropped her eyes. She continued in a softer voice.

"There's something else going on," she said, talking to the can of beer. "There is some other commander with whom I have yet to deal. I know this sounds ominous, overly dramatic, maybe. But there it is. And I don't know *what* it is." She looked up. "Are you going to tell your father *that*? Are you going to tell him that you're mixed up with such a person? Not a happy thought, is it?"

Emily had tears in her eyes. Paul held out his hand to her from across the table, but she didn't take it.

"Sweetheart," he said, *"what* commander?"

"Paul. I—"

"Whatever. I *love* you. My father will love you. Answer me something: are you at all worried about meeting him?"

"No," she whispered, dropping her eyes again. "That's not the issue."

"You never know. *I* might be able to handle the commander."

"You're not with me," Emily said.

"Remember something, Emmy," Paul said, reaching for her hands. "All of our minds are really like two boxes side by side. We're able to roam freely—fairly freely—in *one* of the boxes because that's the box we have reasonable access to. The other is closed. It's shut tight. It's filled with the nightmare of mortality, and the excruciating information we pick up from just peripheral vision *alone*. Forget for a moment what we come across when we're *face* to *face!* That's in there as well, banging around. We only get little peeks into that box, that second box. And if all the tops were flung wide open on all those second boxes, there'd be murder in the streets. I honestly believe that all those second boxes are sealed, simply to perpetuate humanity."

"And I honestly believe the opposite," Emily said, wiping her eyes with the sleeves of her robe. "I want to *see* my commander. Can this be called an ambition? If so, it's the only one I have."

They were quiet for a little while.

"What would happen if you could?" Paul asked, withdrawing his hand from hers.

"Absolution, Paul."

"Absolution," he repeated, not understanding.

"Don't you see?" she said, raising her eyes, finding his eyes. "Insanity."

"Now, do you *know* what *is* possible, in a goofy kind of way?"

Paul waited for their attention. He saw his father's mind receiving Emily tenderly. Franklin saw Paul's eyes following his mind, and said: "We're listening." The team of Franklin and Emily was listening. The idea gave Paul pleasure; how attractively he was reflected by it.

They were gathered in Franklin's garden, waiting until the end of the rush hour to drive up the Pacific Coast Highway and into the Malibu Hills for dinner at El Besame Mucho. Franklin would drive them in his beige Maverick. Told of Emily's Volkswagen, he had shaken his head gravely. "You'll never catch me in one of those. You get thrown around when you go over an olive pit."

At what point along the way had Paul's father, now in his eighth decade, added a cruise in a VW to his list of life-threatening activities? There must have been an hour, or a moment, possibly after such a cruise, at which time Franklin, emerging terrified, had declared to himself that he would not scrunch himself into such a vehicle ever, ever again. Franklin would not: ride on a ski lift or tram of any kind; fly in a propeller plane; pass through the gates of an amusement park, fearing toppling gadgetry; ascend above the twentieth floor of any building in the world; make a right on a red signal under the very signs that permitted it—"You never know where some idiot will come flying out from"; stand closer than twenty-five feet from a color television set in use; swim in the ocean. He would, however, drive his own immaculate automobile up the winding roads of the Malibu Hills, and down again late in the evening, and all the way into town on the Pacific Coast Highway.

"We don't have to go to *that* place, it's just that I heard it was—"

"Don't be silly, Paul," Franklin had said. "It's a nice drive, and I'll enjoy spending the time with the two of you."

"The one of us," Paul had said, laughing, flattering Emily on his father's behalf.

"So what's possible in a goofy kind of way?" Emily asked.

"It's possible that every American mystery is solved by that eighteen-and-a-half-minute gap. For example: Nixon says to Haldeman: 'Bob, we gotta get an extra twenty thousand to Amelia Earhart by next Tuesday.' 'Mr. President, don't forget the ten thousand for Glenn Miller in Tangier by next month.' 'Bob, it's a good thing they didn't discover Pat Buchanan on the grassy knoll.'"

" 'Mr. President,' " Emily added, " 'I'm sorry to have to tell you this, but Judge Crater has the flu.' "

Still in the garden a half hour later, Paul wanted to know if it was remotely possible that Tom Keller and Franklin Kramer had ever run across each other. They were men of the theater, they were travelers, they were New Yorkers. Couldn't it have just been possible that somewhere along the way . . .

Franklin didn't think it was possible. He considered it,

though. He pressed three fingertips to his forehead and thought about it, trying to come up with something; it was an invitingly uniting notion, if only it could be pulled off. "I just don't think so," he finally said. "No," he added, regretfully.

"My father wasn't a Kaufman-Hart man," Emily volunteered. "His sights were set somewhat lower."

"Why does a man decide to express himself through an inanimate object?" Paul asked.

"There's nothing indecent about it," Franklin said.

"I didn't say there was anything indecent about it," Paul said.

"On one level, there *is* something indecent about it," Emily said. "Conceptually, it's sleazy. I didn't know precisely that then. At that time. I just knew something was wrong. In vaudeville, generally, ventriloquists are the low men on the totem pole. I'm not suggesting that they're subjected to any scurrilousness. It's something more malignant than that. There's an *attitude* that the other acts assume, a condescension. I couldn't put my finger on it, but I knew it. And so did my father."

Emily was talking to them as she roamed the garden, looking at the ivy and the daisies and the barren lemon tree. "To answer your question," she said, "I don't think my father ever felt on safe grounds with himself. I don't think he trusted himself out there, out *any*where, unless he was protected by his assistant, over whom he had total control. Well, total control on the surface of things. He wasn't a comfortable man to be around. Had there been television, real eighteen-hour-a-day television, I strongly doubt that we would ever have spoken to each other, except for the basics. He would have sat there watching television. He would have sat there, chained to his chair."

Emily drifted up behind Paul and put her hands on his shoulders. He felt considerably at ease, and filled with sentimental love. These two people had taken to each other at once. There had been a hug from Franklin at his own door. Paul had seen Emily's eyes conceive the hug, call for it, as she stood on Franklin's welcome mat in a pink dress.

"Is it that you want to look like a little girl?" Paul had asked at home, not happy with the pink dress.

"Partially," she had answered.

"And partially what?"

"And partially, fuck off."

"Television might have been a source of revenue for him," Franklin suggested.

"I wonder," Emily said. "I think he would have found it a little too risky, too dreamlike. He was familiar with a stage and an audience and a dressing room and a bus ride. The facts of his life. I think he would have been very much like a silent-screen actor faced with talkies, an actor stuck with some permanent falsetto. In my father's *mind*, you know?"

"Why?" Franklin asked.

"I think because he was addicted to his routine. Life decisions all made, and, like that. He did not take any risks at all."

"You're carrying your share of the family load in that department," Paul said.

"That's how it works out sometimes," Emily said. "Television would have been for *other* people to appear on," she continued. "Television would have been for him to watch. In its early days he sneaked a look at it out of the corner of his eye. And then."

Emily kissed Paul's right temple. He was quite certain that it was the first gesture of affection ever bestowed on him by a woman in front of Franklin Kramer.

"I understand what you mean," said Franklin. "Sometimes new possibilities don't suit certain people."

"Paul's told me about the plays you've written, but I haven't read them yet. I've thought to find them in the library."

"That's a long time ago," Franklin said, with a smile. I

don't think much of them any more. They were dainty trifles, and they don't deserve extensive study."

"I'd like to read them. Do you have them here?" Emily gestured toward the house.

"I think so. In some trunk."

"Emily's incredible. When she's working she sits there for hours. I'd be up and gone in ten minutes." Paul put his arm around Emily's waist. She stood beside his chair. "She's maniacally disciplined."

"Most of it is just nothing, just daydreaming. Staring. Nothing."

"Have you ever written adult stories?" Franklin asked.

"Not yet. Except articles. Things like a piece on McGovern, another on Chavez, Judy Collins. Dainty trifles, as you say."

Emily roamed the garden again, laughing, complimenting; a little restless, Paul thought, as she turned and touched her hair, her short-sleeved pink dress doing the job, rustling a little in a slight breeze.

Paul imagined his father's verdict. "She's a young, thoughtful, and attractive girl, and quite witty, too." But, Dad, she fornicates in filthy canals; she takes drugs, practically *anything*, though not regularly; and, *and*, she goes through lights. Think of that! Right through. Not just traffic lights, Dad. *Moral* lights, *sexual* lights—you name 'em, she goes through 'em. Paul, my son, I don't believe a word of it. It's obvious that she's got an innate sense of decency. That's true, Dad, but only at her convenience. She's a very political girl, Dad. All you have to do is look at the pink dress. Paul, I think it's pretty. Dad, you're right. It's pretty.

The traffic was light on the Pacific Coast Highway, but the sun fought them all the way.

"It's a tough drive at this time of day," Emily said. "You

think you're going north, but you're not. You're actually going due west on account of the bowl of Santa Monica Bay."

Franklin drove cautiously in the right lane. He wore dark glasses. The ocean sparkled in the sunset; it lingered spectacularly in their view, before the rolling hills and the cliffs of Trancas deprived them of it for a moment or so.

Emily, in the front seat, rested her right arm on the windowsill, holding a cigarette in her left hand. Paul sat behind her, occasionally leaning forward to toy with her hair and massage her neck. "Hmn," she said. "Right there, that's it, right *there*. Ah."

Paul gave thought to the ease with which he was able to caress Emily in his father's company. He imagined this fine development taken to its extreme: Emily tumbles into the back seat. Up goes the pink dress, down come the white underpants. She's on him, with her back to the front seat. They're at it in an easy back-seat rhythm. "Kids, please." Or, "I don't think this is appropriate." Both were possibilities; the appropriateness, the *kids*. Would Franklin sneak a rearview-mirror look? Was Emily's ass of any interest to him? Was sex just history to Franklin Kramer, or was there a lingering residue of desire within his sensational heart? At what point on the map does the athlete lose a step or two? At what point on the map does the older gentleman turn to other things, ethereal or cosmic things with no sexual traces, only the important stuff: What are we doing here on this earth? What's to become of us all? Paul remembered his father holding an artichoke to his chest in a supermarket, cradling it. Look here, Franklin could very well have said, this artichoke is sensual and beautiful. Paul realized that no man with a sense of artichoke, seventy-six years old or no seventy-six years old, could be walking around without an interest in Emily Keller's bare ass in a rearview mirror. Raw sex, not just the esthetics. "Kids, please," possible. But, Paul decided, Franklin Kramer was alive and well.

They turned off the Pacific Coast Highway at Point Dume, and made their way into the mountains with Franklin driving slowly, though the road was straight and wide. Maggie had given Paul directions on the phone. On the phone, his first time alone with her, Paul had attempted sexual progress. Lowered voices, jokes at Emily's expense—Paul had tested one out first: "You give Emmy directions to Hollywood and you'll wind up eatin' a hot dog in Central Park." Oh, that was funny! And from Maggie, something interesting: "Emmy can handle a little car, but in a Mercedes she'd be like a little dwarf." A little dwarf, not even a medium dwarf. A little dwarf, incapable of handling a Mercedes, the very automobile Maggie owned. It had been made clear to Paul that Maggie Furth cared deeply for Emily Keller; in the course of their evening together Maggie had shown reverence. Her eyes had told the story. A visit from Emily was a treat, no question about it. They could yap together— "She said, he said that she said—" but Emily held the cards. Maggie, on the phone and alone with Paul, could flirt a bit with Emily's selection. There had been no evidence whatsoever that Emily Keller was incapable of maneuvering a Mercedes-Benz from here to there. There had been no evidence whatsoever that Emily Keller had any kind of history of bolloxed directions in even the dearest kind of way. But there they were, Maggie and Paul, cackling on the wire about old stumblebum Keller. An easy little flirtation. No damage done.

Franklin told them that prisoners of the county jail were up in these hills; Camp Fitzgerald, Camp David Sanchez. One-year incarcerations: years ago, the alimony delinquents; these days, the misinformed, their schemes gone astray, washed-out trouble-makers, the victims of nightmare flights, sirens wailing, roads blocked off, eight hundred dollars of somebody else's loot, tough jabs to the mouths of provocative women with touch-tone phones. Indiscretion after indiscretion, loaded into buses headed for the Malibu Hills, to Camp Fitzgerald, to Camp David Sanchez. They worked in the hills. They made firebreaks, clearing the brush. When the Santa Ana blew in from the northeast and the valleys and the hills ignited and smoke could be seen for miles and the San Gabriel Mountains burned for days and the fires approached the ocean communities from the hills behind Trancas, the firebreaks would deter the wild sparks. Tough right jabs to provocative mouths fought the Santa Ana. Eight hundred dollars of somebody else's loot supplied the troops. Paul imagined himself dangling in a court of law, confronted by Walter Decker and a battery of attorneys. One thousand two hundred and ten dollars of somebody else's loot, and the brightest guy in the media is on his way to the Malibu Hills. And not for dinner with his father and his chickie.

"It's the dark side of the moon up here," Paul said.

El Besame Mucho. Beautiful food. One room, Mexican décor, and Maggie's terra-cotta tiles. Carta Blanca the house beer, but no tostadas, no refried beans. Only steamed clams, or steak and baked potato.

And a one-woman show. A tall, buxom woman named Isolda; the owner, the chef, the waitress, the cashier. A woman in her fifties with long black hair and brilliant white teeth and an open smile. She had casually arranged seven wooden tables. The room was small, noticeably clean, and suggested slow motion. Isolda moved gently, fastidiously, in and out of the kitchen. Her restaurant was filled to capacity, her mood was calm and gracious. She told Emily, who asked, that she was Czechoslovakian, that El Besame Mucho had been on this very spot of land for twenty-two years. She told them all, addressing Franklin, that in the late twenties there had been an amusement park a hundred yards down the road on Lake Enchanto, and that in the late thirties, after the closing of the park, the German-Americans had made their Bund headquarters in the dusty ruins of the tunnel of love. These were facts that Isolda had recited for many a diner at El Besame Mucho. There was a relaxed rat-a-tat-tat about her presentation, a tour-guide slickness. Steamed clams for Emily and Franklin, steak and potato for Paul. Thank you very much, enjoy your meal, Isolda told them. Paul imagined Decker up there: "Strictly *entre nous,* my dear, your place is *charming.*"

Emily was full of questions for Franklin. What kind of a young boy had Paul been? From Franklin's point of view, what kind of a relationship did they have in those years? How did Franklin become a writer?

Franklin told Emily that Paul had been "high-spirited" and that he had had trouble "applying himself" at school, and that was probably because of his mother's illness, which was a "most disturbing thing to have to face at home."

"Your wife's name was Carol?"

"That's right. She was a courageous woman. I think the two of you would have liked each other enormously," Franklin said. "You have a sparkle that she would have enjoyed."

"Paul has told me that you had a very close relationship with her."

"That's the truth. From the beginning, and through her illness and until her death. It was a very successful combination, wouldn't you say?" Franklin looked to Paul for a verification.

"Without doubt," Paul said.

"Do you find that Paul is more like his mother than like yourself? In temperament?"

"I would say that he's a lot like his mother. They have the same kind of imagination. A floating imagination. They're as likely as not to be in China while you're playing gin rummy with them. I've always been more confined to the present and involved with nostalgia of a personal nature. Carol and Paul—very flighty."

Paul was surprised to learn of his father's accurate perception, and was touched by his mother's presence at the table.

"They're both mysterious, too, in ways I don't understand." Franklin smiled.

"What ways?" Emily wanted to know.

"One always expects the unexpected from them, whether it be the use of an unusual word, or a late arrival with a fabulous story attached to it. They always have a number of balls in the air."

Again Paul was surprised, and put on the defensive a little.

"What do you mean by 'a number of balls in the air'?" he asked.

"Secret activities, the nature of which I'm not really sure of," Franklin replied. "Private goings-on. I *know* you, young man." Franklin was having a good time.

"I don't know what you're talking about," Paul said, with a serious face. He glanced at Emily, who wouldn't give him a thing.

Franklin chuckled, and said: "Paul has never fully realized that his old man has eyes and ears."

What a smile from Emily! Clearly, they were a team, a franchise in a league. A winning franchise.

"That's not true. I've always known you were alert."

"Come on now, Paul. 'Alert' is such a condescending word." Emily was right on target.

"We'll forgive him, won't we, Emily?" Franklin patted her hand on the table.

As for Franklin and Paul years ago: "I would say we were close. I think we felt for each other, except for a difficult few years. Wouldn't you, Paul?"

"There were difficult times along the way. But here we are to tell the tale." Paul took a sip of beer.

"Tell me about Paul's women," Emily said, understanding

that on this special night, a hundred yards from Lake Enchanto in late August, with a wonderful little pink dress hard at work, she could yank from Franklin Kramer anything in the world that she wanted

"Paul's women," said Franklin. "That's a tough one."

"Why is that so tough?" Paul asked, observing his role as a rather squeaky offstage voice, a cloutless protester, egging them on with mock indignation, but not absolutely positively out of danger.

"Well," said Franklin, "let me see." He was delighted by the presidency that Emily had arranged for him.

"You don't have to be specific if you don't want to be," Emily told him.

"Do you mean their qualities? What kind of gals they were?"

"Gals. Shit," Paul said.

"What kind of gals," Emily said, very soft, very lovely on "gals."

"To tell the truth, I didn't meet many of them. Nor did I get to know any of them very well, except for that gal named Jennifer."

"Jennifer Rosen," Paul said. "And stop saying 'gals.' You've never used that word in your life."

"He's playing," Emily said, sternly. "Do you think you're the only party-goer at the table?"

"Emily's rather bright," Franklin said, again spraying conspiracy in the air.

"Jennifer Rosen," Emily said. "Paul's mentioned her. She's the one who used to say that everything was 'dynamite.' She had a limp?"

"That's the one," Franklin said, nodding. "She was a very pleasant girl, but no one would ever call her a genius."

"That's funny. Paul said she was real brainy."

"We all exaggerate sometimes." Franklin took a sip of Paul's beer.

"What about this fashion gal?" Emily said.

"A cute little gal. She was older, though. A little on the creaky side."

"Creepy side?" Emily asked.

"Well, I meant creaky. I don't want to be too hard on the gal."

"So, in other words, Paul's gals have been something less than belles of the ball," Emily said, summing up.

"I wouldn't want to go that far. That would be rude, wouldn't it?" Franklin was bouncing around, having quite a night, Emily's obliging teammate, going right along with her, crowning the gal.

"Dad, now you *see*? Emily has seduced you. You've done *nothing* but flatter her."

"What flatters Emily flatters you."

"Even *that* stinks of perfume."

"Gals are real slippery, you know," Emily said to Paul.

Decker was right, the food was terrific. Isolda brought them their clams and steak and offered them free bottles of Carta Blanca. "A gift from Isolda," she said. "Isolda hopes you like the food."

Paul considered the fact that people everywhere were talking of themselves in the third person. Paul likes the food. Paul is happy. Paul is in California. Emily is thirsty. Emily is sleepy. Emily is menstruating. Franklin is getting old. Franklin won't enter a Volkswagen. Franklin misses Lillian. Baby talk, dragged along into adulthood in the name of self-defense. If Emily is thirsty, why, there's nothing to do but bring her a glass of water. If Paul likes the food, why, then everybody should be happy. *Wiggens* should be happy that Paul likes the food. *Carl Furillo* should be happy that Paul likes the food. How could anybody be angry with Paul if Paul likes the food?

"I always had a desire to write. Not necessarily to be a writer," Franklin told them over a coffee.

"I'm not sure I know what you mean," Emily said, with her elbows on the table and her chin in her hands.

During the meal Emily and Franklin had come together in what Paul felt was an extraordinary union. He had contributed to his own exclusion by a respectful lack of interference. He understood that his life was not on the line, and was pleased with his own modest progress to this truth. A professional fulcrum, an agitator, a choreographer out of sheer force of will, he had stepped aside and had allowed Emily and Franklin their own talented improvisation. They had looked each other in the eye. Paul knew that he could never seek out Franklin's approval of Emily; by doing so he would insult their obvious and established glow. And how could Paul confront Emily on Franklin: a simple "What did you think of him?" She wouldn't answer such a question with anything but impatience with the man who asked it. By coffee time it was clear to Paul: there would be, with or without him, communication between Emily Keller and Franklin Kramer. It was easy to anticipate. For Franklin, a grown daughter so late in the game, thrust into his life out of the blue, articulate, uncommonly beautiful, already passed through Customs—Paul had opened every bag, had taken a look in her purse, had drawn her into the back room for more intimate scrutiny. She was as free as the breeze. Franklin's son, the advance man, had issued a Grade-A report. All Franklin had to do was see for himself.

Paul imagined what Emily would say in her bed. Would she inform him that his father was a one-of-a-kind item? An important man? A man filled with life? Paul felt that more than likely she would say: "You never told me."

"At some time, early in my life," Franklin said to Emily, "it became apparent to me that I wanted to express myself with some kind of creating. I felt I had talent as an actor. My school experiences in theatrical endeavors were quite successful, more than just the ordinary appearance in *The Mikado,* or something like that. I liked the idea of writing my thoughts down and having them transmitted to a reader in a book or journal. As I became more involved with the theater I began to realize that what I could do most easily was write plays. I understood the construction of a play. I was well-read in classical theater. And, ah, Chekhov. That's who I wanted to be, let's face it." Franklin smiled and nodded his head. "That's what I had in mind."

"I've got to tell you something, Franklin," Emily said. "A couple of times this evening I've thought of Chekhov in relation to you. Honestly. Not so much what he wrote, but the kind of man I have always imagined he was. Not that my imagination is way out of tune with the truth. It's just that I hold him in high regard. The diligence with which he wrote, the hardness of his winters. And the very fact that he was a doctor. His tremendous respect for humanity. I think that's the key to it. His tremendous respect for humanity."

"I'm very moved, Emily," Franklin said. "That's about all I can say."

When Isolda presented the bill, Emily insisted on paying it. "Next time, next time," she told them both. "Tonight, I want to."

They lingered at their table until they were the only ones left at El Besame Mucho. Isolda, and a small Mexican girl about ten years old, cleared away dishes and attended to order. Encouraging them to stay, the little girl put two candles on the table, each enclosed in blue translucent glass. "Please," she said. "You're welcome not to go."

"You and Paul, I think you'll make out all right," Franklin said suddenly, and after a short lull.

"You never know with gals like Emily," Paul said. "Sometimes it's necessary to drop 'em on the roadside and get on with your life."

"Paul is right," Emily said, and smiled at Franklin. "I better mind my P's and Q's."

Franklin held a match for Emily's cigarette.

"So what do you think, Dad," Paul said. "Do you *really* think we have a future?"

Franklin didn't answer for a moment. He pushed his chair back a little, got himself comfortable. Then he said: "I don't know what a future is these days. There are so many pitfalls, whole new sets of adversities. It seems to me that indecisiveness is running rampant across the land. In my day, you evaluated the data, formed an opinion, and then you went with it. And more often than not you stuck with it. This is not to say that I wasn't open to change. I was. It's just that these days, nobody's sure; they hem and haw and they try for both sides of the avenue. I'm not saying this is bad. The world is all different, as you know. One of the things I get a kick out of is watching immensely intelligent young people's marvelous insights on the way to the wrong conclusions. But who's to say what a wrong conclusion *is*. Certainly not me. Do you have a future? The two of you? What can your old man say? Godspeed. Silly, isn't it? You live in a world that eludes me much of the time. I stick to what I know, a little like *your* father, Emily. But I respect ambivalence because I'm woefully behind the times that have sanctioned it. I'm just a bucket of contradictions, aren't I?"

Paul rested his hand on his father's.

"Thank you for dinner, Emily," Franklin said, smiling at her. "It was a very warm gesture, and I'm sure you know that I understand it and appreciate it."

"I do," Emily said.

"I do, too," Paul said.

At the car, in the dark, Paul took Emily's hand. They stood beside each other for a moment. There was a crescent moon.

The night had grown chilly. They touched each other's fingertips. They kissed each other in Franklin's headlights.

"We're out of here," Emily whispered.

Somehow, confused by a tangle of dark roads—Latigo, Malibu, Kanan—they found themselves descending Encinal Canyon in a pitch-black night. They passed through two tunnels, crawling, Franklin unnerved by the foreign and serpentine route he had stumbled upon. The roadway weaved severely down the steep canyon, cutting sharply to the right, then curling left and down, jutting every which way, confining them to their one narrow westbound lane. They were dropping, inch by inch it seemed, in a treacherous zigzag that silenced them.

Paul, sitting forward, rested his hands on Emily's shoulders. Then he shifted his left hand to his father's right shoulder, holding them both steady. Were there cliffs off to the right? Would they fly over rocks and into space, suspended above the sea, held in midair by some comic force, like characters in cartoons, walking on air, standing on air, taking for granted the safety of the earth below their feet—but wait! No earth below their feet! Whoops! The rocks below. Zip! Crunch! Down they cascade, mutilated into traingles, flattened like pancakes. Whoops!

Paul said: "They shouldn't allow this road. Fuckin'. . ."

Emily said to Franklin: "Do you want me to drive?"

Franklin said: "I'm okay if we go slowly."

Paul said: "It's the dark side of the fuckin' moon."

Silence.

What was off to their right? Their headlights picked up nothing; brush, gravel. Was it sand? There was no railing. A tractor. JOHN DEERE EARTH MOVERS. Big letters. Christina's stream started up here.

A car was coming up the hill on their left. Franklin almost

stopped. The car was moving swiftly. Its lights blinded them. It passed them in a second. They didn't hear a thing.

Emily said: "We've gotta be at *least* halfway down. This comes out about three miles north of Point Dume."

In Las Vegas at some time or other—was it a year ago, or in March?—Paul had stood on the balcony outside the Top-of-the-Strip restaurant, the crown on the Dunes Hotel, watching the giant signboard at the entrance to Caesar's Palace being changed. An enormous *T,* lowered by ropes, fell gently into the back of an open truck. An *O* and an *M* followed, and the five letters of Jones. Before long, the words *ANDY WILLIAMS* were fastened in place, diagonally and in script, to suggest intimacy.

Dear Mr. Williams, Paul imagined in the back seat, you are not intimate, you are false. You are unmoving and unmusical. Sincerely, Paul Knight.

Something on the road in front of them moved; their headlights caught it. An animal of some kind, a raccoon, a fox.

Emily said: "Watch it."

Paul said: "Steady."

Franklin veered to the right, catching the soft shoulder of the road. Frantically, he overcorrected and slipped them into the upbound lane.

Emily said: "Watch it."

Franklin overcorrected. Again. From his maneuverings came speed.

Paul felt the car swerve. The car was losing balance. Paul was shocked to see his mother's face attached to the skin of Emily's face. Emily was on her knees in the front seat. How clear his mother's eyes were. This was all so funny. This would pass away.

The car was on its side. Franklin had lost control entirely. He was thrown against Emily. Paul saw the *T* fall gently into the back of the truck.

The car was moving forward on its side. Paul saw no one in the front seat. They were on an embankment. They were no longer moving. Paul's mind was clear. Accident. Death. Everybody gone. It's happened. It's happened now.

The driver's door was swung wide open. Paul was out, standing by the car. Standing by Emily, whose face was covered with blood.

Paul said: "Help me."

Emily said: "There's no chance in there."

Emily and Paul struggled with Franklin. They pulled him out from the overturned Maverick. They placed him on the gravel in the glare from the headlights.

They laid Franklin on his back.

Franklin was motionless. His eyes were closed.

Paul said: "How do you do pulse?"

Emily said: "No chance." She knelt beside Franklin. Drops of blood fell from her face to Franklin's jacket. She touched his cheek, stroked it with the palm of her right hand.

Paul stood next to his father and Emily. He said: "Daddy."

The *T* was floating. It was caught in a breeze. It was drifting in the air. It landed gently in an open field. A solitary *T* in a field of poppies.

Paul said: "Daddy."

Paul sank to his knees and placed his ear to his father's heart.

Paul said: "Daddy."

PART FOUR

CHAPTER ELEVEN

In the spring the canyons of the San Jacinto Mountains are alive with streams and waterfalls, the melted snow sliding to the valley, endlessly flowing, dribbling, cascading, winding down through the rocks and caves, around the palm trees and saguaro cacti, through the myrtillos and golden barrels and ocotillos. Icy pools lie peacefully below boulders—fairly deep water—safe enough for a naked cannonballer with a cassette machine on a towel on the rock above:

> Everywhere I hear the sound of marching,
> > charging feet, oh, boy,
> 'Cause summer's here and the time is right
> > for fighting in the street, oh, boy.

In the spring the desert colors are purple and orange and white. They are in the hills and by the sides of the roads and in the towns and scattered through the desert itself. Andreas Canyon, Tahquitz Canyon, riddled with empty cans of Olympia beer, are green and charged with running water and rabbits and iguanas and with the tense stillness of an occasional rattler on a rock. There is shade beneath the palm trees and the impression of horse's hooves in the mud. There are slippery logs across the water, and stones just beneath the surface of the streams on which to balance before a leap to a bed of crisp, fallen palm leaves.

There are signs of the autumn fires on the hillsides: scorched brush, black tinder, stretches of barren gray dust; no scampering iguanas, no purple and orange and white. September did it. With the streams and icy pools gone, the fires ravage the canyons, burning methodically for days, sparks leaping over boulders to ignite other hillsides, climbing into the canyons, ascending like mountaineers, fading finally, and dying in November rain. The scars are there when the snow begins to melt.

In the summer the horses of Smoke Tree stable are shipped to Catalina. The tradewinds from the Gulf of Baja bring moist air into the valley. For days on end it is difficult to breathe. In midafternoon the clouds darken. Surely there will be a storm, a bang, a mighty release, and the air will dry, and soon it will be hot and clear. But no. The clouds darken, the wind picks up, the humidity jumps to seventy and eighty per cent. Dribbles of rain; patios display the drops as round dark stains. And lightning, ominous without thunder. The dark stains multiply. Now the patios are wet. The temperature has dropped ten degrees in minutes—it is ninety.

But the wind subsides, the skies lighten. There will be no storm, no release. August, it seems, will live forever in the desert. Retitled September, the days will continue as before. It is only when the heart is heaviest, when all patience is gone, when hope is vanished, that the clouds darken, the wind picks up, the lightning jigsaws through the sky. Then the rain falls. It falls

torrentially, and continues into the evening. The morning dawns a splendid orange. The San Jacinto Mountains appear as glass-crystal miracles. The hot dry winds from the north are blowing by noon. They will sweep the valley clean, and open the shops and restaurants, and return the horses from Catalina, and call back the people from the East who retreated into New England summer. Canadians from Vancouver and Calgary and Toronto will make their way back. The old and the rich and the infirm will arrive again, Los Angeles, Portland, Minneapolis, New York, and Cleveland behind them. There will be bustle up and down the valley. Palm Springs, Rancho Mirage, Cathedral City, La Quinta, Palm Desert. There are spas and lobsters and the New York *Times* in these towns. There are diamonds and Boston ferns and fresh pumpernickel. There are avocados, bean sprouts, private screening rooms, and security officers; Watts lines and San Diego clams and distinguished cardiologists. There is one fleet of seventeen cabs and there are twelve movie theaters; one baseball stadium and about forty Mexican restaurants. There are thirty-six large hotels. There is a shantytown in the north where the few blacks of the Coachella Valley live, and mobile homes to the east, out in the desert a bit, unprotected by the mountains. Beyond Thousand Palms on Ramon Road, further into the desert, is a town called Agua Caliente. The houses are stucco, the rents are low, and the wind blows fiercely at night. The sandstorms, when they occur, are severe; they can rip the paint from cars and surround little stucco homes like snowdrifts. Telephone wires are often blown down; repair trucks are familiar visitors to the dunes.

In Agua Caliente there are swimming pools, a few tennis courts, and two supermarkets. There is one saloon, and a diner called Eat. There are grapefruit trees, and palms, and hummingbird bushes with bright-red flowers. There are solitary trailers off the main road.

There is no fuss or bother in Agua Caliente. There are peo-

ple who have come to sit out the winter, and others who will not make it through the winter. They are amiable and reclusive. For the most part, they are old. They are not rich or poor. They are waiting. They will take no drastic measures, they will incite no riots, they will throw no opulent parties, they will charter no jets, they will pass no legislation.

Agua Caliente, like Indio and Coachella and other towns that line Highway 111, is attended to and lived in by Chicanos. They are the caretakers of the land, the plowers of the fields, the pickers of the grapes and dates. They work in the supermarkets lifting cartons and crates of Gatorade and tomatoes off the trucks from Route 10, the desert's umbilical cord to Los Angeles. They are the gardeners of the Gene Autry Hotel, the Ramada Inn, the Palm Springs Spa. They are the kitchen help at Las Casuelas, Sorrentinos, Casa Camargo. They tend to the private estates of the affluent. They are quiet and friendly and diligent. In Agua Caliente they are half of the populace. They have formed no union, they have distributed no pamphlets, they have declared no intentions. Their intentions, in fact, are to wait with the rest of Agua Caliente. Now and then a Chicano will die in an incident before dawn. How did it happen? No one knows. Who was he, anyway? A passer-through. Where did it happen? In Indio, in Banning, in Thousand Palms. Now and then a group of Chicanos will be killed in an automobile accident. Where did it happen? Bogey Road, Farrell Drive, Tahquitz-McCullum, Pasa Tiempo.

It is said that in Agua Caliente a Chicano named Manny killed a rattler with a thumbtack in front of Eat. How many years ago? No one knows. It is said that the Chicanos plunder from the wealthy homes in the north around the Racquet Club, and steal from the weekend kids in their cheap motel rooms: Timex watches, loose grass in plastic cassette boxes, portable radios, sneakers, cigarettes, Valium. It is said that in June of 1972 a girl named Alexandria Hancock was found raped and decapi-

tated in front of 888 Avenida Palmas, and a witness, a transvestite named Pilot Love, swore the attacker was "a Chicano asshole." Was it true? No one knows, although three numbers of a license plate traced a Chicano to Agua Caliente. "No, man," the owner of the vehicle said, "I was working. You ask them." Where? "Denny's." Till what time? "All night, man."

Agua Caliente, twenty miles from the mountains, nine miles past Route 10, is a prisoner of the desert, held captive by its isolation, by the vastness of the night sky. "Good morning. How are you?" "What a lovely afternoon." "It's raining in L.A., you know." There are swimming pools and patios and air conditioners. But beyond the pools and the patios, beneath the automatic chatter, lies the convenience of surrender. Agua Caliente is dead end.

Paul was playing the piano. The piano was the reason they had taken the house; an ancient Hamilton, an upright that consumed most of the space in the small living room. How odd to find a piano so far out in the desert. "Why a piano?" Paul had asked Valerie Maxwell.

"My husband found it up north. He loved it. Neither of us played, you know."

Valerie was spending more and more of her time at the Botanical Gardens. She found the little house on the property reassuring. Alone now, after her husband's death a year ago, her one remaining contract was with her arboretum in La Quinta. Surrounded by her Palo Verde, her Chuparosa, her variegated yucca, she found that she was less melancholy than in the house in Agua Caliente.

Emily and Paul had spotted her ad in *The Desert Sun*. Valerie Maxwell had interviewed them as they stood by the pool. Paul had spoken soothingly, in what Emily called his oily voice.

Certainly, they would take it for two months. Would she like cash now? Maggie Furth of Trancas would vouch for them. Emily is a writer, and this is an ideal location. Out of the way. Secluded.

"We'll be very careful with everything," Emily said.

Sitting in three old chairs in the living room, they closed the deal.

"You can rest assured that your home is in good hands," Paul said. "May we come and visit you sometime?"

"Of course," Valerie Maxwell said.

She was in her sixties, with crusty desert skin and soft gray hair. She rarely smiled, but her eyes were warm. Paul imagined her on a horse, straight-backed and regal, her quick glance catching invisible creatures and microscopic splashes of color. She wore a white cotton dress and a gold wedding band. She spoke quite softly but was easily heard.

"We lived here for thirty-five years. We were out here before there was anything. You come around the garden anytime you'd like. We've got most of the things you'd care to find."

"Will you be comfortable there?" Paul asked.

"More so every day now. I thought I'd rent this place out a piece to see how it felt." Valerie rested her fingertips on her right temple.

"Well, you've got us for two months at least," Emily said. "I think we're lucky to have found each other."

"What was your husband's name?" Paul asked.

"Charles Dwight Maxwell," Valerie answered. "We were married for forty-four years and there never was a harsh word between us. I miss him."

"I understand," Paul said.

"You know, in these parts you really must have a friend," Valerie continued. "It's a real fine part of the world, but it's got power inside itself. The seasons kind of battle each other, and that can make for trouble. You can't go too far on your own, or you get confused. The two of you, you look like friends. No matter what you do, you're going to have to rely on each other. That's a good thing to keep in mind."

"I'll say," Emily whispered.

"I don't think you're married," Valerie said.

"That's true," Paul said.

"You'll need your friendship. Trust me."

The piano was not in the excellent condition that the ad had suggested. It was out of tune, and several bass notes refused to budge. But it was playable, with an agreeable light action that reminded Paul of Franklin's piano years and years ago.

On a late afternoon Paul sat at the piano with bits and pieces of melodies in his head. He wove them together, and passed by an old song that refused to yield its bridge. He puzzled over it for just a moment, not struggling. His mind wandered. He knew that he wasn't working these days, he wasn't pinning things down; he didn't care to challenge memory. It seemed to him that he was always on the verge of taking a nap.

Valerie Maxwell had removed three paintings from the living room, and one comfortable ragtag chair. The bare walls were easy for Paul; they did not invite scrutiny, and they complemented his lethargy. The room, always dark, looked out on the small swimming pool. There were three orange trees in the yard rich with fruit. A white picket fence surrounded the property. The closest house was well down the road. Paul and Emily were locked in privacy. The word "shrouded" occurred to Paul.

As he played, Paul watched Emily swimming. Back and forth, short laps, an Olympic turn underwater in the deep end. Her nude white behind bopped to the surface. Her persistence made him sleepy.

Paul lay down in the bedroom. It was a hole-in-the-wall, really, just a double bed and an oak bureau. Through partially closed venetian blinds he watched Emily get out of the pool. He lay on his stomach and closed his eyes.

"You're awake," Emily said from the doorway.

"Barely," he said.

"So what's new? Talk to me."

"Sh-sh."

"Please?"

Emily wrapped a towel around herself and sat next to Paul on the bed.

He turned to her.

"Let's go into town for dinner tonight," she said.

Paul took her hand and held it in his.

"Whaddaya say?"

"If you'd like," Paul told her. "What time is it?"

"About five. I really like this place. We could have done worse."

"You're a sweetheart," Paul said.

They carried Franklin, Emily bleeding heavily from a gash in her head.

"October first everything is supposed to come alive in town. You want to go dancing?"

" 'I won't dance, don't ask me,' " Paul said.

" 'When you dance you're charming and you're gentle.' "

" ' 'Specially when I do the Continental.' "

They carried Franklin over a mile.

"Maybe I should get pregnant."

"You're a schmuck."

"Why do you say that?"

"Just because."

They called Maggie Furth from a phone booth.

"Do my breasts look any larger to you? Here, look."

"Don't be so clinical."

"Do they look any larger, is what I'd like to know."

Not a bruise on Franklin. Heart attack. Period.

"Why should they be larger?"

"There's a rumor that the desert sun makes breasts larger."

"Darker."

"That must be it."

Four stitches for Emily.

"A man woke up one day to find he had five penises," Emily said.

"Is this a true story?"

"It's the truth, I swear it."

"Go on."

"So he went to the doctor, and the doctor was amazed."

"I'll bet."

"So the doctor asked how the guy's underpants fit."

"Like a glove, right?"

"Shit. You ruin everything."

They stored Franklin's belongings. They arranged for Franklin's cremation.

"You wanna take a drive?"

"I wanna take a shower," Emily said.

"I'll take a drive, *you* shower. *I'll* wash up, *you* save France."

"Can we go out tonight?"

"Yes. I'll scout around." Paul sat up. Emily moved into his arms. They held each other. Emily kissed him. "Please, no," he said.

Franklin's fortune: seven thousand, one hundred and thirty dollars. No will had been found, no hidden trust funds, no insurance policies, nothing spectacular under the rug. Only this: a novel called The Heat of the Day, *by Elizabeth Bowen, with an inscription in green ink: "To F, with all of my love in all of my heart." And the signature, in letters slightly larger: Lillian Francis Avakian.*

Paul drove west into the sun. The late afternoon was hot and bone-dry. The mountains loomed large directly in front of

him. He imagined himself gathering such speed that he would
forge through them, as they fell over him like waves. He would
emerge at the ocean, between San Diego and Los Angeles, the
car covered with gravel and dust. Children would gather. How
did he do it? Where had he come from? He had come, he would
tell them, from a retreat. They would ask what a retreat was. He
would tell them that a retreat was where you went when you
felt goofy and sad. The wire services would pick up the story.
"Radio and television personality Paul Kramer successfully drove
beneath the San Jacinto Mountains today from Palm Springs to
Balboa. Mr. Kramer made the trip in under two hours in a 1974
Dodge Dart. When asked how he had achieved the impossible,
Kramer, well-known in New York City and surrounding areas,
replied: 'It was God's will.' Kramer, a tall, dark-haired man of
thirty-two, is said to be the first man ever to drive successfully
under any mountain range in the Western Hemisphere. When
asked about his plans, the radio and television personality
replied: 'To be with Emily and see what happens.' Kramer then
drove away, leaving a crowd of a hundred or more onlookers
behind. The Emily referred to by Kramer has yet to be
identified, but a source close to a TV outlet in New York, where
Kramer was employed for several years, has suggested that Mr.
Kramer was referring to the American poet Emily Dickinson,
who died in 1886."

Relationships and will. Franklin's words in the garden. He
had left no will. He hadn't had the will. Ends are beginnings
and beginnings are ends. Will he or won't he? We will see.

And to my son, Paul, I leave seven thousand one hundred
and thirty dollars. And I leave, to my son, Paul, odds and ends.

Sandi to the Dorado to the yellow VW to Emily Keller to
Venice, California, to Maggie Furth and Walter Decker to
Franklin's garden to the Pacific Coast Highway to El Besame
Mucho to Encinal Drive. The villain was here now, driving up
Indian Road in Palm Springs near sunset of an October first,

with a straight Scotch and a glass of beer in mind. How frivolous and shameful a man he was. Paul had no trouble with the word "man." He spoke it out loud in the car. A *man* murders his father, not the child, not the indolent Dodger fan. A full-fledged grownup, whose wanderings end in Encinal Drive on the dark side of the fucking moon. The child Paul watches his mother die and gets it on the air first thing in the morning. The child Paul gives Sandi a buzz and plugs her every orifice with his exaggerated sexuality, leaving her, finally, in Robinson's department store, hearing himself called "buster," and glad to be rid of her.

The child Paul falls for an unstable beauty named Emily. And the child grows. The *man* is not too happy with pink dresses, the *man* sits in the back of the car on the dark side of the moon, a deadly architect, pulling himself out of a wreck without a scratch, to hold his father in his arms by the side of the road. "No chance," Emily had said. Paul held on to his father. And then—what was it Emily had told him then? It was: "We've lost him." Until now, a month after the fact, coasting through a resort town looking for a bar, those words had hidden themselves away. They were the words that had reduced the man's exaggerated sexuality to ashes. In September Emily comforted him. He held her in return, he patted her back and shoulders. Pat pat. Not one orifice did he approach, not one kiss did he surrender. How clear it was to him now: "We've lost him," had shut the door.

Paul wasn't sure if he wished to punish Emily Keller, or make amends, or incarcerate himself voluntarily in some tumultuous institution for the criminally inclined, a gray building in a silent land such as this, with devastating heat, diminished in no way by the little fans in the corners of the rooms. He would be placed in a compartment reserved for the patricidal. In this compartment, on a mattress on the floor, he would be buggered and beaten. Forced to eat his own shit, he would vomit and lie with eyelids taped open on a brick floor so hot that the skin of his back would sizzle and curl.

In a little bar on Amado, Paul had a double Black and White and a Coor's chaser. He was back in the car in ten minutes with the firm conviction that he would not live through the night; his end-of-the-line was at hand. He might as well call Emily and tell her that a body malfunction was just around his corner. He knew it; there was nothing she could do. He would be rather cheerful about it, in fact. He would tell her that he was at peace with himself, and that he loved her.

Paul felt invigorated and amused. He had no one, no one to report to. His actions could no longer be parentally traced. Never again would he imagine his activities through his father's eyes. He was now entirely his own witness, his own best judge of character. His delinquency was a private matter. He would do as he pleased. He was owed this privilege. Strictly *entre nous*, fuck 'em.

Driving south on Palm Canyon Drive, Paul spotted a beautiful woman in a halter and shorts who was standing, reading the Los Angeles *Times*. She was richly tanned and quite thin. Her calves suggested she danced. What Paul found erotic about her was the energy with which she was reading. Her body was taut, perhaps about to spring forward into some compelling choreography. The words in the paper were engrossing her. What she might do next was anybody's guess. Her long black hair obscured much of her face. She was poised, ready to act on the information she was gathering.

Paul stopped in the middle of Palm Canyon Drive to await the verdict. At that moment his was the only car in the block, and he determined to linger and watch. He had no designs on the woman, no intention of signaling to her or securing her. He only wanted to see more of her, to have one good look at her eyes. She glanced up, feeling him frozen on the avenue. She was younger than Paul had expected, and disappointingly uninformed. There was a cheap arrogance to the cut of her jaw, and empty indignation in her pose. She was clearly without wisdom, without an understanding of what was possible. Her eyes betrayed a lazy mind and a stingy heart. She tossed her hair and turned her back to him.

Angrily, Paul drove off. The lazy mind and stingy heart had knocked the whimsy from him, had dispersed his rationales. He found that he was left with a profound despair, and an engulfing rage. He was impotent out here in the desert. He was unable to act on his own behalf. He found Emily Keller repulsive. He saw himself as an aging idiot, self-absorbed, absurdly devious. He would place no call to Emily to announce the conclusion of his life. How laughable a figure he was, entertaining his end-of-the-line in an empty auditorium, with no enraptured crowd to manipulate, and no ground to be gained.

Paul drove slowly into the desert, the sun setting behind the mountains in his rearview mirror. A jet plane, set to land a quarter of a mile north, swooped low above his car. Paul watched it touch the earth, anticipating a ball of fire. When no ball of fire leaped into the sky, when it was clear that the plane was safely down, Paul pulled to the side of the road. He turned off the ignition and stared ahead into the dark folds of the desert. He made fists of his hands. He held the fists to his eyes. After a while, he covered his face with his open hands, and cried.

"Maggie and Walter are going to be down here at the end of the week," Emily told him.

Paul didn't answer. He lay on the bed, reading. He had paid for a library card and had taken books home. He held John Cheever between his eyes and Emily's.

"They want to have a cookout. Where's Deep Well?"

"It's a section of Palm Springs," Paul said, from behind his book.

"That's where Walter's house is."

Paul turned a page.

"Do you want any breakfast?" Emily asked. She was dressed in shorts and a tight blue tee shirt.

"No thanks," Paul said.

"I'm going to take a bike ride. Am I crazy, or is it humid?"

"They're tracking some kind of hurricane in Mexico," Paul said. He rested the book face down on his chest. "That's where the humidity's probably coming from. I didn't know there were hurricanes out here." He smiled at Emily. He felt removed from her, and drawn to her. He wanted her ill at ease and subservient. He was afraid that he would push her too far, that she would see through him, that she would abandon him.

"Do you want any juice?" She stood in the doorway and waited for his reply. She was all business. Juice, or what? It's the middle of October and I've got a lot to do.

Their lack of physical contact was preying on them. Their nudity had lost its charge.

"Thank you, yes." Paul knew to accept this juice of hers. He would push her only so far, and draw her back with his need.

Emily sat beside him on the bed as he sipped apple cider.

"Does it sound like a good idea, Maggie and Walter? I'd like to get out of here and *see* people. I don't care who they are, you know?" Emily spoke quietly, seriously.

"Sure. When?"

"Friday, Saturday. One of those evenings."

"He's such an asshole." Paul let out a little laugh to shield Emily from a surge of anger.

"Maybe we'll make a few bucks, who knows?" she said.

"It's *your* turn."

"We'll see."

"Emily," Paul whispered.

"I'm with you."

"I'm sorry."

"I know."

"This is just now."

"I know."

"I feel sedentary."

"I was thinking about something," Emily said. "I was think-ing that maybe we ought to take some acid together."

"That mushroom stuff?"

"That's all we've got."

"Doesn't it tend to emphasize what you don't want empha-sized?"

"You can always move away. You can always move on to other things. You're not trapped in one spot." Emily rested her hand on his thigh.

"Let's think about it. I like the idea." Paul put his hand on hers.

"I won't pressure you. Honest."

"We'll pick our time."

"Could I ask you something?" Emily leaned forward a lit-tle.

"Of course."

"Have you masturbated in this house?" There was a twin-kle in her eye.

"I haven't," Paul replied. "But I saw you on the grass," he added.

"No shit." Emily blushed. It was her first outstanding blush since their first dinner together.

"It was nice to watch."

"I didn't know." She dropped her eyes.

"I was discreet."

"Too little, too late, turkey."

"*You* should talk."

"I am."

"We'll get it together. Not to worry." Paul squeezed her hand.

"This looks like a good spot," Emily said, lifting her eyes to his. "Did you bring the salt and pepper for the hard-boiled eggs? I mean, this is a good spot, isn't it? Away from the others?"

"Where are we?"

"In a field."

"Okay. I got everything. Including the Milky Ways."

"Do you think we're missed?"

"They're all playing softball. Can I touch you down there?"

"Maybe."

"You promised."

"I'll have to think about it."

"I touched your sister down there."

"I don't have a sister."

"Melanie's not your sister?"

"This isn't working." Emily withdrew her hand.

"Sweetheart, it's all right. At least we tried." Paul pulled her hand to his lips. He blamed himself for the failure. Even at something so natural for them, he was impotent.

"All we need is our rhythm. We'll find it. I know it." Emily caressed his cheek, sensing his futility. "You wait. We haven't even started. We have the rock bottom and the top of the mountain ahead of us."

"You and I will never settle down at the equator, you know that?"

"I do," Emily said.

"That may spell goodnight, folks." Paul looked her straight in the eye.

"Not without a fight," Emily said.

"There are times when I actually think I'm losing control," Paul said.

"I think that that has a great deal to do with anger," Emily said.

They were watching the sunrise from bed. Emily had held him, had touched him. She had felt his body tense and slowly pull away.

"Without you, I don't know what," Paul said.

"Have you thought about going east?" Emily lit a cigarette. After Paul slid from her arms, she had covered herself in a robe.

"You don't get work just like that."

"Make a few calls."

"I have no energy."

"You're babying yourself."

"Come on."

"True."

They were silent.

In a while Paul said: "You want to face a New York winter?"

"I don't much care. I'd like to finish my book is all I know." Emily rested her ashtray on the bed between them.

"There's beer, right?"

"You drink more beer in the night than . . ."

"Than who?"

"Than Walker Percy."

"How do you know?"

"I had an affair with Walker Percy."

"Bullshit."

"Ask me where."

"Where? Or when?"

"Who knows."

"So it's bullshit."

"Not necessarily."

"Where?"

"New Orleans."

"You've never even *been* to New Orleans." Paul gave her a knuckle punch on the arm.

"That's how much *you* know."

"You probably saw a lot of movies with him."

"He's one of the last gentlemen."

"Do you want anything?" Paul left the bed for the kitchen. Emily didn't answer.

"It's true," Paul said, returning to bed with a can of beer. "I associate the taste of beer with early morning."

"I heard on the radio that the storm is moving inland toward Phoenix, and that we might get the edge of it Saturday night and Sunday."

"A good time for tripping, maybe?" Paul turned to look at her in the morning's dim light.

"Wow! Fabulous," Emily said, with a big smile.

"I'm not promising anything."

"What are you, the boss?" Emily put the cigarette out and lit another.

"I'm not the boss," Paul said gently.

"My vote is yes."

"I miss my father," Paul said, in something just above a whisper.

Emily didn't say anything.

"I'm frightened," Paul said.

"I know," Emily said.

"It never occurs to you that that kind of thing will happen within your own experience."

"You know, Paul, I think that most of us are only tuned in to distant stations where all kinds of things are happening to other people. We listen through the static to their heartbreaks as if we were in some well-protected receiving chamber. Do you know what we overlook? That *we* are distant stations for anyone else who comes across *our* transmissions through *our* static. It's all one network; we're all affiliates of the same conglomerate without seeing. We'll go on forever making believe that locally everything is okay; it's just the other folks who've got the bad end of the deal."

"It's the safety of it all. I'm not so sure it's such a terrible thing. We all need armor of one kind or another," Paul said.

"That's the thing," she said earnestly. "I'd like to risk it without armor." She crushed another cigarette in the ashtray.

"Dangerous stuff," Paul said.

"I don't know any other solution," Emily said. "Please. Believe me."

CHAPTER TWELVE

"We've got a deal," Decker said.

"Everybody's real happy," Maggie said.

"What was it like in New York?" Paul asked Decker.

"Pouring rain," Decker said.

They were barbecuing steaks in Decker's back yard. A large swimming pool was surrounded by green Astro turf.

"We'll shoot in New York in late winter. We will make, I do believe, a work of art." Decker, in a polka-dot apron and tennis clothes, poked at the sizzling meat with the corner of a spatula.

"Walter has high hopes," Maggie said.

"Oops, there goes another rubber-tree plant," Decker sang. He was well into a third drink so early in the evening.

Paul received a joint from Emily, and considered Decker's

greeting an hour earlier. "Paul, my good man, I am most sorry," he had said, in a foyer bursting with plastic yellow and red roses.

Paul zeroed in on "good man." Was there any truth to this at all? Good man. A man of goodness, beneficent, concerned for others, a decent guy, a sweetheart. Paul didn't imagine himself as a sweetheart. Paul came first, he knew. Beneficent, yes, but only under reward signs. And yet again, was this the absolute case? Not absolutely, no, Paul decided, as he watched Decker fumble with the steaks.

"Margaret has two roles," Decker was saying, as Paul rejoined him. "Sisters, one twelve years older than the other, who fall in love with the same man."

"Walter flew in from New York today," Maggie said, affectionately.

"My business acumen is, shall we say, intriguingly well-developed." Decker tapped his temple.

"Two Maggies for the price of one," Emily said. "How enticing."

"Come now," Maggie said.

Come now. How nice, Paul thought. The sweetest of protestations, Victorian, dressed to the chin, sitting on the grass beneath one of Franklin's parasols. Come now.

"Where's Christina?" Paul asked Maggie.

"She's home."

"Do you leave her alone?"

"She's a grownup," Maggie replied, with a nice warm smile.

"Tell her I said hello, will you?"

"I'll give her your love. How's that?"

"She's a fine child," Paul said.

"Thank you," Maggie said.

Paul imagined Christina and Debbie Ross together, each wearing earphones, listening to Loggins and Messina as they sat on the floor with their legs crossed, sharing a joint and a bowl of grapes. All grown up.

"Strictly *entre nous,* we've got ourselves quite a meal," Decker said.

They were to eat poolside on Astro turf from a wobbly round metal table under an orange umbrella.

"How about glasses?" Paul said, checking out the table.

"I'd like another Bourbon and soda, if you wouldn't mind too much," Decker said to Paul.

"I'll make you the best drink you ever had," Paul said.

The whole house was carpeted in light green. Paintings of deer and horses hung on the walls. The couches were off-white velvet. On the coffee table: a copy of Mona Nine's one book, *Better Backgammon.*

Paul checked out the three bedrooms. More deer, more horses, and an autographed photo of Joe Namath on the night table near Decker's side of a king-size double bed. A New York Yankee 1974 schedule was Scotch-taped to the bathroom wall near the toilet. In the top right-hand bureau drawer, amidst balls of thick wool winter socks and white silk handkerchiefs covered with little WDs, Paul found currency, loose currency, ten thousand dollars at the very least. Under jockey shorts in the top left-hand bureau drawer, a bulk of hundred-dollar bills was held fast by a gold money clip, inscribed in print: FAITH IN FURTH.

"It's so icky tonight," Maggie said, sipping iced tea at the table.

"We may not see much of the storm, or so they say," Emily told the group. "It's going across Arizona. If it rains here, it'll be late tonight or tomorrow morning."

"Hurricane Celia," Paul said.

"What if the storm shifts?" Decker asked Emily, wiping his hands on his apron.

"Then, I don't know then," Emily said.

"I think, my dear, we'd be in for it," Decker said. He got up, and went into the house for another drink.

"Walter has jet fatigue," Maggie said. "He's been working so hard."

"If it's going to rain all weekend, you shouldn't have come down," Emily said. "This humidity is just awful."

"Walter wanted to come down. He loves the desert."

"But to be locked up indoors."

"Walter watches the footballers," Maggie said, eating the skin of a baked potato with her hands. "He bets. He watches and he bets."

"Does he bet heavily?" Paul asked.

"All I know is, he's on the phone all the time. Minus four and a half, plus two. That's all I hear."

"You never hear the dollars and cents?"

"I think he's got that in some code," Maggie said, most cheerfully. "Anyway, it's not my business."

Paul thought: faith in Furth.

They watched the eleven o'clock news. The Coachella Valley would catch more of Celia than expected. Winds to seventy miles an hour, heavy rain. Fasten down the hatches. Stay indoors. Don't drive. The winds would pick up a little before dawn. The storm would be out of effective range by late afternoon. Have a pleasant day; if not weatherwise, then otherwise.

"Interesting," Emily said.

"Walter's dead asleep," Maggie said.

Indeed, Decker was out of it, overcome by his jet fatigue and his Bourbons and sodas. He had quieted down after dinner, sitting in front of a lively Billy Graham. "This guy's no dummy," Decker had pointed out. "He knows where the bucks are. He and Rufus could have made a deal. And I mean a *deal*."

Now he was asleep in his tennis outfit and bare feet. His toenails, uncut, appeared to Paul prehensile. How was it possible to jam those feet with those nails into shoes?

"Come on, my darling," Maggie said, leaning down to kiss Decker. "Let's get you to bed."

"Whaddaya say?" Paul asked Emily. "Are we out of here?"

"Let's stay," Emily replied. "Let's stay for a while."

Maggie walked Decker carefully down the hall, whispering to him, kissing his cheek. Paul could feel himself in his father's arms in the middle of the night. To the bathroom. Paul could feel his father's strength. Daddy in the dark. Daddy.

"Do you go out a lot? With different people?" Paul asked Maggie when the three of them had long been settled in with their third joint of the night.

"Not a great deal," Maggie said. "Sometimes," she added, after thinking it over.

"Are you in touch with Christina's father?"

"Not a word," Maggie said. "I was real young. The whole business of photography was alluring."

Paul thought how incongruous a word "alluring" was out of Maggie Furth. Her use of it appealed to him. He knew that he rooted for Maggie, not so much to justify her presence in Emily's life—although, God knows, that seed was in the ground —but to magnify for himself her pockets of clarity, her almost involuntary spasms of depth. Her clean white skin and large hazel eyes peering out of words like "alluring" were dazzling and poignant. If Maggie was to be around with any degree of regularity, Paul needed, at the very least, to be occasionally moved.

"It seems that Walter means business," Emily said to Maggie.

"He's a real wonderful man," Maggie said. "He got the whole package together. He found the script on his own, he cooked up a distribution deal in New York. He gave me ten points. Can you imagine?"

"Net or gross?" Paul asked.

"Gee," Maggie said, puzzled.

"He's generous, is what Maggie's telling us," Emily said.

"Emily knows me very well," Maggie said, smiling warmly at her friend.

"But you know me, too," Emily said.

"When did you guys meet?" Paul asked, most friendly, wanting to know all about them, feeling that somehow he had caused a small bit of damage, and now wishing only to set things right.

"Do you know when it was?" Maggie said to Emily. "It was that Christmas on Nicholas Beach Road. Joshua and Andre had that long discussion about—I don't remember what about. It was that night."

"Who's Andre?" Paul asked.

"A friend," Maggie answered.

"Maggie's buddy," Emily said.

"Remember you were dancing? I thought, 'Wow!' "

"And I thought, 'Maggie Furth is a beauty.' "

"Thank you," Maggie said.

Emily got up and went into the kitchen, returning with a tall glass of chocolate milk. She had been sitting next to Paul on one of the velvet couches, and now she slid in next to Maggie, across from him.

"Here you go," Emily said, holding the glass for Maggie, tipping the glass as Maggie drank.

"How richly good," Maggie said, smiling at Emily with a brown mustache.

Paul felt it coming. It was just a matter of Emily leaning close to Maggie.

"Here," Emily said. A nice kiss of the upper lip. Emily's tongue cleared the mustache away. And then a little peck of a kiss on the lips; just a little there-you-go-it's-all-clean kiss.

"More," Paul said, with an innocent smile.

"He wants more," Emily said. "Shall we give him what he wants?"

"Not for him," Maggie whispered. "For us."

Paul said: "Paul doesn't care whose name is written on the package."

It was Emily's kiss all the way. She closed her eyes, Maggie followed. She opened her mouth a bit, Maggie followed. It was Emily's running time, about a minute. It was Emily's follow-through, kisses on the cheek, on the forehead, on the nose, and another kiss on the lips, this time with more passion.

"Now *that's* entertainment," Paul said softly, when the women's lips drew apart.

Emily whispered something to Maggie. Maggie's eyes did not betray the secret.

"Wait," Maggie said. She left the couch and crossed the living room. Carefully, she closed the door to the hall, shielding Decker.

Emily rose, and walked with Maggie to the patio, touching Paul's shoulder as she passed him.

He waited until they were by the pool and undressed, then moved outside and sank quietly into a chaise longue.

The wind had picked up. The orange umbrella was fluttering above the metal table on the Astro turf. The sultry night air hung heavily in the yard. Paul thought for a second of scampering into Decker's room for a handful of hundred-dollar bills. Instead, he stayed where he was. He thought: an embarrassment of riches.

Emily and Maggie slipped into the pool. They talked in low voices. Emily laughed, and Maggie followed with a rich chuckle. More whispering into Maggie's ear in shallow water. Another rich chuckle from Maggie.

They put their arms around each other and kissed, caressing each other's backs.

In a while, Emily slithered away. Paul heard her say, "Come on."

They swam side by side to the deep end. Emily reached up

to the diving board and held onto it, dangled from it with both hands, her back to Paul.

Maggie, with effort—little unsuccessful leaps, and splashes back down into the water—finally made it and held on tightly, less gracefully than Emily, facing her.

They moved toward each other, Maggie partially obscured from Paul's view by Emily's body.

Their breasts touched. They swayed, whispering, their bellies pushed together.

Maggie put her legs around Emily. Their mouths joined in another kiss, their most passionate and accessible.

It occurred to Paul to masturbate right then and there, standing on the diving board above them.

Emily said to Maggie: "Come on."

Maggie said to Emily: "One, two, three."

They dropped into the water at the same moment.

They floated on their backs into the shallow end, so that they were able to stand in waist-high water, and kiss, and touch each other's breasts.

Paul, in a haze of marijuana, imagined his father next to him, sitting with legs crossed in one of the canvas chairs from his garden.

"Notice how they shine in the dark," Paul said.

"They fit together perfectly," Franklin said.

"This is a most enjoyable occasion," Paul told his father.

"I quite agree," Franklin said. "Esthetically, it's pleasing."

"Have I told you lately that I love you?" Paul asked.

"I know you do, and I appreciate it," Franklin said.

"And that I miss you?"

"It's too rare and lovely an evening to foul up with sentiment."

To Paul's surprise, the sharing of the occasion with Franklin was not at all uncomfortable. Finally the moment had arrived for father and son to acknowledge sex, to watch it as companions. The parasols were down. There was total nudity onstage. The facts of life.

Emily and Maggie, their bodies sleek and wet, lay on the Astro turf directly in front of Paul. They lay on their sides, holding each other, kissing each other's mouths.

In a while, Emily turned her face to Paul. "Tell us what to do," she said. "We need your guidance."

"You're both so beautiful."

"Thank you," Maggie said.

"Please tell us what to do," Emily repeated. "We're virgins."

"Maggie, lie on your back," Paul said, gently.

Maggie didn't hesitate. She lay on her back, her head resting in her hands.

"Emmy, straddle her," Paul said, a little more crisply.

"Emmy, run your hands down her body. Her arms, her neck, her breasts. Down to her toes."

Emily did as she was told, caressing Maggie, running her palm lightly over her pubic hair, and down her legs. Emily, at Maggie's feet, kissed them, massaged them.

"Emmy, lie directly on top of her. Kiss her."

Maggie's arms came down to hold Emily's body. They were both breathing quite heavily, licking each other's faces, sucking and biting each other's ears.

Paul fell silent. They were gone from him now, flown away into each other. Paul wondered idly if they would come sooner on Astro turf than on real grass.

Emily and Maggie gravitated easily to each other's genitals. They made love with abandon, seeking out each other with their mouths.

They stayed together a long time, Emily's rectum spread lavishly before Paul, only a few feet away. He could see Maggie's tongue jabbing at Emily's vagina.

Again, his father joined him.

"I think that that young lady, Maggie, is going to have an orgasm," Franklin said.

"Only the fifth recorded orgasm on Astro turf," Paul said.

"Is that so?" Franklin said.

"Watch," Paul said.

There were tears in Maggie's eyes when she came. She came quietly, with an "Emily," spoken softly to Emily's clitoris.

Slowly Emily withdrew, and lay on her side next to Maggie, touching Maggie's breasts tenderly.

"Wait here," Paul said to Franklin.

He went to Maggie and knelt beside her. He leaned down and kissed her eyes. "You are a glorious girl," he told her.

Maggie smiled. She beckoned to him with her lips. He kissed her. He felt Emily's hand slip into his. He held it tightly. Her touch thrilled him. He felt serene and clear-headed. He looked to the patio for his father. "Yes," he said to Emily. "God, oh God, yes," he said into the rain, that only a moment before had begun to fall.

Emily created two little piles of chopped mushroom, moving bits and pieces around with a butter knife. She had found a pewter serving dish that Valerie Maxwell had wrapped in the sports pages of *The Daily Enterprise,* and had stored in a small suitcase under the bed. "It's nice to have a special kind of surface for it," Emily said.

"You gave me more than you," Paul said, poking at his portion with a fingertip.

"They're exactly the same," Emily said. "You have that chunk there that makes it look like more."

"So this is it," Paul said. "What's to become of us?"

"You'll see," Emily said, with a smile.

"Let's just wait a little," Paul said.

They lay on the bed and listened to the rain.

Moments after returning from Decker's house they had stripped off their clothes and had gone after each other voraciously, churning up the dust of Paul's apathy, sweeping it off the bed, and away. "Careful of my head," Emily had been forced to say, in the face of Paul's frenzy.

He had sodomized her energetically, holding her hips securely.

"Easy does it," she had said. "There. Right like that."

"Motherfucker," Paul had whispered, his chest pressed to her back, his lips at her ear.

Suddenly, he had withdrawn. He had knelt above her for a moment, and had flipped her over on her back. Then he had entered her gently.

They had set a slow rhythm, natural for them, and had kept it going, holding each other through their easy conclusions, and beyond, into Paul's tears. "Lover," Emily had said, wiping his tears away with her hand.

Now, dressed again, they lay with their bare feet touching and their eyes wide open in the dark, the candle on the piano in the living room casting only the faintest light into the bedroom.

"How about in fifteen minutes we do it," Paul said.

"What time did we eat?" Emily asked.

"Eight-thirty."

"Six and a half hours ago. It's better after twelve hours without food."

"Do you get nauseous?"

"No."

"Promise?"

"Promise."

They didn't speak for a while; the sound of the rain held them in silence.

"You were very accomplished with Maggie," Paul said, at last.

"How nice of you," Emily said.

"How did you know what to do?"

"You told me."

"I mean the other stuff."

"A woman knows what a woman likes."

"Tell me true: first time?" Paul faced her in the dark.

"No," Emily replied.

"You mean with Maggie?"

"First time with Maggie."

"Who else?"

"No one special."

"Do you like it?"

"I liked it tonight, but I hadn't expected to."

"I see," Paul said.

"Come on, let's take it." Emily sat up.

"You're very accomplished at certain items," Paul said, still lying there. "You probably think this song is about you."

" 'Gavotte' is a nice word in that song," Emily said, standing by the side of the bed.

"Bring it all in here. The stuff, the candle, everything." Paul gathered three pillows together and pushed them behind his back. He slid into a half-sitting position.

In a little while Emily returned with a tray. She put the candle on the night table, and the tray between them on the bed. "Have a sip of orange juice afterward to kill the taste," she told Paul, a bit of the teacher in her voice.

"Does it taste shitty?" he asked, poking at the mushroom again.

"It's not caviar," Emily said.

A spoon for Paul, a spoon for Emily.

It took them a minute or two to clean the pewter serving dish.

"Unpleasant stuff," Paul said.

"Juice," Emily told him.

"Okay. Now what?" Paul asked, when the tray was gone,

and they lay together again, the candlelight flickering in the tiny room.

"We just hang out," Emily said.

"No, I mean, I just feel—I feel better than in a long time."

Emily didn't reply.

"I loved making love. You set everything up, didn't you," Paul said.

"Not necessarily."

"Necessarily."

No reply from Emily.

"Guess what Decker's got in that house," Paul said.

"Tell me what he's got," Emily said. She took his hand in hers.

"Sweetheart, what do you think?"

"I think money," Emily said.

"That's right. Cash. Staggering."

"Where?"

"In the bureau in the bedroom. And I didn't look any further."

"Wouldn't it be fun," Emily said, with a little laugh.

"We'd be thrown in the clink, in fucking *Indio,* or somewhere."

"Just a thought," Emily said.

In a while, Paul got up and went to the window. "The wind," he said. "What time is it?"

"Near four," Emily said, checking her watch by the candle on the night table. "It's been an hour."

"Do you think this is stupid? Taking acid in the middle of the night during a hurricane? We need our faculties intact."

"Our faculties will be fine. So will the students."

"What gall you have, professor," Paul said, pulling the blinds all the way up.

"This is your trip," Emily told him, quietly. "This is for you."

"You've been more than generous today," Paul said, returning to bed.

"Do you want any music?" she asked.

"As a matter of fact . . ."

"Would you like a foot massage?"

"I'm feeling like, in a very good pot-high. Couldn't that be just the resurrection of the grass at Maggie's?"

"How about some music? We have about forty cassettes."

"You program," Paul said, lying down on the spot she vacated on the bed.

Emily went into the kitchen and took the cassette machine from the top of the refrigerator. She set it on the floor of the bedroom.

"I'm feeling good," Paul told her.

"Shostakovich?" Emily asked.

"No Russians," Paul said.

"Wagner overtures?"

"*Christ,* no."

"Just kidding."

"What else? I'm feeling a little spacey, you know that? Are you with me?" Paul folded his hands on his chest.

"I'm with you," Emily told him.

"What else?" he asked.

"Blue Eyes?"

"I think he'd disappoint me. Give me something sure-footed."

Emily found Mozart string quartets in the box of cassettes.

"I'm going under," Paul said. "Are you coming?"

"Everything is just fine, my love," Emily told him, soothingly.

"It's like deep grass."

Emily knelt on the floor by his feet.

"What's that?" Paul asked.

"Cold Cream. Relax."

"How long does the whole thing last?"

"We didn't take much."

"How long?"

"Six hours, tops."

"There's no anecdote?"

"Did you hear the one about Bill Cosby and the fried chicken? Or the night Alexander Butterfield showed up at—"

"*Antidote*, pea-brain."

"No antidote."

"We're stuck, then."

"Pretty nice country to be stuck in, I'd say." Emily squeezed his toes.

"The music is so nice. Ah, this feels good."

"Rainy night," Emily said.

"I can't keep my eyes closed," Paul said.

"You don't want to sleep," Emily told him.

"Will I lose control in all of this?"

"You can always move along. From any stop along the way, you can always move on. And I'm right with you." Emily caressed his ankles.

"But what about loss of control?"

"There'll be no loss of control," Emily assured him.

"Do you promise?"

"I promise."

They didn't talk for a few moments.

Paul focused on the rain. He imagined himself in his New York apartment, lying on his bed by himself, listening to a summer storm. He looked around the room, seeking out details. Easily, he discovered book titles: *The Cape Cod Lighter, Fancies and Goodnights, Witness* by Whittaker Chambers. Paul imagined Alger Hiss going door to door selling vacuum cleaners, or whatever they were. Could he himself endure two trials, the pokey for forty-four months, the vacuum cleaners, after FDR and top security and Courvoisier with Churchill?

Pumpkins, typewriters, guilt.

"Alger Hiss was guilty, Emmy. I'm telling you," Paul said, emphatically. "He'll go to his grave pursuing vindication, but I'm *telling* you he's guilty. I know it now."

"How'd you get there?" Emily asked.

"My room. My books. My mother always wondered about Hiss. She read everything there was to read, kind of like a Hiss freak. I'd forgotten that! My mother was a Hiss freak. My father would bring her everything. All the magazines and everything, so she had a large vocabulary on the subject, a good deal of shorthand stuff."

"What else is in your room?" Emily asked.

"What else is in my room. I have cork on a part of a wall. There's a picture of my father in the garden on Highpoint. I've got some notes up there. I think something to do with Jason Robards. And a snapshot of Michael Holland. You don't know him; he's my doctor and a friend. How much do you think I weigh?"

"I know how much you weigh," Emily said. She had finished with his feet, and now sat cross-legged on the floor by the cassette machine.

Paul shifted to his stomach, reversed himself on the bed, and lay with his feet on the pillows and his chin on his folded hands. "We've got to get a scale," he said.

"A hundred and eighty, right?"

"Around there. You know something? I feel a lot of energy. Like in my loins. It's not sex. It's something else." Paul bounced on the bed a few times.

"Maybe we'll go outside for a little," Emily said.

"Maybe in a while," Paul said.

"Do you want to be alone?" Emily asked.

"Why should I want to be alone?"

"Just for a little while. I'll go in the other room."

"Describe this house to me," Paul said.

"This house has a white front door, and it's on a dirt road called Palm Way. The address is 16 Palm Way. It's odd that the street is called Palm Way, because there are no palms. It's simply a little dirt road off the main drag that's also without palms." Emily lay back and rested her weight on her elbows.

"Go on," Paul said, looking down at her.

"It was built about thirty-five years ago by two nice people from northern California. They had a very good relationship. Valerie and Charles Maxwell. They liked botany, and developed and oversaw a botanical garden in the La Quinta area. Their home is essentially two rooms. One of them has a piano in it. It must have been a symbol to Charles Maxwell, a symbol of the life of an artist."

"Go on," Paul said.

"So," Emily said. "Imagine the years they spent here, in a dime-size bedroom with no furnishings, no embellishments, and no indication of sexuality. None. There's nothing sensual about the house. There's no turn-on in here. They were childless, my guess is by design. I think they were good and close friends mainly.

"And the back yard. Isn't that something? You'd think these people would be the last people on earth to build a swimming pool, but they did, maybe about ten years ago. A plain small rectangle, no stairs in the shallow end. Just a swimming hole, plunked down on a plot of land. A neat little lawn. No patio, no shade anywhere. It's kind of a mystery, isn't it?"

"Let's ask her sometime," Paul said.

"I don't want to know," Emily said, with a smile.

"Go on," Paul said.

"You want to know what the truth is? The truth is that the house is only a passageway. It's like a tunnel through which people pass on the way in and out of each other." Emily sat up again. "Are you okay?" she asked Paul.

"I'm okay," he replied.

Soon, Paul got up and went to the window.

"Do you want to go outside?" Emily asked.

"Yes. I got all this energy."

They stood in the back yard in their clothes, drenched by heavy rain. The wind tore at the orange trees, ripping fruit away.

"This is something," Paul said. "This'll flood the whole valley. They got no drainage system."

Standing by the pool holding Paul's hand, Emily said: "It's getting light."

"It's a lousy little pool, isn't it?" Paul said.

"You want a swim?" Emily asked.

"I don't, I don't think—"

"Take me for a swim," Emily said, in Temmy's voice, Temmy's raised voice, breaking in adolescence.

Paul, stunned, removed his hand from hers.

"What's the matter?" Emily said, naturally. "Cat got your tongue?"

She undressed, pulling off her wet clothing. She put her arms around him and kissed him. "Come on," she said. "I'm with you. All is well."

"I'm a little shaky," he told her.

"Can you hear Dylan?" she asked. "Listen."

Emily had put the cassette machine by the door, left open only a crack to protect against the rain.

> Temptation's page flies out the door,
> You follow, find yourself at war,
> Watch waterfalls of pity roar.

"You said I should program," Emily shouted into his ear.

"You fucker," he said. He moved away from her and took off his clothes.

He ran to the pool and dove.

He surfaced at Emily's belly.

Emily said: "We could be blown away, pool and all."

"Everything's *rocking* in here."

"'Watch waterfalls of pity roar!'" Emily shouted, laughing. "Jesus Jesus Jesus, everything is so light!"

"I want to run around," Paul said.

"Then run around," Emily said.

Paul got out of the pool and ran the length of the yard and back. He did it again, and a third and fourth time.

"That's *gorgeous!*" Emily yelled.

Out of breath, Paul knelt by the pool and held out his arms. "Here," he said.

Emily allowed herself to be hoisted out of the water.

Lying on her back on the grass, she closed her eyes to the rain.

Paul penetrated her immediately. "Just this," he said.

They lay perfectly still, with their arms around each other.

Paul sat alone on the floor in the corner of the living room. He was dressed in bathing trunks and a beige tennis shirt. He slipped his feet in and out of moccasins.

Emily was in the bedroom with the door closed.

"I'll be just fine, thank you very much," Paul had told her. "Go about your business."

"Don't eat anything," she had told him. "You won't like it."

"I will if I want to," he had said.

"That's *your* affair," Emily had said.

The word "affair" stuck with Paul. He looked it up. "Anything done or to be done" was first on the list. It was number six he was after: "An illicit amorous relationship." And as for "illicit": "Not permitted or authorized."

Authorized by whom? A panel of experts, licensed men and women with objective minds? Emily and Paul were *prohibito, prohibitino.* Not sanctioned. There you go. Sanctioned. The

Church prints up the license plates for extra-vehicular behavior. The Church authorizes relationships, permits carnal conduct only with those license plates pinned painfully to bare asses. Would the Church sanction the behavior of Paul Kramer and Emily Keller? What a laugh.

And yet. Paul felt a spiritual presence. The awesome rain in arid territory, the beauty of the mountains as they reached up at the end of each day to slowly pull the sun into their recesses. The arms of the mountains were thin and dark, reaching up into the sky with fragile fingers, many fragile fingers, surrounding the sun.

The ghastly Catholics roaming the land, their dopey Pope in pompous seclusion, had poisoned the entire evolutionary process with their moronic restrictions and absurd edicts. The fetus within a fourteen-year-old black girl on Wadsworth Avenue should, they proclaimed, remain where it was, and grow, and become born. The fourteen-year-old black girl should not be told of what the scientific community—now of course it's the medical community, we all know that—it's what they conceived that should be withheld from the black girl. A good word, "conceived." On target. Language was thrilling every now and then.

"Emmy?"

"What?"

"Would you come in here a second?"

"Are you okay?"

"I don't want to work. I feel myself working."

Emily came to him. "Nobody said you had to work. Just drop it."

"I'm cold."

Emily sat down beside him.

"Do you think we could be flooded?" Paul asked.

"The house? No." She slipped an arm through his.

"My mind is racing."

"Where?"

"I was thinking of my mother. We were on a lake."

"And?"

"It's not true," Paul said.

"What's not true?"

"The lake is true, but that's not where I was."

"What, then?"

"Catholics. My dislike of them." Paul laughed. "I can't be trusted, even with the simplest things. I just threw the lake at you as if you were chasing me through the building, and without breaking stride I flung a chair into the middle of the hallway to impede your progress."

"I have my own chairs, you know," Emily said.

"I was embarrassed by the flimsiness of my thinking. I got hung up on abortions and the Pope. I could have taken it a lot deeper, but I didn't want to work at it, so I called you in here. A lazy man's game if ever I saw one. Just this very conversation is work. I might send you out of the room on some crazed mission just to avoid the new work I've discovered. And then call you right back in when the going got thorny, all the while oblivious to what you needed. So there's a mass of selfishness going on, and laziness, and lying. I'm a raging shambles." Paul leaned over and kissed Emily's cheek.

"This is *your* trip," Emily said.

"What are you up to?" Paul asked.

"I'm up to page ninety-five."

"Have you come to the part where they meet the old man?"

"We don't have to read that far. He only assigned to page a hundred."

"I've read ahead."

"Lie."

"Then how would I know about the old man?"

"Because you talked to Billy Faulk, who's read the whole thing."

"I talked to him, but he didn't talk about the book."

"Then, what did you talk about? I'd like to know."

"We talked about the history test, and that's the God's honest truth."

"What did he say about the test?"

"That it's gonna be all essay."

"How does he know?"

"Because Mr. Garment told him."

"Why would he tell Faulk and not the whole class?"

"Because Garment is a homo."

"You think so?"

"I *know* so."

"How? How do you know?"

"I swore not to tell."

"Please?"

"He made a pass at Faulk."

"Garment made a pass at Faulk? Jesus, what did he do?"

"He tried to kiss him. It was on the lower field and no one was down there."

"What did Faulk do?"

"He got away. So, then, Garment had to tell him it was all essay, and *that's* what we were talking about."

"Ask me anything," Emily said.

"Now we're driving down to Agua Caliente, right?"

"Right."

"Now we're in the living room, right?"

"Right."

"It's eight in the morning, and there's a hurricane, and we've taken LSD."

"We have taken organic mushroom. LSD is a chemical."

"Emmy, but we've taken a drug."

"Ask me anything." Emily faced him.

"What do you want me to ask you?"

In Temmy's throaty coldness, Emily replied: "Ask me what I think of Tom Keller."

"Em?" Paul said.

"You heard me."

"What do you think of Tom Keller?" Paul said, actually making a question out of it.

"I don't think very highly of him."

"And why is that?" Paul asked.

"I think he's spineless."

"You know something," Paul said, "you and I have never really met before."

"We know of each other, that's for sure."

Emily's face was assuming an expression that Paul had never seen. Her eyes were narrowed and her brow was furrowed in what Paul felt to be self-defense. Her lips were slightly puckered, forming lines, almost scars of distrust above and below her mouth.

"Why do you think he's spineless?" Paul asked.

"Because he never took an unknown road, and never gave anyone a look at the truth."

"Many people don't."

"I'm not interested in those people. Only him."

"Would you say that you were friends with him?"

"We had to be a little less than hostile or we couldn't have survived. We spent a lot of time together. But friends? No."

"Did you ever feel helpless in your situation?" Paul asked.

"Ha, I wasn't ambulatory, you idiot. How would *you* feel under those conditions?"

"Frustrated," Paul replied.

Emily stood, and glared down at Paul.

"Did you see your situation as hopeless?" Paul asked, looking up at her.

"Did you know that I was just as tall as Tom Keller? Not too many people know that, so why should I expect *you* to? But it's true."

"What is your height?"

"Exactly six feet."

"No one is *exactly* six feet. Only Jesus."

"You ignorant wimp, that's utter nonsense."

"If anyone's an ignorant wimp, it's you. Look at you, so old now, and still embittered; still raking through the past, cutting Tom Keller down to size. What a waste." Paul looked away.

"If you had gone through what I went through, you wouldn't be so sharp-tongued."

"Why didn't you make friends with the *girl*? At least you would have had somebody—"

"She was nothing but trouble. She was spoiled. She schemed against me."

"She was a kid."

"She had her father's ear. There was no trusting her with anything. She would tell him anything to gain favor over me. She would make up lies, not only about me, but about everybody. She would always get what she wanted. To suggest that I should have been friends with her is utterly ludicrous. She could build trouble out of a deck of cards, a ribbon, a comb, anything, anything at all. It seemed that it would become her life's work. I told her that at the time, you know. I told her she was cruel, that she was sadistic. You don't make friends with a girl like that."

Paul didn't continue. He studied Emily's eyes.

The muscles in her face were beginning to relax.

"What do we do now?" he asked. "I'm all out of questions."

"For the moment," Emily replied.

"I don't know about that," he said, feeling a sharp surge of loneliness. "I feel shut out," he said.

"No need," she said, softly, coming to him, holding him.

"Emily, my hands are shaking."

"No need," she said. "You're the first one I've allowed . . ."

"Allowed?"

Emily didn't reply.

"Pain," Paul said, after a moment.

"Look at it out there," she said.

"You can't see through the rain."

"It'll subside," she said, drawing more closely to him.

"Decker and Maggie are stuck watching football."

"They're chartering a plane this evening, if the rain stops."

"Do you think they'll leave the house just as it is?" Paul asked, resting his arm on her shoulder.

"Good question. Why does the dirty work always fall to us?"

"I want to know something," Paul said.

"And what is that?" Emily turned her face to his.

"Your features became all different."

"Didn't I tell you that we took a drug?"

"Sweetheart, I know you know the truth."

"I'm not lying."

"Oh, Emmy," Paul said. He lay on the floor on his back. "I'm beginning to feel sleepy," he told her.

"We're safe and sound," Emily said, stroking his hair. "Before you realize it, the storm will have passed."

CHAPTER THIRTEEN

The skies cleared in late afternoon. Paul awoke from a deep sleep, thirsty for beer. The digital clock read eleven-thirty. Couldn't be right. The can of Coor's felt warm is his hand. A bottle of Diet Pepsi, a can of tomato juice, were barely cool in the refrigerator. No lights. No electricity in the house. Paul was pleased with this. He felt isolated, unthreatened.

The phone worked. He had hoped it wouldn't. The Dylan cassette was still in the battery machine. He switched to radio. Local news: no power from Indio to Banning Pass. Flooding in the valley. Palm Desert severely damaged by mud and rain. The following roads out: Date Palm Drive, Frank Sinatra Drive—flooding by Los Cocas at the White Water Channel—El Cielo, Monterey Avenue.

Emily was at the pool. Paul watched her from the bedroom window. She was writing in her journal, her feet dangling in the water. She was dressed in rolled-up jeans and the skin-colored leotard she had worn the first night he had come to her house. Paul remembered the crying baby in its mother's arms on Pacific Avenue; and the Oakland Raider tee shirt, the bridge across the canal and into Emily Keller's body, the bridge to Trancas, the bridge to Encinal Drive. If only that tee shirt had read TURN BACK PAUL. Would he have taken its warning to heart? Pardon me, he would have said to the woman with the crying baby. Pardon me, but I'm Paul. Why should I turn back? So you're Paul, eh? The woman would have stopped, the baby's crying would have stopped. Yes, I'm Paul. Well, turn back, Paul. You'll be far better off. Go home and take care of your father. Good day to you.

He dialed his father's number in Los Angeles. "The number you have reached, 475-1868, is not in service at this time."

He dialed Sandi Cummings. Another "Howdy" from the man who answered.

"This is Robert Miller of the Los Angeles Telephone Company," Paul said. "We're taking a survey to find out how many people use the telephone in each home in your area."

"You mean the people who make calls?" The man's voice was pleasant and unsuspecting.

"Precisely," Paul said.

"Well, in this particular apartment, only my wife and myself."

"Your wife?" Paul said.

"It's her phone."

"Our records show that she is employed by Robinson's, the department store."

"Right," said the man, sounding surprised.

"So it's just the two of you who use the phone?"

"Right."

"Thank you for being so cooperative."

"Mighty fine. Thank you."

Sandi was married. Paul, I'm married?

Paul lay on the bed. He wondered if Maggie and Decker were gone, if their house was available for a search, top to bottom. What could Emily and he reasonably expect to find? Decker's distribution of currency could yield God knows what. Perhaps zero; Maggie might have tidied things up. Unlikely, Paul thought. Unlikely unlikely unlikely. He saw himself as cold-blooded, uncaring, treacherous. He made a list of negatives: first of all, he was a thief, pure and simple; always had been a petty thief—a book here, a record there. But now the big time. Second: he cared nothing about Sandi Cummings or her marriage; the news of it had slipped through his mind as rapidly as it had been delivered. Third: a killer. Oh, yes, he knew by now that the facts absolved him, that he overdramatized the issue. And yet, from years ago, from Michael Holland in a Brandeis cafeteria: "There is no such thing as an accident."

And: he was out of work, he was nothing but a drifter, he was a sexual opportunist, a liar, a self-absorbed fantasizer, the insecure lover of a schizoid chickie under whose spell he was quite seriously entertaining a plan drawn entirely of illegality; breaking and entering. B and E. And taking. T.

"Do you think we really should do this?" he asked Emily by the pool.

"It's up to you," she said.

"I say let's skip it."

"If that's what you want."

"Whatcha been writing?"

"Gibberish."

"Can I see?"

"I'd rather not."

"We go to Decker's if you show me what you've got there." Paul gestured at her notebook.

"It's gibberish," Emily said. She handed him the notebook.

The truth was in nightmares, films shown on the inside of her eyelids, reel after reel of films of truth that she watched through thread-like veins. She peered through the spaces between the veins as one would peer through venetian blinds. She saw people walking around and talking together but she couldn't make out what they were saying or what the mood was. Her eyelids presented her with a translucency that prevented a clear view of the films. She had the feeling in the pit of her stomach that the films were sometimes being run backward. She never knew where she was when she came in. Endings, beginnings, she didn't know.

Paul looked up at Emily. "That's not gibberish," he said.

"If Ramon is open, we'll make it fine," Emily said, dropping her eyes.

"They say it's flooded by the high school, but it's passable."

"We'll wait till we get them on the phone in Trancas," Emily said.

"Why are we doing this?" Paul asked.

"Because we're a circus act," she replied.

"Are you all right?"

"Of course," Emily said.

"Could I ask you something?" Paul said.

"What?"

"Do you think it would be helpful in any way to talk with a doctor?" He reached out to touch her knee, but withdrew his hand at the last moment.

Emily looked him in the eye. "I don't want any interference," she said.

"It's not interference."

"I'll be the judge of that," she told him, coldly.

They didn't speak for a while.

"We'll have a good time, you'll see," Emily said, at last.

"That's not quite the whole consideration," Paul said.

"It's close enough, don't you think?"

At ten at night Emily reached Maggie. Had they had any trouble? No, just delay. They had flown into Burbank, the sunset had been terrific, Christina was watching television, Walter was at the Beverly Hills Hotel, Maggie was making spareribs, how was it down there in the desert?

"Say hello to Maggie for me," Paul said to Emily.

"Paul says hello," Emily said.

"Tell him a real nice hi," Maggie said.

At midnight they drove to Decker's house.

"They're unprepared for all this rain," Paul said, as they inched along Ramon Road. "This'll take days to clear up."

They had changed clothes in candlelight, assured by radio that electricity would be restored within six hours. They took a flashlight, and two pairs of Paul's socks for gloves.

"What should be our limit?" Paul asked Emily.

"Let's just see what's around," she said, tucking her legs beneath her on the front seat of the car, as Paul got them started.

The night had turned cool. A wind from the north had begun to blow. It would clear out the Coachella Valley and wipe away the last remnants of moist air. Paul could feel an eastern autumn, an October school night, an after-dinner walk with Franklin. These familiar and reassuring memories flooded his mind and made Emily a stranger. Her private despair was a gray and impenetrable country with demons in the trees. He had wandered inadvertently into forbidden territory, armed only with his own comic deceit, easy prey for her midnight ghosts.

"Turn here," Emily said, "and then right on Mesquite."

They drove in eerie blackness, the headlights their only guide. There were no street lights, no traffic lights, only an occasional flickering candle in a window. They were solitary travelers in the dark evening, moving slowly through much water. Their ominous destination, their own silence in the midst of their excursion, struck Paul as humiliating. The dreadful passing of the summer, the aimlessness of his ill-defined journeys, had finally led to this soggy evening in a empty desert.

"Let's park here," he said, a hundred yards from Decker's house.

"There's no power, therefore no alarms," Emily said. "Isn't that something?"

"You sound like a pro," Paul said.

They walked cautiously, avoiding huge puddles. The night was blacker and stiller than Paul had thought in the car. "Jesus," he whispered.

"What's our plan?" Emily asked, as they approached the house.

"I don't know," Paul said.

"We'll get in because they're careless."

Paul didn't answer.

Front door locked, back door locked. The Astro turf around the pool was slick with rain.

"Do you think he'd prosecute?" Paul asked, checking windows.

"No," Emily said.

"You sure?"

"Yes," Emily said.

"How come you're so sure?"

"Let's keep our voices down," she said.

"Emily, here. Here." Paul felt a stab of excitement at the discovery of an open pantry window.

"What do you know," Emily said.

"Should we put on the socks?" Paul asked.

"I don't see why we need them, really," Emily replied. "What are they going to do, fingerprint us?"

"You never know," Paul said.

When they were both in the pantry, Paul turned the flashlight on again.

They moved through the living room toward the master bedroom.

"What a hideous house," Emily said.

Paul went immediately to the bureau. "Look," he said, shining the light into Decker's socks.

Unlikely unlikely. Maggie hadn't tidied up.

Emily rummaged through the money, spreading it around in the drawer, gathering a rough estimate. "What do you think?" she said. "Well over ten grand."

They left it where it was.

There was nothing entangled with the shirts and tennis apparel in the other drawers but a copy of a magazine called *He and She,* and a handful of Polaroid photographs of Maggie in the nude: Maggie swimming in the nude, Maggie sunbathing in the nude, Maggie watching television in the nude. And Maggie eating in the nude.

"What's on her plate?" Paul asked.

"It looks like scrambled eggs, don't you think?"

"I'm keeping it," Paul said.

"Really?" Emily said, laughing. "Why not one of the more provocative ones?"

"This one is sweet. Just eating like that. Naked. I like it. It's mine forever." Paul slipped the photo into a back pocket of his jeans.

On the night table by the picture of Joe Namath lay Decker's wallet. It bounced into the flashlight's beam, and riveted Paul to his spot on the carpet.

"Christ," he said. "He would never leave it. He'd never
. . ."

"Hello?" Emily said at once, loud and clear. "Anybody
home?"

Silence.

"Anybody home?" Emily repeated.

Again, silence.

"I don't get it," Paul said. "Hold this," he said to Emily,
handing her the flashlight.

Paul went through the wallet. It was the same wallet,
Trojans and all. It contained more than fifteen thousand dollars
in cash, and all of Decker's credit cards. "I don't get it," Paul
said. "Why?"

"Careless is all I can think of," Emily said.

Together they wandered through each room in the house,
not quite believing they were alone.

"Walter?" Emily said.

"Hello?" Paul said.

They turned their attention to other drawers and cabinets.
They went through closets, their socks stashed away in Paul's
pockets.

"Do you know what I'm thinking?" Paul said, after a long
silence. "I'm thinking that this is betting money. That's why
there's so much around. I had a friend, Marty Ackerman.
Smaller scale, naturally. He was always on the phone talking
spread. He was always up to his ass in cash."

They were in the hallway between the living room and the
bedrooms.

"What do you think you're doing?" said a voice from
behind them.

Paul staggered, shaken. His bowels let fly.

In front of him, Emily turned. Paul did, too, his body quak-
ing.

Behind them, at the door to the hall, there was no one. Paul thought for a moment that a shadow moved quickly backward. His flashlight picked up nothing. "Christ," he said, shit dripping down his legs.

In Temmy's voice, Emily said, most casually: "There's no one here but the three of us."

Paul couldn't move. "I've shit in my pants," he said, in a whisper.

"That's quite common under circumstances such as these," Temmy said. "'Many people whose homes have been broken into, return to discover bowel movements on the living-room rug or on the kitchen floor. Not unusual at all."

"I told you never to do that again."

"It was out of my hands," Emily said. "Please believe me."

"Jesus" is all that Paul could say.

"Can I help you?" Emily asked, moving toward him.

"You're *out* of it," Paul said, brushing her away.

He took off his pants and his underpants. He rolled them together, and in the bathroom he wrapped them in a towel, after washing himself with a wet cloth.

From Decker's bottom drawer he removed a pair of bathing trunks. Beneath the trunks, in the corner of the drawer, gone unnoticed during their investigation, were five packets of a hundred hundred-dollar bills each. Paul, stunned, dropped the bathing trunks on the floor.

"Emily," he said, forcefully, "get in here."

"Tell me," she said, coming to him.

"This is what we take," he said. "Now listen to me. Get me some kind of box from the pantry or somewhere. Take the light, I'll stay here. You got it?" Paul spoke quickly.

"Got it." Emily was gone, leaving Paul in darkness, naked from the waist down.

In the blackness, he grappled with Decker's trunks, but toppled over. Resigned to waiting for Emily, he sat on the floor with his knees pulled to his chin.

Franklin drifted through his mind. How could he possibly explain himself to such an honorable gentleman? Paul Kramer, the son of two deceased people, wearing only a blue-short-sleeve shirt with an alligator below the left breast, was sitting on a green carpet in another man's house, awaiting a receptacle for an unthinkable amount of money that he would remove from the other man's house in the company of a beautiful woman with significant psychological difficulties, in the middle of the desert, after an imposing hurricane during which they had ingested a potent mind-altering drug, the very thought of which had always alarmed him in the past. Paul thought that he had lost the thread of respectable conduct. He sat there, baffled, on Decker's carpet. So baffled, in fact, that he emitted a chuckle.

Soon, Emily returned with a small cardboard box and the flashlight.

Paul pulled the bathing trunks on. They drooped below his navel.

Carefully, as Emily held the light, Paul transferred the packets of hundred-dollar bills to the box on the floor.

"We have fifty thousand dollars," he said to Emily. "I want you to know that. That's what we're doing."

Emily didn't answer.

Paul went into the bathroom for his pants, thinking that the photo of Maggie was probably stained. He came back, dropped the towel-wrapped package into the box. The flashlight picked up the words DEL MONTE.

They left the house through the back door.

They walked in silence toward the car.

Just as they reached the car, the street lights flickered on for a moment, were dark again, then burst on, directly above them, cutting through the dark night and forcing Paul to squint.

Paul, holding the box, glanced at Emily. Her eyes were as blank and as milky as a blind man's. She appeared to be looking past him. Her face was lined with fear. She was trembling, slightly.

Paul said to Emily: "I forgive you. I love you."

PART FIVE

CHAPTER FOURTEEN

Paul: Welcome, and Merry Christmas.

Comedian: I like New York in June, how about you?

Paul: You're working against me already?

Comedian: Time is fleeting.

Paul: Why does a woman become a comedian?

Comedian: Money.

Paul: Money?

Comedian: I had wanted to be a teacher.

Paul: And then you changed your mind and became what you are.

Comedian: Hit the road.

Paul: Hit the road?

Comedian: Make big bucks.

Paul: Oh, you mean hit the road comma and make big bucks period.

Comedian: Semicolon.

Paul: Are you going to work against me for the entire program?

Comedian: No.

Paul: Okay.

Comedian: I think you're very attractive.

Paul: That's still working against me.

Comedian: Sort of attractive.

Paul: (chuckles)

Comedian: Not bad, of your genre.

Paul: What is my genre?

Comedian: Oh, not knowing you well, I'd say late twenties, and, ah, singer.

Paul: Singer?

Comedian: Yeah. Someone who's always wanted to be on TV but couldn't quite make it.

Paul: Well, as you know, we're here now on TV.

Comedian: Oh, right.

Paul: Myself having made it.

Comedian: Oh, that's right. You're the fella who comes and goes.

Paul: Why the belligerence?

Comedian: Defensive.

Paul: Why?

Comedian: I can't get work.

Paul: You seem to be working often in this country, not only as a—

Comedian: Crummy places.

Paul: Not true. You worked—

Comedian: It's been two years since I had a good job.

Paul: You directed a movie of your own that received mixed but interesting reviews.

Comedian: Made no money.

Paul: But still.

Comedian: I'm sorry, I'm supposed to be funny here. Let's not talk about the movie. It's a sensitive subject for me.

Paul: Why?

Comedian: The whole world let me down.

Paul: In what way?

Comedian: Not liking it.

Paul: Why do you suppose they didn't?

Comedian: Bored.

Paul: Do you feel it's a boring movie?

Comedian: I think it's a great movie.

Paul: Why do people find it boring?

Comedian: They don't understand the framework. It's an elevated kind of humor.

Paul: You've been compared to Elaine May.

Comedian: *New Leaf* was the only movie I fell out of my seat for, except for *Duck Soup*.

Paul: Is that so?

Comedian: It was very embarrassing. I was with a very dignified gathering. Morticians.

Paul: Morticians?

Comedian: Right out of my seat.

Paul: How did you come to view a movie with morticians?

Comedian: Down flat looking up at the screen. Very embalming moment.

Paul: But how did you come to be with morticians?

Comedian: My publicity director. "Got you a gig," he said. That did it. I honor my obligations. That's why I'm here.

Paul: You are, as I understand it, about thirty-five years old.

Comedian: Thirty-six last month.

Paul: You've been married three times and you have four children.

Comedian: That's true.

Paul: Do the children live with you?

Comedian: No.

Paul: Then, they live with your ex-husbands?

Comedian: They live with him. Them.

Paul: Are you in touch with your ex-husbands?

Comedian: No.

Paul: Do they find you funny?

Comedian: No, they find me pathetic.

Paul: Do you think that if they were to be gathered in a room together—

Comedian: They were at that morticians group! That's who I was with. You knew that, right?

Paul: No. Their general feeling is that you're pathetic?

Comedian: Pathetic. And also pitiful. There's a fine difference there.

Paul: What do *you* think? Are you pathetic, and if so why?

Comedian: No, I don't think I'm pathetic. I think I'm realistic. I think that they couldn't take my view of their collective and individual intelligence.

Paul: I guess what you're saying is that they found you threatening.

Comedian: I think they did. When I was doing well, they found me threatening because I was doing better than they were. When I wasn't, they found me threatening because they knew that I would.

Paul: How about Mort Zukoff, the first one, who was doing far better than you at the time?

Comedian: I can't remember. I was extremely young. I was sixteen.

Paul: You married when you were sixteen?

Comedian: Yes. And I had a child at seventeen. I wasn't ready to be a mother. I have great respect for Mort.

Paul: Do you want to be more of a writer than a stand-up comic? You've done a great deal of work in clubs around the country. Would you prefer directing? Would you prefer—

Comedian: I'm losing my looks. And I would like to be writing.

Paul: I find you attractive.

Comedian: Thank you. Put your money where your mouth is. You don't think that's funny?

Paul: No.

Comedian: Pathetic?

Paul: Pathetic.

Comedian: I usually hit in between the two. Fupathetic.

Paul: Would you say that men and women who wish to be funny are not happy people?

Comedian: It's a cliché, but I think it's true.

Paul: Why?

Comedian: I think that the desire to make people laugh is a desire to make people in some way manic, and focused on you.

Paul: You the comedian.

Comedian: You the comedian. You're not just out for the laugh, you're out for what it is that makes them laugh. Namely, you. I think that that kind of focused wish is the most pathetic thing there is. Not that you want people to be happy. You want people to be happy as long as you are the impetus for their laughter.

Paul: Wouldn't that apply to any performer?

Comedian: More intensely to comedians.

Paul: Why?

Comedian: You're not asking the audience to think about what they're hearing. You're not asking them to appreciate anything except what it is that's making them laugh right then. It's cheap. Later it can be good. I feel that ultimately I could feel better about myself making other people laugh as a writer. But when I'm performing I need them to laugh at me. It's a very instant kind of gratification. And it's very deflating at the same time. You do it, click click. You say: three months ago President Ford granted Richard Nixon San Clemency. Click click. It's living in the air without a net. And that's why I probably haven't been able to stay married, or to stay in one city. It's not a very funny profession. And there's never a sense of, okay, now you can take it easy for a while. It's constantly re-proving yourself, and never feeling that you've quite done it.

Paul: Who makes *you* laugh?

Comedian: My children make me laugh sometimes. I've always admired your channel.

Paul: Why?

Comedian: There's something about it that makes me think that it takes nothing except itself very seriously. Besides, I admire Cornel Wilde.

Paul: You're good and tough this evening.

Comedian: Mild. I watched you interview an athlete. It was Thanksgiving night. You kept saying that it was your first week back. You sounded obsessed with that. You worked it into everything. It was the main thing you wanted to convey, while at the same time showing interest in the athlete.

Paul: You're probably right. I'm self-involved to a great degree.

Comedian: I was eating apples at the time, so I couldn't hear everything you said.

Paul: In American history, there have been very few women comedy writers, or women who devoted their lives to comedy.

Comedian: Well, in the twenties and thirties and forties the women who were funny essentially gave up their lives. Their lives were being funny, then ultimately tragic. There's an awfully big gap between comedy and sex. I think a lot of women have used comedy as a way of entering an asexual field, or a male field. And that to become a successful comedienne was to transcend sexuality, or to co-opt male terms, and make them female. Lucille Ball, basically, is using caricatures of femininity which are not feminine. They are shrieking, crying, and sort of bewildered manipulation. She always gets what she wants. And whatever she wants is something Ricky has. It is not something she decided she wants or needs. She finds a way of getting it. It all has to do with angles and deceit, and scoring in the way we think of the cliché of the stud. It's stacking the cards, or putting the cards under the table. She's always working toward a goal. The goal is always something Ricky can give her. My routines don't depend on men. They depend on people seeing what is ridiculous and laughing at it. I always know that I'm going to be reviewed, which is exhilarating and frightening. Exhilaration and fear are what comedy has meant to me. My mother has always said for me to get a degree and fall back on my teaching. Teaching is boring. You *know* what comes next. I don't like to know what comes next.

Paul: I've recently spent a long while out West not knowing what was coming next.

Comedian: Why did you come back?

Paul: I like New York at Christmas.

Comedian: And so here we are.

Paul: Are you nervous before going on stage?

Comedian: Sometimes. The more I care about an audience, the more nervous I am. I try not to do cheap jokes, like the one I made up about Nixon. I try not to play suburbia, marriage. I like people to learn something from seeing me. Maybe they'll learn that they don't want to be like me. That's something. It's more than they came in with.

Paul painted two of the rooms in his apartment himself, removing books and records from cabinets and shelves, and piling them in the center of the room, and wiping dust away with a wet sponge, and putting them back in a new order. Then he hired two painters from an ad in *The Village Voice*; lesbians in matching red bandannas and coveralls. They were solemn and efficient.

New order: the bed against the opposite wall, the gray and blue couches reversed, the black leather chair out of the back room and into the living room, the gold curtains in the bedroom replaced with white ones, the old upright piano given way for a case of Scotch. Paul didn't feel like playing a piano or passing a piano when he came home late at night. In its place: a huge dictionary on a rolling stand. *Phenology*: The study of periodic biological phenomena, such as flowering, breeding, and migration, especially as related to climate. *Scalawag*: 1. A reprobate; rascal. 2. A White Republican Southerner during Reconstruction. *Longing*: A persistent yearning or desire that cannot be fulfilled.

Emily flew east three weeks after Paul. He watched her emerge from TWA's carpeted tunnel and search the faces for his. She wore a thin brown dress and a yellow blazer. She looked harried and tired and not especially relieved when she spotted him. He put his arms around her and held her.

"You're not dressed for the cold," he said.

"I'm ill-equipped," she said.

Emily liked the apartment. "It's encouraging," she said.

Emily liked the back room, which was to be hers. "I didn't realize how big a place it was. West Side enormous. Plenty of air. And southern exposure? Sunshine in the morning?"

Paul nodded. He hadn't imagined her here, or bundled and shivering in the winter.

In a while, after he had helped her unpack, after he had made steaks and salad, he heard her in the back room on the phone. Her voice sounded metallic. Paul was threatened by the phone calls she made in her back room; reunions, well into night. He was threatened by her knowledge of the city, by her connections to it. In Agua Caliente she had been so solitary and accessible; his confidante. Now there were new names for him to consider, and explanations of the past. It seemed to Paul that Emily carried a heavy population of dependents. Her energy ignited a dozen voices on the other end of the phone, *his* phone. They had been biding their time in her absence, awaiting the return of her buzz. She spoke a special language with each of them; none—as he overheard on the extension, or as he passed through the kitchen pretending business at the sink—corresponded with the way he and Emily behaved together. The difference was in reference and inflection and jive and parentheses and tones of laughter. Did the voices at the other end know about Paul? Were his credentials in order? Was he an acceptable companion for this coveted woman?

"Here are the keys," she had said, almost immediately upon arrriving at the apartment, handing him a small gray envelope. Paul listened to Emily's voice on the phone. He opened the envelope and examined the keys. There were two of them, both with little metal tags: Box 1216, Pacific National Bank, 707 N Palm Canyon Dr. PS, CA 92262.

In the desert they had waited.

Decker had called. Would Paul like to watch the football on Sunday?

Decker and Paul watched two games, from ten in the morning until four in the afternoon. Maggie made them sandwiches on English muffins. Emily sunbathed on a raft in the pool with her top off, distracting Decker in his football chair when she drifted into his sight.

Not a peep out of him. No sad story about being ripped off, no display of an empty drawer, no suspicious glance at Paul. Obviously, he hadn't discovered it yet.

Alone in the bedroom, Paul checked it out.

The bureau was meticulously arranged: cuff links and

some minor jewelry on top, every drawer immaculate. He and Emily had left it in the disarray they had found it.

Paul returned to the living room, and stayed uneasily throughout the afternoon.

"Is he just playing with us, or what?" Paul asked Emily later.

"Could he be so irresponsible?"

"To not even *know*?"

"Hard to imagine," Emily said, flopping down on the bed.

"Could *they* be so irresponsible?" Paul asked.

"I think Maggie's just out of it on this score. I don't think Maggie was aware. Really I don't."

"You know her better than I do. Maybe we're home free." Paul stared out through the venetian blinds at their own little pool.

"Home free is not in our language, honey," Emily said, closing her eyes.

February 3, 1975

Dearest Dad,

I think you'll be happy to know that I'm on the air again in New York. I miss you terribly. I haven't even begun to assimilate the events of California and/or to come to some kind of peace with them. The main thing is that in coming back to New York I was made keenly aware of how much you mean to me. This is where you brought me up, this is where we faced each other, this is where I remember you best—on these streets in your navy-blue overcoat.

Emily is with me. Our relationship is more tenuous now. Our privacy has been diluted by what we know of New York and by what goes on here, so that we don't turn to each other as much as we used to. We both have so many other options that we tend to evade personal issues that someday I'll be able to tell you about (I hope), by calling on the outside people in our lives. How did you live without the phone when you were a young man? The Immediate Gratification Factor is the chief villain in this modern-day world. Come to think of it, you must have, when Henry Ford came along, thought of yourself as living in the modern-day world. What is the ultimate modern-day world if not doomsday?

Sorry for the digression and for the lousy construction of this letter. Did I ever tell you (probably not) that when I was a teen-ager I wrote pornography for myself, knowing I wouldn't show it to anyone? It's true. I'd write real fast and the construction would be lousy. Example (I'll make up something now): Bardot went into the steam room. She lay naked on a towel. He came in and kissed her and lay on top of her and kissed her body and they were sweating profusely and they writhed in the steam with their arms around each other and she whispered to him that he must take her now NOW NOW!

What I'm trying to say is that I know that you're not going to be seeing this letter, so I'm not trying to win points through literary ballet. And yet! I cleaned up the porno. If you'll notice, the only anatomical references are body and arms. I still have a little sexual squeamishness around you, isn't that something?

I see that this letter is nothing but a digression within a digression within a digression, like the mirror at Michael's barber shop that you talked about during one of our evening walks more than twenty years ago. So I'm digressing from a digression, which means that I'm running out of gas. I just wanted to talk to you and tell you that I love you profoundly. And that I regret any sorrow that I ever caused you.

Love,
Paul

Paul addressed the letter to his father's Los Angeles house, and took it with him on a walk through the park. He let it fall gently into a trash can near the shuttered carousel. Maybe it would be found, Paul thought. It was stamped and ready to go. It might be mailed. Wasn't it Beerbohm who mailed letters by tossing them out the window? It was certainly possible that a park attendant might find it and send it on its way. Paul had typed his return address in the top left-hand corner. The attendant might be a viewer of "Paul Kramer Tonight," pleased to help out a man of the media.

1048 Highpoint, Los Angeles, California. Ah, but think of what Paul would have to face a few days later at his mailbox: his returned envelope, covered with bureaucratic notations and postmarks—the scars of cross-continental travel. And: "addressee unknown" diagonally stamped above Franklin's name. Unknown to whom? To the network of government workers into whose hands the letter fell, to Valerie Maxwell and Christina Furth and Loggins and Messina? Paul thought: we are all unknown.

The day was sunny and cold. The wind was still. Paul walked up Fifth Avenue to Seventy-ninth Street, and sat down on a bench on the park side of the avenue.

> Lover, when I'm near you
> And I hear you speak my name,
> Softly in my ear
> You breathe a flame.

If Billings, on American Airlines in May, had told Paul, while shuffling the cards, what the months ahead would bring, could Paul have retreated, stopped the machinery? What's the name of the game, Billings? The name of the game is that you make your own rules, you define your own language, you do the best you can. Franklin's heart would have stopped sooner or later. Emily would have come up with Paul somewhere along the line. And of course, for all his life Paul had been ready to abscond with somebody's funds. California had been the unexpected catalyst.

Walter Decker's money. Fifty thousand dollars in a safe-deposit box in Palm Springs. A secret shared only with Emily. They were letting the money sit there, having agreed to keep it where it was for a year, to test the water in October, to talk about it then.

They were edgy with each other, evasive, unkind. They

quarreled about spoons and tidiness and long-distance calls. They rarely made love. They didn't like each other's friends. Paul walked far too noisily in the hall. Emily left overhead lights on "all the goddamned time."

The answer isn't out the window, Mr. Kramer. The answer isn't Emily Keller or Jennifer Rosen or Sandi Cummings. Paul had known that it was essential that he be covered, plugged into Jennifer Rosen so many years ago. "I am permanently grieved," she had told him in the snow at Logan Airport. He had been covered again, though Jennifer was unaware of it. Paul raced from umbrella to umbrella, from Jennifer Rosen to Sharon Childs, scooping that attractive girl from Michael Holland's basket, racing, permitting only a few drops of solitude to fall on his cheek and slide down to his neck.

Here, with the daughter of a ventriloquist lodged in his apartment, was the artful dodger, Paul Kramer, installed again as an interviewer, an evening interrogator asking about past and present tenses and favorite kinds of music, and hearing about châteaus in the South of France, and San Clemency and marriages at sixteen, while losing his grip on a slithery relationship with a woman who frightened him.

Emily's book hit a snag. She started from the beginning again with a more cheerful narrator's voice. Paul called her Arlene Francis. One night, standing in the doorway to the back room, he called her "a crazy Arlene Francis."

He began to use words like "confused" and "nutty."

"Hey, nut, pass the mustard," he said, as they sat at the kitchen table.

"Is that necessary?" she said.

"Everything is relative," he said.

One morning she came home at dawn.

"Where have you been?" Paul asked.

"Where do you think I've been?"

"Whoring."

"You're right," she said.

"With whom?"

"I've been with Joshua."

"Does he pray when he comes?"

"No."

"I'll bet he prays *that* he comes."

"Cunnilingus is the only thing he's not especially proficient at."

"Why did you go to see him?"

"I wanted something familiar and reassuring."

Emily turned her back to him and took off her sweater.

"Am I a stranger?" Paul asked, near tears.

"You have the answer to that, don't you."

Paul got up from the bench. He walked over to Madison Avenue, half expecting a Good Humor man at the corner. Even on such a cold day he would be glad to have an orange Popsicle, and his father's hand, and Hank Bauer at bat in a bar that no longer was there.

His mother would welcome him home: home from the Château Marmont; from the canals of Venice, California; from Encinal Drive and Agua Caliente; and from his own rambling apartment that he had chosen for himself as an adult. West End Avenue. Mature people pick out apartments and pay rent. Mature people take jobs and lovers and assume responsibility for their own lives and for their children's lives. Paul knew himself to be indecisive and untalented in these crucial areas. He saw himself as forever on the run, seeking cover from unsuspecting women and tolerant friends, lazily shedding light on that which was already illuminated.

He hailed a cab. In the overheated back seat he closed his eyes and thought: Hi, Mommy, I'm home.

CHAPTER FIFTEEN

On a warm day in early March Paul went to see Lillian Avakian. He had checked the Avakians for the phone number he had memorized. William Avakian, 1349 Lexington Avenue, corresponded with AT 9-8980.

In January and February he had occasionally dialed the number, planning to hang up at the sound of her voice. He had called from phone booths in Blarney Stones, from the phone in Emily's room, from the beeper in the studio, from his own room several afternoons in a row. When, at last, there was a reply, he knew that he had found her. There was warmth in her hello, an expectancy without apprehension or disdain. Her hello was declarative—no implication that she had been interrupted, or was out of breath, or had been cornered in a moment of agitation or despair. The quality of her hello made Paul hesitate just long enough to inspire a second and slightly more inquisitive hello, but still a reaction of generosity.

"Lillian," Paul said.

"Yes? Who's this?"

"This is Paul Kramer."

There was a long silence. Paul waited.

"Goodness," Lillian finally said, softly.

"It's nice to meet you," Paul said from a phone booth in the lobby of the Pan Am building. He was aware that she could hear the bustle outside his closed door.

"It certainly is nice to meet you," Lillian said. "I hadn't expected . . ."

"I've called you often."

Lillian didn't say anything.

"Do you think, well, I'd love to meet you."

"Quite honestly, I'm taken aback. Of course. Of course. I teach at Columbia. Would you care to have lunch around there?"

"That would be a pleasure," Paul said.

They made the arrangements.

"I didn't know that your father had told you," Lillian said.

"He didn't."

"I see," she said.

"What do you teach?" Paul asked, wanting to beat the recorded operator.

"Music," Lillian said. "I teach music."

They had agreed to meet at the sundial at one o'clock. Paul was there at twelve-thirty and wandered around the campus. In the pleasant spring weather, he carried his overcoat and thought of Lillian, imagining her as a tall woman in her late fifties, wearing a scarf.

And other thrilling vegetables. His father's words to Lillian.

Paul felt a twinge of embarrassment at barging in on Lillian and Franklin's intimacy, private gifts of Elizabeth Bowen, and summer squash and asparagus and artichokes. For Paul to be intrusive in this way was presumptuous and insensitive. Should he have called? A letter would have been better, giving her the chance to weigh her options and compose a response. He began writing the letter in his head. "Dear Lillian, In going over my father's books and notes after his death, I found your name inscribed in several volumes, and some jottings that indicated the deep fondness he felt for you. It would give me extreme pleasure if you would consider dining with me at your convenience to . . ." To what? Why? To rehash old times in which he hadn't figured? It was none of his concern. He remembered a phrase of his mother's: none of your beeswax. So. It was none of his beeswax.

Paul edited the word "extreme" from his imaginary letter. "It would give me pleasure." Paul thought that everything about himself was extreme; that he was, after all, an exaggeration. Exaggeratedly exuberant, exaggeratedly morose, a man whose appetites were almost always out of hand. He was never centered. He thought of Emily, to whom he hadn't spoken of Lillian, fearing that she would somehow interfere by offering tricky insights for Paul, by going to Lillian on her own, by invading, with her own nimble dance, the secret that Paul had stumbled upon without any help from her.

He sat on the steps in front of the library fifty yards from the sundial, and realized that he trusted Emily not at all, that the need he felt to be covered by her presence was diminishing. He withheld too many things, defended himself too vigorously, attacked her too cruelly. She prayed for absolution from an inner voice, her commander, and equated absolution with insanity. In recent weeks he had seen in his new-found Arlene Francis a desperate pleasantness in the reworking of her book, and in the cheap and ominous smile she wore when she was around him.

There was something frenetic in that smile, and a dithered whirl to her activity. He thought maybe he should talk to her, forgive her, permit her to go bonkers, and lock her up.

Standing in front of him was a small light-haired woman who looked to be around forty. She had a prominent chin and jaw, and a wide white forehead. With her hair pulled back and curled into a bun, her forehead allowed her face a spectacular availability. She had large brown eyes, commanding silky eyes. Paul thought of the word *clean*.

"Hello, Paul" she said, and smiled.

Maybe she was younger than forty. She was just about five feet tall, and not even possibly a hundred pounds.

"Lillian Francis Avakian," Paul said, standing.

Since he had been sitting three steps above her, his advantage in a standing position was immense. Feeling absurd, he sat down again, betraying, he thought, his astonishment and discomfort.

She stayed where she was until he gestured with his hand, inviting her to sit down next to him.

They sat side by side without talking, looking out over the campus.

On the field near Harley Hall two boys were throwing a yellow Frisbee around. The taller and more athletic boy would effect behind-the-back catches, and return the Frisbee from between his legs. Paul thought of Bob Cousy, and laughed.

Lillian turned to face him.

"It's amazing, that's all," he said, meeting her eyes. "Did you ever hear of Bob Cousy?"

"Who is Bob Cousy?" Lillian asked.

"A basketball player from the past. I haven't thought of him in years. The kid over there, the taller kid with the Frisbee, put me in mind of Cousy. Cousy was a marvelous showboaty kind of player. Fancy passes, unexpected moves. I'm just amazed to be sitting here with you and thinking of Bob Cousy."

Lillian smiled and touched her hair.

"I'm sure you know that you're a lot younger than I had imagined," Paul said.

"How old do you think I am?" Lillian held her skirt down against the breeze.

"You look to be in your late thirties. I'm sure this doesn't come as news to you."

"I was born in 1921," Lillian said.

"That's hard to believe," Paul said. "I'm sure you understand that I'm rooting both for and against it at the same time. But I don't mean, I'm not talking salaciously. I meant—"

"Of course I understand," Lillian said.

"I'm extremely pleased to meet you," Paul said, in a moment.

"That's nice of you," Lillian said.

"You teach music here."

"I'm a professor."

"Is *that* so," Paul said, thinking that he couldn't have gotten rid of "extremely" if his life had depended on it.

Lillian didn't say anything.

Paul continued. "Do you have a certain period?" he asked.

"Eighteenth century."

"How long have you been at Columbia?"

"Fifteen years."

"Fifteen years," Paul repeated. Then he said: "Mozart."

"And Haydn," she said, nodding.

Paul considered babbling a bit to display what he knew of what she taught. But he knew that he would be trapped, revealed and trapped, before lunch. Just a bag of wind. There'd be no need for lunch; simply Goodbye, Paul Kramer, and she'd be off.

"What a beautiful day," he said.

"Isn't it," Lillian said.

"I called you on a number of occasions," Paul said.

"Since my husband died I spend most of my time in a studio I rent around here. There's no phone."

Paul had a lot on his mind: a widow. William Avakian had been stored away in Doctors Hospital—Paul remembered his father's letter clearly now. William Avakian in his chair staring out, he imagined, at Gracie Mansion. Also on his mind: a studio. A studio apartment, or what?

"Of what particular use is a studio?" he asked, with a smile.

"It's a wonderful place, well equipped. I own a harpsichord, and a cello, and of course my viola."

Better equipped than Emily, Paul thought.

"It's a peaceful environment, with a skylight and good strong, thick walls." Lillian was gesturing enthusiastically by moving her right index finger in a circle. Paul wasn't sure if the circle referred to the studio as a whole, or the harpsichord, or the good strong, thick walls.

"You're a musician?" Paul asked.

"Yes," Lillian replied, without hesitation.

"What did your husband do?" Paul sought her eyes, wishing to show how open he was, how harmless.

"He was an English professor, and a musician. We shared many of the same interests." Lillian averted her eyes.

"Do you have any children?" Paul asked.

"No."

There was much in the air. Paul had a dozen options. He could get the ball rolling toward lunch, or swoop down right on Franklin's head. Encinal Drive could be dispensed with right there, right on the steps of Columbia University. Paul felt it essential that he clear himself of any wrongdoing, wondering at the same time if Lillian even suspected him of foul play, or knew the details of the accident, and if she did know the details of the accident, how did she get them? The son was in the back seat. There was a girl. Franklin Kramer died at once. The son was in the back seat. The guy on the steps here.

"When did you meet my father?" Paul asked.

Lillian took her time, focusing, or so it seemed to Paul, on an attractive girl in a bright-red beret strolling on College Walk.

"Your mother was alive," Lillian said, turning to him, going right to the heart of the matter. "I'd love a glass of sherry. Would you?"

"You said on the phone that your father never mentioned me to you," Lillian said.

They were seated in a booth in the West End Bar, Lillian with her sherry, Paul with a vodka and tonic. The smell of meatloaf and halibut filled the place. There were several empty booths, and only a handful of people around the bar. The juke-box was quiet, so that the cafeteria clamor from the other side of the room seemed louder than Paul remembered from past visits. It was their only competition, but competition it was, since Lillian's voice was soft, and difficult to pick up across the table.

"He never did. I don't know why." Paul took a sip of his drink.

"He felt it would be disrespectful to your mother," Lillian said. She touched her hair.

"But for so many *years* after she died."

"As you know, Franklin was steadfast about what he felt was correct, or what he felt might be hurtful to anyone else."

"I know," Paul said.

"How did you learn of me?" Lillian smiled, and moved on, past the smile, slipping her eyes away from his. Paul saw that she was tough to catch.

"Quite by accident. Your number was on a pad. Your name was in a book. And there was an occasional incomplete reference from my father."

"What did you think I'd be like?" she asked.

With anyone else, under any other conditions, Paul would

have imagined bits and pieces of flirtation in the way Lillian moved her hands, in the intoxicating flow of her speech. The truth was that sitting across from him in a college bar on a sunny spring-like afternoon, holding a glass of sherry and speaking so softly that he had to lean forward to hear everything she said, was a fifty-four-year-old professor of music, the owner of a harpsichord, the grader of papers, maybe even theses, God knows, and undeniably the lover and companion for many years, maybe twenty-five years, of his own father. How many times in the past had he inflicted gentle talk with inappropriate sexuality? With wives whose husbands stood nearby, with cousins or sisters of hospitalized friends in the lobby of Sloan-Kettering or on a terrace at Lenox Hill or in the waiting room of a hastily acquired cardiologist. Paul had allowed himself to believe that all these women, through a laugh or the touch of his arm or the intimate process of confession, were displaying desire for him—even, upon occasion, lust. His responses were natural, in view of what he thought he saw. The fact that he himself was responsible for the illusion was, all the while, well beyond his grasp. Understandable then, he thought, was his bewilderment and fury at being turned so abruptly away by those malicious provocateurs.

"You want to know what I thought you'd be like," Paul said, weighing several possibilities. "Something like Lillian Hellman," he told her. "Kind of homely and articulate. You turn out to be only articulate, but more softly. I was way off with Lillian Hellman."

"I've seen you on television now and then. Just once or twice. I've never owned a set." Lillian finished her glass of sherry.

"What did you think of me when you saw me?" Paul asked.

"I was interested in how personal the conversation was," Lillian said. "There didn't seem to be an interview going on.

You talked a lot about yourself in response to things. I remember that you were willing to lose points gracefully."

"It's a personal program, no doubt," Paul said, with a chuckle. "That's why some people don't care for it much."

"I don't have much to compare it with." Lillian pushed her glass away.

After a long pause, Paul continued. "When was the last time you saw my father?" he asked.

"August fourteenth, nineteen sixty-nine," Lillian said.

"That long ago," Paul said, surprised.

Noticing Lillian's empty glass, he asked: "Would you like another drink?"

"Perhaps not," she said. "I have a three o'clock engagement."

Paul wondered about the word "engagement." It implied a social meeting. Maybe there were other sons of other fathers who had looked up Mrs. Avakian and were prepared to meet her for the first time this very afternoon. Three other guys, well into their thirties, her fourth and final engagement at seven o'clock at the bar at the Stanhope Hotel. She was refusing a second sherry in fear of being looped at the Stanhope. And yet it was possible that by "engagement" she meant class, or lecture. She was fifty-four, after all, and could have dragged the formality of the word through the years and into the mid-seventies.

"Would you mind if I had another vodka?" he asked.

"Not at all."

As he waited at the bar, Paul noticed that it was two-fifteen. That gave them forty-five minutes, maybe less, depending on the whereabouts of her engagement. She hadn't put aside much time for him. Ninety minutes would do it. Franklin's crass young son, dropping in from the sky with a phone call. Surely her curiosity had at least ninety minutes in its heart.

"Where were we?" Paul said, sitting down again.

"May I ask you something?" Lillian said, surrounding the stem of her empty glass with both hands.

"Are there many things to ask?" Paul said.

"I'd like to know about the last evening," Lillian said.

Paul waited a moment, deciding what to tell her.

"It's something I've wondered about," Lillian said, almost apologetically. Paul heard the apology and urged her away from it.

"Naturally. Of course," he said. "I, uh, you know, it was an especially fine night. We had been to that restaurant up in the hills. I have a girlfriend named Emily, and Emily and my father had just met that night for the first time. They liked each other very much. Dad was very expansive. Just very sweet. That's all." Paul sipped his drink.

"Was it avoidable?" Lillian asked.

"I don't think so," Paul said. "Something moved in the road."

"I see," Lillian said.

"You know what Dad said that night? That the two closest friends he'd ever had were my mother and another woman, someone in the east. When I asked who it was, he said that I didn't know her, but that she was impressive in a number of ways. He didn't expound at any great length. Just that she was impressive. I had the feeling he was understating the case."

"Really," Lillian said.

Paul thought his invention a reasonable gift. He felt that it probably reflected the truth.

"You know, it's about two-thirty now," he said. "Do you want a hamburger or something?"

"Maybe I'll just have another glass of sherry," Lillian said. "But *you* eat. Please. You have something."

"I'm not hungry," Paul said, getting up again, taking Lillian's glass. "I'll be right back."

"I'd like very much to tell you something," Lillian said, as soon as Paul was seated once more.

"Are you sure you're okay for your engagement?" he asked.

"I can be a little late."

"Well then."

"Well then," she said. "I wanted you to know that your father and I were never intimate."

"I see," Paul said, speaking directly into her eyes.

"We were close to each other. We were intimate in other ways, equally important ways."

"I understand," Paul said.

"We would have married. I never told him that, because my husband was alive. I placed a bit more distance between us than was necessary. I live with that mistake."

Ends are beginnings, beginnings are ends.

"He told me last September that he felt very positive about the future," Paul said.

"I'm glad to hear that," Lillian said.

They were quiet for a while.

"When did your husband die?" Paul asked, in a bit.

"Eleven days after Franklin," Lillian said. She touched her hair. She nodded at him without a smile. "Yes," she seemed to be saying with her nodding, her continuous nodding.

"May I walk with you to your engagement?" Paul asked.

"If you'd like. I play chamber music two afternoons a week, not far from here. I would invite you to come, but the group prefers no visitors, and I'm afraid I can't make an exception."

"That's totally understandable," Paul said.

On the sidewalk, the bright sunshine made them squint. Paul thought to use his sunglasses, but felt they would give him an advantage similar to his standing on the steps of the library. He would squint along with Lillian and enjoy no extra privileges.

"I'm glad that you took the time to look me up," Lillian said, as they approached the corner where they would part.

"As I say, I tried frequently."

"The time was more favorable." She touched her hair again, smoothing it back with the palm of her hand.

"I guess there's something I'd like to ask you," Paul said.

They were standing in front of a Chock Full o' Nuts. Paul waited for the roar of a subway train to pass, so that he might hear everything she said.

"My voice is rather weak, I know." Lillian laughed.

"No, no. I was just collecting my thoughts," Paul said.

"I have a feeling I know what you're going to ask me," Lillian said.

"What do you suppose?" Paul asked.

"I think you'd like to know if I ever met your mother, or if she knew about me."

Paul, shocked and pleased, said: "Yes. How did you understand that?"

"What else would you have kept until the last moment?" Lillian put her hand on his sleeve.

"Possibly a number of other things."

"Possibly."

"I'd just like to know. It's really meaningless. It's not a great issue, or it's not—"

"Your mother didn't know. I went to the service before the burial."

Lillian offered him her hand, her left hand. He leaned down and kissed it, his lips touching a gold wedding band that he hadn't noticed all afternoon.

"What will you be playing today?" Paul asked, backing slightly away from her.

"Haydn's Opus Thirty," Lillian replied. "The unfinished quartet. Remarkable, isn't it."

Paul walked downtown on Broadway. He stopped at a fish store and asked that a dozen clams be opened. He ate them standing over a trash can on the corner, letting the shells fall away.

He remembered his father pointing to a seagull in the sky on a summer day in Menemsha.

"Watch," his father said.

The gull, having swooped down to the water, having plucked a clam from the mud, was preparing to break the shell by dropping the clam on a concrete walkway. The wind carried the clam a few feet off course and it landed on grass, intact. Again, the procedure: the clam recaptured, the gull hovering above the walkway, the wind escorting the clam to safety.

"Now watch," Franklin said, his arm resting on Paul's shoulder.

The gull took its time above the concrete. Then it flew a circle, and returned to a spot in the air about two feet from its original station, allowing for the currents of the wind. This time: bull's-eye. The shell smashed down in the center of the walkway, the meat exposed. A final swoop, and away.

"If a bird can do that, you can pass a simple algebra course," Franklin said, squeezing Paul's shoulder. "No?"

He should have told Lillian this. There were many things he should have told her.

A slice of pizza on the next corner. A hot dog three blocks down. A quick Rheingold in a bar. A half hour in the Midtown Theater watching a film call *Honey Bee*. Semen everywhere. Semen all over the country. On Pico Boulevard, and points east. All the way to the Midtown Theater. Semen for three dollars and fifty cents. Semen, unstoppable, irretrievable, except by running the film backward. All that semen returning to all those penises, the ladies and gentlemen disengaging, backing away from the bed or the lawn or the beach or the couch or the ottoman; backing away into their clothes, backing into offices or schoolrooms or into cars. Backing through the credits, and through previous films, backing through meals and marriages and ball games and classes and erector sets and Junket, and into placentas and away, gone, enabling the Midtown Theater and the Pussycat Cinema to peddle *Singin' in the Rain*. No semen out of Donald O'Connor, that's for sure; no come shot for Gene Kelly, who's laughin' at clouds so dark up above.

At home, Paul expected to find Emily, to tell her that he had eaten his way home, maybe embellish it a little with ice cream, a taco, souvlaki. Just one big walking, eating orgy, the semen a secret, Lillian a secret. Paul thought: you can only trust Emily with pizza.

Emily was out. She had written a note and had left it on the kitchen table. It was printed on yellow lined legal paper:

CALL STATION RE DECKER

Paul called the station at once, his hand shaking as he held the receiver.

"Nicki, Paul Kramer. I got a message says you called."

"Did I call? Oh, yes." Nicki was a slow-witted girl with high, pointed breasts. Her eyes were of no particular color, as far as Paul could see. She had short-cropped hair emphasizing the lines of ignorance all over her face that appeared to be drawn with gray Magic Marker.

"Something about Decker somebody?" Paul said.

"Yeah. He doesn't have your number. I wouldn't give him your number. We can't give out—"

"What does he want?"

"He wants to be on your show. He's making a movie? Could that be right?"

"Where is he?"

"The Pierre Hotel. He insisted that he knew you. Do you know this guy?"

"Yes."

"Well, he says he doesn't have your number."

"Thanks."

CHAPTER SIXTEEN

Paul: I know it may embarrass you if I mention your father, but he was a famous man, a self-made man.

Decker: Self-made in many ways.

Paul: Your father was the inventor of Cho-Chews and Kingles and other candies that we're all familiar with.

Decker: That is correct. He was a great American.

Paul: Now, you've carried on the family business, but you've also become a film producer.

Decker: I've branched out. I wanted to widen my horizons. I wanted a larger, shall we say, scope.

Paul: I can understand that. But why film?

Decker: Why *not* film? Film, to me, is an intimate art form of self-expression. I enjoy my coworkers, the men and women of the industry who make it all happen. Film is a living, breathing thing.

Paul: You're here in New York about to shoot a film with the actress Maggie Furth. How did you round her up?

Decker: By persuading her that I had found the right vehicle for her. She is an artist of high quality, in my humble opinion. I want her talents to be on display. Film is a living, breathing thing, and Margaret is a woman of rare depth and insight into the human condition. I am hoping that this project will bring her to the attention of everyone in the film-going community.

Paul: How did you reach her in the first place?

Decker: My dear man, Margaret is a very close friend. She is, how can I say it? She is worldly-wise. We spend long evenings together talking, theorizing. She is, let me assure you, a rare creature.

Paul: I think she's terrific too. Let me ask you this: you've had no experience as a producer of anything. Producing a movie can be a very complex and demanding assignment. Now, I mean this just out of curiosity. What makes you think you can just pull it off, just like that, without having been exposed to the process?

Decker: I think it's a matter of instinct and the innate knowledge of how to handle people, how to deal with certain problems, how to coordinate ideas so that everyone's talents are utilized. I look upon the producer as a stabilizing figure, a man, or in some cases a woman (chuckles), who is capable, by understanding the human condition, of making a team of the people who work for him. Speaking confidentially, I think I can be that man. That is a talent that cannot be learned. It's there or it isn't. It's a kind of basic perspicacity, if you understand my meaning.

Paul: I do. Surely I do.

Decker: May I say, before we go further, that you run a

very entertaining program. When I'm in New York, and I often am, because I commute between Palm Springs and Los Angeles, and the Big Apple, I never fail to catch your efforts. Your efforts are outstanding in the field of television journalism. You have a way of bringing out people in a, shall we say, provocative fashion without appearing overbearing, as some of your contemporaries in your field of endeavor appear.

Paul: Thank you. I appreciate your comments.

Decker: I recall our first meeting. An evening at Margaret's house, am I not correct? What impressed me about you most was your wide range of knowledge, particularly in the field of sports. I don't know if your viewers realize the extent of your knowledge. Do they?

Paul: First of all, I don't feel that my knowledge of *any-*thing is extensive. Just on the average side, and I'm not being falsely modest. Having spoken with you about sports and other things, I honestly feel that you know more than I do about professional athletics. Let me ask you—"

Decker: Strictly *entre nous,* I enjoy the cinema, and the competitive game of tennis, and possibly even criminology, and of course there's always the business world, the world my father taught me.

Paul: (after a pause) Do you see yourself as permanently involved with the production of movies?

Decker: There are many fields of endeavor that I'm interested in. For example, I'm interested in politics. At the moment, we have an unelected President whose incumbency, I think, will be vulnerable in the bicentennial summer of 1976. I can play a waiting game, look over the possibilities, and then move forward toward my man when the time is right. The man in California, Governor Reagan—"

Paul: *Former* Governor Reagan.

Decker: You are absolutely correct. But "former" is only a word. This country, in my humble opinion, is in the mood for a man of conviction. I admire conviction, don't you?

Paul: (After a pause) Depending on the conviction.

Decker: But of course, my dear man.

Paul: Do you see yourself as actively involved in politics, not just as a contributor, but as a personality? Your father was very active during the Depression, and well into the forties.

Decker: To be perfectly candid with you, I see myself as an observer. I think I have the unusual talent of understanding how things work. I can see the chess moves, and when the time comes, I can use whatever influence I may have. As I said before, it's all in the waiting. If you understand my meaning.

"That fat little cocksucker has an interest in *criminology?* Since fucking when, I'd like to know."

Paul was standing in the middle of his living room in the middle of the night. He was holding a Scotch and water, and was facing Emily on the blue couch. She was dressed in jeans and a black turtleneck. She was barefoot and smoking a cigarette.

"And all that shit about waiting for the time, or some garbage like that," he continued.

"A waiting game," Emily said. "He said he could move forward toward his man when the time was right."

"Maybe we're just reading stuff into this," Paul said.

"I'm telling you that even if he knows, he's not going to *do* anything. He's not going to cause me trouble. I'm Maggie's friend." Emily put out her cigarette in a marble ashtray.

"What about *me?*" Paul said.

"You're an extenstion of me," Emily said.

"Extension my ass. Fifty thousand dollars. That's like the net of a ninety-thousand-dollar job." Paul sat down across from Emily.

"You could be right about reading into it, you know. Paranoia strikes deep."

"He's not as dumb as he looks, is he?" Paul glanced at his reflection in the window.

"Hold it a sec," Emily said, slipping a new, unlit cigarette between her fingers. "What to make of the exchange about conviction?"

"Jesus." Paul stood up.

"He likes a man of conviction. And you said that it depended on the conviction."

"What did you expect me to say? Emily? What did you expect me to say?"

"So then it's apparent that he knows. So what do we do?"

"Let's not get into blame. It was a collaborative effort, right?" Paul turned his back to her.

"Who said anything about blame? You got blame on the mind." Emily lit her cigarette.

"I wanted you to know that I'm overlooking the fact that you egged me into it, and that you've egged me into a thousand dumb schemes, and your whole risk stuff is a lot of shit." He faced her again.

"You're such a coward. Something had to be done about you." Emily crossed her legs. "Your whole sabbatical was a fraud. It was a device to call attention to yourself. That's what sabbaticals do, you know. 'Where's Paul?' 'He's on a sabbatical.'"

He didn't respond immediately. He sat down, and stared across at Emily.

Emily continued, staring back at him. "Anyone who brings up blame, I know exactly where he's coming from," she said.

"Let's be calm," Paul said.

"I'm calm," Emily said.

"You're furious and frightened," Paul said.

"I'm frightened, yes," Emily said.

"And furious. Furious at the wrong person under the wrong circumstances."

"Disappointed with the right person under *these* circumstances."

"How have I disappointed you?"

"By reminding me of my father." Emily inhaled deeply.

"In what way?" Paul asked.

"By keeping your feelings to yourself while pretending to be honest and open. You think that by being honest and open about a cup of coffee you're really up front and soul-baring. Your whole life is a series of tricks designed to bamboozle people into thinking you're hot shit, an intellectual, a decent guy, a moral dude. Let me tell you something, moral dude, I know who you are." Emily looked him square in the eye.

"That's pretty serious stuff," Paul said, softly.

"That's right," Emily said.

"Then why did you come east with me, if I'm such a horrible guy?"

"It was a mistake. I knew it from the moment I saw you at the airport."

Paul didn't speak.

"It was a mistake," Emily repeated, with a slight smile. "And also, the thing is . . ."

"What is 'the thing'?" Paul asked.

"Nothing," Emily said.

" 'Nothing' is just shabby bullshit."

"I didn't know quite where I was going with it," Emily said.

"You've hurt me," he said.

"That's the way life is," she said.

Paul got up and went down the hall to the bathroom. He washed his face without looking into the mirror.

In the living room Emily was exactly where he had left her.

"All this because of Decker," he said.

"All this because we've not been talking. We've been skipping around each other. It started in the desert, and that's the truth. When we were left alone, just *alone* in Agua Caliente, our glibness started to dissipate. You can't live in metaphor forever. After a while, it doesn't work any more. I felt that my hands were tied."

"You're condemned by your own words," Paul said.

"Nonsense," Emily said. "When we were down to the brass tactics we—"

"It's 'brass tacks.' "

"I know. It was deliberate." Emily paused, and then continued. " 'Tactics' was right on target."

"Did you come to me?" Paul asked.

"Yes. You bet I did. I wanted to see it out, to challenge us. *Us.* Not just you. So don't get uppity." She leaned way back on the couch.

"You know something, Emily," he said, "you sound so righteous, so contemptuous, and you're so cunning. Really. You undermine every important relationship you get yourself into. You're dangerous stuff." Paul finished his drink.

"That doesn't offend me. Can't you be more aggressive?" She smiled.

"Arlene Francis sitting over there, enjoying life, feeling youthful, fit as a fiddle and ready for love. A big smile for everybody from Bill Cullen on up. What a happy girl you must be, writing your sweet little book about your crazy father and his fucking dummy, and looking around for your commander in your spare time." Paul got up to make another drink.

"You asshole," Emily said, with her teeth clenched, her eyes filled with rage. "Listen to this: I let you in the door and you piss on the rug. Talk about undermining! You'll never know about commanders, you'll never know about forgiveness. And you wanna know something, big shot? You'll never know about God!"

Paul turned away and went down the hall to the kitchen. He was back in a moment with a drink. He said, standing above her: "Tell me about God. I'd like to learn."

"You can't be taught the language, never having heard of the country." She looked up at him in fury.

"For you to invoke God, for you to invoke God is a fucking laugh." He backed away from her. He stood in the middle of the room.

"You really are dumb," Emily said.

"Is that all you can come up with? That I'm dumb?"

"No, it isn't. But I mean it. You have no understanding of me, and we've been together a long time now. The basic essence of you, your basic theme, is a theme of self. You know what I mean? That it's all Paul Kramer. 'The Paul Kramer show.' *Paul Kramer Tonight,* tomorrow, the next day, forever. Your blood doesn't flow into anyone else. And there's no connection between you and the ground you walk on, except if there are rocks or boulders or snow, or anything that stands in the way of you getting to where what you want is. Whether it's to a hamburger, or to a fuck, or to a record, or to a toilet. You're not tangled *into* anything. You get older, you get older, but you don't *know* anything. Just leave Paul Kramer alone and give him what he wants. He'll charm the life out of you and let it go at that. And he'll think he's done a fine job. Paul, listen to me. You'll never begin to understand the conglomerate in which you are only a sloppy and microscopic little twit."

Paul sat down on the couch and held his drink with both hands. He closed his eyes.

"I'm going for a walk," Emily said.

"It's three-thirty in the morning," Paul said, opening his eyes.

She left the room, and reappeared moments later in an overcoat and sneakers. "See ya," she said.

She closed the front door quietly.

So this was the end of Emily. July through March, Paul thought. Just another twitchy little plug-in suddenly aflame.

Again Paul closed his eyes. He tried to suppress tears, but they came, a trickle at first, and then real crying. And thoughts of Emily holding him. Go with the flow, go with the flow, go with the flow, go with the flow.

In a while, Paul got up from the couch and went into the bedroom. He lay down on Emily's side of the bed and stared at the ceiling.

July through March. Emily naked in the pool in Agua Caliente. Emily holding Franklin Kramer under the knees on Encinal Drive. Emily drinking orange juice. Emily in a pink dress.

Paul wished that New York was foreign to her, that she had no place to go, no telephone numbers in her mind, no aces in the hole. She would have to return to him then, her tail between her legs. If he were the only game in town, she'd correct the damage. She would coo to the only game in town. On her knees. Abject. I love you, I love you, I love you, I love you. You're the brightest guy in the media. I need you, oh God I need you.

But Emily Keller's following was enormous. Married couples, for God's sake, would welcome her at three-thirty in the morning. A painter named Judy; Fifteen East Tenth Street. A lawyer named Bob Stockton; Fifty-third and Second. And writers! Steven Murray; Central Park West and Seventy-ninth. Susan Bernstein; West Eleventh Street. Lee Siegal; somewhere on Riverside Drive in the Seventies. And Joshua The Truly Spiritual. Except for cunnilingus, the man was perfecto.

Paul thought ahead. He would look up his fine friend Joan Strasser. He would lay low with Joan Strasser until the dust settled. He was in good shape. Everything would be all right. It wasn't such a terrible thing, this Emily business. All for the good. He was tired of her talking on the phone in the back room, tired of her banging around in the kitchen, tired of her cheap Arlene Francis smile. Paul said out loud: I am tired of her memory.

He got up and made another drink.

He turned on the radio. A man named Wally Adams was taking phone calls on an FM station. Paul had never heard of Wally Adams.

Paul called Wally Adams. "Who do you think the nominees will be in 1976?" he asked Wally Adams.

"That's a long way down the pike," Adams said, live, on FM radio, with no seven-second delay. "I'd have to say that Gerald Ford will step down in favor of John Connally, and that Connally will run against and lose to Hubert Humphrey."

"Wally?" Paul said, his voice elevated in disguise.

"Yes, sir?"

"You're a faggot schmuck."

Paul hung up.

"There are all kinds," Wally Adams was saying on the air. "There are all kinds of sickies out there with a dime to spend. Let's take our next call."

Yes, that's true, Paul thought. There are all kinds of sickies out here. New York City sure has its share.

Connally vs. Humphrey. Paul thought to remember that, to seek out Wally Adams a year from August and throw his opinion back in his face. That is, if Adams was still around. Guys like Adams were radio transients. Another phone, another town, they didn't care. Adams might be hard to track down a year from August.

The phone rang.

Paul let it ring; twice, three times. Maybe someone had heard him with Wally Adams.

No. It was Emily. He let the phone ring. He was telling her that he was in no hurry, that he was in the living room. He imagined he was reading Thurber. This phone call from Emily was interrupting Thurber. Both Thurber *and* Paul Kramer.

Finally, a disinterested "Hello" from Paul.

"Chico?" said an Hispanic voice.

"Yeah," Paul said, disappointed and near tears again.

"Chico?"

"Yeah. I got a cold."

"This no Chico."

"It's Chico."

"Shit. This no Chico."

Click. A hang-up in the middle of the night from the world of the Spanish-speaking. Just click, and gone, leaving Paul alone again. He realized, with embarrassment, that even so ludicrous an exchange, so empty a contact, had moved him, engaged him.

He lay down on the bed, this time on his side. He went over Emily's words. Could he forget what she had said? Was he now stuck with her searing appraisal of his performance? Wasn't it, after all, the *performance* of it all she had scathingly vilified?

He saw himself as the actor she had painted, strolling through crowds of decent, struggling people, people with no facility for posturing. They fought their battles out in the open; they didn't hide behind guile and attitude. They tangled— Emily's very word—in open fields, made their truest feelings felt, all the time, *every* time.

Ridiculous. There were no such fields. Those decent folks had brass tactics of their own. He had been out and around plenty of times without his armor. He was no better or worse than any other guy. On this night, in the winds of Decker's numbing ambiguity, he had been attacked by a shaky girl in more trouble than he could possibly imagine. The key to it was kindness. Kindness for Emily. Kindness.

She came home at six in the morning. He was awake in bed with the light off.

"Hello there," he said.

She didn't speak. Her silence forced him into an apology.

"I'm sorry," he said.

"For what?" she asked, getting out of her clothes.

"We both said some unreasonable things." Paul spoke very quietly. "Could I ask you where you've been? Did you go to Joshua's house?"

"I didn't go anywhere. I took a walk."

For a moment she was naked. Paul could see her breasts in the dark. With her back to him, she slipped on a long-sleeved flannel nightgown.

She left the room. Paul heard the water run in the bathroom sink. Teeth brushing. Silence. The toilet flushing. All in all, five minutes.

She slipped into bed as far away from him as possible.

"Let's talk," he said.

"What about," she said.

"Do you want to leave things as they are?" he asked.

"They are where they are," Emily replied.

Paul sat up and turned on the light.

Emily didn't stir.

"I said I'm sorry for being unnecessarily cruel."

"People with their backs to the wall are invariably cruel," Emily said.

"I didn't feel my back was to the wall."

"*I* did. I do even now."

"You're a cunt, Emily," Paul said.

"Charming," she said. She was on her side, facing away from him.

"Do you want to know what I think?" Paul said.

Nothing from Emily.

"I think you need psychiatric help. And I'll tell you why I think that." He stopped for a moment. She didn't move.

"Don't you want to look at me?" Paul asked.

"I've seen enough," she said.

"Forgetting our relationship," he said. "That has nothing to do with anything for the moment. I think you got trouble. Stuff I can't really get a handle on. Your father, the dummy—"

"Temmy," Emily said, interrupting Paul.

"Temmy," Paul said. "And whatever religious garbage Joshua has stuck into your head. You play with all this stuff, but things are out of control. And under the most difficult circumstances, you blame me for your confusion."

"Is that what you think?" Emily said, sitting up in the bed, pushing two pillows behind her.

"That's what I think," Paul said.

She folded her hands in her lap and took a while before responding. When she did so, she rested her head on the wall and stared at the antique light fixture in the middle of the ceiling. She spoke carefully and without rancor.

"I don't blame you for anything," she began. "For a long time I've been trying to make some kind of an evaluation of what I see as my relationship with a very definite spiritual presence. I can hear my father's voice as it is translated through Temmy. I feel inferior, and guilty, and filled with sorrow. I know that it is the spiritual presence that can grant me absolution, and push me in a very special way into an entirely new world. I have always cherished the concept of that world. I know it's hard for you to grasp, being who you are, and what you've experienced, but I am absolutely sure that the way into that world is through Temmy. If you laugh at the word 'commander,' so be it."

She paused.

Paul said nothing.

When Emily spoke again, it was in Temmy's voice: "You think she's a moron? I'll tell you, she's no moron. The despicable sins of her childhood were very awful things. She was brilliant. Her manipulation of me and her father made a nightmare. She is tortured now, and hoping for forgiveness."

Emily closed her eyes.

Paul said: "Emily."

Emily said: "Sh."

Paul said: "Emily, please."

The room was still. Paul got up and stood at the foot of the bed. He leaned over, and through the blankets squeezed her toes. "I can't think," he said, finally.

Emily, her voice calm, her eyes open and fastened on his, said: "We don't love you any more."

CHAPTER SEVENTEEN

There was a delay at Kennedy because of fog. Drinks were served on the ground. Paul had two Scotches. He asked about his connecting flight in Dallas, and was told that arrangements would be made. He asked what that meant, and was told that he would be given accommodations in Dallas, if necessary. He imagined the accommodations: two single beds in an orange room. Pale-green curtains. Pink towels in the bathroom. Everything off. Missed connections. He would, he thought, be appropriately housed.

Paris. One long, hard pillow to a bed. He was there for the first time, alone. He was nineteen years old. He was shown to his room in a cheap hotel on the Right Bank. He asked the concierge about the douche bowl. "Eez a cheeldrin." Ah, yes. Eeze a cheeldrin. But with no seat. Their little asses would sink right down. They'd wet their cakes in the water. Maybe there was a portable seat in the closet. He looked in the closet. He looked under the bed. He looked behind the radiator. He fell asleep with his shoes on, and woke up in the middle of the night, terrified.

Paul had barely made it in time for the last flight out. Flight 95. Three and a half hours to Texas. Thirty-nine minutes *in* Texas. Flight 397 to Los Angeles. Arrival at 2 A.M. He was going with no plan. Sandi Cummings was married. Howdy. No cover. No minimum. Maybe howdy was out of town on a business trip. A business trip to *Dallas*. How about that? Oh, Sandi, I've missed you. You look wonderful. Young. You look *young*.

It was a rocky flight. Paul stayed fastened in his seat. He was sitting next to a short man in a white shirt and a thin tie.

"Bumpy," Paul said.

"It's a bitch," the man said. He was around fifty. He was drinking ginger ale. He wore a diamond ring on his right pinky.

"You heading to Dallas?" Paul asked.

"Fort Worth," the man said.

"What's in Fort Worth?"

"My son. They got him jailed."

"Why?"

"He killed a girl."

"He killed a girl?"

No reply.

"When did it happen?" Paul asked.

"This morning. I don't know much about it. They say he shot her. Golly."

"I'm real sorry," Paul said. The "golly" had been filled with despair.

"I don't know what to tell you," the man said.

"Don't tell me anything if you don't want to."

"It was only a figure of speech."

"Oh, I see," Paul said.

"I don't think he'll talk to me," the man said.

"Why not?" Paul asked.

"We're not close."

"How old is he? may I ask."

"Twenty-eight."

"Does he live in Dallas? I mean Fort Worth?"

"I don't know. He lives all over." The man looked at Paul for the first time. He had kind blue eyes and a slight mustache.

"Did he call you?" Paul asked.

"The police. Not the boy." The man turned his face to the window.

"What did they—"

"They said he wasn't talking. That he wasn't saying a word. They found my name on him."

"Where do you live?"

"Great Neck."

A father's name on a son. Maybe on a little folded-up piece of paper, like Millay's poem. In a wallet filled with other little folded-up pieces of paper: women, window washers, car dealers, bookmakers. Father. Tissue-thin emergency lines exposed in Fort Worth, Texas; unfolded, maybe torn in the process. Women: Vegas, San Diego, Houston, God knows, all over.

Father. Great Neck, Long Island.

"Mr. Father?"

"Speaking."

"Sergeant Tom Diehl, Fort Worth, Seventeenth Precinct. We got your son. He killed a girl."

"My son?"

"You Mr. Father?"

"He killed a girl?"

"Shot her."

"I'll be down tonight."

Paul asked for a third drink and was refused. Two to a passenger. American Airlines again, with their wax toilet paper and their "two to a passenger."

"Would you mind?" Paul said to the man. "Would you order a drink? And I'll give you the money? Usually they don't enforce this."

"Sure," the man said.

The stewardess' name was Nancy. She served the man a J&B, and looked coldly at them both.

"Isn't there some kind of age limit in your profession?" Paul asked Nancy. "I was reading only yesterday that there's a certain cutoff point."

Nancy waited a moment before replying. She said, finally: "There are all kinds of passengers."

Wally Adams felt there were all kinds of sickies. Out there. Paul was out there with his third drink, on his way to the biggest state in the union, behind schedule, destined for a Ramada Inn, traveling with the father of a killer. Paul thought: everyone is a screwball.

"His mother is brokenhearted," the man said.

"I can understand," Paul said.

"God bless her."

"Yes," Paul said.

"She wanted to come, but I wouldn't let her. She packed everything for me." The man glanced at Paul with pain in his eyes.

"So you don't have any idea how long you'll be down," Paul said.

"I don't have any idea at all. It's like walking into hell." The man chuckled bitterly. "With three suitcases."

Paul imagined lots of thin ties and white shirts. Suits of muted colors in which to face the family of the deceased. Boxer shorts in which to pace the hotel room, in which to make long-distance phone calls. Lawyers in Great Neck summoned by a man in boxer shorts in Fort Worth.

Three bags full.

Paul had no bags. Just the slacks and blue pullover and denim jacket he wore. And *The Magus* in a pocket of the denim jacket. And two keys to Box 1216 of the Pacific National Bank, 707 N Palm Canyon Dr. PS, CA 92262. After all, he would face no silent son, no family of the deceased. Only the embers of Emily would confront him. They rode with him now, on Flight 95. A night coach fare for the embers.

She had moved away that afternoon. Joshua had her back, he knew. Joshua would help her through this, putting things in order for her. Paul imagined Joshua in a kimono; etheral, tender, the deepest river, the profoundest thinker, the purest teacher, the holiest friend.

And all that crap.

"I'm going out west," Paul had said to Emily, from the beeper phone in the studio.

"When?" she had asked.

"Right after the show," he had said, dramatically. "I'll take care of everything."

"Fine," she had said.

"Emily," he had whispered.

"Be well, Paul," she had said, after a long pause.

In a while, the man offered to buy Paul another drink.

"I wouldn't mind, quite honestly," Paul said.

Nancy was icy with another little bottle of J&B.

"Sure is nice to meet a drinking man on a plane," Paul said to her, with a smile.

"I hope you're having a pleasant trip," Nancy said. Pure ice.

"It's getting progressively better," he said.

Paul closed his eyes. He felt mellow. He was stuck with a song. He saw the song in a rocking chair in his brain, its tiny legs neatly crossed. The song was smoking a corncob pipe. It was dressed informally in corduroy pants and green cashmere sweater. A nice consistent rocking.

> You're all dressed up to go dreaming
> So don't tell me I'm wrong;
> What a night to go dreaming,
> Mind if I tag along.

Paul drifted to sleep.

> You certainly know the right things to wear.
> You certainly know the right things to wear.
> You certainly know the right things to wear.

He awakened to the captain's voice on the speaker above him.

The captain was saying that it was pouring rain in Dallas. They were circling. It was a thunderstorm, that's all. Just sit back, relax.

"What's your business in these parts?" the man asked.

"Government work," Paul replied.

"Oh. Government work," the man said.

"We may have a break in the Kennedy assassination," Paul said.

"Do you mean that?" the man said, facing Paul.

"I wish I could tell you more," Paul said.

"Golly," the man said.

"I know you have trouble of your own," Paul said. "But you just watch your papers over the weekend."

"What's your name?"

"Bill Cunningham," Paul said.

"You look a little like a man on television."

"I know," Paul said.

Paul wanted another drink. Obviously, there was no chance on this plane. Nancy's last laugh, that was for sure.

"I can't tell you how much I wish you well," Paul said when, fifteen minutes later, they were taxiing to the gate.

"I haven't seen him in three years," the man said.

"I didn't know that," Paul said.

"It's true," the man said.

"How old was the girl? Do you know?" Paul asked.

"Only fifteen, Bill."

In the terminal Paul discovered that his connecting flight had been delayed an hour, and now longer, as a new plane was being rolled into service.

No Ramada Inn. No reading *The Magus* in an orange room. No masturbating at seven in the morning onto hexagonal bathroom tiles.

Paul found a bar, and ordered a beer and a straight Scotch. He sat on a stool and thought about ten-gallon hats. Why ten gallons? Probably, he imagined, because they held ten gallons of whiskey. Think of it. But wait just a minute. Ten gallons. Ridiculous. Ten gallons was a tremendous amount of whiskey. Paul studied a ten-gallon hat across the room. It would hold, he figured, a quart. Tops a quart. Something called a one-quart hat wouldn't fit into the Texas traditions of large, wide, bombastic. What about two gallons? Even four gallons? More credible. He imagined describing the hat to Emily: "It's a felt hat, I think, with a huge crown and a wide brim, and anyone who puts one on his head or anywhere near his head for more than four and one-half minutes is an asshole. I love you, Emily."

Paul called home with his credit card.

"Credit card number 222 7458 074 R, as in 'regret,'" he told the operator, wearily.

It was a quarter of three in New York. There was no answer. He let it ring endlessly, imagining the sound of it in his apartment. Would the acoustics in the back room be altered even slightly by the removal of Emily's bags and trinkets? Maybe a little hollower sound. Maybe an echo: "EMILY." "emily."

Paul called the Sports Phone.

". . . Celtics 101 . . . Rangers 2 . . . have traded . . ."

Paul didn't listen. It was the sound of the voice he was after; a voice awake in the night, rattling off scores, shoving them together in sixty seconds.

". . . update at 3 A.M."

That young man was a veritable beaver, somewhere in the city; checking the wires, following leads in the dead of night, letting Paul, in a phone booth in Dallas, Texas, have it straight. The facts. That man at Sports Phone had the facts.

Paul imagined his own facts distributed in the same way:

. . . "Kramer left on American Airlines Flight 95 for Dallas, Texas, tonight, where he'll connect with Flight 397 to Los Angeles. He's had several drinks and is feeling lonely as he waits, in the much-used Texas air center, the second leg of his unpremeditated journey. Update at 4 A.M."

In January he had been given Goldie Hawn's phone number in California. He had memorized it. He tried it from Dallas.

A service picked up.

"I'd like to leave a message for Goldie," Paul said.

"Please hold," he was told.

Were they actually going to get Goldie herself? He had never met Goldie; had nothing to say to Goldie. Were they trying to locate Goldie? Was she secretly listening on an extension?

"What's the message?" The voice at the service was a man's. He was quick and formal. Nothing but the best for Goldie.

"Tell her Bob Green called from New York," Paul said. "Tell her that we have acquired the rights for the musical version of *Tea and Sympathy,* and would like to discuss it with her. Tell her we'll reach her tomorrow. And tell her we're talking Truffaut."

Back at the bar, Paul had a good time mulling this over. He longed for Emily to know. He was sure that he could convince her to place a follow-up call, maybe even talk to Goldie, actually sell her on the idea, then call Earl Wilson, and they'd read about it the next day. Easy to do. Remarkably easy to do.

Paul finished a double Scotch, and wandered out of the security area.

The long corridor was bustling, even in the middle of the night. Drab Texas children trailed behind their parents. A baby cried, way down at the other end, a piercing airport sound, a deep-night wail, out of sight, around the bend. There were infants shrieking all over the world, tangled up in blue. At Logan, at LAX, at Orly, at Heathrow, shrieking, tangled up in blue. Emily's favorite new Dylan song. She had learned the words. "Tangled up in Blue." An unlikely torch song for Paul Kramer in Texas. He imagined Tony Martin giving it a go.

Paul had to stand in line to re-enter the terminal through the security gate. Tears came to his eyes. He wanted to sleep, holding Emily.

He passed through the gate and set off the alarm. He did it again, and a third time. Finally, he removed his belt and breezed through. He thought that quite soon a second gate would be required, by order of the Government of These United States. Same size, same shape. The alarm would be set off on moral grounds. Paul knew that he would never pass safely through such an installation. He would have to give up flying. He would have to take trains and drink their Nehi and stare out the window at cows and get just a little nauseated trying to read. As he boarded Flight 397, he thought that maybe right now, even though it was late, there was a man in a laboratory somewhere in the country putting the finishing touches on this new device. Moral Grounds. The MG gate. There'd be a stink in the Senate, but the bill would be passed after weeks of debate. The MG gate. It would be tried experimentally in Sacramento and Jacksonville. And then the big towns: Chicago, Boston, and finally New York. JFK. Paul could still get out through La Guardia, but only for a month or so. And a week later, Newark. And then it would be all Amtrak for the brightest guy in the media.

Paul asked for a pillow, and closed his eyes at once. The flight was almost empty. He stretched out on three seats.

His friend, the song, was back. There it was in its rocking chair, back and forth, back and forth, legs still neatly crossed. It was wearing loafers.

> If I say I love you
> I want you to know
> It's not just because there's moonlight,
> Although, moonlight becomes you so.

Things would be all right. Things would be okay. Paul turned his face to the seat to hide the tears that now flowed heavily onto his hands, onto his wrists.

He wakened with a half hour left. He went to the bathroom and talked to his reflection as he urinated. "What do you have to say for yourself?" he asked. "So you want to lead a band? I see. The first thing you've got to do is to get your shit together. Get organized, man. John Fowles is organized, why not you? John Fowles is so fucking organized!"

Outside the lavatory he discovered the liquor cart stashed in a metal locker. He removed four little bottles of Cutty Sark, loading his pockets. He returned cautiously to his seat, home free. Home free, Emily.

In the airport Paul called Decker's Palm Springs number. There was no answer. He called his own home in New York. There was no answer. He called Maggie Furth's house. A little girl answered. He knew at once that it wasn't Christina.

"Is Maggie there?" he asked.

"She's in New York," the little girl said.

"Is Christina there?"

"She's asleep. Want me to get her?"

"No. I'm a friend of her mother's. What are you doing up so late?"

"Listening to records."

It was Debbie. Must be Debbie.

"All alone?"

"Everybody's asleep."

"Who's 'everybody'?"

"The maid and Christina. And me. I'm awake."

"I can hear the music."

"Yeah."

"Loggins and Messina?"

"Seals and Crofts."

"Oh."

"Who's this?"

"Just a friend of Maggie's."

"Okay. Well, I gotta go."

"Okay. Goodnight, Debbie."

"Hey."

Paul hung up, pleased.

In the phone booth, with his back to the terminal, he drank one of the Cutty Sarks and left the empty bottle on the counter.

He took a seat in the lounge and opened *The Magus*. His eyes didn't focus on the words, though he read sentences and turned pages.

In a short while he put the book away. He stared at an arrival/departure screen that hung above the information desk in front of him. He saw that Denver would be in for a busy day. And why three flights to Hartford? What went on in Hartford? He would have asked but for the absence of an official.

It was quarter of four. With the exception of two other men about his age, one asleep in a lumber shirt and jeans, the other reading *Newsweek* through thick horn-rimmed glasses, he was alone in front of Gate 30. Gate 30 would be activated, he discovered, at nine in the morning: Phoenix, Dallas, Baltimore,

Rochester. Was it possible, Paul wondered, to be continuously airborne with the exception of stopovers of no more than thirty minutes? It seemed like a project that would have appealed to someone by now. Weeks and weeks in the air, money no object, zigzagging across the country, a local paper picking the story up first, and then a network, and then everyone, a hundred journalists gathered at each arrival zone for a quick glimpse of the perpetual passenger. Paul himself would be that man. "Why are you doing this?" he would be asked time and time again as he scrambled for his next flight. "Fear of landing," he would reply, on the run.

On the run. Even now he was on the run, zigzagging across the country with his private gremlins keeping up with him, nipping at his heels. They were scattered invisibly throughout the lounge, waiting expectantly for his next shrewd maneuver.

His next shrewd maneuver was to sit on the railing of the moving sidewalk while killing another Cutty Sark. He let the empty bottle ride with him on the railing. He whisked it off at the last moment and dropped it into a trash can near Avis.

From Avis he rented a Camaro and drove to the Beverly Hills Hotel.

The lobby was empty except for Milton Berle, who sat on a couch reading the Los Angeles *Times*.

Paul went to the front desk.

"Paul Kramer from New York," he said.

"Do you have a reservation?" he was asked by a pleasant-faced young man in a green jacket.

"Yes."

Much searching by the man in the green jacket.

"When was the reservation made?" Paul was asked.

"Three days ago. My secretary made it." Paul was trying to be helpful.

"I don't . . ."

"I stay here often. It's almost automatic."

"I don't have it. Wait a minute, please." The man took a look at some papers on another desk. He came back to the reservation window with a smile. "Mr. Kramer, I'm sorry, your reservation doesn't seem to be here. I'm from New York and I know you. How long will you be staying?"

"Just one night. I got in a half hour ago. Long delays, let me tell you."

"Do you have any baggage?"

"I don't," Paul said. "I have a morning meeting, and I'm gone."

"Very well, enjoy your stay."

"I'd like to pay in cash," Paul said.

Paul gave the cashier sixty of his one hundred and fifty dollars.

"How are things in New York?" the cashier asked.

"Harassed," Paul said.

A bellboy greeted him with a key.

"I'll find it," Paul told the bellboy, giving him a five-dollar bill.

Paul's eyes met Berle's. Paul had interviewed him three years before. From his seated position, the newspaper masking all but his eyes, Berle nodded, almost imperceptibly.

In his room Paul took a shower and lay down on the bed. Then he placed a call to the city desk of the New York *Times*.

"Have you heard anything at all about Jacob Javits taking his own life?" Paul asked.

"Nothing like that at all." A New York voice.

"I have it on pretty good authority," Paul said.

"Who are you?"

"It's of no concern. But if I were you, I'd get hopping on this story."

"Who are you?"

Paul could hear anger. "I'd rather not give my name," he said, "but if you insist, I'm calling at Milton Berle's behest."

"Milton Berle?"

"Milton Berle," Paul repeated, with irritation.

"What has Milton Berle got to do with anything?"

"More than you'll ever know."

"Is this a joke?"

"It's no joke, my man."

"Hey, we're tied up here."

"Remember, my man: Berle and Javits. Check the *Post* today. You'll see."

Paul got dressed. Putting the key on the bureau, he left the room.

He found his way to the garage, and up the ramp to the front of the hotel. An attendant brought his car.

Paul drove down Crescent Drive. He crossed Santa Monica and stopped at a phone booth in the village.

He used his credit card to call Lawrence Tellman in Boston.

"This is Dr. Tellman," said Lawrence Tellman, bright and chipper at eight-thirty in the morning.

"The light at the end of the tunnel is the light of the oncoming train," Paul said. "Or at least that's what Robert Lowell thinks."

"To whom am I speaking?" Tellman asked.

"It matters not."

He hung up and got back into the car.

On Olympic Boulevard Paul found an open diner.

He sat by himself at a filthy counter, quickly putting away three large glasses of tomato juice.

He continued east on Olympic, made a right on Fairfax, and hit the Santa Monica Freeway, which was already busy with early-morning traffic. He searched the radio dial for rock 'n roll. He had in mind "The Pinball Wizard." He wondered why; why, out of the blue "The Pinball Wizard" should occur to him. Pinball. Wizard. The Who. He could find no clues in the words. A blind boy. Maybe it was the blind part of it. No sight. Darkness. Blackness. Maybe.

He settled on a song he didn't know. It was loud, and that was the important thing. He sought out loudness, good tough rock 'n roll loudness, through West Covina, Claremont, Pomona, Ontario, all the way down on Interstate 10, past Colton to the Palm Springs turnoff, Highway 111. Suddenly, Paul realized that it was daylight; that he had missed the sunrise.

He switched the radio off in Banning Pass, and drove in silence. The morning was clear. He opened the window and felt the warm desert breeze.

A flashing red light appeared behind him.

Cop.

A nice man in dark glasses. "May I see your license and registration, please?"

"It's a rented car." Paul opened the glove compartment. "Is this the registration?"

"That'll do it," the cop said.

He studied Paul's license and registration without speaking.

"Okay?" Paul said, finally.

"Where were you heading so fast?"

"Just to get some sun," Paul said, with a smile.

"You passed a number of vehicles."

"I didn't know that. It's my fault entirely."

The cop wrote a ticket.

"How fast was I going?" Paul asked, conversationally.

"Seventy-five." The cop didn't look up.

"I'm going back to New York late today. Can I pay this by mail?" Paul was filled with smiles.

"You can do that," the cop said. "This ticket will reflect sixty-five miles an hour."

"How can I thank you?" Paul said.

"Right," the cop said. "Enjoy the sun and take it easy." He tipped his dark glasses with his index finger.

Paul tipped his temple with his index finger. "Bye-bye," he said.

Paul drove slowly away. Bye-bye, Mr. Cop. Bye-bye from an adult, a motor vehicle operator, a jobholder. Bye-bye, Mr. Cop. Bye-bye, Mr. DiMaggio. Bye-bye, Judge Sirica.

Paul took a room at the British-Ritz motel. The décor was inexpensive Mexican. The eight-foot pool was surrounded by plastic daisies. Paul paid twenty-five dollars for a room with a single bed, a fold-out couch, and a radio.

He showered again. There was no hot water. That was the British part, he thought.

He drove to the airport.

At the airport he called Decker's Palm Springs number. There was no answer. He called his own apartment in New York. There was no answer. He called the Beverly Hills Hotel and asked for Milton Berle. Berle picked up the phone after three rings. His voice was filled with sleep.

"Milton," Paul said.

"Yes, hello?"

"Bob Green here," Paul said.

"Hi, how are ya?" Berle said.

"Javits is dead."

"Javits who?"

"Jacob Javits."

"Oh. I'm sorry. Awful."

"He took his own life."

"Awful. Awful."

"Do you have any comments?"

"Who's this again?"

"Bob Green."

"Yeah. Bob. Well. It's awful. He was a great man," Berle said, composing himself.

"What do you think was his biggest contribution?" Paul asked.

"I think his zest for life," Berle replied.

"Milton?"

"Yes?"

"God bless you."

"Thank you."

In the gift shop Paul saw a plastic yellow shopping bag with the words P.S. I LOVE YOU emblazoned above a drawing of the sun wearing sunglasses. He bought it for fifty cents.

He returned to his room at the British-Ritz motel.

He opened the two remaining bottles of Cutty Sark and poured them into a plastic bathroom cup. He added a few drops of water, and sat down on the edge of the bed. He sipped his drink slowly. He went to the window and looked out at the empty pool. There was no one around at all. There were no strollers.

The British-Ritz motel had ten rooms. Paul thought it a possibility that he was the only lodger. The idea depressed him, appalled him. He finished the drink in two gulps, put the key on the bed, and left, walking through a back alley around a Mexican restaurant.

Ninety-one degrees at eleven o'clock. He stayed with the Ray Conniff Singers for only a moment. He tried one or two other stations before turning the radio off.

He decided to drive out to Agua Caliente. He made a left on Ramon with that intention, only to circle back to Indian Avenue, feeling tears approaching.

He stopped at a deli for a package of potato chips.

"I'll never know why he did it," a pretty young girl was saying to the clerk. "How can you live with a guy with a burrito for a brain?"

Back in the car, Paul imagined a brain squeezed into a burrito shape. The consistencies were similar, he thought. A bean burrito, kind of brain-like, mushy, malleable. He imagined his own brain as a bean-and-potato burrito. Meatless. Basically lard. It all came down to lard. Everything came down to lard.

Paul was ushered into the vault of the Pacific National Bank at eleven-thirty.

Left alone in a very small carpeted room, he transferred fifty thousand dollars from the safe-deposit box into his plastic yellow shopping bag.

He was asked to sign two cards and one slip of paper. Emily and he had signed them together in October. He looked at their signatures: Paul Knight. Emily Keller. She had worn a blue tee shirt and had held his hand.

Parked in the mall, he ate the potato chips.

He opened the shopping bag and glanced at Decker's cash. He counted six thousand dollars before tiring of it. He dropped crumbs of potato chips between one-hundred-dollar bills, and laid the bag on the seat next to him.

From the lobby of the Palm Springs Spa, Paul dialed Decker's number. There was no answer.

Paul parked a block away from Decker's house.

Carrying the yellow shopping bag, he walked the rest of the way with his shirt off in the hot afternoon sun, wishing to appear touristy, at ease. He imagined Decker with some elaborate videotape equipment, getting it all down, adding music later, maybe the Ray Conniff Singers themselves.

"Now, you see there, officer, he's going toward the house now. You see?" Decker would be standing in a darkened projection room. The officer would be seated with a notebook in hand. "Now, look at this," Decker would continue, gleefully, "he's about to enter *illegally*. It's right there in front of you, as you can plainly see."

Paul took a glimpse over a waist-high brick fence. He circled the house, checking windows. Clearly, no one was around. The house looked uncared-for. Leaves and pebbles covered the front walk. The water in the pool looked yellow and ancient.

Paul tried the window that Emily and he had used, but found it locked.

He tried a sliding glass door to the living room.

It opened slowly.

He gave it a second strong push, and ducked inside.

A piercing alarm sounded at once.

Immediately Paul darted into the back yard. For a moment he stood frozen. He was covered with perspiration.

The phone rang. He let it ring twice. Then he raced inside and picked up the receiver.

"Yes?" he said, out of breath.

A man's voice said: "Westinghouse Security. May I have your name and your abort code?"

Paul said: "My name is Bob Green, and I know the abort code, give me just a second. I was told what it was and I seem to have forgotten it."

The voice said: "What is your abort word?"

A word. An abort *word*. Paul's mind ran through Decker's language. "Maggie," he said, enthusiastically.

Silence.

Paul said: "How stupid of me. That was *last* year's abort code. Code word. *Word.* Cho-Chews. Right? *Kingles.* I know: *Christina!*"

"Fella, you're—"

Paul shouted: "Wait a minute! Hold on a second! Listen to me."

"Yeah."

"I do not know the code word. I am a thief."

Paul hung up.

He raced into the bedroom and opened the bottom drawer of the bureau. There were Decker's bathing trunks, Decker's underwear shirts, Decker's jockstraps.

Paul laid the yellow shopping bag on top of everything, removing a one-hundred-dollar bill for the speeding ticket. Then he closed the drawer with a bang.

He was in the car two minutes later.

He was off.

He made a left on Sunrise. He drove all the way up to Tachevah. He took another left over to Caballeros at a diminished speed; touristy, at ease.

In Colton, he pulled off the freeway and put his shirt on.

Decker's code word. Rufus? Perspicacity? "Maggie" had been a good guess.

Paul laughed. He sat there on the side of the freeway and laughed.

At a gas station in San Bernardino he drank three Cokes, and asked for the key to the men's room.

He sat on the toilet with the lid down, and covered his face with his hands. For a moment he thought he would vomit, but the feeling subsided.

He thought: ends are beginnings and beginnings are ends.

He thought of Lillian playing the viola. He thought of Emily kissing Maggie's chocolate mustache.

He sat on the lid for a long time, not moving, his palms pressed to his temples, his elbows on his knees.

When he got back in the car he found a sticky ice cream stick on the driver's seat. He put it in the pocket of his denim jacket.

He drove directly into the setting sun. He couldn't believe it would be dark soon.